THE CLAN CALLING

By Wendy Terrien

The Adventures of Jason Lex
Chronicle One
THE RAMPART GUARDS

Chronicle Two-Jason
THE LEAGUE OF GOVERNORS

Chronicle Two-Sadie
THE CLAN CALLING

"The Fate Stone"
A short story in the anthology
TICK TOCK: SEVEN TALES OF TIME

"Light"
A short story in the anthology
OFF BEAT: NINE SPINS ON SONG

THE CLAN CALLING

CHRONICLE TWO-SADIE
IN THE ADVENTURES OF JASON LEX

A NOVEL BY

WENDY TERRIEN

CAMASHEA
PRESS

CAMASHEA PRESS | DENVER, CO

Camashea Press
PO Box 621252
Littleton, CO 80162
Library of Congress Control Number: 2017908333

Printed in the United States of America

For Vanessa
May you forever be proud of your strength

ONE

Changes

S adie glanced at her classmates passing in the hallway. They had no idea how close they came to being wiped out, incinerated, erased. She heard snippets of their conversations about football games, and papers they had to write, about teachers, and where to go after school, about how gross the latest lunch was in the cafeteria. But no one mentioned Skyfish. Or the Rampart. Or that her best friend, Jason Lex, can shoot blue bolts of electricity out of his hands.

Totally clueless. Not exactly how she'd imagined ninth grade would be, but it was just as well. Her classmates would freak out if they knew who and what lived around them, hidden by the Rampart.

Sadie met Jason at their lockers. "From Mamo." She handed him an apple from her grandmother's garden.

"All this healthy stuff is going to kill me." Jason grinned, took a bite. "Tell her thanks, as usual."

"I will. And she'll be glad to hear you are actually eating what she sends." Sadie snapped her locker shut.

"Hey, if it's good, as in tastes good, I'll eat it."

Sadie and Jason headed to the lunchroom where Jason tossed the apple core in a trash bin near the door. They grabbed seats and Sadie unpacked her lunch. Jason pulled a protein bar out of his bag and peeled back the wrapper.

"Seriously, that's all you're eating?" Sadie asked.

"I had an apple."

Sadie rolled her eyes. She looked across the room. "Ugh. Here comes Derek Goodman."

Jason looked over his shoulder. His lip curled.

Derek sneered. "What are you looking at?" He and two of his friends stopped behind Jason.

"I was trying to figure out what smelled so bad," Jason said.

Derek sniffed the space above Jason's head. "It's you, the slime-ball that beats up his own weakling brother."

Jason bolted out of his seat and stood inches away from Derek. "Take that back."

"Or what?"

Jason pressed his fists into his thighs. His chin jutted. "Take—That—Back."

"Not—Gonna—Happen. For all we know, you've done something to your sister, too. I heard she hasn't been in school for like a month."

Jason's knuckles whitened and he glared at Derek.

"Jason?" Sadie wanted him to take a breath, to take a step back. Given Jason's power, she knew this could get bad fast. For everyone.

Jason shook his head. "You're not worth it."

"No? How about now?" Derek shoved Jason into the table.

Jason sprang into a fighting stance. Sadie rushed to his side of the table.

"What's going on here?" Coach Martel grabbed Derek's shoulder from behind. "You. To the principal's office."

Derek moved toward the exit. Coach turned to Jason. "Are you all right?"

"Yeah. Fine." Jason straightened and relaxed.

"Okay. Good man." Coach patted Jason on the back. "Don't forget basketball tryouts are in a couple of weeks."

"Thanks, Coach."

Sadie doubted Jason would try out for the basketball team. He was focused on his training for the Guards. Maybe too focused.

Coach Martel nodded. "Now, if you'll excuse me, I have a problem to escort to the principal's office. Again." The last word he said under his breath.

Lunch period was almost over and most of Sadie's classmates left for their next period. Sadie stepped closer to Jason. "Della's still having a hard time?"

Jason wadded his trash and tossed it into the nearby bin. "Yeah. She's awake half the night, she starts crying at the weirdest times. She was playing fetch with Shay yesterday and lost it when Shay wouldn't drop the ball for her."

"Is there anything I can do?" The bell rang and Sadie picked up her lunch bag.

Jason looked at his hands. The skin on his palms was shiny and smooth, newly healed from being burned when he'd tried to save his mom. "Nah. Dad's trying to figure it out. Thanks, though." He turned toward his next class. "See you later."

"Yeah, see ya." Sadie spun on her heel and headed to Algebra. She didn't want to disappoint Mrs. Bauer by being late.

✳ ✳ ✳

After the last bell, Sadie exited the school and watched a few parents picking up their kids. Parent stuff reminded her that she was different. Sadie didn't have parents. But she had Mamo and that's what mattered.

She walked down the street toward home. In front of her house, a tall man with gray hair and matching beard smiled and nodded at Sadie, then eased himself into a red SUV. Sadie didn't smile back, or wave, or nod her head. She didn't know the man. And she knew pretty much everyone. Salton wasn't a big town.

"Mamo, I'm home." Sadie dropped her backpack in the foyer and headed to the kitchen. "Mamo?" The kitchen was empty. She dashed upstairs. Mamo was lying on her bed. Sadie tapped lightly on the open door. "Are you awake?" she whispered.

Mamo's eyes slitted open. "Yes, come in. Sit with me." Mamo patted the bed beside her.

"What are you doing up here?" Sadie asked.

"I thought I'd lie down for a few minutes."

"Are you okay?"

"Of course," Mamo said. "Just wanted to rest my eyes."

Rest her eyes? That's a new one.

"So you probably didn't see that man out front," Sadie said.

"What man?" Mamo cleared her throat.

"Gray-haired guy. He was getting into a car when I walked up."

"Must have been visiting a neighbor. You didn't recognize him?"

"No," Sadie said, "and it's weird he'd park in front of our house if he's visiting someone else. It's not like there are tons of cars parked on our street."

"Maybe he was drawn to the shade of our pine tree," Mamo said.

Maybe, except there was no shade when I saw him.

Mamo rubbed her temples. She grimaced.

"Are you really okay?" Sadie pressed the back of her hand against Mamo's forehead like Mamo had done to her whenever she hadn't felt good. "Are you sick?"

"I'm fine, I'm fine." Mamo took Sadie's hand in hers. "Just a little headache."

"Again?" This was the third headache in two weeks, and Mamo never got headaches. She never got sick.

"It's nothing. I already feel it fading. Now tell me about your day. Everything okay at school?"

Sadie shifted to face Mamo. "Well, no Skyfish attacks or surprises from parents trying to destroy all of us, so that's good." Sadie chuckled.

"And how is Jason handling everything? Is he still doing all right?"

"Seems like it, but he spends so much time on his training for the Rampart Guards that we don't get to talk much. He barely eats at lunch now because he says he doesn't want to be too full for training. Oh—he said thank you for the apple."

Mamo pushed herself up to sitting. "Maybe I need to send food for him every day." She closed her eyes.

"I think you need to see a doctor. You're pale, and I can tell you don't feel good."

Mamo's complexion was pasty, almost gray. Her hand felt cool in Sadie's.

"Just a little flu bug, I think. No doctor necessary. Good food and good rest will fix me right up." Mamo pushed herself a little higher against the headboard. "Maybe you could bring me a cup of the veggie soup we made, and hot tea with some of our fresh honey. You know our honey fixes anything."

"Sure thing. I'll be back in a few minutes." Sadie rose and headed to the doorway. She looked back at Mamo. Her eyes were closed again and Sadie's throat tightened.

She prepared the food, including a serving for herself. It was early for dinner, but she wanted to be with Mamo. Homework could wait. She'd have plenty of time to get her work done before bedtime.

Sadie carried the tray into Mamo's room.

Mamo opened her eyes. "Smells delicious."

She set the tray on Mamo's lap. "Of course it's delicious. I'm a highly skilled re-heater of soup." She smirked.

"I've taught you well." Mamo took a sip of tea. "Mmm. Just what I needed. Now tell me about school today, boring as it was without any mayhem."

"Jason almost got in a fight with Derek Goodman. He was picking on Jason about the Skyfish attack, the one at school when it seemed like Jason tried to hurt Kyle." Sadie sipped her soup from a mug.

"Glad to hear it was only an almost fight," Mamo said. "And poor Derek."

Sadie's head jerked. "Poor Derek? What about poor Jason? Derek is so annoying bringing up stuff he knows nothing about, and he's such a jerk to everyone, even his friends. Of which he has maybe two, and I'm surprised he has that many."

"People like that usually act the way they do because of other things going on in their life. It has nothing to do with Jason, or you, or anyone else at school."

"I don't know about that," Sadie said. "I think he's just mean."

"Maybe you should talk to him sometime."

"Um, no thank you. I'd rather not go out of my way to ruin my day."

Mamo pressed into Sadie's hand. "Hmm, well, maybe you'll change your mind if the opportunity presents itself."

Not likely. Sadie changed the subject. "So what are we doing this weekend?"

Mamo pushed her bowl away and leaned into her pillows. "You don't have plans with your friends?"

"Well, sure, we talked about some things. But I wanted to check with you first."

"I can plan around you and your friends."

"Yeah, I know. But you and I are a team. Two for one and one for two, right?" She and Mamo had adopted their own version of the Musketeers' motto.

"Always, my dear. But I'm not sure how I'll be feeling this weekend, so go ahead and make plans with your friends. We'll adjust our plans later." Mamo's eyes scrunched.

Sadie touched Mamo's forehead again. "How can I tell if you have a fever?"

"I don't. I'm fine."

"You feel kinda warm to me." Sadie moved the tray off the bed. "I'm going to call the doctor."

"No, no. I'll be just fine in another day or two." Mamo shifted down into the pillows. "A little rest and I'll be right as rain and back in the garden with the beehives."

Mamo's breathing was short, shallow. It seemed like she hurt everywhere, not only in her head.

"If I tell the doctor your symptoms—"

"A couple more days, Sadie, okay? I just need to rest." Mamo closed her eyes.

"Okay." Sadie rose from the bed and picked up the tray. "I'll let you sleep. I'm going to water the garden and do my homework. Call if you need anything."

"Thank you, sweetheart. I don't know what I'd do without you."

I feel the same way, Mamo.

✳ ✳ ✳

Sadie woke early the next morning. She had a text message from Jason: "See you at school. Staying at Uncle A's. Dad and Della headed to London."

Wow. That's huge. Sadie didn't text back. They wouldn't meet up to walk to school since Uncle Alexander's house was in a different direction. She'd ask Jason what was going on when she saw him at lunch.

She climbed out of bed and got ready, then checked in on Mamo. She was sound asleep, resting comfortably. Even though she hadn't eaten much of her soup, she did drink her tea and her headache had improved. Sadie hoped it stayed that way. She left a note in Mamo's office and headed out.

✳ ✳ ✳

"Sadie, wait up." Vanessa Barnes dodged students and hurried to where Sadie had stopped in the hallway. She'd been friends with Vanessa since first grade when Mamo met Vanessa's mom through home schooling connections. The girls followed the same lesson plan, went on home schooling field trips together, and both transitioned to public school when they were ten.

"Hey, Nessa," Sadie said. "Ready for the history test?"

"Yeah, I think so. I was up a little late studying, but I feel good. Maybe not bright-eyed but definitely bushy-tailed so I count that as a win." She flicked her brunette ponytail and grinned.

Sadie chuckled. "So I can count on getting a better score than you."

"Like that's new," Nessa said. "But I'll be a very close second, and I may just shock you one of these days and amaze you with my super-intelligence."

"You already do that, every day," Sadie said.

They dashed into Mr. Bond's History class. He was in room number seven, and he'd added two zeroes, cut from construction paper, in front of the number on his door. He drank water from a martini shaker during the day, and always included an extra credit question on his tests that had something to do with James Bond. He usually wore bow ties, but not with a tuxedo. More often than not, Sadie saw him in plaid shirts and brown corduroy pants. And his first name wasn't James. It was Bruce.

Sadie and Nessa sat in their assigned seats, Nessa's directly behind Sadie's.

"Welcome to History Headquarters, students. I trust you've trained for today's test and will score at least eighty percent correct lest you otherwise end up in the pool of sharks swimming beneath our floor." Mr. Bond straightened a stack of papers on his desk.

"Whatever." Stevie Harkness, one of the not-so-bright football players, tipped back in his chair, teetering on two of the four legs. "Like, bad guys have the sharks, not James Bond."

"Whoever's in charge of Headquarters gets to decide what's under the floor. I've also decided that you get to hand out the exams since you apparently enjoy trying to be helpful." Mr. Bond picked up the stack and waved it in the air. "Come and get 'em."

Stevie huffed and clunked his chair onto all four legs. He shuffled to the front of the room and snatched up the tests.

Sadie took her copy and flipped to the second page to see the extra credit question: In what country does the opening scene of the James Bond novel, Carte Blanche, take place?

Yes. Two extra points. Sadie mentally fist-bumped the air and wrote her answer: Serbia.

Twenty minutes later, Sadie stood to walk her exam up to Mr. Bond. She jumped when Stevie snorted, waking himself from a nap. The class laughed. Mr. Bond sighed. He'd seen that from Stevie plenty of times before.

Sadie returned to her desk and glanced at Nessa. Her head was down on her forearm. Sadie kicked Nessa's foot.

Her head popped up. "Oh my god," Nessa whispered. She shot a look at the clock.

"No talking, Ms. Barnes," Mr. Bond said.

"Sorry." She mouthed the word and started scribbling answers on her paper.

Sadie sat. *Jeez, she must have been more tired than she thought. She's never done that before.* Nessa's pencil tapped and scratched and whisked behind her. *Please let her have enough time to finish.*

The bell rang and Nessa ran her exam to Mr. Bond's outstretched hand. She retrieved her backpack from her desk and walked out with Sadie.

"What happened?" Sadie asked.

"No idea. I don't even remember feeling sleepy. I was taking the test and then I was in Nap-land. I'm so glad you woke me."

"Me too. How do you think you did?"

"No extra credit this time," Nessa said. "But otherwise I think I'm good."

"That's a relief. And you're feeling okay?"

"Totally," Nessa said. "Nothing like a good power nap in the middle of an exam to get the batteries recharged. Hah." She blew out a breath.

The girls weaved through the crowded hallway.

"Are we on for the lake this weekend?" Nessa asked.

"I think so. Mamo isn't feeling that great, so we don't have any set plans."

"Sorry she's sick. But if she feels better, bring her along. She's cool." Nessa skipped left to avoid a teacher coming out of her classroom. "And then we'll have a ride instead of needing to ride our bikes. Plus she brings the best snacks."

"She does have the food thing down," Sadie said.

"Here's my stop." Nessa peeked into the classroom. "Ooh, substitute teacher. French should be a cakewalk today. Or, I mean, *c'est du gâteau*. I think." She laughed. "See you at lunch?"

"Yep. I'll save you a spot."

"And I'll be there. Think maybe there'll be a Jason-Derek rematch? I was bummed I missed that yesterday."

"I really hope not," Sadie said. "And you didn't miss that much." *Especially compared to everything else you've missed.*

Sadie wished she could tell Nessa about the Rampart, the cryptids, the secrets. But she'd promised Jason and his family to keep her lips sealed. At least Mamo knew the scoop.

"Yeah, well, one of these days I'd like to see Derek get what he deserves." Nessa stepped into the doorway of her French class. "Later."

"Later." Sadie continued down the hall to English. She passed the janitor's supply closet, though Mr. Whitfield liked to call it his office.

"Good morning, Sadie," Mr. Whitfield said.

"Good morning. Office is looking good." Sadie smiled.

"Thank you. You know how I like a clean and organized space." He chuckled and pretended to straighten a pile of disheveled rags on the shelf.

"On top of it, as always." Sadie waved. "Have a great day, Mr. Whitfield." She continued to her next class.

As she rounded the corner, a woman she didn't recognize ducked into a classroom across the hall. She was slight, only a bit taller than Sadie. Her hair was dyed purple.

Huh. Another sub.

That didn't happen at Salton High very often, especially one with purple hair.

Sadie hurried home after school. She dropped her backpack in the foyer. "Mamo?" She spotted her out the kitchen window.

Mamo was in the garden. She wore a straw hat tied with a royal blue scarf, khaki shorts, and a peach-colored T-shirt that said, "Ask me about the birds and the bees." She piled zucchini into the basket next to her.

Sadie stepped outside. "You're feeling better." She hugged Mamo.

"Right as rain, just as I said." Mamo looked up at the sky. "Which is exactly what we could use more of these days. This Indian summer won't let go."

"I'll water the garden after I do my homework," Sadie said. She nodded at Mamo. "I haven't seen that shirt in a while."

"You asked me not to wear it in public, so I tucked it away. But I figured it would be just fine for gardening."

Sadie felt her cheeks flush. "It was a little bit embarrassing when we ran into Mrs. Bauer at the grocery store.'"

Mamo laughed. "It's only meant to get people into a conversation about actual birds and bees and their importance to our food supply."

"I know. But we'd just had 'the talk.'" Sadie laughed too. "Anyway, that was years ago. Wear it wherever you want." Sadie paused. "But maybe when we're not together."

"Oh, you're really growing up." Mamo smirked. "Help me carry in the zucchini."

Sadie lifted the basket and they walked inside.

"You get after your homework. I'm going to slice some of these and we'll sauté them with onions for dinner. We're also having trout and salad. Sound good?"

"Sounds great." Sadie grabbed her backpack from the foyer. She returned to the kitchen for a glass of water.

Mamo was hunched over the sink but straightened quickly when she heard Sadie behind her. She turned toward Sadie. "Forget something?"

Sadie took a glass from the cupboard. "Just water." She placed the glass under the dispenser in the refrigerator door. "You okay?"

Mamo dismissed the question with a wave of her hand. "I was just stretching my neck. It's a little tight from too much time in bed. That's all."

Sadie nodded. "Okay." She went upstairs. She wanted to believe Mamo was fine.

But something nagged at Sadie's gut and wouldn't let go.

TWO

Attack

Early the next morning, Sadie's phone buzzed with a text message from Jason: "Going to London to help Dad and Della. Back in a few days."

Sadie responded: "Everything okay?"

"Probably. Not sure. Weird coin stuff. Tell you when we get back. Dogs and Kyle at Gma Lena's."

"I'll stop by, help with dog walks."

Jason replied: "Thx. Talk later."

It hadn't even been two days since Jason's dad took Della to London, hoping the League of Governors could help her feel better. It seemed odd that Jason and his uncle needed to go after them so soon. But "odd" was kind of their normal lately. Like the League of Governors—the secret organization that governed the relationship between humans and cryptids. It had been around for hundreds of years, though most of the world didn't know it existed. Most didn't even know cryptids like Bigfoot, Skyfish, and Ahool existed and lived among humans. But for Sadie and Jason, it was all normal.

Sadie dressed and checked on Mamo. She was sleeping. Sadie eased her door closed and went downstairs. She made eggs, toast with homemade raspberry jam, and poured herself a glass of almond milk. Mamo was still asleep when it was time to leave for school, so

Sadie wrote her a note and stepped into Mamo's office to leave it on her computer. Her hand brushed the trackpad and the screen came to life.

A new post for Mamo's blog, The Beesy Gardener, sat open with only two lines written. Next to it, the Messages window displayed a note received last night at nine-thirty from someone known as CDubya: "Let's talk again soon. This is important to both of us."

Mamo hadn't sent a reply.

Who is CDubya? Sadie scanned her memory for anyone in town with the last name of Dubya, or if she'd heard Mamo mention the name before but came up empty. She clicked "Sleep" and shut off the screen.

✳ ✳ ✳

The end-of-day bell rang and the silence of the halls morphed into chatter, and laughter, and banging locker doors. Sadie took out her phone and called Mamo.

"Hello, sweetheart." Mamo sounded good, energetic.

"Hi. How are you feeling?"

"You really need to stop asking me that. I'm the one that takes care of you, remember?"

"It goes both ways, Mamo," Sadie said. "And you slept in this morning."

"Just catching up on my beauty sleep." Mamo chuckled. "Nothing to worry about."

"Okay. Well, I was thinking I'd stop by Mrs. Fallon's house and see if she needs some help with the dogs. Jason and his uncle had to go to London, and she has both Shay and Finn."

"That's a great idea. I talked to Lena earlier today, and she's got quite the full house. I'm sure she'd appreciate the visit. I've got a few errands to run, so I'll see you at home later. And how about I pick up pizza for dinner?"

"Yum, yes. Onions and mushrooms please."

"Consider it done. See you later. Love you."

"Love you, too. Bye." Sadie ended the call.

Shoot, I was going to ask her about CDubya. She made a note to remember when she got home.

A few minutes later Sadie arrived at Jason's grandmother's house. She heard the dogs barking and growling in the backyard so she skipped ringing the doorbell and let herself in through the gate. Two white pit-bull-mix dogs raced toward her, stopping only inches before they barreled her over.

"Whoa, you crazy dogs." Sadie laughed and hunched down. Shay, the younger of the two, had some black on her face and paws, but otherwise she was as white as Finn. Shay was almost as big as Finn, but still mostly puppy. She licked Sadie's hand, then face, then hand again, her tail wagging like seeing Sadie was the best thing ever.

"Okay, okay, it's great to see you, too." Sadie dodged a lick to her eyeball. "Sit, Shay."

Shay pretended to sit, her butt not quite on the ground.

"All the way," Sadie said.

Shay scooched two inches backward and planted herself.

"Good girl, Shay." Sadie scratched her behind her ears. "Now go find your ball."

Shay sprang and dashed away. Sadie turned her attention to Finn who'd sat as soon as she'd reached Sadie's side, waiting for her turn.

"Hello, beautiful girl."

Finn lowered her head and pushed it into Sadie's thigh. Sadie scratched her ears and under her collar. "How's my good girl?" Finn's tail swished against the cobblestone walkway, flicking leaves and dirt. Sadie kissed the top of her head.

"Let's go find Mrs. Fallon, okay?"

Finn pranced ahead of Sadie, leading the way to the back patio. There sat Jason's grandmother, Lena Fallon, Jason's brother, Kyle, and another guy Sadie didn't know. He seemed about her age.

"Sadie, thank you for stopping by." Mrs. Fallon gave Sadie a hug.

"You're welcome. Hey, Kyle." Sadie waved at Jason's brother.

The other guy jumped from his seat, his hand outstretched. "I'm Brandon, Brandon Shaw. I'm a friend of Jason's from his old neighborhood."

"Oh yeah, hi." Sadie shook his hand. "He talks about you all the time."

"Likewise. And you look just like your pictures," Brandon said.

"Huh?" She felt her cheeks warm. Was she blushing? Why was she blushing?

"Some selfies you guys took. I told him to send me a pic."

"Oh. Wow. Well, I guess I should have asked the same of you. I mean of him, of you. I mean for a picture of you." Heat from her cheeks traveled to her neck and chest. "Okay, I totally hope you know what I mean."

Everyone chuckled.

"Of course, yeah," Brandon said. "No worries." He returned to his seat.

Shay dropped a ball at Sadie's feet.

Oh, thank you, Shay. Sadie threw it across the yard and Shay sprinted after it.

"Nice throw," Brandon said.

"Uh, thanks." Sadie wondered for a second if she should explain that she'd played softball. But she caught herself.

"So, you're visiting?" Sadie asked.

"Brandon's parents have been called out of the country for a few weeks," Mrs. Fallon said. "They'd arranged for Brandon to stay with Jason and Kyle while they were gone. But with Jason's change in plans, Brandon will stay here with us until everyone gets back. They should be home in a few days."

"What about school?" Sadie threw the ball again for Shay.

THE CLAN CALLING

"I usually travel with my parents since they're away a lot on business. But sometimes it doesn't work out, like this time, so my parents talked to the school, and now my teachers give me my assignments via the web," Brandon said.

"That's cool. Do your homework whenever," Kyle said.

"Yeah, as long as I get it done on time. And don't slack." Brandon stroked Finn's head.

"We'll make sure of that." Mrs. Fallon smiled at Brandon. "Sadie, have a seat. Can I get you a lemonade? Or some water?"

Sadie dropped her backpack and sat in the chair nearest her. "No, thanks, I'm good. I guess the dogs don't need to be walked?" She watched Finn and Shay who were wrestling and play-biting each others' ankles.

"Kyle took them this morning after we got back from the airport. Plus, they've been running around all afternoon. I expect exhaustion to hit any time now," Mrs. Fallon said. "Then again, I've been thinking that for more than an hour."

The dogs leaped onto the patio and raced around the circle of chairs, Finn on Shay's heels. They zipped onto the grass and tumbled into each other.

Sadie laughed. "Yeah, they're definitely close to exhaustion."

"Are they always like this?" Brandon asked.

"They have their moments, but they're not usually quite this worked up." Mrs. Fallon shaded her eyes against the sun. "I think they're putting on a show for you."

Sadie hung out for another hour and checked her phone again for messages. Nothing from Mamo, but Sadie wanted to be there when Mamo got home.

She stood. "I guess I better get going. Mamo's bringing home pizza."

"Lucky." Kyle and Brandon spoke in unison.

Mrs. Fallon *tsked*. "You poor boys. You'll have to suffer through

17

our evening with only hamburgers and salad. How will you manage?" She winked at Sadie.

Shay and Finn collapsed in a shady corner of the yard. "Looks like the show is over," Sadie said. "Let me know if you want me to stop by tomorrow or whenever."

"Thank you, Sadie. Even if the dogs don't need to be walked, we always love seeing you." Mrs. Fallon stood and patted Sadie's back.

Sadie picked up her backpack and let herself out of the yard. She headed down the street toward home.

The strange red SUV was parked in front of her house again, but she didn't see the man anywhere nearby. She turned up the walk to her front door. It was open.

Weird.

"Mamo?" Sadie glanced into Mamo's office, then continued through to the kitchen. It was empty except for two fresh pizzas smelling of cheese and Italian spices.

Sadie went upstairs. "Mamo?" Maybe she was in bed? *Please don't let her be sick.*

She stepped into the doorway of Mamo's room. Mamo lay on the floor, not moving. The SUV-man was hunched over her, his hands on her neck.

Sadie's heart hammered. "Get away from her!" She fumbled for her phone.

The man turned toward her. "Call for help." He returned his hands to Mamo's neck.

"Stop!" Sadie lunged and swung her leg, round-housing a kick into the man's thigh. He hollered and dropped to one knee, grabbing his leg.

Sadie launched a front kick intended for the man's chin. He blocked with his forearm.

Sadie sprung back and kicked again, aiming for his back.

The man spun and grabbed her leg. "Stop," he said.

She twisted out of his hold and reset her fighting stance. "Get away from her." She hit the emergency call button on her phone.

"Just let me talk to you for a minute."

Sadie heard the distant voice when her call connected. She moved the phone to her ear but didn't take her gaze off the intruder. "There's a man in my house. He's hurt my grandmother. She might be—" A gasp of air strangled her for a second. "I think she might be dead."

"She's not dead. She needs an ambulance," the man yelled.

"Are you safe?" the dispatcher asked.

"I don't know. He won't leave."

The man put his hands in the air. "I'll go outside and wait in the front yard. Don't leave Willene's side."

How does he know... "He said he'll go outside," Sadie said into the phone.

"Do you know CPR?" the man asked Sadie.

She nodded.

"Check her pulse, make sure she's breathing, do CPR if you need to."

Sadie nodded again. The man hurried out of the room.

She scrambled over to Mamo and felt her neck. "He left," Sadie told the dispatcher. "I'm checking her now."

"Don't hang up. Set the phone down and put it on speaker."

She followed the dispatcher's instructions.

"Do you feel a pulse?"

Sadie pressed harder into Mamo's neck. A slight beat thumped into her fingertips. "Yes. Yes, I feel her pulse."

"And she's breathing?" the dispatcher asked.

She held her hand under Mamo's nose, watched her chest. It rose, but just barely. "Yes, she's breathing, at least a little. Please hurry."

"Police and ambulance are already on their way."

Sadie heard the sirens approaching. "I hear them, I hear them." She kept her focus on the slight rising and lowering of Mamo's chest.

"Good. Just stay on the phone with me until they get there, okay?"

"Yeah, yeah, okay. Okay." Waves of adrenaline crashed through Sadie's system. Her stomach churned.

Soon the paramedics were in Mamo's room asking Sadie to step aside. She watched them from the doorway. They checked her vitals, radioed in stats, referred to Mamo as "unconscious Caucasian woman, approximately fifty to fifty-five years of age."

"She's sixty-four, she just turned sixty-four," Sadie said.

"Correction. Patient is sixty-four," the paramedic said into his radio.

Mamo, you have to get better so I can tell you they thought you were only in your fifties. Proof that you look ten years younger than your real age, just like you always say. Sadie's nails pressed into her palms. "Is she going to be okay?"

"We're doing everything we can," one paramedic said. They lifted the stretcher and moved toward the door. Sadie followed them down the stairs and out of the house. SUV-man stood by his car, talking to Sheriff Gunderson. Sadie ignored him and climbed into the ambulance with Mamo.

An hour later, Sadie sat on the edge of a chair in the waiting room at the hospital, anxious to hear from a doctor, a nurse, anyone. She tried watching the too-loud television hanging in the corner but the old sit-com couldn't hold her attention. Her knee bounced. A few minutes later, the outside doors opened and Mrs. Fallon walked in with Brandon. Sheriff Gunderson was just behind them.

Mrs. Fallon rushed over and scooped Sadie into her arms. "I'm so sorry. Thank you for calling me. Have you heard anything yet?"

Sadie shook her head. "Nothing."

"That's okay. These things can take time." Mrs. Fallon directed Sadie back into a chair and sat next to her.

Brandon sat next to Mrs. Fallon. "I hope it's okay I'm here. I just wanted to help if I could."

"Yeah, it's fine," Sadie said. "Thanks."

Sheriff Gunderson stepped up to their seats. "Sadie, I need to ask you a few questions."

She scooted back in her chair and faced the Sheriff. "All right."

"The man who was in your house? He says his name is Connor White, and his ID matches his claim."

"Okay?" She shrugged.

"He says he's a friend of the family."

"He's lying. I don't know him. And neither does Mamo." Sadie crossed her arms.

"How can you be so sure about that?" the sheriff asked.

"Because I saw him in front of our house yesterday, and I asked her about him. She didn't know him."

"He was at your house?" The sheriff jotted in his notebook.

"He was parked on the street in front of our house. He must have been scoping it out or whatever it is criminals do." Sadie tilted her head. "You arrested him, right? He hurt my grandmother."

"We have him at the station. We're still talking to him."

"But I saw him standing over her. He had his hands on her throat." She shifted forward in her chair.

Mrs. Fallon put her hand over the top of Sadie's.

"He tells a different story," the sheriff said. "Says he was visiting when your grandmother got dizzy. He helped her upstairs and that's where she collapsed. What you saw was him checking for a pulse."

"But he—no. We don't know him." Sadie's body tensed.

"I understand. He also says you kicked him, dropped him to one knee."

"He wouldn't get away from Mamo."

"And you tried to kick him again?" the sheriff asked.

"Yes. He wouldn't leave." Sadie kept her gaze locked on the sheriff's face.

"Well, we're going to keep talking to him, checking out his background. And we'll talk to your grandmother when she's able." The Sheriff put his notepad in his pocket. "I'll keep you posted." He nodded at Mrs. Fallon and left the hospital.

"Why doesn't he believe me?" Sadie asked Mrs. Fallon.

"I'm sure he does. But it's his job to check and double check. That's all." She stood. "I'm going to go ask the nurse if they've heard anything yet."

Sadie nodded.

"Man, I'm really sorry about your grandmother. What is it you call her?" Brandon asked.

"Mamo. It's Irish for grandmother."

"Cool," he said. "And damn, you're like a badass or something."

"Huh?"

"Kicking that guy's ass. Not backing down. I'd probably be running if I found some strange dude in my house."

"I just, I was just…I have my blue belt in Tae Kwon Do. And I didn't think about it. I just needed to do something."

"No, absolutely," Brandon said. "That's awesome."

Mrs. Fallon returned from the nurses station. "The doctor's on her way to speak to us, then we can see your grandmother. The good news is she's awake."

"Is there bad news?" Sadie asked.

"The good news is all I know. Let's see what the doctor says."

Another door opened and a woman in a white doctor's coat walked in. "Sadie Callahan?"

"Yes, that's me." She stood. The doctor looked at Brandon and Mrs. Fallon. "They're with me."

The doctor nodded. "Your grandmother is conscious. We're still running tests to find out what happened, and that's going to take a bit more time."

"Okay," Sadie said.

"We'd like to keep her at least overnight, maybe longer depending on what we find. But she's insisting on going home tonight," the doctor said.

"Oh, Willene Callahan," Mrs. Fallon said to no one in particular. "Can we talk to her?"

"Yes, and I hope you'll convince her to stay. Until we know more, I don't want to risk a similar episode." The doctor placed a pen into her coat pocket. "I'll take you to her now."

They followed the doctor through the door and down a corridor. She directed them into Mamo's room. "I'll check back in a few minutes."

Sadie hurried to Mamo's side. She had an IV in her arm, and machines beeped behind her. Sadie examined Mamo's hands, careful not to grab where medical devices were clasped or attached.

"You look far more worried than is warranted," Mamo said. "I'm perfectly fine." She squeezed Sadie's hand.

"You're in the hospital." Mrs. Fallon put her hands on her hips. "Perfectly fine people aren't often found in hospital beds."

Brandon stood behind her, near the door.

"I just had a momentary setback with the flu and ended up here," Mamo said. "A bit of an overreaction, if you ask me. And I don't know why they moved me into this room. They said I can go home."

"That's not what the doctor told us." Sadie sat taller. "She wants you to stay."

"Nonsense. Look at that monitor." Mamo pointed to the screen near her head. "Pulse is normal. In fact it's better than normal for a woman my age. And my blood pressure is normal, too. There's no reason to keep me here."

"Willene, please don't be stubborn," Mrs. Fallon said. "Listen to the doctor."

Mamo's brows furrowed. "I have been listening to the doctor and every other person that's poked and prodded me since I got here.

And none of them can find anything wrong. So why stay? I'd much rather be home, in my own bed, if I even need to be in bed at all."

Mrs. Fallon pressed her lips flat.

"Is anyone going to introduce me to the young man hiding in the corner?" Mamo craned her neck to see around Mrs. Fallon. "I'm guessing you're Brandon? Lena told me you were coming to visit."

Brandon waved and took two short steps forward. "Hey, yeah, hi. I'm Brandon. Sorry you're sick?" He shrugged and turned to Mrs. Fallon. "Should I wait in the hall?"

Mamo answered. "Of course not. Any friend of Jason's is a friend of ours. Lena's told me all about you, so you're practically family. And now I guess we're even better friends since you've seen me in my lovely hospital smock. Not the most flattering look but I've never been too hung up on worrying about how others rate my fashion, as I'm sure Sadie can tell you."

"So true," Sadie said.

Brandon laughed. "Okay, then, well it's great to meet you, and, yeah." He shuffled closer to Sadie.

Mamo eyed the two of them for a moment.

"What?" Sadie asked.

"Hmm? Oh, nothing," Mamo said.

"Well, then what about that man?" Sadie asked. "He says he knows you."

Mamo scrunched her eyes. "I don't think it's a good idea for you to talk to him."

"So you do know him?" Sadie withdrew her hand from Mamo's. "Who is he? Why was he at our house? Why didn't you tell me about him?"

Mamo cleared her throat. "I didn't want him around you. I told him to leave town."

"But who is he?" Mamo didn't keep secrets from her did she?

"Someone I knew a long time ago. He just showed up a couple of days ago."

"So he *was* at our house yesterday." Sadie stood.

"Yes, but—"

"Then you flat out lied to me when I asked about him." From the corner of her eye, Sadie noticed Brandon moving toward the door.

"I thought he was going to leave," Mamo said.

"He *is* a bad guy. That's why you don't want him around me. And he was trying to hurt you." A breath caught in Sadie's throat.

Mrs. Fallon put her arm around Sadie's shoulders.

"No, he didn't hurt me, Sadie," Mamo said. "He just needs to go."

Sadie opened her mouth to ask again about who SUV-man really was, but the doctor entered the room.

"So, what's the verdict?" she asked.

"She's staying," Sadie and Mrs. Fallon said in unison, while at the same time Mamo said, "I'm going home."

"Mrs. Callahan," the doctor said, "please listen to your family and friends. They want what's best for you."

"Have your tests found anything wrong with me?" Mamo asked.

"No, but we'd like to run more tests."

"Is there any sound medical reason to keep me in the hospital?"

"Mrs. Callahan, you lost consciousness, your pulse dropped to a dangerously low level, and your breathing was shallow. We don't yet know the cause, but I prefer you stay here, at least overnight, so we can monitor you."

"I was just dehydrated. But now you've pumped me full of fluids and I'm fine. I'd like to be discharged." The look on Mamo's face indicated the discussion had ended.

The doctor turned her attention to Mrs. Fallon.

She nodded. "I'll help keep an eye on her."

A few minutes later, Mamo was dressed and ready to go. A nurse brought a wheelchair and insisted Mamo sit in it for transport to Mrs. Fallon's car.

At home, Sadie and Mrs. Fallon helped Mamo into bed and she quickly fell asleep.

Mrs. Fallon pulled Mamo's door almost closed. "I'm going to drive Brandon home, then I'm coming back here and spending the night in the room with her so you can get some rest."

"You don't have to do that," Sadie said.

"Yes, I do. Instead of school, you'll have to take care of her tomorrow, and you'll need your rest, okay?"

"Yeah, okay." Sadie stretched. "I'll text Nessa and ask her to get my assignments for me."

"Good," Mrs. Fallon said. "Hopefully you'll only miss Friday, and we'll have Willene back to her old self by the end of the weekend."

Sadie nodded.

Mrs. Fallon hugged her. "You're doing great, Sadie. You hang in there, okay? We'll get through this."

Sadie nodded again and yawned. "Okay. I'll sit with her until you get back."

Brandon waved at Sadie from the bottom of the steps, and he and Mrs. Fallon left. Sadie crept into Mamo's room and eased into a padded rocking chair pulled close to the bed. She watched Mamo's breath, her chest rising and falling, willing it to keep going, keep going, keep going...

THREE
Mamo

Sunshine seeped through the blinds on Sadie's windows and warmed her face. She smelled blueberry pancakes. *Why does the sun smell like blueberry pancakes?*

She opened her eyes and let them adjust to the light, then stretched her arms above her head, yawned, arched her back, and rolled onto her side, letting her eyes close again. She smelled coffee.

Oh. Mamo's making breakfast. Sadie sat up and swung her feet onto the floor. The memories of the night before rushed in. *But she's supposed to be resting.*

Sadie pulled on a hoodie and headed downstairs.

Mrs. Fallon flipped pancakes, a steaming cup of coffee on the counter next to her. "Good morning. Did you sleep well?"

"Yeah, thanks." Sadie filled a glass with water. "Smells good."

"Hmmm. The look on your face says otherwise. You don't like pancakes?" Mrs. Fallon took a sip of coffee.

"Sorry. It's just, I was hoping Mamo was down here." Sadie climbed onto a stool at the kitchen island.

"Would it make you feel better to know your grandmother is awake? And she's quite full of sass this morning, so she must be improving." Mrs. Fallon laughed. "She actually had the nerve to send me to the kitchen with a specific breakfast order."

Mrs. Fallon and Mamo had been friends forever, and Sadie knew how much they enjoyed bantering with each other.

"Speaking of which, would you get me some tomatoes and basil from the garden?" Mrs. Fallon asked. "It seems her highness would also like a Caprese salad with her pancakes. I don't see how they go together, especially for breakfast, but far be it from me to deny her highness's wishes."

"Sure." Sadie hopped off the stool and headed outside.

The heat of the morning sun coaxed garden scents from everything around her. She smelled mint, and basil, and soil. Tomatoes and freshly mown grass. The hum of the beehives soothed her like a meditation. Sadie breathed deep. She hunched and used her thumbnails to snip basil leaves, then plucked three ripe tomatoes.

She moved closer to the beehives and circled them, checking for anything odd or out of place, anything that might indicate a problem, but everything seemed in order. She watched the bees departing for their workday, ready to collect pollen for the hive. The buzzing dwindled as more bees flew off until there was barely a sound at all. *Must be more bees out of the hive than I thought. Early risers today.*

She returned to the kitchen. Mrs. Fallon served pancakes and syrup and put the plate on a tray along with a glass of water and a cup of coffee. "Please take this up to Willene, and tell her I'll have the Caprese for her in a few minutes." Mrs. Fallon yawned.

"You don't have to do that. I'll make it after I come back down." Sadie picked up the tray. "You've been up all night. You must be tired."

"Not at all. I'll grab a little catnap later and be just fine." Mrs. Fallon washed the tomatoes. "I'll have the Caprese done in two shakes, and then I'll be out of your hair." She smiled. "I'll check in with you later, okay? And you be sure to eat some of these pancakes, too. I made plenty."

"Thanks, Mrs. Fallon. For everything."

"Of course. That's what friends are for." She added a napkin to the tray. "Off you go. Willene will be happy to see you. And you call me if you need anything."

✳ ✳ ✳

Sadie backed into Mamo's room, pushing the door open with her elbow. "Good morning."

Mamo sat up in bed. "Good morning. Oh good, Lena made me blueberry pancakes." She reached out for the tray.

"Didn't you order them?"

"Yes, but Lena doesn't always do what I say if you can believe that." She balanced the tray on her lap.

"I'm shocked." Sadie smiled and plopped into the rocking chair, propping her feet on the box springs of Mamo's bed. "And I'm supposed to tell you your Caprese salad is coming."

"Perfect." Mamo took a bite of pancake, savoring the flavor. "Mmm, these are good. Maybe I need to go to the hospital more often."

"Oh, please no," Sadie said. "That was not fun."

Mamo laid her hand on Sadie's leg. "I know. I'm sorry about that."

"You seem like you're feeling better. Are you?" Sadie asked.

"Yes, I am. I'd get up right now except I promised Lena I'd take it easy, at least for today."

"And I'm holding you to that promise. Today your bedroom is my classroom."

"Would you like some help on your lessons? It would be just like the old days when I homeschooled you," Mamo said.

"You. Resting. Remember? And thank you, but I've got it under control." Sadie stood. "I'm going to get your salad."

Sadie returned and found Mamo lying on her side, the breakfast tray next to her. She was sound asleep.

Weird. Sadie set the salad on Mamo's tray and carried it all down to the kitchen. The scent of fresh basil tempted her. *I can make more for her later.* Sadie ate the Caprese and wrapped three pancakes in paper towels. She grabbed her laptop, a glass of almond milk, and the pancakes, and went back upstairs, plopping down in the hallway outside Mamo's door. She didn't want to risk waking her but didn't want to be too far away either.

A few hours passed. Sadie worked on her Algebra and English assignments, with a break every hour to check on Mamo and be certain she was still breathing. Sometimes between checks, Sadie heard Mamo's soft snore which made her smile. She would tease Mamo about that as soon as she had the chance.

The doorbell rang. Sadie dashed down the stairs to answer it before the visitor rang again. Sheriff Gunderson stood on the stoop.

"Good morning, Sadie. Wondering if I could have a few words with your grandmother," he said.

"She's sleeping."

"I don't want to disturb her. But please give me a call when she's awake—"

"Sadie, who's at the door?" Mamo called from her room.

"Hold on one sec, sheriff. Come in." Sadie gestured for him to wait in the foyer. She went up to Mamo's room. "It's Sheriff Gunderson. I'm sorry the doorbell woke you."

"Nonsense. I shouldn't be sleeping this much anyway." Mamo smoothed stray hairs away from her face.

"He wants to talk to you," Sadie said.

"That's fine, send him up."

Sadie waved to the sheriff from the top of the stairs. She followed him into Mamo's room.

Mamo held up one finger then turned to Sadie. "Would you be a dear and get me some ice water?"

"But I—"

"And that salad you promised earlier. That sounds perfect right about now."

Sadie glanced from Mamo to the sheriff, then back to Mamo. "Okay." Sadie exited the room. In the kitchen, she layered tomato, mozzarella, and basil, and sprinkled it with olive oil and balsamic vinegar. *Why did she want me out of the room?* She filled a glass with ice water and carried everything upstairs.

Sheriff Gunderson stepped into the hall. "You'll be happy to know everything is okay, and your grandmother was never in any danger from Mr. White. It's best you talk about it with her, but we won't be pressing any charges against him." He put his hand on Sadie's shoulder. "You have a good rest of your day. I'll see myself out."

Sadie pushed into Mamo's room and set the tray down. "What is happening?"

"It's too dark in here. Open the blinds, would you?"

Sadie pulled the cord and light flooded through. "Why aren't they pressing charges?"

"Mr. White didn't try to hurt me."

"Okay, then why was he here? Who is he?" Sadie's face felt hot. "Why didn't you tell me you knew him?"

"Like I said, he's someone I knew a long time ago. I never expected to see him again, and I thought he was on his way out of town, so there was no reason to tell you more." Mamo sipped her water.

"What is he, like an old boyfriend or something?" Sadie crossed her arms.

"He's someone I was very close to once, but haven't been for a long time. I barely know him anymore, and he's not part of our lives. Okay?"

Sadie stared at Mamo, her thoughts racing. "I guess."

Mamo tapped the rocking chair. "Come sit with me while I eat this delicious salad."

The chair creaked when Sadie sat.

"The sheriff told me you used your Tae Kwon Do skills on Mr. White." Mamo took a bite of salad. Her eyes twinkled.

"Yeah, but I couldn't stop him. He blocked me twice after I landed my first kick." Sadie rocked the chair.

"I suspect your instincts told you he wasn't a real threat. He didn't counter-attack did he?"

"No."

"There you go. Reason to stand down, right?" Mamo asked.

"Yeah, I guess so."

"Well, I know so. And I'm proud of you for taking the action you did."

Sadie smiled. "Thanks, Mamo."

"Let's just hope that's the most you'll ever have to use those skills in your lifetime. Though I'm comforted to know you can put them into action if needed." Mamo looked out the windows. "Big clouds off in the distance. Might be a storm coming. How about you head out to the garden and harvest whatever's ready to be picked while I finish my salad?"

"Okay." Sadie stood. "Do you need anything else before I go?"

"No, but you can bring me some chocolate chip cookies when you come back up."

"Done," Sadie said.

✳ ✳ ✳

Sadie grabbed one of the baskets stacked on the back porch and walked into the garden. She stopped and closed her eyes, feeling the warmth of the sun mingle with the fall breeze blowing across her skin.

"Sadie." A man's voice.

Sadie jumped and spun toward the sound. Mr. White stood by the gate.

"What are you doing here?" she asked.

"May I come in? I'd like to talk to you."

"I think I can talk to you just fine with the gate between us."
Sadie's heartbeat hastened.

"I need your help," he said.

"I don't even know you. And aren't you supposed to be leaving town?"

"I'm not going anywhere while your grandmother is sick." He ran one hand through his hair. "And I need your help to get her better."

"She's already getting better." Sadie bent and plucked cucumbers from their vine. "She just needs a little more rest."

"She doesn't get sick, does she. Isn't this illness of hers unusual?"

Sadie jerked to face him. "How do you know that?"

"Because I know Willy, and I know this isn't normal," he said.

Willy? Sadie squinted. "And how do you know her?"

"Our relationship goes all the way back to—"

"No." She held up her hand. "Forget I asked." *Relationship?* "She told me you don't matter to her, to us." Sadie returned to the cucumbers.

"I care about Willy, your grandmother. Together, you and I can help her get better," Mr. White said.

"We're fine. She's fine. Please go." She picked zucchini.

"She's going to get worse, but I can stop that from happening. You must convince her to let me do that."

Sadie stood. "She's not going to get worse, and you need to go, right now. Or I'm calling the sheriff and tell him you're trespassing."

"Please listen—"

"Go!" Sadie pointed toward the street.

Mr. White sighed and walked away.

Sadie crumpled to her haunches and sucked in deep breaths, balancing herself against the handle of the basket.

FOUR

Threats

S adie took two more deep breaths, in through her nose and out through her mouth. Cleansing breaths, as Mamo called them. *Shake it off, he's gone.*

She checked the plants around her and zeroed in on the yellow squash. Her phone dinged.

She pulled it from her pocket. Two texts showed on the screen. The first was from Jason: "Landed. Saw Tower of London sort of. Secret pass code didn't work. Cabbing to some friend of Uncle A's. Still looking for Dad and Della."

Sadie's brows scrunched. *Secret pass code?* She typed her reply: "Huh? Landed I get. And still looking I get. Confused about the rest."

Jason wrote back: "Sorry. Complicated. More later."

Hopefully, that means more detail later, and not more confusion later.

Her second text was from Nessa: "How's the throwback to home-schooling going? Miss you in the real world. :)"

Sadie replied: "Miss you too. All good here. Don't have too much fun without me."

Nessa: "Never! Xoxo"

Sadie put her phone back in her pocket and continued working her way through the rest of the garden. Soon she had a basket laden with fresh vegetables. She carried them into the kitchen, washed her hands, then put two chocolate chip cookies on a plate. She was about to close the cookie jar when she decided to add two more.

Mamo called to her as she climbed the stairs. "Is that the cookie fairy I hear on approach?"

"Yes it is," Sadie said. She slipped into Mamo's room. The shades were closed again. "I thought you wanted those open?"

"The light was bothering me a little." Mamo ogled the cookies. "Oh—it looks like we're splurging today." She clasped her hands together.

"I figured it was a special day since we're kind of homeschooling again." Sadie handed Mamo a napkin. The silver charms on Sadie's bracelet clinked against the plate.

"It makes me happy that you love your mother's bracelet enough to wear it every day," Mamo said.

Sadie sat on the edge of the bed. "I know it's weird, but I sometimes feel like I know her a little bit, like she's with me if I wear her bracelet." Sadie rotated the chain around her wrist. "I mean, I know she was thinking about me, that they both were when Dad bought her the baby rattle charm after I was born." She tapped the rattle and tiny beads pinged inside.

"It's not weird at all. Of course, she's with you. They both are. I just wish they'd lived to see what a wonderful young woman you're becoming." Mamo squeezed Sadie's hand. "I have an idea. Put off your school work for a while, and let's start planning those trips we've been talking about."

"Seriously?" Sadie asked.

"One hundred percent. We've put them off long enough."

"But I thought you didn't want me leaving town. Remember how upset you were when Jason and I went to the sugar mill a few weeks ago?" Sadie smirked. "And that was barely a mile over the Salton border."

"That may have been a bit of an overreaction, and you seemed to have survived it, so I suppose you can handle a trip to California or Mexico, or—do we have a list of everywhere we want to go?" Mamo asked.

"Right here." Sadie jingled the bracelet.

"Ah yes—the places special to your parents."

Sadie grinned. "Okay, there's Mexico, like you said, where they went on their honeymoon." She touched the silver sombrero charm, then the diploma. "And UCLA where they met—plus that means Disneyland, too, right?" Her eyebrows rose.

"Of course. I haven't forgotten."

When Sadie was little, Mamo had promised to take Sadie to Disneyland. She said it was something Sadie's parents had always wanted to do with her.

"And then there's the big trip to Australia to see where Mom was from," Sadie said. She didn't have a charm for Australia and hoped to find one during their trip.

"Australia is going to take a lot of planning," Mamo said. "We probably need to put that further out on the schedule for now."

"Yeah, okay. Makes sense."

"But let's figure out the other two. Where do you want to go first?" Mamo asked.

"Let's do them in order, so California first since that's where Mom and Dad met and got married. Plus, Mom lived most of her life there after she moved from Australia."

"That's very sound logic." Mamo took a bite of her second cookie. "How about we go when you're on spring break?"

Sadie clapped her hands. "Really?"

"Absolutely. I can't think of a better plan for spring break, can you?" Mamo asked.

"No. Nothing." Sadie popped off the bed and danced around the room. "I'm going to Disneyland, I'm going to Disneyland." Many of her friends had already been to Disneyland, and finally, she'd get to go there, too.

Mamo laughed. "All right. How about you do some research and find us some flight options, figure out where you'd like to stay, and start putting ideas together about what we should see? I'm going to take a little snooze."

"I can do that." Sadie took Mamo's napkin and plate. "And over dinner, I'll tell you what I found."

"Perfect," Mamo said. She eased herself from sitting to lying. "I can't wait to hear all about it."

Sadie moved into the doorway.

"Oh, and one other thing," Mamo said. "I lost track of my cell phone in all the hubbub. Would you find it and make sure it's charging? I think it's in the office."

"Sure thing. I'll take care of it. Have a good nap."

"Thank you, sweetheart."

Sadie pulled the door partway shut and went downstairs. After putting the plate in the dishwasher, she went into the office. Mamo's phone sat next to the computer, already plugged into its charger. *That was easy.* Sadie clicked the trackpad and the screen woke up.

There was a new note from CDubya in the Messages app. *Dang, I keep forgetting to ask about him.* Sadie clicked on the app: "Willy— you have to talk to me. If you don't listen, you're going to get hurt. Is that what you want?"

A tingle ran down Sadie's spine. This "CDubya" threatened Mamo.

CDubya...Connor White. The C matches, but Dubya? Dubya... White...CWhite...CW...W...dubya. CW is CDubya. He's just playing with the pronunciation.

Sadie printed the message, then she copied and pasted it into an email to herself. She called the sheriff's office. "I'd like to speak with Sheriff Gunderson, please."

"He's out on a call right now," the dispatcher said.

"This is Sadie Callahan. I need to tell him Connor White threatened my grandmother."

Sadie heard typing on the other end. "I see you had a recent altercation with him. Are you safe right now?"

"Yes," Sadie said. "I just saw a note from him to my grandmother. He said she'd better listen to him or he was going to hurt her."

"And where is your grandmother right now?"

"She's asleep."

"Okay. Stay inside and make sure all the doors and windows are locked. I'm sending an officer to your home. Don't open the door for anyone who doesn't identify themselves as one of our deputies, understand?" the dispatcher asked.

"Yes."

"Okay. Someone will be there shortly."

"Thank you." Sadie disconnected the call. She pressed the number for Lena Fallon.

"Hello, Sadie. Is everything okay?"

"I found a note from Connor White, saying he's going to hurt Mamo," Sadie said. "I called the sheriff's office and they're sending someone over right now."

"Oh...are you sure that's necessary? What did Willene say?" Mrs. Fallon asked.

"She doesn't know yet. She's asleep, I found the message on her computer."

"Tell you what. Why don't you send it to me, and I'll take a look at it. Maybe we don't need to bother the sheriff's office just yet."

"I know what I read," Sadie said.

"It could be some sort of misunderstanding. I think we need to talk to Willene first."

Mamo did say she knew him, and she didn't seem scared of him. "Yeah, okay." *Probably best to get Mamo's take on things.*

"I'll call the sheriff's office for you and explain the situation. And I'll come over later and we can talk to Willene together," Mrs. Fallon said.

"That's okay. I'll talk to her."

"Are you sure?"

"Yeah, I'm sure. Thanks, though," Sadie said.

"Call me if you need me."

"I will. Bye." Sadie disconnected the call.

A minute later, Mamo's phone buzzed. There was a message on the screen from Mrs. Fallon to Mamo: "Willene, you need to talk to Sadie about things."

Jeez, I said I'd talk to her. Sadie slid the phone across the desk. She stared at the message from Connor White. She read it, and reread it, and read it again. *How is that not threatening?* Finally, she closed the Messages window. Mrs. Fallon was right—it was best to talk to Mamo first.

Sadie opened a browser window and brought up Disneyland's website, exploring places to stay and learning about the events on the calendar. Then she visited UCLA's site and imagined her parents meeting there, how maybe they sat on the lawn under one of the big trees or attended a football game together. She wondered how things would be different if they hadn't died in that car crash. Would they live in California and spend time at the beach each weekend? Would they go to Disneyland whenever they wanted? Would Sadie have a little brother or sister?

She closed the browser. She'd seen enough for today. Disneyland, UCLA, and the beach. Those three places would make the trip perfect. Sadie could hardly wait to put her hands in the ocean and her toes in the sand with Mamo.

Just her, and Mamo, and the trip to California. That's all she needed.

✹ ✹ ✹

Mamo slept through the rest of the afternoon. For dinner, Sadie made sandwiches, reheated vegetable soup, and sliced fresh tomatoes, sprinkling them with garlic salt and pepper. She poured two glasses of ice water and added a sprig of mint to each, one of Mamo's favorites.

She carried it upstairs and stepped into Mamo's dark room. "The dinner fairy is here," Sadie said. She set the tray on a dresser. "Mamo?" Sadie opened the blinds partway and a splash of early evening light peeked through, though the sun would soon be down. Sadie clicked on a lamp next to the bed. "Mamo? Dinner?"

Mamo thrashed in the bed. Sadie shrieked and jumped back.

"Monsters. Stay away." Mamo flopped to her left side, then her right. "Burden. Her. A burden."

Who's a burden?

Sadie rushed forward and pressed into Mamo's shoulders. "Wake up."

Mamo shifted and a necklace Sadie didn't recognize glinted, then dropped back inside Mamo's top. Sadie shook her shoulders. "Wake up, Mamo. You're having a nightmare."

"What?" She grabbed Sadie's wrist and twisted. "Where are they? They're coming."

"Aah! You're hurting me!" Sadie cried out.

Mamo's eyelids sprang open. She gasped and released her hold, then reached for Sadie and drew her into an embrace. "I'm so sorry. Are you okay?"

Sadie nodded and pulled herself free. "I'm fine." She stepped back. "But are you okay?" She rubbed her wrist.

"Oh, your wrist. Let me see." Mamo held out her hands.

Sadie hesitated, then moved closer and placed her wrist in Mamo's palms.

Mamo examined the skin on both sides. "I don't think it's anything too serious. Does it hurt to shake it?"

Sadie flicked her arm back and forth. "No."

"That's good. Oh, I'm so sorry. I was having a terrible dream." Mamo scrunched her eyes and leaned back.

"You didn't answer my question," Sadie said. "Are you okay?"

"That dream left me with a doozy of a headache—"

"No." Sadie swallowed. "Are you going to get better?"

Mamo stopped rubbing her forehead and pushed herself up in the bed. "Of course, sweetie. Of course I'm going to get better. It was just a bad dream." She patted the bed beside her and Sadie sat. "I'll be better before you know it, and these few days will become a distant memory." She stroked Sadie's arm. "Alright?"

"Yeah, alright."

She's going to get worse. Connor White's words replayed in her head.

"And right now, something smells delicious, and we have travel plans to discuss."

Sadie half-smiled. "We're having sandwiches. And soup. And water with fresh mint." She hopped off the bed.

"My favorite," Mamo said. She closed her eyes and breathed deep.

"Should I get you something for your headache?" Sadie asked.

"No, no. All I need is some good food and good company. And I have that right here. Now tell me about our trip."

Sadie decided to hold off about the note from CDubya. She relayed everything she'd researched about their trip and gushed about the Disneyland hotels, and the beaches, and the UCLA campus. Through it all, Mamo was her regular self, excited to hear Sadie's ideas and make plans. But Connor White's voice wouldn't stop playing in the back of Sadie's head.

She's going to get worse.

FIVE

Nightmares

Mamo slept late on Saturday, but insisted on getting out of bed and "making a day of it." She made brunch of waffles, eggs, and a mixed berry salad, and served it on their back patio.

Bees buzzed between nearby pots of flowering plants.

"How are the hives? Do the bees have enough honey for the winter?" Mamo asked.

"I think so. But you might want to check them," Sadie said.

"Not necessary," Mamo said. "You're one of the best beekeepers I know, and if you say the bees have enough for the winter, then the bees have enough for the winter."

Sadie smiled. "That's if winter ever comes. The weather report said it's supposed to be in the seventies again today."

"Ah, it's coming. There's just the slightest edge of cold air on the breeze. I didn't feel it a few days ago, but it's there now," Mamo said. "Can you feel it?"

Sadie turned her face into the breeze. "I think I do, yeah. Weird."

"Not weird. Mother Nature. She's always sending us messages. We just have to listen." Mamo stabbed a strawberry and bit into it.

"Hey, can I talk to you about something?" Sadie asked.

"Always."

"It's about Connor White."

"You don't have to worry about him, sweetie," Mamo said.

"Okay. But is he CDubya?"

Mamo tilted her head. "You saw something on the computer?"

"Yeah, from CDubya. In Messages. Is that him?"

Mamo wiped her mouth with her napkin. "It is."

"Well, he said he's going to hurt you." Sadie swallowed hard.

"I'm sure that's not right."

"No, it is right. Look." Sadie pulled up the emailed copy of the note. "Right there. If you don't listen, you're going to get hurt."

Mamo sighed. "He's talking about my feelings, sweetheart. Not about me physically getting hurt."

Sadie's brow furrowed. "But why? Why is he talking about your feelings when you don't even know him that well?"

"Honey, there are some things that are best left to grown-ups," Mamo said. "This is one of those things. It's nothing serious, and it involves my life from long before you ever came into it, okay? I have everything under control, and you need to stop worrying about it."

"Are you sure?" Sadie asked.

"Absolutely. Wisdom is one of the gifts that come with growing older and I have loads of it. Everything is fine." She released Sadie's hand and ate a bite of waffle. "Did you get enough to eat?"

Sadie nodded. "Yeah, thanks."

"We should do this every weekend. Until it snows, of course."

✳ ✳ ✳

Mamo declined dinner that evening saying she'd tired herself out trying to do too much. She went to bed early.

Some hours later a scream pierced Sadie's sleep. She bolted up, rushed to Mamo's room and flipped on the light.

Mamo was standing in the center of her bed swiping at the air. Her eyes were shut. "Stay back. Stay back. I won't let you." She swung her fist.

"Mamo," Sadie called.

Mamo's arms flailed like she was fighting someone. "No. Get off me." She twisted her body and kicked. She teetered near the edge.

Sadie rushed over and held up her hands. "Mamo."

Mamo righted herself and moved to the center, her eyes still closed. She kicked some more.

Sadie scanned the room for something, anything that would help her wake Mamo without making her fall off the bed. Or cause Sadie to get kicked in the head.

Maybe a spray bottle?

"Aaaaaahhhhhh," Mamo screeched. "Get away."

Sadie shuddered and rushed to the laundry room. She grabbed the bottle and set the nozzle to stream.

Please work.

Mamo stood near the middle of the bed, her pillows behind her feet. Sadie squirted Mamo's ankles, firing as fast as she could.

"No, no," Mamo said. She bent forward to swipe near her feet and toppled over, onto the bed.

Sadie closed in and squirted Mamo's face.

"What? What?" Mamo's eyes opened.

"Sorry." Sadie eased back.

Mamo stared. "Sadie?" She wiped water from her face.

"Yes?"

"You're okay?"

Sadie stepped to the edge of the bed. "Yes, I'm okay. You just had another bad dream." She helped Mamo turn around and lie back on her pillows. She plucked tissues from a nearby box and handed them over.

"But I didn't," Mamo said, dabbing the remaining drops from her skin.

"Yeah, you did. See? You're in your room, I'm here with you. Everything's fine." Sadie untwisted the covers and pulled them over Mamo.

"You're really okay?" Mamo touched Sadie's face.

"Yes, and so are you."

"I thought you were gone. I thought they took you."

"Who?" Sadie sat.

"The Clan. They came for you." Mamo scrunched her eyes. "I couldn't protect you."

The Clan? "I don't think you're all the way awake, Mamo. Do you know where you are?" Sadie felt Mamo's forehead. It was warm and clammy.

"I'm with you, right where I want to be," Mamo said.

A smidge of relief eased into Sadie. *That's more like it.*

Mamo grabbed Sadie's arm. "Promise me you won't go in the forest." Her eyes widened.

Sadie's stomach flipped. *This is not good.* She pulled at Mamo's hand. "Please let go."

"Promise me," Mamo said.

"I promise I promise." *We don't even have any forests. Just cottonwoods and scrub oak.*

Mamo released her grip. Sadie stood.

"Oh, sweetie, I'm really tired. Would you mind turning out the light?" Mamo asked.

Sadie scanned Mamo's face. Her expression was normal, calm, Mamo.

"The light? Sadie?"

"Uh, yeah. Of course." Sadie switched off the light and returned to her room.

✳ ✳ ✳

Screams woke Sadie three more times that night, but none of the incidents were as bad as the first. Mamo didn't stand, didn't punch, didn't kick. But she thrashed in her bed until Sadie could wake her and calm her. After the second scream, Sadie didn't bother going back to her room. She dozed in the rocking chair next to Mamo's bed.

There were no more screams after four a.m. The sun rose but Mamo didn't want to get up. She used the bathroom, then went right back to sleep. Sadie made breakfast and ate it in Mamo's room. The plate she'd prepared for Mamo went untouched. Sadie brought Mamo water, tea, a glass of lemonade but Mamo refused it all saying her stomach felt nauseous.

Sunday night brought more violent nightmares. Sadie planted herself on the floor of Mamo's room and barely slept between outbursts.

Monday morning came, and Sadie sat in the chair next to Mamo's bed. She texted Nessa: "Mamo still sick. Please tell office. Will bring excuse note later."

Nessa replied: "Got it. I'll give you my class notes and get your homework. Need anything else?"

I need Mamo to get better.

She typed: "No. All good. Thx."

Sadie hesitated, then texted Haru, a friend and Kappa, a cryptid with the power to heal: "Hey Haru—how are you?"

Haru responded: "I'm good. In Tokyo with family. Everything okay?"

She answered: "Yeah totally. Just saying hi. Have fun."

Her shoulders sagged.

Mamo's eyes opened. She blinked.

"Hi, good morning. Can I get you anything?" Sadie asked.

"Who are you?"

"It's me. Sadie."

Mamo rolled on her side, her back to Sadie. "Don't lie to me."

"I...you're tired. I'll let you rest." Sadie rushed out of the room. She leaned against the wall in the hallway and sucked in two deep breaths. They shuddered out.

What if she doesn't get better? What if she...

"Stop it, stop it," Sadie said to herself. "You can't think like that. Of course she'll get better." Sadie rubbed the back of her neck. It was tight, knotted. "I just need to think about something else." She went downstairs and removed her math book from her backpack. She opened to the page of problems assigned on Friday. She ran the formulas through her head and scratched notes on the paper beside her. Her vision blurred and she blinked fast to clear it and focused again. She made a few more calculations. Her eyelids drooped. Her thoughts jumbled. She fell asleep.

Ding-dong.

"Huh?" Sadie sat up and reached for her phone while her eyes adjusted to the light. The screen on her phone was blank.

Someone knocked on the front door. Sadie jumped up and hurried to answer it. Mrs. Fallon stood on the front porch.

"Hey, good morning, Mrs. Fallon. What are you doing here?" Sadie asked.

"Good afternoon, dear." She stepped inside. "I called Willene but didn't get an answer, so I stopped by to see how she's doing."

"Wait—afternoon?" Sadie glanced at the time on her phone. "Oh my gosh." She dashed up the stairs and pushed into Mamo's room. She was sound asleep. Relieved, Sadie stepped back into the hallway.

Mrs. Fallon looked up from the bottom of the stairs. "Everything okay?"

"Yeah, fine." Sadie walked halfway down the stairs and stopped. "I mean, no." Her eyes filled with tears. "No, everything is not fine."

Mrs. Fallon waved her forward. "You're exhausted. C'mon, I'm going to fix you something to eat. And you tell me what's going on with Willene. She's not feeling better?"

Sadie shook her head and continued to the bottom of the stairs. Mrs. Fallon put her arm around Sadie's shoulder and led her into the kitchen. She sat her down at the kitchen island and cracked eggs into a frying pan. Sadie relayed all that had happened since Friday.

"For a while, she was totally better, and we had waffles, and she told me I was good with the bees," Sadie said. "And then everything went crazy."

"What did the doctor say?" asked Mrs. Fallon. She buttered toast and sliced an avocado.

"She won't let me call the doctor. She said she didn't need one."

"Hmm. And you didn't think about calling an ambulance when she got really bad?" Mrs. Fallon added berries to the plate and placed it in front of Sadie.

"I did think about it. But she sounded so crazy, I was afraid. I was afraid they'd lock her up somewhere and I'd lose her." A hiccup of air scuttled out.

"Oh, Sadie, I wish you'd called me." Mrs. Fallon sat next to her.

"I didn't want to bother you." Sadie picked up a napkin and wiped a tear from her cheek.

"You are not a bother. Never. Okay?"

Sadie nodded again.

"Okay. Here's what we're going to do. First, you eat. We need to get a hot meal in you. And then you're going to take a shower and get cleaned up. That'll work wonders."

"That does sound good," Sadie said.

"Then we're going to get yours and Willene's things together, and move you both to my house."

"I don't think Mamo will be okay with that. She'll want to stay here."

"She can want anything she likes, but it's not her decision," Mrs. Fallon said.

"We can't make her do something she doesn't want to do." Sadie tucked a tangle of hair behind her ear. "She's in charge."

"If Willene were thinking straight, and healthy, and able to take care of herself, I would agree with you. But she's not. That means you have to make the decision that's right for both of you. From where I stand, you need some help. Kyle, Brandon and I—even the dogs—can give that to you."

Sadie bit into her toast. Melted butter trickled down her throat. "I've never gone against Mamo."

"This isn't like disobeying a rule. This is big life stuff, Sadie. It's about doing what's right for everyone's health and welfare, yours and Willene's, and making decisions that others aren't capable of making. Do you see?" Mrs. Fallon asked.

"Yeah, I think so. But still..." She took a bite of eggs. "We always decide things together."

"And when she's healthy, you'll do that again."

"She's not going to listen to me," Sadie said.

"She has to. You're the reasonable one right now." Mrs. Fallon rinsed the skillet and put it in the dishwasher.

"But what if she doesn't? We should probably just stay here." Sadie sipped her water.

"You spent the whole weekend here, just the two of you. How did that go again?"

Sadie thought about the nightmares, the screaming, and sleepless nights on Mamo's floor. "It was horrible and hard." She swirled her fork through yolk on her plate. "But telling Mamo I've made a decision without her, that's going to be really hard, too."

"As hard as this weekend has been?" Mrs. Fallon asked.

"Probably not," Sadie said. "But what if she throws a fit?"

Mrs. Fallon smiled. "There's no what if. We both know she'll throw a fit. But she's all bark. And I've got your back."

"Okay," Sadie said. "Finish food, then shower, then tell Mamo we're moving. Let's do this."

✳ ✳ ✳

"Absolutely not. We're staying right here." Mamo tried to sit up, then reversed the action. "And shut off the overhead light, please."

Sadie switched off the light and turned on a lamp. Mamo angled away from it.

"I've already packed some things for you—pajamas, your toothbrush, your shampoo. And Mrs. Fallon is here to drive us," Sadie said.

"Tell her she can drive herself home." Mamo mumbled into her pillow.

"I'm standing right here, Willene."

Mamo half-opened one eye. "Did you put this idea in her head?"

"It's the right thing to do, and you know it. You can't expect Sadie to continue taking care of you. She needs rest, and she needs to be at school," Mrs. Fallon said.

"I can take care of myself, thank you."

"Is that so? When was the last time you bathed? Your room smells like Jason's gym bag."

Mamo didn't answer.

"Willene?" Mrs. Fallon stepped to the edge of the bed. She shook Mamo's shoulder. "Willene?"

Mamo rolled on her back and opened her eyes. "Oh, hello. You look pretty today, Lena."

"Thank you, Willene. Are you ready to go?" Mrs. Fallon signaled Sadie to get Mamo's bag.

"Go? Where are we going?"

"We're having a sleepover at my house. Don't you remember?" Mrs. Fallon helped Mamo stand. "It was all your idea."

"Oh, right...but what about Sadie?" Mamo asked.

"She's coming, too."

"That's good." Mamo stood. Her necklace swung outside of her pajama top.

Mrs. Fallon sucked in a breath. "Willene, you're wearing that necklace."

"Should I take it off of her?" Sadie asked.

"No, leave it," Mrs. Fallon said.

"It's helping me, Lena. I can feel it." Mamo clutched at the pendant.

Mrs. Fallon walked her toward the bedroom door. "I'm glad, Willene. I'm glad."

"Are you sure I shouldn't take it off? Maybe she'd sleep more comfortably without it," Sadie said.

"No, it's a healing stone. It helps her."

Not very much it doesn't.

✻ ✻ ✻

Sadie and Mrs. Fallon managed to get Mamo moved, bathed, and dressed in fresh pajamas. They tucked her into bed, and Mrs. Fallon offered to make Mamo something to eat. Mamo drank some broth, but refused anything more. She was soon asleep.

Mrs. Fallon ordered Chinese food for everyone else. The order arrived, and Sadie fumbled her way around the kitchen learning which cupboards held plates and glasses, and what drawer had silverware as she helped set the table. She heard Finn and Shay scrabble up the stairs from the basement. They both came into the kitchen.

"Finn and Shay hang out in the basement by themselves?" Sadie asked.

"Nah," Brandon said. "They were outside."

"But...how?" Sadie had only seen the dogs go in and out through the back door.

"I wanted to make sure they could get in and out whenever they needed," Mrs. Fallon said, "But I also wanted to avoid the draftiness of a dog door in the kitchen. So instead, the dogs can go through the basement where they have a ramp to a dog door into the window well, and steps that go out of the window well into the yard. It's rather impressive, if I may say so myself."

"Mrs. Fallon's a creative genius." Brandon pulled out a chair and sat.

"I don't know about that," Mrs. Fallon said. "I came up with the idea, but it took people smarter than me to make it work."

Sadie slumped into a dining room chair. "That is awesome." Shay belly-crawled under the table and lay on Sadie's feet.

Kyle walked in. "Yes. Egg rolls." Kyle took three and put them on his plate as he pulled out his chair.

"I know you're a growing boy—"

"Uh...hello, Grams." Kyle stared at Mrs. Fallon.

"Excuse me. A growing young man. But there's enough for two egg rolls per person, so please give one of those to Brandon."

Brandon grinned and held up his plate. "You may serve me."

Kyle picked up an egg roll, pretended to lick it and plunked it on Brandon's plate.

"Thank you, sir." Brandon took one more from the container and passed it to Sadie. "Two left. All yours."

"I am so tired, I don't know if I have the strength to chew." She reached for the container, grasping where Brandon already had his hand. She jerked her hand back. "Oh, sorry." Sadie felt warmth flush her face.

"Oh yeah, er, no. It's okay." Brandon turned the container so a space to grab was clear for Sadie.

She set the container down. "Uh, I think I'll stick with the noodles. I probably won't choke on those if I fall asleep mid-bite." She looked at Mrs. Fallon. "But the egg rolls smell really good."

Mrs. Fallon smiled. "You head up to bed when you're ready. After all, I do expect you to go to school tomorrow."

"Can't think of anything I'd rather do," Sadie said.

"You are such a geek." Kyle took a giant bite of egg roll.

"Thank you," Sadie said.

Later that evening, Sadie sent a quick text to Jason: "Super crazy here. Hope London is good. Say hi to everyone for me."

She was too tired to wait for a response, plus it was probably the middle of the night in London anyway. Sadie switched off her bedroom light.

✳ ✳ ✳

There was no message from Jason the next morning.

Weird.

Sadie gathered her bathroom stuff and peeked into the hallway. It was strange to be in a house with boys. She didn't want to see anything she shouldn't see, and she for sure didn't want anyone to see her naked, or half-naked, or any other kind of naked. She scuttled into the bathroom and locked the door behind her.

After Sadie got ready, she saw Mrs. Fallon in the kitchen and asked if they should make a bathroom schedule.

"Not to worry," Mrs. Fallon said. "Kyle and Brandon are both staying in the basement, and they have their own bathroom down there. You and Willy share the bathroom you used this morning, and I have my own in my bedroom." She added cream to a cup of coffee.

Relief washed over Sadie. "Oh, okay. That makes it easy."

"Even more so when Willy is feeling strong enough again to bathe on her own," Mrs. Fallon said. "But she'll get there."

"Yeah," Sadie said. And the sooner, the better. She tucked her phone in her bag and headed to school.

✳ ✳ ✳

"My girl is back." Nessa skipped to Sadie and linked arms as they walked down the hallway to class. "That was too many days apart."

Sadie nudged Nessa's shoulder. "I totally agree."

"How's your grandmother?"

"Not that great." Sadie unlinked to open her locker. "But we're staying at Mrs. Fallon's house now, so I think that will help."

"With Kyle? You're so lucky," Nessa said.

Sadie swapped out her books and picked up her lunch. "Seriously? I thought you were over your crush."

Nessa sighed. "I thought so, too. But I think I heart him."

"You crack me up." Sadie shut her locker. "After you meet Brandon, you'll probably tell me you heart him, too." She moved down the hall but Nessa grabbed her arm.

"Wait—who's Brandon?"

"A friend from Jason's old neighborhood. He's staying with them for a while."

"And is this old friend cute?" Nessa asked.

"Yeah he's, I mean..." Sadie shrugged. "He's okay, I guess."

Nessa's jaw dropped. "Ooooh, you like him."

"What? I mean sure, I like him. He's nice." Sadie stepped into the flow of students.

Nessa faced Sadie and walked backward. "No, you like-like him." She grinned. "He's a hottie, isn't he. What color is his hair?"

"Black, I guess." Sadie picked up her pace.

"Is he tall?"

"I don't know, he's a little taller than me, I think."

"Tall, dark, and hottie. Perfect. And is he smart?" Nessa side-stepped the janitor's bucket. "Please say he's smart. I know how you like the smart boys."

"I haven't even talked to him that much. Only when he came to the hospital—"

Nessa grabbed Sadie's arm and pulled her off to the side. "Hold on. You're telling me he came to the hospital when your grandmother was there?"

"Yeah, but he was with Mrs. Fallon."

"Was Kyle there?" Nessa asked.

"No, but—"

"Oh my God, Brandon is a total keeper." She hugged Sadie. "I'm so happy for you."

Sadie laughed. "For what?" She continued to her class and Nessa fell in step next to her. "Because I talked to a boy for five minutes?"

"You can tell yourself that all you want, Sadie Callahan. But you like him. And he likes you. No way he comes to the hospital if he doesn't like-like you. And you're both adorable. It's a match made in heaven."

"You're ridiculous," Sadie said.

"We shall see." Nessa stopped. "Oh, this is me." She stretched her back and yawned. "You can see how excited I am for art class today. I'm so not inspired. See you at lunch?"

"See you at lunch. I'll save you a spot."

Sadie still had a minute before the bell, so she poked her head into the janitor's closet-office. "Mr. Whitfield?"

He sat on an overturned bucket in the back corner. He was snoring.

"Oh." Sadie pressed her lips tight and tiptoed toward the door.

The snoring switched to sputtering. "Sadie?"

She turned back. "I am so sorry. I just wanted to say good morning."

"No worries, no worries. I'm not sure what came over me." Mr. Whitfield removed his cap and rubbed the top of his head. "I'm real glad you woke me. Now I wonder where my mop bucket got to?"

"I saw it. It's just down the hall, not far from my locker."

He nodded his head. "Ah, right. I remember being down there, cleaning up a soda spill. Strange. Not real sure what happened after that, but I'm sure it will come to me. Anyway, you best get to class."

"Yeah, I gotta run. Have a good day." Sadie felt a flush in her cheeks. She hoped she hadn't embarrassed Mr. Whitfield.

Algebra passed slowly, like honey poured in winter Mamo liked to say. Sadie's mind wandered. She wondered how Mamo was doing. She'd passed the night without any nightmares which seemed like a good sign. Hopefully, she'd feel like eating something tonight.

A snort sounded behind her. The class laughed. Debi Banks, head cheerleader, sat up in her chair and wiped her nose. "Why is everyone staring at me?"

"They seem to find it amusing that you were sleeping, and snorting, in my class," Mrs. Bauer said.

Debi gasped. "I was not."

"You totally were." One of the guys near her seat flipped his cell phone around and showed her the screen. Her snort sounded from the video.

"Oh, my God, please delete that." Debi reached for the phone.

The kid yanked it back. "Already uploaded."

"My dad's gonna kill me." Debi covered her face with her hands. "Please. Please, take it down."

"No way. I'm going to get a ton of likes with this." He high-fived his friend.

"Okay, class, settle down. Mr. Smith, please consider Ms. Banks' request. There's no reason to embarrass anyone. Not to mention the fact that phones are not to be used during class time."

The bell rang. Sadie scooped up her books and headed to the cafeteria. Nessa waved at her from across the lunchroom and Sadie made her way to the table.

"What's for lunch today?" Nessa asked.

"Not sure. Mrs. Fallon made it for me." Sadie unzipped her lunch bag. She unpacked apple slices, carrot sticks, and a turkey and Swiss sandwich on whole grain bread. "What about you?"

"Same old same old. Peanut butter and strawberry jam. And chips." Nessa dropped the chips on the table. "I need to step up my game. Yours looks much better."

"I'll swap halves with you." Sadie held out half of her turkey and Swiss.

"Sold." Nessa handed over her half. "You take such good care of me."

"You're lucky to have me." Sadie smiled.

"Oh, hey—I'm helping plan the winter dance," Nessa said. "We're meeting after school today. You should totally do it with me."

"Can't. I need to get home and check on Mamo. Plus, I want to help Mrs. Fallon with whatever. She's being so nice, letting us stay there."

"Mmm-hmm." Nessa raised one eyebrow and bit into her sandwich.

"What?" Sadie asked.

"Is Brandon going to be there helping Mrs. Fallon with whatever stuff, too?" Nessa said in a sing-songy voice.

"Oh seriously." Sadie wiped apple juice off her fingers.

"I've got a good feeling about you two," Nessa said.

"I don't know how that's possible since you haven't even met—"

A snore roared behind Sadie and she bounced in her seat. Students at the table burst into laughter.

Sadie turned as Stevie Harkness shot from his chair. "What the—"

"Dude," one of his friends said, "you're going to break windows with that thing."

"What thing?" asked Stevie.

"You were totally snoring like some old grandpa or something." His friend laughed harder.

"No way." Stevie joined in. "I don't even remember falling asleep. That's hilarious, dude."

Sadie turned back to face Nessa. *Weird. And I thought I'd had a rough weekend.*

"Did you see the video of Debi Banks?" asked Nessa. "That is so embarrassing. I'm so glad that wasn't me."

"Yeah, I was there. She seemed really upset."

"Her dad is kind of a jerk to her about school. Wants her to be a doctor or something and she has to get straight As in everything, but for sure in math and science," Nessa said. "He might make her quit cheerleading."

"That would suck." Sadie wadded her trash.

"Totally." Nessa finished her chips and handed the empty bag to Sadie. "To add to your trash wad, please."

"Very good, your highness." Sadie smirked and snatched the bag from Nessa's hand.

"Thank you." Nessa yawned.

"Are you tired?" Sadie asked.

"A little, I guess. Lunch makes me tired." Nessa stood. "And history class right after is not going to help."

Sadie tossed their garbage into the bin. "Yeah...lunch plus history can be rough."

✳ ✳ ✳

After school, Sadie walked to Mrs. Fallon's house and knocked on the front door.

Mrs. Fallon opened it. "No need to knock, Sadie. You come right on in like it's your own home."

Sadie stepped inside. "Thanks, Mrs. Fallon. How's Mamo?"

"She slept all day but woke up about thirty minutes ago. She must have known you'd be home soon." Mrs. Fallon smiled and took Sadie's backpack off her shoulder. "You go on up and see her."

Sadie walked into Mamo's room. She was sitting up in her bed.

"You look good." Sadie hugged Mamo. "How do you feel?"

"Much better. Maybe I just had to get out of that germ-laden room."

"You mean your bedroom at home?" Sadie asked.

"That's exactly what I mean. We need to clean that whole place. Have the carpets shampooed, wipe down the walls with vinegar and water, and wash all the bedding. Kill all the bad bugs."

Sadie sat. "You really think that's going to fix things?"

"Well, look at me. I'm doing better aren't I?" Mamo asked.

"Yes, but maybe that's because you've been asleep for most of the last four days." Sadie smiled. "Have you eaten anything?"

"Lena is making me something right now. I'm not very hungry, but she made me promise I'd try to eat at least a little."

"I really like her." Sadie tucked her hair behind her ears.

"Because she tells me what to do?" Mamo chuckled.

"Yes, that. But also, she's just so nice," Sadie said.

Mamo squeezed Sadie's hand. "That she is, sweetie. That she is. She's good people."

A few minutes later, Mrs. Fallon entered the room with a tray. "I'll start you off easy with some soup and crackers, and we'll see how you do." She set the tray on Mamo's lap.

"Thank you, Lena."

"I guess sleep did a little something for your manners." Mrs. Fallon put her hands on her hips.

"I think you can cut me some slack for being under the weather. I did have a fever." Mamo sipped some soup. "Mmm, and this is good."

"I'm glad you like it," Mrs. Fallon said. "Consider yourself slacked. And if you keep up the good behavior, as warden, I may even grant you an early release from the horrible torture or being waited on hand and foot. But I'm keeping you for a couple of days at least."

"I don't think—"

"Zip it. Quiet. Don't waste that slack I gave you."

Mamo rolled her eyes. "Fine. I'm your obedient guest." She took another sip of soup. "But I'll show you. I may even come downstairs later and join in the fun."

"And we would love it if you did," Mrs. Fallon said. "Sadie, please bring the tray down when your grandmother is finished. And the rest of us are having dinner in about half an hour."

"Okay. Thanks, Mrs. Fallon," Sadie said.

Ninety minutes later, Mamo was seated in the living room with everyone. She sat in a recliner, a blanket over her lap. Mrs. Fallon sat across from her on the sectional along with Sadie and Brandon, and Kyle sat in an armchair angled across on Brandon's right. Finn curled herself on the couch next to Mrs. Fallon, and Shay slept between Sadie and Brandon, her head on Sadie's lap.

Kyle passed his phone around the room, showing the video of Debi Banks' snort.

"Oh, that poor girl." Mrs. Fallon got up and handed the phone to Mamo. "She's probably mortified."

"But it's so funny," Kyle said. "She must be the only girl who snorts."

"I've been known to snort a time or two in my day." Mamo brushed a hair from her forehead. "And they always show up when I'm having the time of my life, laughing my head off, so I don't mind them one bit."

"Even if someone recorded it and put it on the internet?" Sadie asked.

Mamo thought for a moment. "If it was me laughing, I'd be perfectly fine with it. But that's not what this video is. This video is meant to embarrass someone. She should have the choice about whether it was posted or not."

"Even though it's so funny," Kyle said, not really meaning the question as a question. "Brandon, back me up here."

"Don't get me wrong, I think it's hilarious," Brandon said. "But I get what Mrs. Callahan is saying. If it's embarrassing, the person in the video should decide about it being uploaded."

Mamo toyed with the pendant around her neck. "I knew I'd like you, Brandon."

Sadie smiled. "Where did you get that necklace, Mamo?"

She dropped it back inside her top. "Oh, it's old. Been sitting in my jewelry box for years."

"I don't remember seeing it before," Sadie said.

"Haven't worn it in a long time. But I noticed it a week or so ago and felt inspired to wear it, maybe show it off a little."

"It's a healing stone?" Sadie asked. "Do you think it's working?"

Mamo snapped her gaze to Mrs. Fallon then back to Sadie. "It's working like gangbusters. I feel like we should all go dancing. Who's with me?"

"Very funny," Mrs. Fallon said.

A snore growled from across the room. Kyle's head was tipped back, his mouth hung open. Another snore rumbled out.

Sadie nudged Brandon. "We should totally record him." She looked from Kyle to Brandon. He was asleep too, but not snoring.

Huh. Weird.

She directed her attention to Mrs. Fallon. Her head drooped sideways nearly touching Finn's. Her eyes were shut.

"What is it with everyone falling asleep?" Sadie asked Mamo.

Mamo didn't answer. She sat motionless, her eyes shut, her mouth closed.

Sadie bit her bottom lip. She stroked Shay's head, called her name. The pup lifted her head an inch then dropped it back onto Sadie's lap.

Sadie's heart skipped and pulsed faster.

"Mrs. Fallon?" Sadie reached right and pulled on Mrs. Fallon's arm. "Mrs. Fallon?"

Mrs. Fallon didn't stir.

Oh my god what is happening?

Sadie's mind raced. People falling asleep at school, and now here. Is there a gas leak or something in the air? But that wouldn't happen both here and at school. And why would she be awake when everyone else was passed out?

No, there's no way...is there? She held her breath. *I'm the only one unaffected. Am I doing this? No. No, that's crazy.*

Brandon stirred. Kyle snored again.

Sadie scanned the room for Skyfish or some other cryptid that made people sleep, though she didn't recall any cryptid who had that kind of effect. And she didn't expect to see Skyfish unless there were a lot of them, which meant a different kind of problem.

There was no one in the room who didn't belong there.

Sadie startled when she noticed movement at her side.

"I'm gonna record him." Brandon stood and pulled his phone out of his pocket.

"I...uh..." Sadie looked at Kyle then back to Brandon.

"It'll be funny, right? I won't post it or anything," Brandon said.

"I'm glad to hear that." Mrs. Fallon was sitting up. She was petting Finn as if she hadn't missed a beat.

Brandon crept across the room and recorded for about thirty seconds.

Kyle lifted his head. "Dude, what are you doing?"

"You were totally snoring." Brandon stopped the recording and walked back to his seat.

"No way. I've been awake this whole time," Kyle said.

I wish everyone had been awake this whole time. Why don't they remember?

"Nope. I have video proof right here." Brandon raised his phone and hit play. Snoring sounded from the speaker.

"That's someone else," Kyle said.

"Not even. I'd show you but I don't want you to delete it." Brandon tucked the phone back in his pocket.

"Hey, you guys?" Sadie watched Mamo. She hadn't moved.

"Whatever. Then I don't believe you have anything." Kyle leaned back.

"Hey," Sadie said. "Mamo is still asleep." She jumped up.

"*Still* asleep?" Mrs. Fallon asked.

Sadie crossed the room to Mamo. "I mean, she's asleep."

"We've probably worn her out already," Mrs. Fallon said. "We should get her up to her room."

Sadie pressed Mamo's arm. "Mamo, wake up."

Nothing happened.

Sadie shook her. "Mamo. Mamo, wake up."

She didn't budge or twitch or mumble.

Mrs. Fallon hurried over and picked up Mamo's hand, patting it. "Willene, c'mon. Wake up now." She felt Mamo's forehead. "Willene?" She pressed her fingers into Mamo's neck, searching for a pulse. She turned to Brandon. "Dial 911."

Sadie stepped back, her hands flew to her mouth.

Oh my god, did I do this?

I...I killed Mamo.

SIX
Alarms

Sadie backed away and stared at Mamo.

Mrs. Fallon continued saying Mamo's name and patted her hand again, then her cheek.

Brandon spoke into his cell phone, his voice tense. "Yeah, that's the right address." He paused. "For sure, yeah, I'll stay on the line."

Mamo stirred.

"Oh, she might be waking up," Brandon said.

"Willene, c'mon now." Mrs. Fallon brushed Mamo's hair back with her hand. "Can you hear me?"

Mamo raised her head. "Don't tell me we're doing each other's hair now?" She pushed herself higher in the chair. "I'd rather have a mani-pedi if you don't mind."

Sadie scrunched her eyes shut. *Oh, thank goodness. She's okay. She'll be okay.*

Mrs. Fallon exhaled. "You gave us a bit of a scare, Willene."

Mamo clamped her hands on her head. "My hair looks that bad, does it?"

"Hardly," Mrs. Fallon said. "But we couldn't wake you up."

"Should I cancel the ambulance?" Brandon asked.

"No," Mrs. Fallon said. "I'd still like the paramedics to take a look at her."

"What? Don't be ridiculous, Lena," Mamo said. "It was a little cat nap. Tell them not to come, Brandon."

"Ignore her, Brandon." Mrs. Fallon turned back to Mamo. "My house, my call."

"You're making a mountain out of a speck of dust on the head of a pin, if you ask me," Mamo said.

"I didn't ask you." Mrs. Fallon walked away from Mamo. "I'm getting you a glass of water."

Mamo looked across the room at Sadie. "What are you doing all the way over there?"

"I just..." A pit formed in Sadie's stomach.

"Come over here and help me defend myself." Mamo smirked. "Clearly the power is going to her head."

"I'm good right here," Sadie said. "I don't want to get in the way." *I need to stay away from her.*

"You're never in the way," Mamo said.

Sirens approached.

"I mean, you know, the paramedics. I'll get the door for them." Sadie hurried out of the living room and through the foyer. She opened the front door.

An ambulance pulled up to the curb and two paramedics jumped out. Sadie directed them toward Mamo. She watched from the doorway as they asked Mamo questions and took her vitals.

Brandon walked over. "Are you okay?"

"Yeah. I just want to give them plenty of room," Sadie said.

"You have that covered."

"What do you mean?"

"You're not even in the room," Brandon said. "I don't think you can give the paramedics much more space without leaving the house."

"Oh." Sadie shifted her weight. "I guess that's true." She faked a laugh.

"I thought maybe you were freaked out by everything."

Heat faded from Sadie's skin. "What do you mean?" *Did he see me do something weird to make everyone fall asleep?*

"It's gotta be scary to see someone in your family so sick," Brandon said. "And having an ambulance come by for the second time? That would freak me out."

"Oh, right." Sadie nodded. "Yeah, it's really hard. Mamo is my only family."

"Seriously? No aunts or uncles or cousins?"

"Nope. It's just the two of us." Sadie's chest tightened.

"Wow, I'm really sorry. At least you have Jason's family though. Seems like you're pretty close," Brandon said.

Not the same thing.

"But look at your grandmother with the paramedics." Brandon gestured into the living room. "I wouldn't worry about her too much."

"I will not go anywhere with you two young men, nice though you are," Mamo said. "I'm perfectly fine right here."

The paramedics stood and asked Mrs. Fallon for assistance.

"Is there any indication of something wrong?" Mrs. Fallon asked. "Anything off in her vitals?"

"No, ma'am. But given her history—"

"My history is that I've always been healthy, and I'll be healthy again with a little more rest," Mamo said.

"We'd like to ensure that," one of the paramedics said, "by taking you to the hospital for a few more tests."

Mamo tucked her blanket around her hips and settled deeper into the reclining chair. "I'm in for the night, gentlemen."

"It's no use," Mrs. Fallon said. "She's an expert when it comes to bull-headedness."

Mamo *tsked.*

"We'll keep an eye on her," Mrs. Fallon said. "I'm sorry we bothered you."

"Not a problem. That's what we're here for." The paramedics gathered their gear and headed toward the door. "Don't hesitate to call us again if needed."

"Thank you." Mrs. Fallon closed the door behind them and returned to the living room. "I suppose that's enough excitement for one day."

"Yeah, I'm kinda wiped." Kyle stretched his arms over his head.

Sadie's shoulders tensed. *Stay awake, please stay awake.*

"Me too." Brandon yawned.

Sadie gasped.

Brandon's jaw snapped to close. "What? What is it?"

Everyone looked at Sadie, including the dogs.

"What's wrong, sweetie?" Mamo asked.

"I...uh...I'm super tired. I'm going to bed." Sadie spun on her heel and headed to her room. She sat on the end of her bed. *I'm overreacting. There's no way I'm making people fall asleep. That's impossible.*

Someone scratched on her door. Sadie opened it and Shay bounded in and jumped on her bed. She circled three times and lay down, wagging her tail.

"I think a puppy snuggle is exactly what I need, Shay." Sadie kissed the top of Shay's head. "And hopefully I don't make you fall asleep against your will." Sadie changed into her pajamas. "It's been a hard few days, and everyone's tired. Me especially." She climbed into bed. "I'm so sure I thought I was making people fall asleep. Like that could even happen. So dumb. But everything will be okay. Right, Shay?"

Shay moved closer to Sadie, tucking her back into Sadie's belly. Sadie stroked Shay's side. "You're a good girl."

Good girl.

✳ ✳ ✳

The alarm woke Sadie and she got ready for school. It was going to be another warm October day. Shay stood and stretched and followed Sadie downstairs.

Mamo and Mrs. Fallon sat at the kitchen table.

"You're up." Sadie kissed Mamo's cheek. "I assume you approved her being out of bed, Mrs. Fallon?" Shay scratched on the back door and Sadie opened it. Finn ran across the grass and tackled Shay on the patio.

"Warden Fallon gave me a pass only for breakfast, then it's back to bed for me." Mamo yawned.

Sadie froze.

"Which is probably a good call," Mamo said. "I don't want anyone else summoning the cavalry every time I feel a nap coming on."

Sadie glanced at Mrs. Fallon. She was wide awake and smiling at Mamo.

"Nice to see you being a bit more cooperative." Mrs. Fallon sipped her coffee. "I'm counting on that attitude sticking around for a while."

"And by attitude, I think you mean sparkling personality." Mamo chuckled and turned to Sadie. "How are you this morning? You seemed a bit out of sorts last night."

Sadie dropped her shoulders. "Oh, I was tired. It's been kind of crazy." She filled a glass with water.

Mrs. Fallon stood. "That it has. But we're all in this together now." She pointed Sadie toward the table. "I've got eggs and toast for you."

Sadie sat. "Thank you. Where are Kyle and Brandon?" A worry spiked her mind. "Are they still asleep?"

"They were both up early," Mrs. Fallon said. "Brandon is online meeting with one of his teachers, and Kyle already left for school to do something with the football team."

"Oh. Great," Sadie said.

Mrs. Fallon set a plate filled with scrambled eggs, toast, and a cup of yogurt with raspberries in front of Sadie. The fragrance of fresh raspberries made her mouth water.

"This looks really good, Mrs. Fallon." Sadie dug into the eggs.

"Lena does an okay job in the kitchen." Mamo winked at Sadie.

"Remember who's choosing what you eat for the next few days," Mrs. Fallon said to Mamo.

"I know, I know," Mamo said. "Just having a little fun. You're a better chef than I am, Lena, and you have been for a long time. You know I'm jealous."

"No way I'm better, but I appreciate the compliment," Mrs. Fallon said.

"And on that high note, I think I should return to my room and sneak in a morning snooze." Mamo pushed herself to standing.

Sadie stood to assist.

"I'll help her, Sadie," Mrs. Fallon said. "You finish your breakfast."

"Yes, eat." Mamo held onto Mrs. Fallon's arm and stepped around the table. "Your brain and body need that good fuel for the day."

"Okay." Sadie hugged Mamo. "I'll see you after school."

"That you will," Mamo said.

Sadie had almost finished her breakfast when Mrs. Fallon returned to the kitchen.

She noticed Sadie's empty plate. "You were hungry. Let me get you some more eggs."

Sadie held up her hand. "Oh no, I'm good. That was yummy." She stood. "I need to get going anyway." Sadie put her dishes in the dishwasher and picked up her bag. "Mrs. Fallon, have you heard from Jason? I sent a text a couple of days ago but he still hasn't responded."

Mrs. Fallon pulled a dishtowel off the rack. "Alexander called me the day before yesterday. Said they'd had a bit of trouble getting into League headquarters, something about an expired password or something." She dried a pan with the towel. "But everything's fine now. They're meeting with the League about Della. I guess she and Zachary are there, and simply had trouble with their phones being unable to make international calls."

So maybe my last message didn't get through. Weird that the League doesn't have WiFi.

Mrs. Fallon repeatedly wiped one spot on the pan, her brow furrowed.

"Are you worried about them?" Sadie asked.

Mrs. Fallon looked up. "Hmm? Oh, no. Alexander seemed a bit off, but they had a long journey and I doubt they'd had any rest since they arrived in London. I'm sure they'll get everything sorted out and be home in no time."

"That's great," Sadie said. "Maybe I'll try texting Jason later."

"Alexander said they would get upgraded phone plans though he does still tend to be forgetful at times." Mrs. Fallon chuckled. "I suppose his phone will remind him the next time he tries to call the US."

"Hah, very true," Sadie said. "Thanks again for breakfast, and for everything. I'll see you after school."

"Of course. Have a good day," Mrs. Fallon said.

Sadie snapped her locker shut. She slung her bag over her shoulder and waved at Mr. Whitfield who was emptying a trash bin as she hurried through the halls to Mr. Bond's history class.

"Good morning, fellow agents." Mr. Bond picked up a piece of chalk. "Today we're starting our lesson on the War of 1812." He dragged the chalk at the end of the number two across the chalkboard.

"I don't get it," Stevie Harkness said.

"That's why you're here, Mr. Harkness." Mr. Bond leaned against the front of his desk. "We're going to learn about the War of 1812 so you will, indeed, get it."

"But how did they even fight?"

"It's safe to say they used guns and ships and other standard wartime tools."

"Huh?" Stevie teetered backward on his chair. "How does a number hold a gun?"

Mr. Bond's brows furrowed. "Not following, Stevie."

"The numbers. Eighteen and twelve." He clunked forward in his chair. "How do they hold guns? And why are they even fighting?"

One corner of Mr. Bond's mouth turned up. Students laughed and Sadie pressed her lips tight to keep from smiling.

One of Stevie's friends turned toward him, grinning. "Dude, are you serious?"

"What? Yeah, I'm serious," Stevie said. "It's a totally good question. Do you know the answer?" He jutted his chin at his friend.

"He's talking about the year 1812, not the numbers eighteen and twelve." His friend punched Stevie in the arm.

Stevie's mouth hung open and he looked at Mr. Bond. "You really need to enun...enunsh...you really need to sound out your words better, Mr. B."

Mr. Bond cleared his throat. "Your feedback is noted. Now that we have that cleared up, let's dive into the War *of* 1812. Please—"

The fire alarm screeched making Mr. Bond drop his chalk.

"Calmly, everybody," Mr. Bond yelled above the din, "outside, please. Do not push. Do go to your designated area."

The sound pierced Sadie's ears. *Why does the alarm have to be so obnoxious?* She stepped into the crowded hallway. Nessa scooted up from behind and linked her arm with Sadie's.

"I'm here to save your life." She smiled and pulled Sadie forward.

"I think my hearing needs saving, too," Sadie hollered.

Nessa quickened her step and Sadie kept up the pace. "Then the faster we get outside, the better."

Sirens sounded and a fire truck rounded the corner into the main driveway of the school.

"Guess they're putting on the whole show for this test," Nessa said.

A few seconds later, two squad cars and an ambulance sped up the drive.

"I don't think this is a test." Sadie searched for smoke but didn't see anything. She and Nessa scurried around the corner of the building and moved closer to the emergency vehicles.

Paramedics rushed to five students on the ground. They coughed and gasped for air.

"Oh my god." Sadie pulled Nessa forward.

"He needs help over here!" Coach Martel signaled another paramedic. The coach was kneeling next to Mr. Whitfield who held his hands over his eyes and wheezed for air.

Sadie let go of Nessa and ran to Mr. Whitfield. "What happened? Can I help?"

"Stay back, please." The paramedic blocked Sadie and Nessa with his arm and hunched next to Mr. Whitfield. He placed an oxygen mask on Mr. Whitfield's face and flicked a flashlight in his bloodshot eyes. "Can you hear me, sir?"

Mr. Whitfield nodded.

The paramedic checked his pulse. "Try to take slow, deep breaths." He continued checking Mr. Whitfield's vitals.

Mr. Whitfield shut his eyes and inhaled deeply. He coughed out the air.

"You okay?" the paramedic asked. "Feel like you're getting enough air?"

Mr. Whitfield nodded again.

"Good deal. Deep, steady breaths for a few more minutes, okay?"

"Okay." Mr. Whitfield's voice muffled through the plastic. He coughed and took another breath.

Coach Martel patted Mr. Whitfield's shoulder and stepped back while the paramedic continued to work on him.

"Is he going to be okay?" Sadie asked. "What happened?"

"He's in good hands," Coach Martel said. "And we're not sure exactly what happened. There was a trashcan in the hallway billowing fumes. A few students with hall passes got sick." He gestured toward the students near the school's front door. "One of them fell into my room or we might not have discovered the issue as soon as we did. I hate to think what would have happened if we hadn't cleared the school before the end of the period."

"How did they even get there? The fumes, I mean," Nessa said.

Two paramedics helped Mr. Whitfield into the ambulance.

"We don't know, but you can be sure we'll figure it out," Coach Martel said.

"Sounds like some idiot doesn't know how to do his job if you ask me." Derek's voice came from behind them.

Nessa turned. "I'm one hundred percent sure no one asked you."

Derek ignored her. "That old janitor dude is dangerous. You guys need to fire his ass."

Sadie glared. "Like you know anything about him, Derek."

"I know he mixed vinegar and bleach in that trashcan. Saw him do it."

"Is that right?" Coach Martel put his hands on his hips. "Then you must have had a hall pass. Let me see it."

"I...uh..." Derek shoved his hands in his pockets. "I guess I lost it."

"It's uncanny how often you lose a hall pass." Coach Martel stepped toward Derek and put his arm around his shoulder. "And I'd love to hear more about your knowledge of chemistry. Seems like you have a real talent."

"I didn't do this." He threw off Coach's arm. "It was that dumb janitor. I swear."

Coach Martel placed a hand on Derek's shoulder. "Let's talk about it in the principal's office." He directed Derek toward the school entrance.

"This is so stupid," Derek said as he passed Sadie and Nessa.

"I agree with you there, Derek." Coach Martel held the door and they disappeared into the school.

"He is such a jerk," Nessa said. "I can't believe he tried to poison people."

"That does suck." But something bugged Sadie. Derek was an expert-level jerk but trying to hurt random people didn't seem like his style. He kept his jerk-ness more focused on those he decided to hate—like Jason. *Could Mr. Whitfield have made a mistake with chemicals?*

School officials closed the school for the rest of the day so the building could be cleaned and the chemicals cleared. Sadie received a text from Mrs. Fallon saying she was coming by to get her and Kyle. When they got home, Sadie and Mrs. Fallon went into Mamo's room, escorted by Finn and Shay, to tell her what happened.

"Thank goodness no one was seriously hurt," Mrs. Fallon said. "All the affected kids are home now, but Gabriel is still in the hospital." Mrs. Fallon and Mamo were both old friends of Mr. Whitfield's.

"You know he doesn't have any family in town," Mamo said. "We should go see him. I'll get dressed." She swung her legs off the bed. Shay's ears perked.

"I will go see him," Mrs. Fallon said. "You will stay put."

"We'll make it a short visit. I'll be fine." Mamo stood and took a step toward the closet.

"Back in bed or I'll push you in that closet and lock the door."

Mamo huffed. "Lena, he's a dear friend."

"And I'll deliver your best wishes." Mrs. Fallon pointed at the bed. "Go."

Mamo opened her mouth to speak.

"No." Mrs. Fallon's arm still pointed. "In."

Mamo shut her mouth and returned to the bed.

Sadie smiled. "Can you teach me how to do that?"

Mrs. Fallon winked. "That's exactly what I'm doing."

"Oh great," Mamo said. "Now you have my own granddaughter conspiring against me." Her eyes twinkled.

"And the next step is to praise Lena for performing the task we asked of her," Mrs. Fallon said.

"Good job, Mamo." Sadie kissed Mamo's forehead.

She laughed and flicked her hand. "You two conspirators better be on your way before I change my mind and decide to take Finn and Shay for a run or something."

Sadie smiled. "I'll check on you later."

Sadie was doing homework in the kitchen when Mrs. Fallon got home from visiting Mr. Whitfield. Both dogs greeted her, their toenails clicking on the floor.

"How is he?" Sadie asked.

"He'll be fine." She hung her car keys on a hook by the door. "They're keeping him overnight for observation."

Sadie closed her notebook. "Does he know who did this?"

"He's afraid he did it, but he doesn't remember very much."

"What do you mean?"

Mrs. Fallon filled a glass with water. "Well, he said he remembers needing to clean out the trash bin because of the smell of a forgotten tuna fish sandwich or something, so he emptied the trashcan and went to his supply closet to get vinegar." She took a sip of water. "The next thing he remembers is standing in his supply closet unable to find any vinegar. He happened to check his watch and was surprised to see nearly twenty minutes had passed, or so he thought."

Twenty minutes? Did he fall asleep again, like yesterday? Like yesterday. A knot formed in Sadie's stomach.

"Since he didn't see any vinegar, he grabbed a bottle of bleach and poured some of it into the trash bin," Mrs. Fallon said. "He was about to drag the bin outside and add water when he was overcome with fumes."

"From the bleach?" Sadie asked.

"From the bleach mixed with vinegar—the vinegar was already in the trash bin."

Sadie gasped. "Oh, no. Didn't he smell the vinegar?"

"He said he already had the container of bleach open, and that's all he could smell." Mrs. Fallon wiped at a drip of condensation on the glass. "I'm worried about him. If he's forgetting things..."

He's gotta be okay. She stared at nothing. Her mind whirled.

"Sadie?"

Her attention snapped back to the conversation. "Huh?"

"Did you see Mr. Whitfield today?" Mrs. Fallon asked.

"Oh, uh, only to wave good morning to him," Sadie said. "I didn't talk to him or anything. But I did talk to him yesterday and he seemed totally fine." She didn't want Mr. Whitfield to get in trouble. Or get fired.

"I'm glad to hear that." Mrs. Fallon stood. "I'm going to let Willene know what's going on, if she's awake." She yawned.

Sadie held her breath.

"And if she's not awake, I may curl up for my own little catnap before I start dinner." She walked out with Finn and passed Brandon as he came into the kitchen.

"Hey, Sadie. Cool, you're doing homework too." He plopped his computer and books onto the table. "I hate homeworking alone."

"Yeah, hey." Sadie pushed aside her stuff to make more room.

Brandon stopped midway to sitting. "Wait—am I invading your space?" He straightened. "I can study somewhere else."

"No, there's plenty of room here." She scooted her chair away from Brandon's.

"Are you sure? The look on your face said you were kind of bugged."

"I'm sorry," Sadie said. "Stressful day at school, and I was thinking about...other stuff."

"Yeah, I heard about the for-real fire drill." Brandon opened the lid of his laptop. "Glad you're okay."

"Oh, yeah thanks. But I wasn't in that part of the school. "Sadie pushed her hair off her face. "And luckily everyone is going to be fine." *Or at least I hope so.*

"Do you think they'll have school tomorrow?" Brandon asked. "Maybe you'll get to do the homeschooling thing with me. Mrs. Fallon is an excellent lunch lady."

Sadie laughed. "I bet she is. Though she probably wouldn't want us to take over her kitchen table all day."

"True," Brandon said. "But it would still be cool to have a fellow student in the house." He typed something into his computer.

Sadie opened her notebook and returned to the history assignment she was doing when Mrs. Fallon got home. She pulled her laptop out of her bag and searched for information about the War of 1812. Stevie Harkness popped into her head and she was about to tell Brandon the story when he yawned.

"You're tired?" Sadie stared at Brandon.

"I guess," he said. "Though I think it's more likely I'm just hungry." He yawned again and checked the clock on his screen. "Dinner's not for a while. Maybe I'll grab a snack." He stretched and yawned a third time.

"I'm, uh, I need to check on my grandmother." Sadie lowered the lid on her computer and stuffed it into her bag. "I think I heard her call me." She closed her notebook and tucked it under her arm. Shay raised her head off the dog bed.

"I didn't hear anything," Brandon said.

"Well, I'm supposed to check on her now anyway." Sadie stood and flung her bag over her shoulder. "I'll see you later. At dinner."

She hurried out of the kitchen and up the stairs to her room, Shay on her heels. Sadie threw her bag down and sat on her bed. Shay jumped up and sat next to her.

"Shay, tell me I'm being totally stupid." Sadie put her arm over Shay's back and scratched her chest. Shay licked Sadie's cheek. "I'm not sure if that means you do think I'm being stupid, or you don't think I'm being stupid."

Shay licked her again.

"Okay, I am being stupid because how would I be making people fall asleep? It's not like I'm magic or something." Sadie leaned against her headboard and Shay turned toward her. "And hello, even if I got to choose some superpower, who picks the ability to make people fall asleep?"

Shay yawned.

"Oh no, not you, too."

Shay shook.

"Maybe I'm just super boring." Sadie folded her arm over her eyes. "Everyone in the house fell asleep yesterday evening, even you, Shay." Sadie stretched and stared at the ceiling.

But what about Mr. Whitfield?

She sat up and reached into her bag for her laptop. With a little searching, Sadie found numerous articles about the dangers of working in the janitorial industry. There were plenty of items to explain the problems Mr. Whitfield might be having. But something still gnawed at her.

She initiated a new search about cryptids. There are so many different types in the world, she was certain she didn't know details about all of them. She scanned her results. No cryptids with the ability to make people fall asleep.

She scratched Shay behind the ear. "I need to talk to Mamo. She'll be interested in what I found about the janitor stuff, and maybe we can help Mr. Whitfield."

Sadie pushed the other idea, the crazy thought that she could actually be making people fall asleep, out of her mind and walked down the hall to Mamo's room. She opened the door and saw Mamo asleep, a soft snore coming from her mouth. Sadie pulled the door closed and peeked into Mrs. Fallon's room. She was asleep, too.

Sadie's head spun. *It's nothing. They're just tired.*

She went to her room, picked up her bag and headed downstairs. Kyle had gone to a friend's house, but maybe Brandon would talk through the information with her.

Sadie and Shay walked into the kitchen and found Brandon with his head down on his folded arms, sound asleep.

Oh no. "Brandon?" Sadie stared at him. He didn't budge. "Brandon?"

Still no movement.

I didn't...I can't... She hurried to the back door, grabbed Shay's leash and harness, and rushed outside.

A few minutes later, Sadie and Shay were in the hidden cove along the banks of the canal that she and Jason shared as a meeting place and hangout. The light inside glowed golden as the sun shone through the yellow autumn leaves of the surrounding bushes. Sadie sat, and Shay stretched, her butt in the air, before dropping to her belly.

"This can't be happening. Why do I even think this is happening?" Sadie pulled a dried leaf off its branch. "Making people fall asleep—that's not even a thing. It makes no sense." She opened her laptop and searched "making people fall asleep superpower." The results showed magic spells, gods, and comic book characters that all had the power of making people and animals fall asleep. "Okay, it's kind of a thing. But since I'm not a witch, or a god, or a comic book character, I'm not making people fall asleep." She shut her laptop and stuffed it back in her bag.

Shay's tail wagged across the dirt. She stared at Sadie and panted.

"Next thing you know, I'll think you're magic, Shay." Sadie rubbed Shay's ears. "Not that you aren't über-talented with all the training you're doing with Jason and Finn. You'll be catching bad humans and bad cryptids before you know it."

Shay wagged harder.

Sadie took out her cell phone and texted Jason: "Hope you're good. Need to talk to you. Text when you can." She put her phone back in her bag. "How about we stay here for a while, huh, Shay?"

The pup rolled on her back for a belly rub.

"I'll take that as a yes." Sadie scratched Shay's chest and pink tummy. "You're a good girl. And you're awake, which makes me feel even better."

Shay righted herself and placed her head on Sadie's leg.

A breeze raised bumps on Sadie's arms. "Cools off quickly when the sun starts to go down. We won't be able to stay too much longer, but we'll get home in time for dinner. Deal?"

Shay scooted closer so her body ran the length of Sadie's leg, radiating heat.

"You're better than an electric blanket." Sadie petted Shay's head, then took her laptop back out of her bag. She revisited the results of her sleep search and clicked on link after link. She read every page, looking for anything that might indicate a real ability to make people around her fall asleep without her effort. She checked for any record of body odors causing such a phenomenon, or unusual electrical energy, or even psychic power. But Sadie didn't find anything of significance. Even actions that produced similar behavior to what she was seeing, like hypnosis, required a conscious effort.

People falling asleep around her the last couple of days had to be a coincidence—there was no other logical explanation. And Mr. Whitfield must have had a momentary lapse and made a mistake. Everyone makes mistakes.

Sadie packed up her computer.

Shay sprang to her feet and froze, staring through the branches and startling Sadie. A muted growl rumbled in Shay's chest.

Adrenaline spurted through Sadie. She followed Shay's gaze but the tangle of branches and low light of dusk made it impossible to see anything.

What is it? Sadie didn't dare say the words aloud.

Shay remained fixed on whatever she watched.

Sadie crawled to the opening of the cove behind them. She gave a light tug on Shay's leash and Shay followed her out but kept checking on something she sensed on the other side of the bramble. A few seconds later they cleared the thickness of the bushes and moved onto a path.

Shay stopped. Sadie pulled on her leash but Shay wouldn't budge. She stared toward the edge of the canal.

"C'mon, Shay," Sadie whispered. She tugged again but she might as well have been trying to move a boulder.

Another growl rolled through Shay's chest.

"I don't think there's anything—"

Something big jumped and crashed through the woody branches. Shay yanked and Sadie fell into the brush but held tight to Shay's leash. Branches scraped and Sadie flung one arm over her face to protect her eyes. She heard the thing splash into the canal. Shay pulled hard but couldn't move fast through the thick scrub. Sadie held tight and pulled herself back and up. A dark, furry figure scrambled up the other side of the bank and ran.

"What is that?"

The figure faded from view. Shay relaxed and turned toward Sadie. She licked her face, sat, and wagged her tail.

"What was that thing?" Sadie thought about the cryptids she knew from training with Jason. Bigfoot flashed in her mind. But they've never been seen here before. That had to be a dog, or maybe a bear.

"It was a bear, right Shay?" Sadie pushed herself to standing. Her arms stung and bled where they'd been scraped.

A bear that runs on its hind legs?

It had to be a bear.

Light wind carried a kiss of the coming winter across her skin. Sadie pulled a hoodie out of her bag and slipped it on, and she and Shay headed home. She looked forward to telling everyone about their bear encounter, about how Shay had warned Sadie and was ready to protect her and how the bear must have known it didn't stand a chance.

Sadie just hoped everyone would be awake when they got there.

SEVEN

Worse

Sadie unhooked Shay's leash as soon as they arrived back at Mrs. Fallon's house. She opened the front door. "We're back."

Finn trotted over and Shay bit at Finn's ankles, chasing her into the living room for a wrestling match.

"We're in the kitchen," Mrs. Fallon called.

Relieved at the sound of her voice, Sadie dropped her bag at the foot of the stairs and continued into the kitchen. "You'll never guess what we saw—"

Brandon and Kyle were seated at the table. Standing next to Mrs. Fallon near the refrigerator was Connor White.

Sadie's shoulders tensed.

"Thank you for your time, Lena," Mr. White said. "I'll be in touch." He lifted his jacket off the back of a chair. "Nice to meet you, boys. And nice to see you again, Sadie."

Sadie didn't answer.

Connor White let himself out the front door.

Sadie crossed her arms. "What was he doing here?"

"He wanted to see how your grandmother was feeling." Mrs. Fallon took a pitcher of iced tea out of the fridge.

"Mamo is none of his business. Did he talk to her?"

Mrs. Fallon carried two filled glasses to the table. "No, she's asleep."

Sadie grabbed the other glasses of iced tea and set them on the table. "Good. Besides, I thought he was supposed to leave town."

"He has some other things he wants to take care of first." Mrs. Fallon opened the oven door.

Brandon jumped up from his seat. "Can I help?"

"Jeez, dude, you're making the rest of us look bad," Kyle said. "Are you trying to get adopted or something?"

"What? No, I just—"

"He's doing his part to chip in and I appreciate it." Mrs. Fallon handed oven mitts to Brandon. "Please dish the macaroni and cheese onto the plates for me. And Kyle, if you can be bothered, would you grab the salad and dressing from the fridge and put it on the table?" She gave him a look that said it was more of an order than a question.

"Alright." He stood. "But tell me again who that guy is?" He looked from Mrs. Fallon to Sadie.

"Someone Mamo used to know." Sadie plopped into a chair. "That's all she's told me."

"But you know him, right, Grams?" Kyle asked Mrs. Fallon. "At least it seemed like you did."

Mrs. Fallon knows him, too?

"It's a..." Mrs. Fallon wiped her hands on a towel. "It's Willene's story to tell, not mine."

Brandon set a plate in front of Sadie. "You don't like him."

"What's to like? I've caught him in our house, he snuck up on me in our yard, and Mamo told him to leave town."

Mrs. Fallon rehung the towel. "He snuck up on you?"

"Well, maybe it was more that he startled me when I was outside a few days ago," Sadie said. "He came to the back gate when I was in the garden and told me Mamo was going to get worse." Sadie's stomach flipped as she thought back to everything that happened since then. "But she isn't."

"Hmm..." Mrs. Fallon seemed to be staring at something on the floor.

Muscles in Sadie's neck tightened. "Mamo is getting better, right?" Sadie asked. "Mrs. Fallon?"

"What? Oh, of course she is, yes."

"See what I mean?" Sadie shifted her chair into the table. "How can I like someone who tells me Mamo is going to get sicker?"

"That is creepy," Brandon said.

"Right?" Sadie appreciated the validation.

"Well," Mrs. Fallon said, "I think he's genuinely concerned about your grandmother."

"I dunno." Kyle carried his plate back to the table and sat. "I'm on the side of creepy."

"Regardless, he's gone now." She served herself some salad. "And we're all here so let's enjoy our dinner."

Sadie listened to the conversation around her, relaxed a little and laughed at Brandon's stories, and groaned when Kyle told a dumb joke. She thought about telling the bear story but decided it wasn't that interesting. Besides, she couldn't get Connor White off her mind. Who was he to Mamo and why hadn't she told Sadie about him before? And why not tell her now?

She and Mamo never had secrets.

I'll ask her about him again tonight. She always said we could talk about anything.

Dinner finished without anyone yawning. Sadie smiled to herself. *I'll tell Mamo about my sleep-thing, too. She'll crack up at me thinking I have some weird power to make people fall asleep.*

Kyle had dish duty so he cleared plates. Sadie excused herself from the table and walked toward the stairs.

Brandon caught up with her. "Hey, do you want to watch a movie or something?"

"Sure," Sadie said. "I'll come back downstairs after Kyle's done cleaning up."

"Or, we could just watch a movie," Brandon said. "Kyle could join later if he wants, or watch something else in his room or whatever."

"Oh. I..." Sadie's stomach felt like bits of macaroni were pinballing into each other. "I need to talk to my grandmother about stuff."

Brandon shuffled backward. "Yeah, no biggie. Maybe later."

Or I could talk to Mamo in the morning... "No, I'd like to watch a movie—"

"Another time." Brandon was almost back in the kitchen. "I'm gonna help Kyle." He disappeared around the corner.

Sadie glanced at the ceiling. *I definitely screwed that up.* She went upstairs. *I'm such a dork.*

She eased into Mamo's room. Mamo was deep asleep and the covers were smooth around her. It seemed like she hadn't moved in hours. Sadie tiptoed out and stood in the hall.

Now what? I can't go back downstairs already.

She went to her room, opened her laptop and searched on the name Connor White. She got over thirty-eight million results. She typed another search string: connor white willene callahan.

Fewer results, but many were from years before Mamo was born, or they were obituaries, which obviously weren't applicable. Sadie added Mamo's maiden name, Tressa, to the search and the results thinned. She scanned the screens finding nothing until a link to a yearbook caught her eye. It was from Mamo's school in Maine. Sadie clicked the link.

Yearbook pages opened before her. Sadie searched the document for "Tressa" and found a photo of a young Mamo on stage, frozen in a moment of dialogue she was delivering as Puck in *A Midsummer Night's Dream.*

Sadie surveyed Mamo's costume. "How did she keep all those leaves on, and in the right places?" She printed the photo to show Mamo later. It was the only photo of Mamo in the yearbook. The space where her sophomore photo should have been was blank except for the words "Photo Not Available."

Next Sadie searched for Connor White and found a portrait in the senior class section. She enlarged the image and moved her face closer to the screen. The kid in the photo was scrawny and had straight brown hair past his shoulders. The Connor White Sadie knew was tall, broad-shouldered, with a rounded face. And whatever color his hair used to be had long been transformed to the silvery gray it was now.

He looks kind of the same in the eyes...maybe around the mouth?

She printed the photo of Connor White and set it with the one of Mamo as Puck. She looked through the rest of the yearbook but didn't find anything that might link the two of them together. If that was the same Connor White, and if he and Mamo knew each other, there was no evidence in this yearbook.

Sadie did some more searching but came up empty.

Shay rounded the corner into Sadie's room and jumped onto the bed.

"Is it that time already?" Sadie checked the clock. It was nearly ten p.m. "I guess I was at it longer than I thought. Down the internet rabbit hole again and not much to show for it." She shut her laptop.

Sadie peeked into Mamo's room but she was still asleep. Sadie returned to her bedroom and changed her clothes, brushed her teeth, and went to sleep.

❋ ❋ ❋

A screech jarred Sadie awake. Shay leaped to all fours and barked at the wall separating Sadie's room from Mamo's. From across the hall, Finn's deep bark joined Shay's.

Oh no.

Sadie scrabbled into a hoodie. Mamo wailed. Shay barked harder and ran to the door with Sadie close behind. Mrs. Fallon came out of her room and they all rushed to Mamo.

She thrashed in her bed, her eyes shut tight. "No. Don't do it. Get out." She pulled at her own hair. "No! I told you to get out."

Sadie's skin chilled.

Mrs. Fallon grabbed Mamo's arms. "Willene. Wake up."

Mamo fought against Mrs. Fallon's hold. She tried to punch, to scratch, but Mrs. Fallon didn't loosen her grip. "Willene," she yelled. "Wake up."

Mamo kicked underneath the blankets. Sadie tried to grab onto her legs but Mrs. Fallon shook her head. "Stay back, I've got her."

"But—"

"It's okay. She'll wake up soon." She pressed Mamo's arms down.

Mamo lifted her head and bit at the air. "I won't let you do this." She snapped her jaws.

"What about a spray bottle?" Sadie asked. "That worked for me."

"Yes, in the laundry room," Mrs. Fallon said. "It's sitting on the dryer."

Sadie dashed down to the laundry room. She ran into Brandon on the way back up.

"What's happening?" Brandon asked.

"Mamo." Sadie kept running. She heard Brandon's footsteps behind her.

"Where?" Sadie aimed the bottle of water.

"I will stop you." Mamo snarled the words.

"In the face." Mrs. Fallon dodged an attempted head butt from Mamo.

Sadie squeezed the trigger fast and hard, squirting Mamo's forehead and cheeks and mouth.

Mamo sputtered and twisted in the bed but didn't wake.

Sadie kept spraying, drenching Mamo's face and neck while Mrs. Fallon held tight.

A moment later Mamo's fight changed from attack to defend. "What? What's happening?" She tried to move her hands to block the stream of water. "Lena?"

Mrs. Fallon released her hold and Sadie stopped the spray. She stared at Mamo.

"What happened?" Mamo asked, her voice almost a whisper. She wiped away water with the back of her hand.

"You were having a nightmare." Mrs. Fallon turned to Brandon. "Would you mind grabbing a towel from the linen closet?"

He hurried out of the room and returned a few seconds later with a towel and a blanket. He took the water bottle from Sadie and put the blanket around her shoulders.

She curled her arms into the warmth. "Thank you."

Brandon nodded.

"Do you remember what you were dreaming about?" Mrs. Fallon asked.

"Oh Lena, it was—" Mamo noticed Sadie and Brandon. "Confusing. I don't remember. It's all blurs now." She sat up and handed the damp towel to Mrs. Fallon who dried drips of water from her own skin.

"It was a bad one, Willene."

Why does she sound like she's mad at Mamo?

"I'm sorry for the trouble." Mamo rubbed her forehead. "It did give me a little headache."

"Willene..."

Mamo raised her eyes to Mrs. Fallon. "It was only a dream."

"Hmm." Mrs. Fallon walked over to a dresser. "We need to get you into dry pajamas."

Mamo waved Sadie over. "There's nothing to be worried about."

"You keep telling me that, but it's not helping," Sadie said.

Shay let out a little whine.

"Oh, sweetie." Mamo held her arms wide. "Do you mind a hug from your soggy grandmother?"

Sadie gave a little laugh. "No, I don't mind." She opened the blanket and encircled Mamo. Cold water from Mamo's neck sent a shiver into Sadie.

Mrs. Fallon set pajamas on the bed next to Mamo. "You two go back to bed. I'll help her change and get resettled."

"Isn't there anything I can do?" Sadie asked. "I could make tea or something."

"No need, no need," Mamo said. "I'm going to follow Warden Fallon's instructions and let this headache settle down.

"Uh, okay." Sadie kissed Mamo on the cheek. "Love you. I'll see you in the morning."

"Yeah, goodnight." Brandon followed Sadie and Shay out of the room.

Sadie stopped outside Mamo's door. Connor White's voice played in her head: *She's going to get worse.*

Is that what's happening?

"Are you okay?" Brandon touched Sadie's arm.

She refocused on her surroundings. "Uh, sorry. Yeah, I'm fine."

"Do you want some water or something?" Brandon asked. "Or I know where Mrs. Fallon has a secret stash of cookies. Benefit of being home all day."

Sadie needed to think. She needed to figure out what to do next. "I'm going to try and go back to sleep."

"Okay," Brandon said. "I'll probably be up for a while if you change your mind. Kind of wide awake now."

"Thanks." Sadie turned toward her room then paused. "Oh, and Brandon?"

He looked at her from the top of the stairs.

"Thanks for the blanket," Sadie said. "That was really nice of you."

"No problem. Goodnight." He went downstairs.

She returned to her room and climbed into bed with the blanket still around her. Shay lay down next to her.

It was just a nightmare.

Sadie flipped onto her stomach and pulled the edge of the blanket over her head. *But Mamo wouldn't talk about it. And she's scary. And the nightmares a few days ago happened when she was worse than she is now.*

"She is not getting worse." She punched her pillow and Shay raised her head. "Sorry, Shay." Sadie shifted onto her side and draped an arm over Shay's back.

Sadie scrunched her eyes and tried to ignore the thoughts playing over and over in her mind. *What if Mamo doesn't get better?* She told herself she was overreacting, being stupid, being too sensitive. But she couldn't fight the endless loop in her head.

She grabbed her laptop and searched. Sadie clicked through pages and found all the results led to the same basic point: kids without any living relatives ended up in foster care.

Foster care? A chill crawled through Sadie's body. *I would have to move. Where would I go? Who would even want me?*

She pushed the laptop aside and slid deeper under the covers. *I'm being ridiculous. That's not going to happen.* Air hiccuped in Sadie's chest. She bolted to a seated position, startling Shay. "I will fix this."

Sadie started a new search for things that heal people and found remedies from chicken soup to herbs to something called reiki. She bookmarked pages and made short notes about topics to study further. But there was so much information. If Sadie knew exactly what was making Mamo sick, whether it was flu or a bad cold or something else, she could pinpoint the best treatments. She'd ask Mrs. Fallon about that in the morning.

There was one other person Sadie needed to talk to—Connor White. *I want to know why he said Mamo would get worse.*

"And whatever is making her sick, I'm going to stop it."

EIGHT
Needs and Wants

Sadie's phone beeped the arrival of a text message. It was from Nessa: "No school—yay! I should come over."

The notification about school being canceled for additional cleaning arrived less than five minutes ago. Nessa hadn't wasted any time.

"You want to do homework together?" Sadie smiled at her response.

"LOL no! To hang out with you, and maybe other people. But really my BFF."

Sadie typed back: "Hah. I can't promise Kyle will be here."

Okay but I bet Brandon will be...right by your side. ;)"

"Butterflies fluttered through Sadie. "Whatever. I have no idea where he'll be."

"Let's find out."

Sadie thought about her plans to help Mamo. "I have some stuff to do, but after noon is good."

"See you BOTH then."

Sadie let Shay out of her room, then showered and dressed. She stuffed the high school photos of Mamo and maybe-Connor-White into her desk drawer and grabbed her bag with her laptop. She peeked in on Mamo, wished she was awake, and went downstairs.

"Good morning," Mrs. Fallon said. "Did you get the message about no school today? You can go back to bed if you want to. We did have a bit of a rough night."

"I'm good." Sadie dropped her bag next to the doorway. "Did you get any more sleep?"

Mrs. Fallon topped off the coffee in her cup. "Some. I stayed in Willene's room to be certain she was okay."

"I should have done that," Sadie said. "I'm sorry."

"Not at all. That's why you're both here, so we can help each other." Mrs. Fallon held her cup with both hands. "And I have plenty of hot coffee so I'll be just fine."

Sadie put a slice of whole grain bread into the toaster. "Mrs. Fallon, what's going on with her? She seems like she's getting better, then weird stuff happens and she's scary and..." Sadie quaffed a cry that threatened to spill out.

Mrs. Fallon set her cup on the counter. "Are you okay?"

"I just want to know what's wrong with her." Sadie took butter out of the refrigerator. "Is this walking pneumonia or something? How can we fix her?"

"I wish I could tell you the answer," Mrs. Fallon said. "But we have to give it time."

Sadie removed a plate from the cupboard. "It's taking too long."

"Aw, dear Sadie." Mrs. Fallon lifted Sadie's hair and smoothed it down her back. "Hang in there. Things will turn around." She reached for a jar sitting on the counter. "This is honey from your hives if you'd like some."

"Thanks." Sadie buttered the toast and drizzled honey on top.

"And we'll keep taking it one day at a time, okay?"

"Okay." Sadie smeared the honey into the half-melted butter.

"Speaking of keeping things moving along," Mrs. Fallon said, "we need a few items from the store. Would you mind picking them up this morning? Maybe Brandon can go with you. I heard him stirring downstairs. Kyle's still asleep, and who knows when he'll decide to roll out of bed."

"Did we wake him up last night, too?" Sadie couldn't keep track anymore of what seemed like normal sleep and what seemed weird.

Brandon walked in with hair sticking out, styled by pillows and sheets. "He's just lazy."

"More likely it's that pesky teenager gene," Mrs. Fallon said. "It seems to be the same from one generation to the next."

"So, I should go back to bed." Brandon yawned.

"Except that your school didn't get canceled today, did it?" Mrs. Fallon asked.

Brandon poured himself a glass of orange juice. "No. Stupid internet."

"Even so, you do have some flexibility in your schedule," Mrs. Fallon said. "I need some help from you and Sadie today."

He glanced at Sadie. "Oh, sure thing. As long as it doesn't involve picking up dog poop."

"Thank you for that excellent idea," Mrs. Fallon said. "You and Kyle can do that this afternoon."

Brandon's shoulders dropped.

"But this morning I need a grocery store run," Mrs. Fallon said. "Just a few things that will fit in a couple of backpacks. You can borrow Kyle's bike if you'd rather not walk."

"That would be good," Sadie said. "I need to stop by our house anyway, and I can get my bike, too."

"Perfect. I'll text the list to you." Mrs. Fallon picked up her phone.

✳ ✳ ✳

An hour later, Sadie and Brandon were heading to Sadie's house. Brandon rolled Kyle's bike alongside him, and his hair had been smoothed back to where it was supposed to be.

"We're here." Sadie directed Brandon up the walkway. He leaned the bike on the front porch and they went inside. "I just have a couple of things to do."

"No problem," Brandon said. "I'm in no hurry to get back to school work. Or dog poop."

"I don't blame you." Sadie dashed upstairs and threw one of her Tae Kwon Do uniforms into her bag for her next lesson, along with a framed photo of her and Mamo at the county fair when their roses won a blue ribbon. She went back down to the office and turned on the computer.

Brandon looked in. "Jason said you have beehives."

"Yeah, they're out back." She entered the requested password.

"Can I check 'em out?"

Sadie snapped her gaze from the computer to Brandon. "You're not scared?"

"Of bees? No, they're cool."

She smiled. "Jason thinks they want to kill him."

"Are you serious?" Brandon laughed. "He told me he was going to help you harvest honey."

"Well, if he can figure out how to do that from his house, then I guess he'll help us some day," Sadie said. "But so far he hasn't been closer than thirty feet to the hives."

"Hilarious." Brandon grinned. "I am totally using this against him."

"You should. He deserves it." Sadie opened the messaging app. "Go down the hall and through the kitchen to the backyard. You can't miss the hives. I'll be done here in a few minutes."

"Great. See you out there."

Sadie clicked on Mamo's account and scrolled to the string of messages from CDubya. The last one was the note that suggested Mamo was going to get hurt.

Should I really do this? She thought about everything that had happened with Connor White. She wasn't sure she could trust him. *I need to know what he meant.*

Sadie clicked in the text box and typed: "This is Sadie. I would like to talk to you, please." She pressed enter and watched the cursor blink in the empty box. The app said the message was delivered.

She waited. No response came.

Sadie picked up her phone and flicked through the screens, trying to distract herself. She opened a game then closed it without playing. She checked the weather.

Still no response from her message to Connor White.

What do I do now? I can't sit here all day. Sadie thought about her options. Maybe she could use Mamo's phone and try again later.

She moved to close the app when a chime sounded the arrival of a response: "I'm glad you texted. I can stop by around four p.m."

"Ok but not Mrs. Fallon's house. My house."

"See you then."

Sadie deleted the message, shut down the computer and went out the back door.

Brandon was bent over with his hands on his knees, staring into an opening of one of the beehives. The insects entered and exited the hive, flying close to his cheeks. Brandon didn't flinch.

"Don't move," Sadie said.

"Why? Is there a bee on me?" Brandon froze but didn't seem anxious.

"No. But I have to get a photo of you for Jason." She tapped the camera icon on her phone and zoomed in.

"Should I smile?"

"If you want to," Sadie said. "Anything that shows bravery and courage as opposed to being a huge baby like he is."

Brandon grinned and gave a thumbs up.

Sadie snapped the photo. "Perfect. I'm sending it now."

"Shoot me a copy?" he asked.

"Sure. What's your number?"

He gave her his number and Sadie added Brandon to the message. "On its way." She walked closer to Brandon and the hives. "Can you hear them in there? Even though it's October, it's warm enough that some will still go out looking for pollen. But the rest should be buzzing around in there." She leaned into the hive and he followed her lead. A low hum resonated from inside.

"I hear them," Brandon said. "That is so cool." He stepped to another hive and listened again. "Yep." Then to another. "I hear these guys too."

"I'm glad to hear it," Sadie said. "That means things are probably all good in there."

"Hah—I see what you did there," Brandon said. "Glad to hear it. The bees? Hearing the bees?"

Sadie rolled her eyes. "I didn't mean it that way." She leaned into the hive again. "I hope I could come up with a better play on words than that." The buzz diminished. *That's weird.* She pressed her ear close and the buzzing faded to a few individual bees rather than a larger group. "Huh." She moved to another hive. The buzzing again faded as she listened. At a third hive, the same thing happened. *Am I imagining things?*

"What is it?" Brandon was at the far end of the row.

"I'm not sure," Sadie said. "It's almost like they're—" She straightened. A tingle ran over her skin.

"Like they're what?" Brandon asked.

"Can you hear the bees in the hive nearest to you?"

He listened. "Loud and clear. There have to be tons of bees in there." "You're sure?"

"Totally," Brandon said. "Why?"

Sadie walked to the hive near him and leaned close. The distinctive buzz hummed then faded. She jumped back and turned to Brandon. "Are you tired?"

"What? No," he said. "I mean, I didn't sleep that much last night, but I feel okay."

"You don't feel like yawning? Or taking a nap?"

"No, I'm good." Brandon ran his hand over his hair. "Why? Are you tired?"

The bees shouldn't be this quiet.

"Uh, no. I'm not tired." Sadie moved away from him and hurried toward the house. "We should go."

"Yeah, okay." Brandon caught up with her and held the back door. "Don't forget your bike."

"Right," Sadie said. "Go through the front and lock the door for me? I'll meet you in front of the garage."

"Sure thing."

Sadie paused inside the garage. *Did I make the bees fall asleep?* She rubbed her eyes. *No, this is just stress. I've got to pull it together.* She shook off her thoughts and rolled her bike into the driveway.

"Ready to go?" Brandon asked.

Sadie mounted her bike. "Yep. Follow me."

"Not if you're too slow. Then you'll have to follow me."

"Oh really?" Sadie didn't wait for a response. She pumped the pedals and sped away from Brandon. She heard him scramble onto the bike behind her.

Sadie raced along the streets toward the grocery store. She zipped around corners and jumped curbs. A quick glance showed Brandon about twenty feet back. She pushed the pedals harder. A minute later, she skidded to a stop in front of the store.

"Nice," Brandon said. "But you had a head start."

"Sorry." Sadie breathed hard. "I thought you'd be a stronger rider."

Brandon smirked. "Oh, okay. Now I know what I'm up against, and I demand a rematch."

"No problem." She pushed her front tire into the bike rack. "We can race back to—" A figure in front of the hardware store caught Sadie's eye. It was Connor White, and he was talking to a woman wearing a ball cap. She seemed familiar, but Sadie didn't have a clear line of sight to the woman's face. The pair stepped into the store.

"That's weird," Sadie said.

"What is?" Brandon asked.

"Oh, I just saw that Conner White guy." She locked the bikes to the rack and wondered what a visitor in town needed to buy at a hardware store.

A few minutes later they'd finished the shopping and raced to Mrs. Fallon's house. Sadie beat Brandon into the yard.

She dropped her bike and raised her arms in the air. "Woo hoo! Undefeated!" She hunched to let her body recover.

"I think you kind of cheated," Brandon panted, "when you went off road." He flung his backpack and flopped onto the grass.

"Who said we couldn't go off road? I don't remember that being a rule."

"Fair enough. But I might demand another rematch." He rolled onto his belly. "Except not today. Definitely not today. And probably not tomorrow either."

Sadie laughed. "Whenever. You just let me know when you think you've recovered enough."

"Well, hello, and what do we have here?" Nessa stood on the sidewalk.

Sadie straightened. "Oh my gosh, is it noon already?" She walked over and hugged Nessa.

"I'm a little early. Or I'm just in time, depending on how you look at it." She smiled at Sadie then turned to Brandon. "And you must be Brandon. I'm Vanessa, but everyone calls me Nessa."

He stood and held up his hand. "Hey, yeah. Nice to meet you."

He grabbed his backpack and reached for Sadie's. "I'll take the groceries in." He headed into the house.

Nessa smacked Sadie's arm. "He is *cute*."

"Well, yeah, I never said he wasn't." Sadie rubbed where Nessa had hit, pretending it hurt.

"But you never said he was *that* cute." Nessa raised her arm to smack Sadie again, but Sadie side-stepped and Nessa missed her mark. "And what were you guys doing out here? I saw a lot of heavy breathing."

"Oh my gosh, just come in." Sadie put her bike away. "And please be on your best behavior."

"Best is my only behavior." Nessa followed Sadie inside.

Mrs. Fallon was in the kitchen putting away the groceries. She greeted Nessa with a hug and asked her if she'd like some lunch.

"I can't pass up that offer," Nessa said. "I'd eat all my meals with either you or Sadie's grandmother if I had my choice."

"Still eating a lot of takeout for dinner?" Sadie asked.

"Yeah. It was fun at first but I'm kind of over it." Nessa's mom had a new job that kept her on the road, and her dad wasn't much of a cook.

"I'm going to say hi to Mamo," Sadie said, "and I'll come back down and help with lunch."

"Oh, Sadie, I'm sorry but she just fell back to sleep a few minutes ago," Mrs. Fallon said.

Jeez, she's sleeping so much.

Brandon walked in. "All washed up. What can I do?"

"You can go get some schoolwork done," Mrs. Fallon said. "I'll bring you a sandwich."

"I just thought—"

"Don't make me report an unexcused absence." Mrs. Fallon raised one eyebrow but her eyes were more teasing than serious.

"Yes, ma'am," Brandon said. "Back to the grind." He waved at Sadie and Nessa.

A bark came from the backyard. Sadie opened the door and Finn and Shay ran through the kitchen, down the hall, turning into the living room.

"I swear those two should be skin and bones considering how much they chase each other," Mrs. Fallon said. "What are your plans for the afternoon?"

"I don't know." Sadie looked at Nessa. "Watch a movie or something?"

"Yeah. And maybe Kyle will want to watch it with us," Nessa said. "And Brandon, if he's not studying." She nudged Sadie.

"Kyle is at a friend's house." Mrs. Fallon took out bread and deli meat for sandwiches.

"Boy friend or girl friend?" Nessa asked.

"Oh my gosh," Sadie said.

Mrs. Fallon chuckled. "It's not my place to talk specifics about Kyle's whereabouts, but I will say that I don't think you have any competition to worry about."

"That's good news." Nessa slapped her hands together in mini applause.

Sadie and Nessa ate lunch with Mrs. Fallon. Afterward, Sadie considered waking Mamo but decided against it. Mamo wouldn't sleep this much if she didn't need it.

She went back downstairs and watched a movie with Nessa, then Nessa headed home. Sadie had an hour before she had to meet Connor White.

Brandon came up from his room in the basement. "Another school day done. I'm even ahead of schedule on homework so my weekend should be stress-free."

"No-homework-weekends are the best," Sadie said.

"Yeah. Maybe we can do something?"

"Hah—don't even think I'm going to help you go clean up dog poop right now." Sadie folded a throw Nessa had used during the movie.

"No, I mean this weekend," Brandon said. "Maybe we can do something this weekend."

Sadie's stomach flip-flopped. "Oh. I...uh..." *Is he asking me out? Like a date?*

"I mean if you want to." He put his hands in his pockets. "And if you're not busy. With your grandmother or whatever."

"No. I mean yes. I mean..." Sadie stopped and reset. "I would like to do something with you."

"Yeah? Okay. Cool."

"But I do have to see how things are with Mamo." *And make sure she's okay with me doing something with Brandon, which she totally will be because we're just friends.*

"Of course," Brandon said. "We can play it by ear and see what works."

Sadie smiled. "That'd be great. In fact, I'm going to go check on her right now."

"And I have dog poop duty, so I'll go do that. Have you seen Kyle?"

"I don't think he's home yet."

"Figures," Brandon said. "He will pay since I'm getting stuck doing the dirty work alone." He headed toward the back door. "Talk to you later."

After peeking in on still-sleeping Mamo, Sadie grabbed her bag out of her room and texted Mrs. Fallon. "Forgot something at my house. Taking Shay, be back in a few." She slipped out the front door.

Ten minutes later she was home. She sat in the office and noticed for the first time how much it smelled like Mamo, like lavender and honey. Sadie noticed Mamo's scent the most when she came in from being in the sunshine. In her office, the aroma seemed to have soaked into the walls, the carpet, even the desk.

There was a knock on the front door and Shay sprung to her feet. Sadie checked the clock. *Right on time.*

Connor White stood on the porch. He wore navy pants with a red sweater over a white shirt, and a mocha-colored blazer, the same outfit he was wearing when she saw him outside the hardware store.

Sadie stepped outside and pulled the door shut behind her. "We can sit out here." She directed him to a wicker rocking chair, and she sat on the porch swing. Shay curled up on the floor next to Sadie.

"I was very happy to hear from you," he said.

I hope I'm not going to be sorry I did this.

"Is Willy okay?" Connor White asked.

"She sleeps a lot." Sadie kept her feet planted on the floor. "But Mrs. Fallon says she's getting better."

"And how are you feeling?"

"What do you mean?" Sadie shifted in her seat. "I'm not sick."

"No, but you're going through a lot," Connor White said. "I'm just wondering if you're feeling any different?"

"Different?" *That's a weird question.*

"With your grandmother being sick, and being away from your home...maybe you're feeling different? Or stressed?"

"I didn't message you to talk about me, Mr. White."

"No, of course not. Please forgive me." He rubbed his hands down his thighs. "And please, call me uh...Conner. Please call me Conner."

"Okay, Conner." It felt odd to call an adult by his first name, especially when she didn't know him well. "I want to know why you said Mamo was going to get worse."

He flicked his wrist. "Forget I said that. Everything I'm hearing says I was wrong."

"So you believe she's getting better?"

"There's no reason to think otherwise. I don't know how, but it sure seems like she's managing it somehow."

Managing it? "You mean healing? She is getting better?" Sadie asked.

"Yes." He leaned into the couch cushions. "You tell me she's getting plenty of rest, Lena said she's eating well, and the nightmares have disappeared."

Air caught in Sadie's throat.

Conner leaned forward. "What is it? Is she having nightmares again?"

"How did you know she was having nightmares?"

He stood.

Shay's ears perked.

"Did she have another one?" Conner asked. "When?"

"Last night." Sadie's hands chilled.

"Did she wake from it?" His eyes widened. "Has she been awake since the nightmare?"

"Yes. Yeah, we squirted her with water."

He paced across the patio. "And you're certain she was awake? Fully awake."

"Yeah." Bumps skittered across Sadie's skin. "Mrs. Fallon stayed with her for a while after that."

"Good. That's good." He rubbed his hand down his chin. "I wish she would listen to me." He mumbled the words.

"What is happening? What are these nightmares?" Sadie asked.

He mumbled more and continued pacing.

"Mr., er..." She sprang to standing and Shay matched the movement. "Conner!"

Conner stopped and had an expression on his face like he was surprised Sadie was there.

"Tell me what is happening," she said.

"I need to see her."

Sadie crossed her arms. "Just tell me."

His face softened. "Sadie, I can't tell you anything. And I need to talk to Willy."

A wave of exhaustion dropped Sadie back into the swing. Shay whimpered and pressed her head against Sadie's hand.

"Oh, my dear girl," Conner said. "I wish I had some words of comfort for you."

She looked up. "Tell me she'll get better. Tell me I won't lose her."

"I'll tell you she *can* get better." He sat on the edge of the couch. "But it's up to her."

Somehow Sadie knew he meant something different than getting plenty of rest and eating chicken soup. "What can I do?"

"I need to see her," Conner said. "Now."

Sadie nodded.

"I have a car out front."

Sadie locked the house and she and Shay climbed into the SUV. Conner turned the ignition and headed down the block. Silence hung between them until Sadie thought of a question.

"Who was the woman I saw you talking to at the hardware store today?"

Conner shrugged. "Uh, I'm not sure what you mean. Perhaps you saw someone else."

"No, I recognized you."

"Ah right, the hardware store. Odd though it is, they carry a brand of gum I can't find anywhere else." He turned on his blinker.

"Who was that lady?" Sadie asked.

He shook his head. "I don't recall talking to anyone in particular. Perhaps you saw me say a passing hello to a stranger."

Except that you walked into the store with her.

"You talked for longer than a hello."

"You must be mistaken." Conner pulled up in front of Sadie's house.

Uneasiness oozed through Sadie.

Mrs. Fallon met them in the foyer. "I saw your car pull up." She glanced from Sadie to Conner. "What's going on?"

"I need a few minutes with Willy," Conner said.

"Of course," Mrs. Fallon said. "But I—"

He dashed up the stairs.

Brandon walked in and stood next to Sadie.

Mrs. Fallon turned to her. "You look upset. What happened?"

"Is Finn inside?" Sadie asked. "I think we need both dogs inside." She wanted all the help they could get in case Conner turned on them.

"I'll get her." Brandon hurried toward the back door.

Sadie told Mrs. Fallon about her conversation with Conner. "If she dies—" Sadie choked back a sob.

Mrs. Fallon pulled Sadie into an embrace. "There will be no talk of dying. We have no reason to believe it deserves any consideration."

"But if she doesn't want to get better—"

"Of course she wants to get better. She loves you."

Finn raced in and tackled Shay, then sat and wagged her tail. Mrs. Fallon released Sadie. Shay nudged Sadie's thigh and licked her hand, then grabbed a squeaky toy and tossed it in the air. Finn caught it and dropped it at Sadie's feet.

"They're trying to cheer you up," Mrs. Fallon said.

"Can I do anything?" Brandon asked. "Should I bring you another squeaky toy?"

A smile forced its way onto Sadie's face. "That's okay. One squeaky is enough for me." She picked up the toy and tossed it across the room. Shay zipped off in pursuit. "I'm going up to Mamo's room."

Her bedroom door was shut, but Mamo was awake. Sadie heard her talking to Conner, though she couldn't make out what Mamo was saying.

Conner's voice was booming and clear. "Willy, you're being ridiculous. You can't keep this up."

Mamo responded with muted voice.

"I don't care. You need to accept the way things are going. What you're trying to do is impossible."

Mamo again, still not loud enough to hear.

"The price is too high," Conner said. "You need to stop this."

Mamo's voice grew louder, more insistent, but Sadie couldn't catch her words.

Conner's steps clunked across the floor. "You can't keep this to yourself. It's not fair to you, to me, and especially not to Sadie."

Keep what to herself? What is she hiding?

"This is a decision to be made by everyone involved," Conner said. "And everyone includes Sadie."

Mamo's voice spiked. "As if she has any say in this at all. She has none and you know it."

Sadie slumped against the wall. *Me? Mamo won't listen if I tell her I want her to get better?*

"You know I'm right, Willy," Conner said. "You're hurting a lot of people, and you're still going to fail." His footsteps moved toward the door.

Sadie scrambled and ducked inside her bedroom.

Mamo's door opened.

"I'll be back tomorrow," Conner said.

"Don't bother," Mamo yelled from her room.

"Not your decision." Conner stomped down the stairs.

Sadie stepped back and fell onto her bed.

Mamo's doing this on purpose.

She pressed the heels of her hands into her eyes.

Mamo doesn't care if she leaves me. Alone.

NINE

Sovereignty

Sadie pulled a pillow over her face. She wanted to scream into it, and she wanted to punch it. She yanked the pillow off her face and flung it, knocking over the photo of her and Mamo.

Good. I hope it broke.

"What was that?" Mamo called from her room. "Are you okay, Sadie?"

"Like you care." Sadie jumped up and slammed her bedroom door. She fell back on her bed.

A few seconds later, her door opened. Sadie sat up.

Mamo leaned against the doorframe. "What's this about?"

"Shouldn't you be in bed sleeping or having a nightmare or something?" Sadie moved to her desk and woke up her laptop.

Mamo sighed. "I'm sorry you're so upset. What can I do?"

Sadie heard her shuffle to the bed and sit. She ignored Mamo's question.

"C'mon now, you don't want me to catch my death of cold being out of bed for more than five minutes, do you?" Mamo asked with a note of teasing.

"Haven't you already done that?" Sadie kept her back to Mamo.

"Already done what?"

Sadie flicked her hand. "Whatever. Forget it."

"Sweetie, talk to me," Mamo said. "We tell each other everything."

"Do we?" Sadie spun in her chair. "Then who is Conner White and why haven't you ever told me about him before?" She thudded her laptop closed. "And why don't you care if I end up alone?" Her eyes flooded with tears. She turned away from Mamo and pressed her sleeve to her cheeks.

Mamo's arms wrapped Sadie's shoulders from behind. She didn't smell like Mamo. She smelled sour.

"No." Sadie shrugged out of Mamo's hug and stood. "Leave me alone."

"Not until you talk to me."

"You first," Sadie said. "Why are you so sick?"

Mamo moved back to the edge of the bed and sat. "This is just a bad virus or something." She pulled the edges of her bathrobe closed across her thighs.

"Conner White doesn't think so."

"He doesn't know anything," Mamo said. "And he needs to mind his own business."

"But who is he? Why is he even here?" Sadie clutched the back of her chair.

Mamo gazed at her hands, then looked up at Sadie's face. "There are things—"

Someone knocked on the wall outside Sadie's open door.

"I'm sorry to interrupt," Mrs. Fallon said. "But Willene needs to be in bed."

"But—" Sadie held up her hand.

"You can talk in her room," Mrs. Fallon said.

Mamo stood. "I agree that bed is the better place for me to be."

"You agree with me?" Mrs. Fallon took Mamo's arm. "I must remember to write about this moment in my memoir."

Sadie sank as she watched Mamo walk away.

"I'll deny the moment ever happened." Mamo shuffled a few steps and stopped. "Oh...oh, I'm a little...a little light..." Her head lolled and her knees folded.

Mrs. Fallon tightened her grip and kept Mamo from falling.

Sadie rushed over and lifted Mamo from the other side. "What happened?"

"She passed out. Let's put her on your bed for a minute."

Fear erased Sadie's anger.

Mrs. Fallon rubbed Mamo's hand. "Willene? Willene, can you hear me?" She stroked her cheek.

Mamo woke. Sadie helped get her into her bed, and Mrs. Fallon suggested they let her rest. They went downstairs.

Kyle came home and Brandon harassed him for ditching dog poop duty. Kyle said something about being too smart to end up with that chore, and Mrs. Fallon told him he'd clean up the yard without Brandon's help next time. A short time later they all ate dinner together, but without Mamo. Sadie didn't hear much of the conversation. All she could think about was losing Mamo. After dinner, she took soup up to Mamo's room but she was deep asleep.

Sadie returned the tray of food to the kitchen, excused herself, and went to bed early, tossing and turning most of the night.

✳ ✳ ✳

Sadie overslept.

She checked the clock, bolted out of bed, and raced through a condensed morning routine including a quick check on a sleeping Mamo.

She left Mamo a note:

Sorry I was mad.

Love, Sadie

Part of her was still angry. But the angry part wasn't as strong as the worried and afraid parts.

She hurried to school without breakfast. She scrambled into her Algebra class ahead of the teacher, Mrs. Bauer, who she'd scooted by in the hall.

The bell rang less than a minute later but Mrs. Bauer still wasn't in the classroom.

Chatter around Sadie bounced between Mrs. Bauer's absence, and the accident Mr. Whitfield had caused. No one minded the extra time off, and one kid joked that he wished Mr. Whitfield would have accidents like that every week. Sadie didn't join in the laughter.

Apparently, Mr. Whitfield was resting at home now, but she hadn't heard about when he would be back at work, if ever.

The classroom door opened and the vice principal entered. The laughing and talking quieted.

"Mrs. Bauer had an accident on her way into class," the vice principal said.

She was right behind me.

Whispers tittered through the classroom.

"She's fine, but she's not teaching today, so you all get to enjoy my company this morning. As I don't have a prepared lesson, we'll use the time to work on assignments, starting with the exercises at the back of chapter five."

While everyone got out what they needed to do their assignments, the vice principal motioned a student into the classroom. The girl took her seat near Sadie and leaned toward another student.

"It was so weird," the girl whispered to her friend.

Sadie shifted, tilting her head to hear better.

"Mrs. Bauer stopped walking in the middle of the hall and I practically ran into her. Then she yawned and it was like someone snapped their fingers and she was a big heap on the floor. I had to help her. That's why I'm late."

"That is so embarrassing," the friend replied. "Is she still in the hallway?"

"No, she totally woke up like two seconds later and went to see the nurse. They're driving her home."

She passed out? A twinge snaked through Sadie's gut. She shook off the thought and focused on her algebra problems. She searched for the value of X, and tried to calculate Y but her mind kept wandering back to Mamo, and people passing out, and sleeping too much, and the quiet bees, and Connor White. Sadie shut her eyes and told herself everything was fine, or would be when Mamo got better.

If she wants to get better.

She clenched her jaw and refocused on her assignment.

A thump sounded. Sadie turned. The girl who'd told the story about Mrs. Bauer was asleep at her desk, her forehead flat on the surface, and her arms hanging at her sides.

Sadie gasped. She looked at the girl's friend. Her head hung forward and her eyes were shut.

No, no, no. Sadie's heartbeat spiked.

She scanned the students nearest her. Three others seemed to be asleep. She glanced at the vice principal in the front of the room but he was awake and reading a book. Students farther away from Sadie were also awake and working on their algebra problems.

She wanted to run out of the room. But Sadie forced herself to remain and pretended to look at the assignment in front of her. She didn't want to call attention to herself, or to the other students who would get in trouble if the vice principal noticed them sleeping. She kept her head down and raised her gaze only to check the minutes as they ticked off the clock one....by one...by one...

The bell finally signaled the end of class. The sleeping students awoke and moved as if they'd been awake the whole time. Sadie shoved her things into her bag and rushed out of the room. She went straight to the school office, not even stopping at her locker.

Sadie wrote her name on a log sheet. "I'm sick. I'm going home." She dropped the pen.

"Have a seat. I'll call your parents," the woman said.

"No, I don't need a ride or anything." She lifted her bag onto her shoulder. "I'll go straight home."

"Hold on. It's policy to—"

Sadie scurried out of the office and into the hallway. She dodged students and tried to avoid bumping them. She jammed her hands into her pockets and moved faster.

Nessa's voice called from behind her. "Sadie—hey. History class is this way."

Sadie didn't respond other than to keep moving away, giving a short wave. She increased her pace. She banged through the exit. She held her bag tight to her side and ran.

Sadie hurried up the steps of her house. She shut the door hard behind her, locked it, and collapsed onto the floor. The silence of the empty house enveloped her, the quiet broken only by her breathing. She rubbed her temples.

What is happening to me? Why is everything so crazy?

Sadie pulled her phone out of her bag and examined her recent texts to Jason. They showed sent, but not read. She typed a new note: "Weird things are happening. Please call."

She clicked off the phone and stared at the empty foyer. If she and Mamo were here, at home, the entry table would be decorated with a display of gourds and dried flowers. They would be planning their Halloween costumes and probably figuring out the details for their spring break trip. Instead, the entry table held a vase of wilted old flowers, Sadie'd practically forgotten about Halloween, and she'd had no conversations with Mamo about their trip since Mamo had first suggested it.

Nothing felt right.

Sadie pushed herself to standing and went into the office. She started the computer, determined to find information that would help her figure out what was going on. She conducted a new search on "sleep powers" and received the same results as before. She hunted for more information on Conner White but found nothing new. She reviewed Mamo's emails and messaging history but everything was standard and boring and bland.

"Crap." Sadie shoved the trackpad. "How is this not working?" Her web skills always helped her find what she needed. But not this time.

She went upstairs and threw her bag in her room. She passed the door to Mamo's empty bedroom on her way back downstairs and stopped. She stepped inside the doorway. Mamo's scent filled her head but the fragrance was dull, fading, almost stale.

Sadie gazed around the room. She'd never spent much time in here without Mamo, and discomfort oozed in like she'd stepped onto property with a "No Trespassing" sign. Mamo never said Sadie had to stay out of her bedroom, but she knew Mamo wouldn't want her to snoop. She walked across the room and reached for the top dresser drawer.

Her phone rang. Sadie jumped.

She took the phone out of her pocket—it was Mrs. Fallon. Sadie concentrated on softening her voice to make herself sound sick, and answered the call. "Hello?" Sadie faked a cough.

"Are you okay? The school called saying you left because you're not feeling well," Mrs. Fallon said. "Where are you?"

"Oh, sorry I didn't call you. I'm at my house. I don't feel that great, but I'm okay."

"I'll come and get you."

"No," Sadie said. "I don't want to get anyone there sick." She coughed again. "Especially with Mamo already being as sick as she is, I don't want to give her any more germs."

"But you can't stay by yourself," Mrs. Fallon said.

"I've done it before." Sadie crossed her fingers that Mrs. Fallon wouldn't ask Mamo if this was true. "I'll keep the house locked and stay inside. I'm just going to take a nap."

Mrs. Fallon paused. "I don't know..."

"Really, I'll be okay. I can't be around Mamo anyway, I mean, so I don't make her even sicker." Sadie sniffed.

"Well, all right. That's fine for now," Mrs. Fallon said. "But please call me after your nap and we'll talk about whether or not you'll stay overnight by yourself. I want to discuss it with your grandmother."

Sadie cringed. "Can we keep this a secret? I don't want her to worry."

"She'll wonder where you are."

If she wakes up for more than five minutes. "Tell her I'm doing school stuff, that I'm helping Nessa plan the next dance or something." Sadie surprised herself at how fast she came up with a story.

Mrs. Fallon was quiet for a long moment. "I don't think we should be telling untruths to your grandmother, do you?"

"No..."

"So let's take it one step at a time," Mrs. Fallon said. "You're sure you're okay?"

I'm definitely not okay.

"I will be, and being in my own bed will help a lot. I'll call if I need anything, or text or something. I promise."

"Okay. But I expect to hear from you later today anyway, even if you don't need anything."

"I can do that," Sadie said. "No problem."

"Get some rest. I hope you feel better soon."

Sadie thanked Mrs. Fallon, ended the call, and exhaled. She had at least a few hours where she could stay away, where everyone would be safe because she wasn't around. But she wished she knew what was happening so she could make it stop. Sadie held up her hands and looked for anything different—blue sparks or an odd glow or something strange with her fingernails. Jason noticed things like that before he knew he was a Rampart Guard. Maybe things were changing on her body that she didn't realize. But everything was exactly the same as it always was.

She dropped her arms. "This is so stupid. Like I'm getting some super-cool Rampart Guard power or something. Because, you know, everyone gets a superpower someday." She spun and walked out of Mamo's room. "And mine is to make people fall asleep without even trying. And getting people hurt or in trouble or make them lose their jobs. Whatever." She set her mind to ignore everything but normal stuff and went to her room to get her Algebra book and finish the assignment from class.

She stopped.

I can't ignore it. I have to figure out what's going on.

She walked back into Mamo's room. She fought with the voice in her head that said she shouldn't snoop.

She's not going to find out. She's not here, and she's not coming home anytime soon. I'm totally safe.

Sadie eased forward and opened the top drawer of her dresser. It was filled with underwear and bras. "Okay, didn't really need to see those." She moved through the rest of the drawers and found nothing but socks and T-shirts and long underwear for winter.

The attic fan switched on and Sadie startled. "Jeez. Stupid fan." She reminded herself the house was locked, and no one could get in without her knowing it.

Sadie returned to her search. The nightstand held a book on beekeeping Mamo had read a million times already. It was the same one she'd given to Jason a few months ago to help him be less afraid of bees. A second book, titled *A History of Yowie in the Americas*, sat underneath the first. Sadie figured Jason must have shared the book with Mamo when he returned the book on beekeeping. Also in the drawer was a pad of paper, a couple of pens, and a stack of bookmarks with pictures of endangered animals that Mamo had collected over the years.

Sadie shut the drawer and moved to the walk-in closet. It was jammed with clothes, from gardening clothes to lounge clothes to "make myself look snazzy" clothes that Mamo wore for parties and events. There were blouses and sweaters, pants and scarves, and they ranged in color from pastels to jewel tones, with a minimum amount of beige in the bunch. Mamo always said she thought "beige" should be renamed "drab" because any beige top made her look and feel drab whenever she wore it. With the exception of khaki pants, she'd banned beige from her wardrobe.

Shoes sat on a rack along the closet wall, and in one corner of the closet was a floor-standing jewelry chest about four feet high. Mamo laughed that any burglar who took her jewelry and thought they'd scored big would be in for a rude awakening after they saw what they had. Mamo didn't own anything of value except for her wedding ring, which she still wore. Everything in the chest was inexpensive costume jewelry. But she'd acquired a lot of it over the years and kept it all in this chest. Every few months Sadie would hear Mamo comment that she was going to sort through the jewelry and give most of it away but it hadn't happened yet.

Sadie examined the contents. There were earrings in the top compartment, then bracelets and necklaces and pins below. Two bottom compartments were big enough to hold small purses and clutches. Sadie tried on a couple of bracelets and returned them to their spot. She pulled out a favorite clutch, black and beaded and sparkly, then pushed aside another bag to squeeze the clutch back into the drawer. A small box underneath caught her eye.

The box was cardboard and plain, like the simple gift box given with the purchase of inexpensive jewelry. Sadie jiggled it—it seemed empty. She ignored a pang of guilt about snooping, opened the box and found a note:

Dear Willene,

As you requested, the hawk's eye pendant has been shamanically worked to help you transmute and ground the power. But be warned—the pendant can only do so much. To push it and yourself beyond your limits means breaking the laws of nature and you know how that will end. I suggest you use the time the pendant grants you to prepare your granddaughter for what is to come. I wish you both only the best.

Blessings,
Gwilla

Sadie reread and reread and reread the note. What did it mean? The power...was that the power of Mamo's illness? The note had to be referring to the pendant Mamo was wearing, but what did this Gwilla person mean?

Mamo is sicker than she's said, and this pendant—is it keeping her alive?

Sadie read the note again.

And Mamo should prepare me for...for her death?

Cold shivered through Sadie. She dropped the paper and covered her mouth. Her eyes welled, her breathing shortened.

She's dying. Mamo's dying, and she doesn't want to tell me. She wiped wet streams off her cheeks. *And I've been horrible to her.* Air hiccupped into her chest. She picked up the note, scrambled out of the closet, and hurried to her room.

Sadie sat on her bed and texted Mrs. Fallon: "How is Mamo?"

"Still sleeping. You okay?"

"Yes. Lying down. Talk later."

No point in going to see Mamo right now. Sadie set her phone down and opened her laptop. She typed "Gwilla shaman" into the search engine. Pages of results came back. Sadie scanned them, but none led her to anything that made sense.

Sadie smacked her palm on her bed. "Why isn't this working?" She entered more terms and clicked through more sites. She learned about the hawk's eye stone and confirmed it assists with healing. She searched shamanism and learned that shaman are people who practice divination and healing. She educated herself about the meaning of transmutation and grounding. But nothing gave Sadie any useful clues about the note or the person named Gwilla.

She hurried downstairs and checked the Contacts on Mamo's computer but found no matching entries.

"Crap." Sadie pounded her fist on the desk. Ninety minutes had passed and she hadn't discovered any way to help Mamo. If she could just talk to this Gwilla person, maybe Sadie could fix things.

Her throat constricted.

She knew there was no way to fix things. There was no way to stop Mamo from dying. Sadie laid her head on her arms and cried.

A text message arrived on Sadie's phone from Conner White: "I stopped by to see Willy. Mrs. Fallon said you're not well."

"I'm fine." Sadie grabbed a tissue and wiped her eyes.

"I need to talk to you."

"To tell me Mamo's going to die?" Sadie watched her screen. A minute passed before an animation showed he was typing a response.

His message arrived: "You don't understand."

"Then explain it to me." She was tired of grown-ups not answering her questions and then telling her she didn't understand.

"I can do that."

She stared at the message Conner had sent. What did he have to say?

Conner sent another message: "I'll come to you. Are you still at your home?"

Sadie didn't know why Mrs. Fallon told him where she was, but Sadie didn't want him here. She didn't want anyone here but Mamo. "No, I'll meet you somewhere."

Another minute passed. "Brandon wants to come with me, okay?"

He was still at Mrs. Fallon's house. Sadie typed back: "Okay."

"The Salton Spoon? Thirty minutes?"

Hunger gurgled through Sadie. She hadn't eaten anything today. "See you then."

Sadie went upstairs, brushed her hair, and splashed cold water on her face hoping to make her eyes less puffy and red. She didn't want anyone to know she'd been crying, especially Conner White.

✳ ✳ ✳

Sadie arrived early and sat on a bench outside the restaurant to wait. She glanced up from her phone and said hello to neighbors she knew, which was everyone she'd seen so far. As she said goodbye to the postal worker who also lived on her block, Sadie noticed a woman across the street with long, purple hair.

She's that substitute teacher I saw.

The woman looked at Sadie then averted her gaze.

Sadie recognized the ball cap the woman wore. *She's the lady I saw talking to Conner White at the hardware store.*

Sadie stood and waved. "Hey."

The woman didn't respond. She kept walking.

"Excuse me." Sadie checked traffic and dashed across the road. "Ma'am?"

The woman turned into an alley, her pace quickening.

Sadie increased her speed and followed the woman around the corner. But the woman was gone.

There's no way she just disappeared.

Sadie continued down the alley, looking through the windows of businesses that had alley access, but didn't see the woman with the purple hair in any of them. She reversed direction to head back to the restaurant.

The woman stepped out from behind a dumpster.

Sadie skittered backward.

"You need to come with me." The woman wore black leggings, black boots, and a black peacoat. Her dark purple hair flowed past her shoulders.

"Who are you?" Sadie's muscles tensed.

"I'm a friend." The woman reached toward Sadie.

She moved away. "Jumping out at people in alleys isn't really a friend-thing to do." Sadie assessed her surroundings without taking her eyes off the woman.

"I can help you."

"Help me with what?" Sadie asked.

"Everything."

What did Conner tell her? "You'll have to be a little more specific."

"I can help with what's happening to your grandmother, and to you. I can make it stop." The woman put her hands in her coat pockets.

"But how—"

"Come with me. We'll talk."

Tingles crawled up Sadie's spine. "We can talk here."

The woman smiled. "I understand your hesitation but don't worry. I'm a friend of the family. And the information I have is better shared someplace nicer than an alley. We can get milkshakes or whatever sounds good to you. Are you hungry?"

Sadie's stomach rumbled. "Wait—whose family are you a friend of?"

"Your family."

"I don't know you." Sadie's mind spun.

"It's a long story." The woman offered to put her arm around Sadie's shoulders. "And I'll bet it's one you will love hearing." Her smile warmed.

Sadie stared at the woman. She wanted to hear what the woman had to say. But Conner was coming to meet her and said he had things to tell her.

"You can come with me to The Salton Spoon," Sadie said. "We can talk there with—"

"That won't work." The smile dropped off the woman's face.

"Well, I'm not going anywhere with you."

"Then we'll have to do this the hard way." The woman lunged and grabbed Sadie's arm. She yanked and spun Sadie into a chokehold.

Sadie smashed her foot onto the woman's toes. She yelped and weakened her hold. Sadie slipped her fingers under the woman's arm, increased pressure, and wrenched her arm forward, scrambling out of her grip.

The woman grabbed Sadie's hair. Sadie back-kicked the woman in the gut. Her grasp released. Sadie spun to face her, fists up. The woman rushed forward and Sadie ducked. The woman corrected and kicked. Sadie blocked with a grab to the kicking leg and twisted the woman to the ground. The woman sprang up and punched. Sadie blocked and counter punched. The woman teetered then scrambled back.

Sadie solidified her stance, ready for the next attack. But the woman stilled, straightened, and pulled her arms tight around her. A second later, her form softened, condensed to an orb, and morphed into a black bird. A starling.

How...

The starling hovered then changed direction.

A four-legged blur blew by Sadie and launched. The bird veered but Shay caught a tip of wing in her teeth. The starling screeched and flapped. Shay yanked. The bird screamed and aimed its talons at Shay's eyes but couldn't connect. It flapped harder and feathers scattered, freeing the bird from Shay's mouth. It fluttered higher and moved away, its flight stuttered from the damage.

Shay pushed her tongue forward, flicking black feathers to the ground. She wagged her tail.

"Where did you come from?" Sadie's adrenaline levels dropped. She hugged Shay's neck.

"Sadie."

Brandon and Conner hustled toward her from the street.

Brandon got to her first. "Are you okay?"

"Yeah. Maybe a few bruises." Dizziness washed over her. "And I need to eat something. And maybe sit down."

He grabbed an old crate next to the dumpster. "Here."

"Thanks." Sadie sat and Shay plopped down next to her. Sadie picked off a piece of feather stuck to Shay's nose and scratched her behind the ears.

Conner shuffled up to them and leaned against the wall. "What happened?"

"Pretty sure that's for you to answer," Sadie said. "She's your friend."

"I'm not sure what you mean," Conner said.

"That woman you were talking to at the hardware store," Sadie said. "She attacked me."

"Merinda? That's not possible."

"So that's her name. She didn't bother to tell me," Sadie said. "And at least you admit you *were* talking to someone when I saw you," Sadie said.

"I—" Conner exhaled.

Sadie turned to Brandon. "Please tell me you saw what happened here, in the alley, what she did."

"Uh, you mean you kicking ass and her turning into a freakin' bird that almost got munched by Shay? Yeah, I saw that. At least the end of it." Brandon thumbed at Conner. "And he saw it, too. Don't let him tell you any different."

Conner ran his hand through his hair. "It seems we have more to talk about than I thought."

✳ ✳ ✳

A few minutes later they were seated at a table on the patio of The Salton Spoon. The lunch rush was over, and they had the whole sunny patio to themselves. The waitress brought glasses of water for everyone, a bowl of water and chew stick for Shay, and took their order.

Sadie felt grime and stickiness on her hands. "I'm going to use the restroom." She pushed away from the table.

"Good idea, especially after touching things in that alley," Conner said. "I'll do the same."

Brandon agreed to stay at the table with Shay, and wash up after they returned.

Once out of Brandon's line of sight, Conner asked Sadie for a word. "Some of the things I have to share with you are...sensitive in nature. Maybe you'd rather wait until we can talk in private? Without Brandon?"

He's trying to get out of this. "No, I don't want to wait."

"But there are things you might not wish for him to know."

"He saw a woman turn into a bird. And he knows Mamo is sick. I don't think there's anything else you could say that he shouldn't know." Sadie pushed on the bathroom door.

"What about the sleeping?"

Sadie froze.

"That's happening, isn't it?" Conner asked. "People around you are falling asleep?"

She released the door and faced him. "I...you know about that? That's for real?"

"I suspected. And yes, it's real."

Every instance of unusual sleeping friends and family flashed through Sadie's mind. "Can you fix it? Make it stop?"

"Of course, my dear," Conner said. "It's not permanent. My goodness, what a mess that would be if it were."

Sadie exhaled. "Oh my gosh, thank you for telling me. I've been freaking out." Without thinking, she hugged Conner then caught herself and quickly let go.

"Oh, well, yes, that would be a lot to deal with on your own, without any guidance. Your grandmother—"

"What is it, some kind of weird puberty thing? Does it run in the family or something? Mamo must have spaced telling me about it because she's been so sick. And you can totally talk about it in front of Brandon," Sadie said. "He'll probably think it's funny. Oh my gosh, I feel so much better." Her mind raced.

"Yes, but—"

"I read articles about what hormones trigger sleep. I wondered if I should be tested to see if those hormones were coming out of my pores or whatever, but it seemed like a total long shot."

"Hormones are related, but—"

"It's got to be a rare condition," Sadie said. "I did tons of research and didn't find anything that helped explain it. But this is good. I'm so glad you told me. And telling Brandon is cool because he saw a woman turn into a bird, and that's way weirder than me making people fall asleep at random. Right? I'll see you back at the table." She entered the ladies room.

Relief flooded through Sadie. She wasn't some mutant. She would outgrow this and get back to normal.

At least as normal as she could be without Mamo.

She went to the sink, picked a black feather out of her tangled hair, and washed her hands. She used a towel to wipe a smudge of dirt off her neck. She smoothed bits of hair that were flipping and twirling in odd directions, tucked it behind her ears and returned to her seat.

The waitress brought their meals and said she'd be back in a few minutes to check on them. After she left, Conner stabbed bits of salad with a fork and took a huge bite.

"Do you need me to ask questions?" Sadie asked. "Because I can do that. I have a million of them."

"I'm betting one of them is about how a person freaking changes into a bird, am I right?" Brandon took a drink of water.

"That is one of the questions, yes." She switched her focus to Conner. "You ready?"

"Just wanted to get my thoughts together," he said. "There is much to tell."

"I'm all ears," Sadie said. "How about starting with why that Merinda person tried to kidnap me?"

"For what it's worth, I don't believe that was her intention," Conner said.

"Uh, pretty sure when someone tries to force you to go with them, kidnapping is the intention." Sadie sipped her water.

"No," Conner said. "Merinda is a friend. She's here with me to help. But she's a bit on the impatient side."

"Help with what?" Sadie asked.

"As I said, there is much to tell."

"Fine," Sadie said. "Then start at the beginning."

"Much easier said than done. But I think a proper introduction makes a good starting point." Conner held his hand out to Sadie. "I'm your Great-Uncle, Conner White."

Sadie's jaw dropped. "Excuse me?"

He withdrew his hand. "Your great-uncle. I'm Willy's brother. Her older brother, in fact. A bit of information she happily reminds me of whenever she can."

She remembered the yearbook photos. "But your names...her maiden name isn't White."

"Different fathers, same mother," Conner said. "But that's more a technicality than anything. My dad died when I was very young and my mother married Willy's dad, my step-dad, and she and I were raised together."

"Why didn't Mamo tell me this?"

"There's a bit more to it, and Willy should tell you the rest of that story."

Sadie slumped in her chair. "I'm tired of everyone pushing off my questions. And Mamo's too sick to talk to me for more than a couple of minutes anyway."

"That's just it, Sadie," Conner said. "She won't be sick anymore."

A lump caught in Sadie's throat. "What are you saying? There's a cure for whatever she has?"

"Yes. It's you."

She closed her eyes and tried to think. "I don't understand."

"Me neither," Brandon said. "How is Sadie a cure for her grandmother?"

Conner canted his head from one side to the other. "Willy won't be happy with me telling you..."

Sadie leaned forward. "Please. Just spill."

He looked at Brandon, then locked his gaze on Sadie. "Our family is part of a long-lived Clan, and from our family line within the Clan, our leaders are chosen."

"Clan as in kilts, and crests, and plaid stuff?" Brandon asked. "A friend of mine back home is from Scotland and they have tons of plaid stuff in their house. And a huge sword mounted on the wall." He nudged Sadie. "Is she getting a sword?"

"Not that kind of clan," Conner said. "We're more...specialized."

"Specialized how?" Merinda's transformation came to Sadie's mind. "Oh my god, you're bird people. Like Merinda."

Brandon's eyes sparked. "More like a flock than a clan."

"Not quite that specialized." Conner took a sip of water. He signaled the waitress. "Could I get a—" He glanced at Sadie and Brandon. "A club soda, please." She nodded and left.

Conner continued. "Think of our Clan as a tribe, a society of people like the African tribes or the Native American tribes in the Americas. Our Clan is but one of many."

"I get that," Sadie said.

"Do you all live together, like in a commune?" Brandon asked.

"Many choose to live close to each other, others prefer distance," Conner said. "But all are subject to the Clan's laws and leadership. And there is an element to our Clan that involves certain abilities like you saw with Merinda."

"Cool." Brandon grinned.

"The selection of our leadership also has a supernatural element to it." Conner dabbed his forehead with his napkin.

"Double cool," Brandon said.

Sadie watched him for a moment. Ever since she'd met Jason and learned that cryptids were real, she was used to weird stuff that the rest of the world didn't know about. But Brandon didn't seem to be even a little surprised about what he was hearing.

"Okay, so supernatural elements, like what?" Sadie asked.

"The power of the Sovereignty. An ancient system created by our Clan ancestors that oversees and selects our leaders."

"Seriously?" Sadie asked. "You're telling me there's some magic that finds the chosen one from every generation or something?" She used air quotes for "the chosen one."

"A form of magic, yes," Conner said. "But there's no predetermined chosen one, as you call it. And no certainty that any one person shall lead. The only criterion is that the leader comes from our bloodline, and after many generations, the pool is quite large."

The waitress walked up and set the club soda on the table. Conner sipped the drink until she was out of earshot.

"A new leader is selected when the current leader is deemed unfit to serve," Conner said. "This can happen because the leader falls ill, or dies, is injured, or otherwise incapacitated. In most cases, leaders serve for the remainder of their lives after their selection. There is no set time to be the Clan leader, and in fact, entire generations have been skipped because the leader remained sound." He bit into a French fry and stared at the steam rising from the fry as he chewed. "There is one more condition that calls for a leader to be replaced, and that is when the power of the Sovereignty deems the leader's moral character to be damaged or corrupt. I'm afraid that is what we're facing now."

"What do you mean?" Sadie asked.

"Our history tells of a time when war between Clans was common. Thankfully, peace was negotiated, and hundreds of years have passed without conflict. We've lived well and happy, safe in our communities." He took another sip of his drink. "But I'm sad to say our current leader wants to return to the old ways. He has hidden his agenda well over the years, but some Clan members saw through him and fled. Many stay and continue to fight for what is right, but I fear we are losing the battle." Conner rubbed the bridge of his nose. "The Sovereignty has sounded the Calling, its choice for a new leader, but the selected member is one of those who fled, and the Calling has not been able to connect. Without the new leader to replace our corrupt one, all that is good about the Clan will vanish."

Heat flushed Sadie's cheeks. "Oh my god...Mamo."

"What about her?" Brandon asked.

"She's one of those who fled," Sadie said. "She's who the Sovereignty is looking for."

Everything made sense now. This was why Mamo never wanted to travel, why she didn't talk a lot about her childhood.

"That's why she's so sick, right? The Calling is for her, but she's fighting it, or she's not strong enough for it or something. You need to tell them to stop."

"That's not quite it," Conner said.

"Well, just make them stop." Sadie pulled out her phone. "Let me call Mamo." *I hope she's awake.*

Conner held his hand over her phone. "Hold on. There's more to tell."

She stopped and set the phone down. "What is it?"

He straightened his napkin in his lap. "You're right about the Calling, about the power flowing into Willy, and her not being strong enough."

Sadie picked her phone back up. "We have to do something."

Conner raised his hand. "She's too weak to handle the Calling because the Calling is not meant for her, Sadie. It's meant for you."

TEN
Secrets Told

"...what did you say?" Sadie asked.

Conner cleared his throat. "The Calling is meant for you."

"Whoa." Brandon leaned back in his chair.

"That doesn't make any sense," Sadie said. "I'm only fourteen. And Mamo would have told me."

"She should have told you," Conner said. "And the fact that she didn't tell you is precisely why she's been so ill."

"She's sick because she kept a secret?"

"The secret has been a heavy burden to bear, so perhaps some of her illness can be attributed to that." Conner straightened the napkin in his lap. "But it's mostly because she's been intercepting the Calling, and all its energy and power, and redirecting it into herself. And she's not strong enough. But now that you know, her burden will lessen."

"Does she want to lead the Clan?" Sadie asked.

"No, Sadie. She did it because she wants to protect you."

"Protect her from what? Sadie could totally be a good leader," Brandon said.

Sadie's eyebrows raised.

"I mean, if she wanted to do it," Brandon said. "But that does seem like a lot to ask of her."

"Indeed, the challenge is great," Conner said. "But we trust the Sovereignty to make the right choice."

Sadie felt like her thoughts were riding a carousel. She gripped the edge of the table.

Conner continued. "Many trust the Sovereignty and the Calling. But those who are loyal to our current leader are outraged at the Sovereignty's call for his replacement. Rumors abound that some of his followers have banded together to stop the Calling. We believe they've succeeded in carrying out this type of mission in the past though we have no proof."

"How can they stop it?" Brandon asked. "Elect their own candidate?"

"There is no election," Conner said. "The process established by the Sovereignty identifies the ideal leader."

"Then how did they stop it before?" Sadie held her water glass with both hands, cooling her palms.

Conner swallowed. "We believe they eliminated the candidate."

"Eliminated...as in killed?" Sadie asked.

"Yes." Conner pushed salad around his plate.

"Oh my god," Brandon said. "Did you know the last candidate?"

Conner kept his eyes on his food. "I did."

"Did Mamo know him...or her, too?" Sadie asked.

"She did," he said. "Very well."

Sadie's chest tightened. "Who was it?"

Conner paused and swallowed again. He looked up. "It was your dad, Sadie."

Sadie gasped.

"No way," Brandon said.

Conner nodded and returned his attention to his plate.

"That can't be right," Sadie said. "My parents died in a car crash." She lowered her head trying to see Conner's face. "They were in a car crash. I was there. In my car seat."

He raised his eyes. "We believe the car was sabotaged. And that the objective was to kill both you and your father because the Calling would likely pass to the closest in your father's bloodline if he were not able to serve."

"If that were true, the Calling should have gone to Mamo." Sadie's voice thinned.

"It doesn't work that way," Conner said. "The Calling moves down the bloodline, not up. It had already passed over your grandmother to select your father."

Sadie pulled at the silver charm bracelet around her wrist. "Do you know this for sure? That the bad guys killed my parents?"

"Yes," Conner said. "But there is no hard evidence, no physical proof, so we couldn't take action. It's one party's word against another's."

Sadie tried to think. Everything felt crazy, but at the same time felt like the truth, which made her feel even more crazy.

"Who is this jerkwad aaa—bsolutely sucky leader?" Brandon asked.

"His name is Garrison Devine," Conner said. "He's—"

"I'll say it," Brandon said. "Gary's an ass."

"Yes. And calling him 'Gary' is a crime punishable with the loss of your tongue."

Sadie couldn't believe what she was hearing.

Brandon flung his arms up. "You have to be freaking kidding me."

"No," Conner said. "His leadership skills leave much to be desired."

"But then...he...the bloodline..." Sadie pushed her plate away. "He's related to us."

"Yes." Conner pressed his fingers against his eyelid.

"Oh, no way," Brandon said.

"How?" Sadie asked.

Conner swallowed. "Garrison Devine is my and Willy's uncle, our mother's brother."

"Wait," Brandon said. "No offense, but if he's your uncle, doesn't that make him, like, ancient?"

"He's quite youthful for his age," Conner said. "Good genes."

"More like evil genes. You're saying he killed my parents to stay in power." Sadie forced down a lump that had formed in her throat.

Conner sighed and stared at his fries. He nodded.

"I need to go." She pushed away from the table.

"Hold on, let me pay the check." Conner beckoned the waitress.

"I'll be outside." Sadie headed toward the exit.

Brandon followed. "I'm coming with you."

Sadie plopped onto the bench she'd waited on earlier. She stared at the bracelet that used to be her mom's, fingering the heart charm her dad had bought. *They were murdered.*

"Hey, do you want me to go?" Brandon asked, thumbing over his shoulder. "This is super big family stuff. I totally understand if you want me gone."

"Huh?" Sadie focused on Brandon. "Oh, no don't go. I'm glad you're here. It's good to have you hear everything, too. So I don't think I'm losing it. I have no idea if I can ever talk to Nessa about any of this since it's so out there." She noticed the still empty seat beside her. "Wait—unless you *want* to go? If you're not comfortable or whatever—"

"What? No, I'm not uncomfortable, not even a little. I'm in." He sat on the bench.

Sadie scooted sideways to give them both plenty of room. "I have a question."

"Shoot," Brandon said.

Sadie paused. "Why are you so okay with all of this? I mean, it's completely crazy."

"Oh, I...my parents have told me about stuff. They're archeologists so they know all sorts of things about old curses, and people who did magic, and weird ceremonies and things. And they tell me a lot about it. Like tribes—there are tribes that shrink heads, which you've probably heard of, but do you know how they do it? They peel back the flesh and pull the skull out, and that part is basically garbage so they toss it. Then they sew stuff shut and actually boil the head—"

"Okay, okay, I get it. But those are from a long time ago, right?" Sadie asked. "Stuff like that doesn't happen anymore."

"Well, not officially. But sometimes my parents say things that make me wonder. Anyway, I always think the crazy stuff they talk about is pretty cool."

She paused. "Have you ever talked to Jason about those kinds of stories? Or does he have some he tells you?"

"What?" He shrugged and switched his gaze to the building across the street. "I don't know. Maybe? I don't remember."

"He *has* told you," Sadie said, "about the cryptids and the Rampart."

Brandon eased back into the bench. "He swore me to secrecy."

"Jason's uncle is going to kill him for telling you."

"He doesn't have to know," Brandon said. "And it's not like I didn't keep the secret since you already know everything."

"How did you know that?"

"Are you kidding? You're in practically every story." Brandon turned on the bench to face her. "It would have been hard to leave you out."

A breeze blew Sadie's hair around her face. She tucked it behind her ear. "Actually, I'm kind of relieved. It's a hard secret to keep."

"Good." Brandon smiled. "Then I've got your back. And if we see any—what are they called? Skyfish? I won't even freak out."

"Yeah, well we can only see them when they're in large groups. And if that happens, you probably should freak out. And I guess we should both freak out if this Garrison guy ever shows up."

"Noted," Brandon said.

Conner came out of The Salton Spoon. "All set. Let's go see your grandmother. Though I have a feeling she won't be too happy to see me."

✸ ✸ ✸

Mamo stood on the front porch, fully dressed and with her arms crossed.

"Wow," Sadie said. "She must be feeling tons better." Conner telling Sadie about the Calling did help Mamo, just like he said it would.

"Except she looks kinda mad," Brandon said.

Conner parked the car. "As I assumed she would be."

The three of them got out of the car and approached Mrs. Fallon's house.

"What did you do, Conner?" Mamo's eyes flashed.

He held up his hands. "Take it easy, Willy. Everything's fine."

Mamo moved her hands to her hips. "Is it? Everything is fine because what—you're smarter than everyone else? You have psychic powers? Do you have any idea what you've done?"

Sadie and Brandon stepped aside to let Conner go first.

"I told Sadie the truth, and it was the right thing to do," Conner said.

"That was not your decision to make, and you know it."

"You're wrong about that, Willy." Conner stopped at the foot of the steps and stared at Mamo. "When you put yourself in danger, when you became irrational and put your own life at risk, it sure as hell became my decision." His voice was serious, tough.

Mamo pursed her lips.

"Mamo?" Sadie took a few steps toward her. "You're feeling better? You look...like yourself." Her stomach fluttered.

Mamo's shoulders relaxed and she motioned Sadie over to her, pulling her into a protective hug. "I am. I'm much better."

"That's good, right?" Sadie felt Mamo's too-thin frame through her shirt.

"It's all perspective," she said. "Let's go inside." She directed Sadie through the front door and gestured for Brandon to follow. Mamo left Conner to enter last.

Mrs. Fallon stood in the foyer. She smirked at Sadie. "You look like you're feeling better, too."

"Uh, yeah." Sadie bit her bottom lip. "I'm good."

"That must have been some nap." Mrs. Fallon winked.

"All right, let's get to it," Mamo said. "Everyone have a seat."

The group shuffled into the living room.

"There is one thing I need to do before we start." Mamo reached behind her neck and unclasped the hawk's eye pendant. She hung it around Sadie's neck. "This is for you."

Sadie gazed at the stone. Blue and green light glinted from within, refracted by late afternoon sunlight streaming into the room. She didn't say anything. After reading the note from Gwilla about the pendant, she wasn't sure what to think.

"She doesn't need that," Conner said.

"It's not a matter of need," Mamo said. "The pendant is a gift from me to Sadie. And any benefits that come with it are merely icing on the cupcake."

"I saw the note," Sadie said. "The one that came with the pendant."

Mamo was taken aback. "Well, this is a day full of surprises."

"I'm sorry I snooped—"

Mamo held up her hand. "Nope, there's no need to be sorry. I put you in a tough spot, trying to keep some big secrets from you. I have to say, I'm actually a little bit proud of you for taking the initiative to try and figure things out on your own."

Sadie released tension she didn't realize she was carrying.

"And speaking of secrets, we need to get all of them out in the open," Mamo said.

Brandon shifted in his seat.

"As for you," Mamo said, looking at Brandon.

138

"Right. I should go." Brandon stood.

"Hold on a minute," Mamo said. "Lena tells me good things about you, and she knows your parents quite well."

Sadie didn't realize Mrs. Fallon had anything more than a casual relationship with Brandon's parents.

"And it seems to me you're pretty far down the road already with family secrets..." Mamo tilted her head. "Am I right?"

"Well, uh..." Brandon fidgeted with his hands.

"That was a rhetorical question, young man. No answer needed," Mamo said. "As far as I'm concerned, I'm glad to have you stay but it's really up to my granddaughter."

She focused on Sadie. "There is much more to tell, and some of it may be worth hearing on your own and choosing to share later."

"He can stay," Sadie said. "We've come this far."

"Glad to hear it," Mamo said. "Everyone needs to be aware of what's going on."

Kyle walked in the front door. "Hey, Grams. I came as fast as I could."

Mrs. Fallon directed him to a seat. "Thank you, Kyle. You need to be part of this conversation, too."

Really? Even Kyle?

"Sadie, please bring me up to speed about what you've learned so far," Mamo said.

She relayed what had happened and what Conner had already shared.

When Sadie got to the part about Merinda, Mamo interrupted and looked at Conner. "And why, exactly, did Merinda grab Sadie in the alley? Has she lost her mind?" Her voice pitched up.

"I think it was just a misunderstanding, but I texted her," Conner said. "She's on her way over to explain. And apologize."

Sadie's gut pulled tight.

"That should be interesting," Mamo said. "She's been high-strung since she was a kid."

"You've known her that long?" Sadie asked.

Mamo nodded. "She lived with us for a while when her mother was, well, she wasn't able to do much in the way of parenting. And Merinda didn't have a father readily available either. So Merinda was our foster-sister for a few years. We consider her part of the family."

"We were always close, even after she moved home," Conner said.

"You more so than me," Mamo said, "but that's a story for another time."

"What about my parents?" Sadie asked. "Is what Conner said about the car accident true?"

Mamo's shoulders dropped. She took Sadie's hand in hers. "Yes, sweetie, we believe it is. And that's when we realized how corrupt things really were, and I decided it was best to hide you."

"Without anyone else's counsel." Conner crossed his arms.

"It was for the best." Mamo took a deep breath. "I am sorry we left without saying goodbye, Conner. I do regret that."

"That's when we came to Salton?" Sadie asked.

"Yes," Mamo said. "With some assistance, I was able to cloak us within the town so the Calling couldn't find you."

"Which is why we never went anywhere." Sadie touched the pendant around her neck.

Kyle scooted forward. "Wait—you've never been anywhere outside of Salton? Seriously?"

"Nope," Sadie said. "Not even a little bit outside the borders, until Jason and I went to the sugar mill a couple months ago." She remembered the stomachache that hit her not long after they passed the *Thanks for visiting Salton* sign. "And I felt sick."

"That was the Calling," Mamo said. "There are feelers out all over the world searching for you. When you left the protected area many of them hit you at the same time, overwhelming your system. I know Haru helped you with his healing power, but I'm not sure exactly how. And I never asked because I didn't want to call his attention to the situation." She sighed. "I don't know what would have happened if he hadn't been there to intervene."

"So I broke the spell, or whatever it was that was hiding us." Sadie pushed deeper into the couch.

"More like cracked it, which was enough for Conner to find us. But I knew it was only a matter of time before the Calling, and our enemies would also find us if I didn't do something. That's when I came up with what I thought was a brilliant plan of redirecting the Calling to me," Mamo said.

"I question how brilliant the plan was," Conner said, "seeing as how you would have died."

"Well, it seemed brilliant at the time." Mamo brushed her hands on her thighs. "I was committed to making it work, especially after you contacted me. I believed it was only our family connection that aided you, and that I could still stop the others from coming."

Flashes of Mamo yelling in her nightmares weaved through Sadie's memory. "These others—that's who you saw in your nightmares, that's who you were worried about."

"That wasn't just worry," Conner said. "She was battling them in her nightmares."

Mamo *tsked*. "Do you have to tell her every little detail?"

"Yes," Sadie said. "If you're not going to tell me, then yes he does have to tell me every little detail." She glared at Mamo.

Her face softened. "You're right. I'm sorry."

"So you're fighting them off in your nightmares, and you're trying to intercept the Calling, and you're practically about to keel over through all of this," Sadie said. "But why? Why can't we just tell the Sovereignty or the Calling or whoever that I don't want to be the leader and to leave us alone?"

"Yeah, totally," Brandon said. "She can decline the nomination or whatever."

"There is a process that allows that," Conner said. "But it's not something we can count on."

"Why not?" Sadie asked.

Mamo paused. "The corruption of the current leadership team runs too deep. Even if you officially dismiss the Calling, Garrison won't stop."

"What does that even mean? He can keep the stupid leadership job. I don't want it."

"But the Calling wants you to have it," Mamo said. "And that is a powerful force for Garrison to fight. The only way he and his followers win that fight is to eliminate candidates."

Sadie pressed her lips together. "Like my parents."

Mamo moved over and put her arm around Sadie. "Yes."

"Hold on." Brandon jumped up. "You're saying even if she declines everything, he *still* wants to kill her?"

"That's exactly what we're saying," Conner said. "And maybe me and Willy as well, for good measure."

"No way," Kyle said. "This is like Mafia stuff or something."

"Very similar," Conner said. "You see, our family has certain abilities and powers that are enhanced, stronger than most in our Clan, and with the Calling, those powers would exceed Garrison's. Once the Sovereignty deemed him corrupt, the progression of his powers has been stalled, maybe even diminished. He knows this and has been protecting his position by eliminating members of our family. Those who have fled seem to be safe, but anyone who has returned to the Clan and expressed an opinion not to his liking has met with certain...accidents." He leaned back in his chair. "I've kept my head down and my opinions to myself which up to now has kept me off his radar screen."

"And now that his followers know where I am, they're coming." Sadie pulled her knees close to her chest.

Shay trotted in from the kitchen and climbed up on the couch next to Sadie, pushing her head onto Sadie's lap. Sadie rubbed Shay's cheek.

"They don't know yet," Mamo said, "or they'd already be here. And we do still have one trick up our sleeve."

"Willene, we talked about this," Mrs. Fallon said. "You can't run."

"We can. It's better than waiting for them to show up and hope to fight them off."

Mrs. Fallon blinked, keeping her eyes shut for a moment. "Being on the run all the time is no life for Sadie."

"What choice do we have?" Mamo asked.

Mrs. Fallon raised an eyebrow. "I believe you mean what choice does Sadie have."

"I don't want to be the leader." Sadie waved her hands in the air. "No way."

"See? She doesn't want it," Mamo said.

Conner blew out a breath. "She can't make that decision without knowing everything."

"Jeez, there's more?" Kyle asked. "Wait—is Sadie an android or something? I just saw a movie about androids taking over the world."

Mamo ignored Kyle. She looked from Mrs. Fallon to Conner and back to Mrs. Fallon. "Fine." She turned to Sadie. "The information they're referring to is that you—"

The doorbell rang.

Conner stood. "That's probably Merinda."

A minute later, Merinda stood in the living room and held one arm close to her side. She gave a small wave with her uninjured arm. "Hi, Sadie. And Conner. And Willy. And everyone else. Thanks for letting me come over and clear the air." She didn't smile.

"You're welcome," Mamo said, her voice flat but firm. "Have at it."

Merinda stepped closer to Sadie.

Shay's head popped up and her ears perked. She fixed her eyes on Merinda.

Merinda stopped where she was. "Uh, is the dog friendly?"

"Depends," Brandon said.

"Okay..." Merinda stayed where she was. "Sadie, please accept my sincere apologies about earlier. I had no intention of hurting you."

"You didn't." Sadie kept her expression neutral.

"Well, that's good," Merinda said. "It's just that I came here with Conner to talk to you and Willene, and to hopefully convince you to return to the Clan with us. Both of you." She wrung her hands. "Um, I was a little frustrated that things were taking so long, and I stepped out of bounds by trying to talk to you on my own."

No one said anything.

"I didn't tell Conner what I was doing, so I was kind of stressed about that because I knew he'd be mad at me. But I figured it would be okay if I convinced you." Merinda shifted from one leg to the other and back. "And then when you wouldn't go with me to talk, well, I thought if I could make you go somewhere with me, and make you listen to what we had to say, then you would decide to come with us."

"So you *were* trying to kidnap me." Sadie gaped at Mamo then back to Merinda.

"Sort of? But not really," Merinda said. "I mean, it was a good kidnapping, not a bad kidnapping because I just wanted to talk to you to help make things right."

Brandon jutted his chin.

"Is your arm going to be alright?" Mamo asked.

Merinda tucked the arm closer. "I think so."

"Well, good for you," Mamo said, her voice still hard. "And lucky too, because if I had been in that alley with Sadie, I would have snapped that wing right off of you."

Merinda took two steps back. "I'm sorry. I thought I was helping."

"Thank you for apologizing, Merinda." Mamo stood. "Sadie, do you accept Merinda's apology?"

"Yeah, I guess. Sure." Sadie pulled Shay closer.

"My granddaughter is a kind and caring person," Mamo said. "I am following her example and accepting your apology as well. But if you ever pull a ridiculous stunt like that again, you will answer to me. Do you understand?"

Merinda's eyes widened and she nodded. "Yes, I understand."

"Thank you for stopping by," Mamo said. "Conner will see you out."

Conner directed Merinda out of the room.

"As for you, Shay," Mamo said.

Shay lifted her head.

"If that ever happens again, feel free to do more than pull out a few feathers."

Shay's tail thumped twice on the couch and she placed her head back on Sadie's lap.

Conner returned to the group after Merinda left. "You were a bit harsh, don't you think?"

"The woman tried to kidnap my granddaughter," Mamo said. "She should know better."

"Yes, but she is still family—"

"Can we stop talking about Merinda?" Sadie sat higher. "Mamo was about to tell me something else when the doorbell rang."

"Yes." Mamo took a seat in a chair opposite Sadie. "Conner told you our Clan has certain abilities. You saw Merinda change into a bird."

"What?" Kyle asked. "How did I miss that part of the story?"

Brandon leaned over. "I'll tell you later."

"Anyway," Mamo said, "before I tell you more about our Clan, and about you, please know this first—you have a choice. None of this is set in stone. You are not locked into anything."

"Okay..." Sadie's heartbeat thumped in her chest.

"Most in our Clan have the ability to shape-shift like you saw Merinda do," Mamo said. "And a few are capable of magic, but that is a rare quality."

"Oh my god, I'm so glad I came home for this." Kyle grinned.

Mrs. Fallon gave him a look.

"Sorry," Kyle said. "My bad."

Sadie refocused on Mamo. "Can you shape-shift? And Conner?"

"We can, and I can do some magic," Mamo said. "But there's more to it than that."

Kyle covered his mouth with his hand.

"Okay, so like what?" Sadie asked.

"Can you show us right now?" Kyle scooted to the edge of his seat. "How about turning into a horse? But that's probably too big for the living room. How about a tiger?"

"Kyle." Mrs. Fallon's tone was cold.

"Sorry, Grams, but this is so cool."

"Be quiet and listen, or go downstairs to your room and hear nothing," Mrs. Fallon said.

"Okay, okay, I'll zip it," Kyle said. "I'm a fly on the wall."

Mamo switched her attention from Kyle to Sadie. "Your ability to make people fall asleep is part of who we are as well. That ability is just coming in for you, and it doesn't work exactly right when it starts, especially since I was messing with the proper order of things by intercepting the Calling."

"So it's not something I'm going to outgrow." Sadie's stomach flipped.

"No, but it's not really a sleep power, and it is something you can learn to control," Mamo said.

"I don't want to make people fall asleep." Sadie jumped up, startling Shay. "I don't want to make people do anything. I want to be me. Just Sadie."

Mamo stood and took Sadie's face in her hands. "And you can choose that, absolutely. No questions asked."

"Willy, you're pussyfooting around the information she needs," Conner said. "Tell her."

Mamo scrunched her face at Conner, then relaxed it. She took Sadie's hands in hers. "Sweetie, we are Yowie, and an especially powerful line of Yowie at that."

Air caught in Sadie's throat.

"Have you heard Jason talk about Yowie?" Mamo asked. "Do you know what we are?"

Sadie gave a slight nod. Her voice squeaked. "Like Bigfoot."

"That's right. Like Bigfoot, but from Australia. Our Clan is all Yowie. Merinda, me, Conner, your mom and dad—all of us."

Mamo squeezed Sadie's hands. "And Sadie, so are you."

ELEVEN

Family

S adie pulled her hands away from Mamo. "Yowie? How can I—?" She crossed the room and leaned into the back of a chair. "This doesn't make any sense. You're not...furry." Sadie folded her arms across her belly.

"Many of our kind choose to live in human form." Mamo moved close to put her arm around Sadie.

Sadie shrugged away. She glanced at Brandon. His mouth was open, his eyes wide.

I'm a monster.

"Please, Mamo, please tell me this is some kind of joke." Sadie moved back to the couch and sat next to Shay. "I promise I'll laugh. You really got me with this one. Please..."

Mamo sat on the other side of Shay and touched Sadie's arm. "This isn't a joke, sweetie. This is who we are. And I'm sorry I couldn't keep it from you."

Sadie gulped air and raised her eyes to Mamo's. "So what's going to happen to me? I'm going to turn when the moon is full or something?" She held up her trembling hands. "Is this some kind of fake body that's going to disappear?" Her voice cracked.

"No, no, no." Mamo brushed Sadie's hair off her shoulder. "You have a choice. You were born in this body, as human, and you can choose to keep it and live a fully human life."

"Okay, that's what I choose." Sadie slapped her thighs. "Human. Done."

"I strongly urge against that," Conner said.

"And I don't really care what you think." Sadie scratched Shay's ears. The room was silent around her.

Mamo spoke. "I wish it was that simple, sweetie. But the Calling, and Garrison...they complicate things."

Sadie leaned into Shay. "I'll promise him, Garrison, I'll sign something, anything, that says I'll stay out of it. I won't bother him. I won't even come near wherever they are for the rest of my life."

"That won't work," Conner said.

Mamo snapped her attention to him. "Give me a minute, would you? Don't push her."

"She needs to know." Conner's voice was firm.

"I'm getting to it," Mamo said.

"Are you? Because hiding for the past fourteen years and not telling her anything just says avoidance, avoidance, avoidance." Conner rubbed his hands down his face. "We don't have much time left."

Mamo held up her hand. "Stop. Just stop."

"I'm not going to stop, Willy. The family needs her. You and I need her." Conner paced across the room and back. "They are coming for her one way or another, and if we're not prepared we'll get everyone in this room killed."

Nausea flowed through Sadie. "So, I can't really choose."

"You can, and you will." Mamo knelt next to Sadie. "And you have time to think about it. You don't have to decide today or even tomorrow."

Conner threw his hands in the air.

"When does she have to decide?" Brandon asked.

"An excellent question," Conner said.

Sadie shifted her eyes from Mamo to Shay.

"When she's ready," Mamo said.

"Oh, Willene," Conner said. "Stop coddling her. She's a strong young woman. Stronger than you know."

"I know how strong she is." Mamo's eyes flashed. "I raised her."

Mrs. Fallon crossed her arms. "The two of you sniping at each other isn't doing any good for Sadie."

Sadie waved her hand. "Yeah, seriously, just tell me. What is the rest of the deal?"

Mamo sat on the coffee table and faced Sadie. "You are the last in our direct bloodline."

"But at the restaurant, Conner said there were lots of people, or whatever, in our bloodline."

"Yes, but they are branches of the family tree if you will. We are the trunk," Mamo said. "And in the trunk is a great deal of power. The farther away from the trunk the branches reach, the more diluted that power becomes."

"So the sleep power I have, that's because we're the trunk."

"Yes," Mamo said. "Though the sleep power is actually developing into the power to erase people's memories, in order to protect both you and them."

"Why would I need to do that?"

"For example, if someone accidentally sees you in Yowie form," Conner said. "Seeing such things tends to upset people, and we find it's better to reset their memory. Then they don't say anything to their friends and family, and consequently, aren't seen as a cuckoo bird."

Sadie cringed at the idea of ever looking like a big, hairy creature.

"Only some in the Clan have that power," Mamo said. "And while all can shape-shift between Yowie and human, a few can also shift to other forms."

"Like Merinda," Brandon said.

"Exactly." Mamo addressed Sadie. "Some have enhanced strength, some have great speed, and some, like me, have healing and regeneration power."

"Or you did until you burned up most of it when you intercepted the Calling, against my advice," Mrs. Fallon said.

Sadie's brow furrowed. "You did? You lost it?"

Mamo touched Sadie's knee. "It will return in time."

"And I...I would have the power to erase people's memories." Sadie hated the idea of messing with other people's minds.

"You will have that whether you choose Yowie or not," Mamo said. "That's already forming within you. I'll teach you how to use it."

"Cool," Kyle said. "You can help the teachers forget to give us tests." He held his hand up to high-five Brandon. "Am I right?"

"Yeah. Whatever." Brandon high-fived Kyle but stayed zeroed in on Sadie.

Mrs. Fallon eyed Kyle and cleared her throat.

Mamo continued. "But that's not all, Sadie. If you choose Yowie and accept the Calling, you'll eventually have all the powers I mentioned and more."

"What?" Sadie scooted deeper into the couch and pulled Shay close.

"It's our family's power plus the Calling," Conner said. "In time, your power would be unmatched. This is why Garrison wants you eliminated."

"But why wouldn't Sadie have powers right away?" Brandon asked. "Does she have to earn them or something? Like in video games?"

"No special quests," Mamo said. "She simply has to live her life and embrace the powers when they come. And Sadie, I would be right by your side to help you learn about them, and manage the powers, even enhance them."

"And if I say no, everything stays like it is except for the memory thing, right?" Sadie asked.

"Yes," Mamo said.

"No," Conner said. "She can't defend herself in this form."

Mamo stood and faced Conner. "We'll protect her."

"We can't protect her from what's coming, and you know it." Conner put his hands on his hips. "We need her to protect us."

"Huh?" Sadie leaned forward.

"She's fourteen years old," Mamo said. "She's too young."

"Fourteen-shmorteen she's the same age as you when your healing power started to develop," Conner said. "And as far as I'm concerned, she's more mature than you were at that age."

"That may be true," Mamo said, "but there's more going on here than when I was her age."

"And the time to prepare her for it is now. They don't care how old she is," Conner said. "You may have delayed the inevitable, but we need her ready and on our side or it's the end of all of us."

"We'll find another way."

"We've been searching unsuccessfully for another way since her parents were killed," Conner said. "What makes you think that's going to change anytime soon?"

"Enough," Mamo said. "Sadie needs to decide on her own terms."

"Wait." Sadie covered her eyes with her hands then focused on Conner. "What did you mean about me protecting you?"

"Sweetie, you don't need to worry—"

"Garrison's power, even with the stay of the Sovereignty, is immense." Conner sat on the edge of a chair and leaned toward Sadie.

Mamo glared at him.

Conner clasped his hands and continued. "Our informants tell us he wants to expand his rule beyond our Clan to other Clans and then to human populations. And no one can stop him. No one that is, except you."

A chill raced through Sadie's veins. "But I can't—"

"Not like this, as human, no," Conner said. "But once your powers are in place..."

Mamo placed her hand on Sadie's knee. "Don't think about—"

"You said they're already looking for us." Sadie twisted a section of her hair. "How long until they come?"

"If you accept the Calling, you'll be cloaked until ready," Mamo said. "There's no knowing how long that will be."

"Just like that?" Sadie asked. "I say whatever magic word to be a Yowie and do this Calling thing, and then I go to school every day like it's no big whoop, and hope I don't suddenly grow hair on my knuckles while I'm taking an Algebra test? Or accidentally wipe Nessa's memory? Or do something that gets Mr. Whitaker in trouble again?"

Sadie stood and walked across the room. "Is that why we needed Kyle here for this? So he can monitor me at school and tell you if I've turned into a monster? And is Brandon's job to watch me after school or something?"

Mamo held out one hand. "Sadie—"

"And who's supposed to protect them from me, huh? What happens when I change into a monster and hurt one of them? Have you thought about that? Or maybe you just lock me in a cage or something until I settle down."

"I wanted them here, Sadie," Mrs. Fallon said. "I don't believe in secrets." She eyed Mamo. "Especially when it's a secret that impacts all of us."

"Because I'm putting you all in danger?" Sadie covered her mouth with her hands.

"No, sweetie." Mamo tapped the seat next to her.

Sadie didn't sit. She looked at Conner. "How much time do we have? For real?"

"As Willy said, if he knew where you were, they'd be here already," Conner said. "We have some time but I don't know how much."

"And when time runs out some big band of ape-people charge in here and grab me? Or kill me? Or kill everyone?" Sadie's lip quivered.

"Nobody's in danger. And you're tired," Mamo said. "This is too much for one day."

Tears welled in Sadie's eyes. "I think it's probably too much for any day."

"Why don't you go upstairs," Mamo said. "Lena's ordering pizza and I'll bring some to you after it arrives, okay?"

"But—"

Mamo stood and put her arm around Sadie. "Take a little time to yourself. We'll talk more later."

"It's just that I don't...I can't...I'm not sure what to do," Sadie said.

"We'll come up with a plan, don't worry." Mamo hugged her. "None of this is as bad as it feels to you right now. We're going to be fine, me and you and everyone else here."

Sadie nodded again. "Okay."

"I'll be up in a little bit," Mamo said.

Shay followed Sadie upstairs.

Sadie sat at her desk and opened her laptop. She typed "yowie" into a search field and held her finger above the enter key but didn't press it. "All that will tell me is that Yowie are big and hairy and ugly. I already know that. I don't need to see it." She closed the computer. Her gaze drifted to the picture of her and Mamo at the state fair. Knowing the truth about her family made Sadie feel like everything in her past had been a lie. Being Sadie seemed like a long game of dress up she didn't know she was playing.

"This is all so stupid." Sadie put the picture face down. "I wish I could go back in time. I wish I could make this all go away. I can't be a Yowie." She remembered Brandon's face when he heard the news. "I'm a total freak."

Sadie lay on her bed and thought about going to school, moving back home with Mamo, studying for exams. None of it seemed normal anymore. She folded her arms over her face. Shay jumped onto the bed next to her, licked Sadie's cheek, and thrust her head under Sadie's arm. Warm air flowed over Sadie's face as Shay exhaled.

"I can't do it, Shay. I just can't." Sadie shoved aside an image of herself transformed with claws, and fangs, and fur. She thought about Nessa and keeping this secret from her, even without accepting the Calling. "It's hard enough to keep all of Jason's secrets. And if I ever slip up, or she sees Mamo as a Yowie or something, she will flip out."

But Sadie had never seen Mamo as a Yowie, or even a hint that she could change into something covered with fur. Or hair. Or whatever it was. So maybe the secret could stay hidden. "Maybe it hurts to change. Maybe that's why she never does it." Sadie scratched Shay's neck. "Whatever. I'm never going to find out for myself. I just want to forget all of this. No way I'm doing it."

Sadie wondered why her parents had chosen to be Yowie. She never knew them, but she had pictures of them from throughout their lives. Back at the house were photos of her mom as a child in Australia before her family moved to the United States. And pictures of her dad with Mamo when he was a kid, playing on the beach in California. There were yearbooks from both her parents' high schools and photos of the two of them after they met in college. And no pictures where they appeared to be Yowie, not even for Halloween—the one day a year where Sadie thought the Yowie-thing might be cool. But that was it. Her parents were Yowie and that didn't save them from dying. Why choose to be a monster?

Sadie knew she was being unfair. She'd learned cryptids looked different and acted different, but they weren't necessarily mean or scary or bad. Still, imagining herself as an ugly, hairy beast brought only one term to Sadie's mind: freak.

I can't believe I'm a cryptid. What will Jason think?

A knock on the door startled her. "Come in."

Mamo entered with a plate full of pizza. "I come bearing gifts." Shay stood on the bed and leaned toward the food, her nose wiggling as she assessed the plate.

"None for you, Shay." Mamo set the plate on Sadie's desk. "But there's a special dinner waiting for you downstairs."

Shay leaped off the bed and hurried out to find her meal.

Sadie moved to her desk chair. "Thanks for bringing my dinner up here." She bit into a slice of veggie pizza.

"It's the least I could do after everything I've put you through," Mamo said. "I'm so sorry."

"At least you're not going to die now." She halted before taking another bite of pizza. "You are getting better, right?"

Mamo sat on Sadie's bed. "Yes, it looks like you're stuck with me for a while." She smiled. "Once Conner told you about the Calling, my power to intercept it was snuffed out. The Calling has found you and will continue to empower you unless you decline."

"And how do I do that?"

"There's a short incantation I'll teach you when you're ready," Mamo said. "A couple of sentences and you're set either way."

Sadie set the slice down. "Am I horrible if I don't want to do it? That I don't want to be a Yowie like you and my parents?" Her voice quivered.

"Of course not." Mamo leaned closer. "It's a tough choice for any of us, but normally we don't have to make it until adulthood. You've had this thrust upon you at fourteen and all the weight of the Calling on top of it." She rubbed Sadie's back. "It's too much. Which is exactly why I tried to protect you from it."

"But what about what Conner said? That my power as a Yowie can get rid of Garrison Devine?"

"Don't even worry about that," Mamo said.

"So, it's not true. There's another way to stop him."

"We will find one." Mamo slapped her hands on her thighs. "We've lasted this long and we'll keep fighting until we win."

"But you've been hiding."

"Yes." Mamo rubbed Sadie's shoulder. "And we will have to hide again."

"You mean leave here?" Sadie asked. "Leave Salton?"

"It's the only way." Mamo stood. "And we'll have to do it without telling Conner or Merinda, or anyone."

"But Jason, and Nessa, Mrs. Fallon..." *And Brandon.*

"No one," Mamo said. "To tell them would only put them in danger." She stepped to the window and looked out. "In fact, we might need to adjust their memories before we go."

"Like, erase us? Make them forget us?" Sadie's stomach felt like a twisted rubber band.

"It's the only way to keep everyone safe." Mamo picked up the face down photo of her and Sadie. "I've always loved this photo of us. Those are two huge grins right there."

Sadie ignored the comment. "Where would we go?"

Mamo placed the picture upright. "I have a few ideas. It will be someplace small, like Salton, where I can manage another cloaking spell."

Another place I can never leave.

"And I'll have to stay there forever?" Sadie asked.

"No," Mamo said. "Eventually the Calling will select a new candidate and you'll be released."

"But if I decline it right now, why wouldn't it find someone else *right now*? Then we can stay in Salton."

"Because of your age, the Calling won't be so quick to officially accept your decision," Mamo said. "The refusal of your Yowie heritage will defer those qualities from developing, but the Calling will wait until you've passed into adulthood to officially accept your refusal.

The point being that, as an adult, you might come to a different decision."

I don't know how I'd ever agree to being a Yowie.

"So we'd have to hide for four years." Sadie thought she could maybe deal with waiting until she was eighteen, though the idea of losing her friends triggered a tightening in her chest.

"Eleven years, until you're twenty-five."

"What?" Sadie sank in her chair. "Are you sure?"

"I promise you, it will fly by," Mamo said. "Time goes by faster as you get older."

"Not if I can't go anywhere, like on our spring break trip, or to college, or even stick my toe across the town-of-wherever border." Sadie shoved the pizza away.

Mamo sat and placed her hands on Sadie's knees. "I know this is hard. But it's the best choice for everyone. I can keep you safe."

Sadie stared into Mamo's eyes.

"One for two and two for one, right?" Mamo set her hand on Sadie's knee.

More than anything, Sadie wanted to be with Mamo, to be with her family. She was the only real family Sadie had.

"One for two and two for one," Sadie said.

"There you go." Mamo stood. "I understand how you feel about all of this, sweetie. I do. And you know how I feel as well." She lifted the hawk's eye pendant and held it in her palm. "But with this around your neck where it belongs, we have some time. So don't feel pressured to do anything just yet." She set the pendant back in place on Sadie's chest. "Let's take a few days to let things sink in, go through our normal routines, and see where that takes us."

"I don't need to think about anything," Sadie said. "I know what I'm going to do."

"Good. Then it will be that much easier in a few days when we pull the trigger on your decision." Mamo moved toward the door. "Okay?"

"Okay."

Mamo stepped into the hallway. "Will I see you downstairs later?"

"I don't think so." The idea of seeing everyone right now, especially Brandon, made Sadie anxious. "I'm going to stay up here, maybe go to bed early."

"Then I'll see you in the morning," Mamo said. "Love you."

"Love you, too, Mamo."

Sadie woke to her alarm the next morning. She got ready for school, repeatedly checking her arms, and hands, and legs for any unusual hair growth, and decided to wear long pants and a hoodie. The more covered up she was, the better she felt. She practiced her new mantra in her head: no sleeping, no sleeping, no sleeping. She hoped it would work on everyone around her.

She walked into the kitchen. Mamo was cooking eggs. Brandon stood up from the table and carried his plate to the sink.

"Good morning," Sadie said.

"Good morning, sweetie," Mamo said. "I'll have some breakfast ready for you in a couple of minutes."

"Hey." Brandon walked past her. "I've got to go video call my parents. See you later."

"Yeah, see ya." Sadie watched him leave the room. *Probably doesn't want to spend too much time with monster-girl.*

"How did you sleep?" Mamo asked.

"Amazingly well." Sadie sat at the table. "Where's Mrs. Fallon?"

"She's on a phone call with someone in London."

"Jason?" Sadie's texts to Jason still showed delivered but not read.

"I'm not sure," Mamo said.

Sadie wished she could talk to Jason about everything that had happened. He was used to weird stuff. Though he'd still probably look at her differently. There was no getting around the monster part, even if she did turn it down.

Mamo put a plate of eggs, toast, and fresh berries in front of Sadie. "It feels good to be back in the kitchen, making myself useful."

"And it's good to have you back," Sadie said.

Mamo scrubbed eggs off the skillet. "I haven't felt this good in a long time. In fact, I think we should get out of Lena's hair and move back home. Whaddya say?"

Sadie smiled behind her napkin. "I say yes. For sure yes."

"Then it's a done deal. We'll pack up and head home."

"I'll get my stuff ready and we can go as soon as school is out."

Mamo tilted her head. "Well, unless things changed dramatically while I was ill, you don't have school on Saturday."

"Saturday?" Sadie checked the calendar on her phone. "Oh my gosh, I've never been so thankful for a weekend. I was freaking out about making people at school fall asleep again."

"The pendant is helping to balance that for you," Mamo said. "You don't have anything to worry about. And I'll teach you how to control the power so you can manage it going forward, even without the pendant."

Relief washed through Sadie. She didn't care how the pendant worked. She was just glad it was there.

Mrs. Fallon walked in, her brows scrunched tight.

"Everything okay?" Mamo asked.

"I'm not sure," Mrs. Fallon said. "I'm told by the League of Governors that everything is fine, but I need to go to London to see for myself."

"That's a big trip," Mamo said. "Did you talk to Alexander or Jason? Or Jason's dad?"

"I have," Mrs. Fallon said. "But something seems off. And this little excursion of theirs has turned into too much of an extended trip if you ask me. I need to understand why and hear their reasons for myself."

"What can I do to help?" Mamo asked.

"I know you're anxious to move home," Mrs. Fallon said. "But would you mind staying here a couple more days with the kids? That is, if you feel up to it. I promise to make this trip as quick as I can."

Sadie's spirits sank.

"Of course not," Mamo said. "You do what you need to do. I've got the home front."

"Thank you, Willene." Mrs. Fallon took a banana from a fruit bowl on the counter. "There's a flight to London tonight. I'm going to go book the ticket now, and I'll keep you posted on my schedule."

Sadie thought about her texts to Jason. Why was he talking to his grandmother on the phone, but not responding to Sadie's messages?

"Best laid plans," Mamo said.

"Huh?"

"Our plan to move home." Mamo hung a dishtowel on the oven door handle. "Looks like it's not happening just yet."

"Yeah," Sadie said. "Kinda sucks."

"Yes, it does," Mamo said. "Not that Lena isn't a wonderful hostess and friend. But maybe we can head over to the house anyway, and check on the garden. What do you think?"

"That'd be good." Sadie ate the last berry off her plate. "Plus, I saw a bear wandering around. We should check the hives and maybe do something to protect them."

"A bear?" Mamo asked. "In town?"

"Yeah, I saw it when I was out with Shay."

"Has anyone else seen it?"

"I don't know. I haven't really asked anyone about it with everything else going on."

"Right," Mamo said. "Makes sense." She stared into space, seemingly focused on something that wasn't there.

A worry skittered through Sadie's belly. "Mamo? Are you okay?"

"What? Oh." She smiled and flicked her wrist. "Just thinking about having some of that delicious honey of ours. It's been too long. How about we head over in, say, thirty minutes?"

Sadie relaxed. "Sounds good."

❋ ❋ ❋

Sadie and Mamo walked through their garden, pulling weeds and picking the last few tomatoes that grew in the warmth of the unusually temperate autumn.

"Hard to believe we still have tomatoes at this time of year," Mamo said. "Let's take these back to Lena's and add them to a salad for dinner.

Sadie put them in a basket. They moved over to the beehives. The hives hummed like it was the peak of summer.

"They weren't this loud a few days ago," Sadie said. "I worried I was putting them to sleep."

"You probably were," Mamo said.

"What? Seriously?"

"No reason your power is limited to humans. At least for now." Mamo pressed her ear against a hive and listened. "That may change once your power is fully fleshed out, but for now I'd guess you could make anyone fall asleep, bees included."

Sadie remembered the night in the living room at the Fallon house when even the dogs were deep asleep.

"At least that was likely the case before you had the pendant," Mamo said.

"Because it's grounding, and invigorates my body and soul?" Sadie quoted one of the web pages she'd seen on the hawk's eye stone.

Mamo put her hands on her hips. "I guess you really did do a lot of research while I was, shall we say, not myself."

"I didn't get very far." Sadie put insulation on top of one of the beehives to prepare the hive for colder weather.

"Doesn't seem that way to me," Mamo said. "You're making me feel like I'm not as clever as I thought I was, trying to hide things from you."

"So don't hide things from me."

"Lesson learned, my dear granddaughter. Lesson learned." Mamo reached out and Sadie handed her a piece of insulation. "We're lucky winter's held off as long as it has since we hadn't weatherproofed our friends just yet."

"I would have done it." Though Sadie wondered if she really would have, given everything that had happened over the last couple of weeks.

"I don't doubt that for a second," Mamo said. "I know you love the bees as much as I do."

Sadie smiled. She did love the bees. And she loved being in the garden with Mamo. It felt good. It felt safe. It felt normal.

"Hello there." Conner's voice called to them from over the back gate. "How are two of my most favorite Callahans?"

Sadie's muscles tensed.

"What a not-so-coincidence," Mamo said. "Come on in. We're just finishing up."

Conner opened the gate and stepped into the yard. "I thought I might swing by and see if I could treat you two to brunch on this fine Saturday."

He seems strangely calm, and friendly, compared to last night.

"We had breakfast not too long ago, but would you care to join us for some iced tea or coffee?" Mamo asked. "With a lovely view of our backyard?"

"I'd be delighted," Conner said. "Iced tea for me if you have some."

"Of course we have some," Mamo said. "Give me a few minutes to brew it and we'll be all set. Sadie? Do you want something?"

"Iced tea's great." Sadie walked to the patio and plopped into a wicker rocking chair.

Mamo whispered something in Conner's ear then went inside.

Conner sat on the flowery-cushioned couch.

"What did she say to you?" Sadie asked.

Conner paused and gazed at the garden. "She seems to think I'm here with another attempt to lure you to my side."

"The side of becoming a Yowie? No thank you," Sadie said. "There's nothing you can say to make me change my mind."

He watched a bee working late blooming flowers in the patio pots. The bee settled on one bloom, gathered pollen, then buzzed to the next flower searching for more of its bounty. "May I show you something?"

Sadie shrugged.

Conner took out his phone and tapped the screen. "I received an email this morning. This video was attached." He handed his phone to Sadie and asked her to hit play.

The video sprang to life. A little girl sat in a sandbox with her brother. A moment later they jumped up, climbed the steps to the top of a slide, and slid down. The girl ran to the swings and asked her daddy to push her, higher and higher.

"The kids are your second cousins," Conner said. "On your dad's side."

Sadie scanned their faces, searching for a resemblance. She and the kids all had the same dark hair, and maybe their eyes were similar, too. She watched them run to the slide again.

"They're really cute, but—"

"No. No!" The yell came from the voice behind the camera, the voice that must have been the kids' dad. The view skewed as the camera dropped. A man raced into the frame toward the children. "Leave them alone. They're just kids."

Another voice came from off screen. "Are you Grant Callahan?"

"Yes. Please don't hurt my kids. I'll do whatever—"

Bright light filled the frame. When it cleared, three piles of ash sat where the kids and their dad were only seconds ago.

Sadie gasped.

Conner took the phone from her hand. "This is what we're facing. Methodical extermination."

"There's nothing I can do about it," Sadie said. "Unless you need someone to fall asleep."

"No, you can't help now," Conner said. "But choose your family, choose Yowie and accept the Calling, and you can change this path." He waggled his phone.

"Mamo is my family."

Conner canted his head. "We are your family. And we need you."

Mamo came out of the house carrying a tray. "Here we go. Freshest iced tea in town." She glanced from Sadie to Conner and set the tray down. She focused on Conner. "What did you do?"

"I don't know what you mean," he said.

"Did I not ask you, only minutes ago, to keep your opinions to yourself?" Mamo picked up a glass of tea and thrust it at Conner. Several drops splashed out of the glass and ran down the side.

He took the glass. "I did nothing but share a family email."

"And an unpleasant email at that, given the looks on both of your faces." Mamo handed a glass of tea to Sadie. "Are you okay?"

Sadie faked a look of dismissal. "Totally. He showed me a video with some cute kids." She sipped her tea.

"Hmm." Mamo wiped off drops of tea that had splashed onto her hand and looked at Conner. "Are you going to behave yourself or should I ask you to leave right now?"

Conner raised his right hand. "I solemnly swear I have nothing but the best intentions and only want to spend time with my family." He placed a slight emphasis on the last word of the sentence. "After all, look at you, Willy. You're the picture of health, we're together, and I'm finally getting to know my darling great-niece. What more could a man ask for?"

Mamo sipped her tea and set it down on the table. "What more indeed."

The white light and piles of ash replayed in Sadie's mind.

TWELVE
Freak

The rest of the weekend slogged by. Sadie tried to distract herself from thinking about Yowie and the Calling. She spent time on homework, but the video of the kids kept replaying in her mind. She hung out with Mamo and told her she didn't want to talk about any of it, but Sadie found herself examining Mamo's features for anything unusual, anything hairier than it should be. And Sadie played with Finn and Shay but wondered if Finn had ever seen a Yowie in her work tracking cryptids with Jason's uncle. And what would Finn or Shay do if they saw Mamo in Yowie form? For that matter, what would Sadie do?

Brandon kept to himself spending most of his time in his room. Sadie saw him at dinner, but even then he didn't talk much. He never again brought up the idea that he and Sadie might do something together this weekend.

He thinks I'm a freak. Because I am.

Nessa had texted about getting together. Sadie declined. She wanted to spend time with Mamo and told Nessa she'd see her at school on Monday.

Nessa replied: "Are you sure it's not Brandon you really want to spend time with?"

Sadie replied: "Totally sure. Only Mamo."

A response from Nessa arrived: "Sure. Because grown-ups are way more fun to hang with than cute boys who like you."

Sadie didn't write back.

Monday arrived and marked seventy-two hours without any Sadie-triggered sleeping incidents. The pendant was working. She got dressed and headed for school.

Sadie opened her locker when someone grabbed her from behind.

"My Sadie." Nessa hugged her hard. "Happy Monday."

"Is there such a thing? A happy Monday?" Sadie hugged her back.

"Well, I'm happy to see you, and you're happy to see me," Nessa said. "And it's Monday. So happy Monday."

"I guess you're right." Sadie shut her locker.

"Wait—what's up?" Nessa planted her feet. "You are not yourself."

Sadie shrugged. "I'm just tired. I didn't sleep that great last night."

Nessa tilted her head. "You sure that's it? Seems like something more going on to me."

What would Nessa do if Sadie spilled the whole story? *Oh yeah, and I also found out I'm a freakazoid monster, and so is everyone in my family, and someone probably wants to kill us. No big whoop.*

Nessa would stay away. Like Brandon.

"Nothing else. Just tired," Sadie said. She stepped into the flow of student traffic and walked to first period with Nessa.

To Sadie's relief, the class went by without one weird thing happening. The teacher showed up on time. No one fell asleep. Then the bell rang and she and Nessa made their way to their next class.

The Biology room smelled like old pickles. Sadie and Nessa took their seats at a station set with two trays, scissors, scalpels, and plastic forceps.

"You will come to order." Ms. Feinstein hammered a gavel onto a block on her desk. "Order, please. Settle down."

The class quieted.

Ms. Feinstein placed the gavel in a stand that kept it upright with the mallet in the air. "This is a special day, one that I quite enjoy every year, and I'm confident you'll enjoy it as well. Today we'll explore the inner workings of our friend, the grass frog."

Nessa leaned close to Sadie and whispered. "Not sure the dead frogs think we're very good friends."

Sadie agreed and wished she'd remembered to have Mamo sign the form excusing her from the exercise. She felt bad about the frogs being used this way.

"Derek is bringing each of you your specimen," Ms. Feinstein said. "You will wait until all frogs have been distributed, then you will follow my instruction and we will dissect together."

Derek splatted a preserved frog onto Sadie's tray, reached over and plopped another one in front of Nessa. "Don't worry about the smell. These ain't near as bad as the ones I've caught around my house." He sneered.

Sadie rolled her eyes.

Derek finished handing out frogs and returned to his stool at the station he shared with one of his friends.

"All right, class. Place your frogs on their backs," Ms. Feinstein said. "The first step—"

The door to the classroom opened and the vice principal poked his head into the room. "Sorry about the interruption. Can I see you for one minute in the hallway?"

"Of course." Ms. Feinstein addressed the class. "Do not, I repeat, do not do anything until I return. I'll only be a few minutes."

"I wonder what that's about?" Sadie scanned the room to see if everyone was awake.

"I heard she's up for some award," Nessa said. "Maybe it's about that."

Metal clanked behind them.

"I challenge you to a duel." Derek picked up his scalpel and pointed it at his friend.

The friend snatched his scalpel off the tray and jabbed it at Derek. The two scalpels clinked against each other. Derek swung and his scalpel pinged off the other one. His friend copied the move and struck Derek's.

Students at nearby seats scooted farther away.

"Do they seriously think this makes them look cool?" Nessa rested her head on her hand.

"No idea," Sadie said. "But it definitely makes them annoying."

"*More* annoying," Nessa said.

Derek yelped and dropped his scalpel to the floor. He grabbed onto the underside of his arm. "You cut me." Derek glared. Blood seeped through his fingers.

"I didn't mean to." The friend tossed his scalpel onto the tray. "Dude, I'm sorry." He reached forward.

Derek spun away from him. "Get off me." More blood dripped onto the floor.

Sadie grabbed paper towels and rushed to Derek. "Let me see."

"I got this." He jerked his arm away.

"You need to stay calm," Sadie said. "I'll apply pressure." She turned to Nessa. "Get Ms. Feinstein."

Derek moved his hand away. Sadie suppressed a gasp when she saw how deep the wound was. The gash quickly filled with blood and she pressed the towels against it. Seconds later, the white towels reddened as the blood soaked through.

Where is Ms. Feinstein?

Derek stared at Sadie's hand on his arm. His skin paled.

"Are you okay?" she asked.

Derek grimaced. "Yeah. Whatever. This is nothing." He swallowed hard. "But you're pushing too hard. It feels weird."

Ms. Feinstein rushed in. "What happened?" She hurried over to Derek.

Nessa entered the room. "Sorry. She was way down the hall."

"I had an accident," Derek said. "It was totally an accident."

Ms. Feinstein took over for Sadie. "How bad is it?"

"Bad," Sadie said.

Derek shrugged. "I guess. And it was feeling kinda weird until a second ago."

"Weird how?" Ms. Feinstein asked. "Numb? Can you feel your fingers?"

"Yeah, it's just—"

"Let's get some fresh paper towels on it and I'll walk you to the nurse's office," Ms. Feinstein said. "Sadie, will you grab some for me?"

"Sure." Sadie handed more towels to Ms. Feinstein.

"Here we go." Ms. Feinstein lifted the soaked towels from Derek's arm revealing a small cut that was no longer bleeding.

"What the hell?" Derek looked from the wound to Sadie.

Sadie's jaw dropped. *Oh my god.*

"Regardless of your injury, you will watch your language," Ms. Feinstein said.

"She did something to me." Derek jutted his chin at Sadie.

"It seems to me she stopped the bleeding, and a good thing, too," Ms. Feinstein said. "We hardly need you passing out." She assessed the amount of blood on the floor. "I am surprised such a small wound would bleed that much. But the wound itself is nothing to worry about."

"It was bigger." He focused on Sadie. "Tell her."

"I...I think it just seemed worse than it was," Sadie said. "With all the blood."

"You did something to it," Derek said.

"Oh for heaven's sake, Derek," Ms. Feinstein said. "Do you think Sadie has some magical power or something? Perhaps she's a witch. And if so, I wouldn't be surprised if you were the first on her list of people to turn into a toad. Of course, I'd never endorse that sort of behavior." Ms. Feinstein pulled him to standing. "Seems to me you should thank Sadie for helping you and leave it at that. Now let's get you to the nurse."

"Uh, may I be excused to go wash my hands?" Sadie asked.

"Of course," Ms. Feinstein said. "In fact, class, given today's events, our dissection is canceled."

Groans sounded from a few of the students.

"Please take yourselves to the library for the remainder of the period," Ms. Feinstein said. "You will check in with the librarian and I will follow up with him to ensure you all followed my instruction. Off you go."

Nessa followed Sadie out of the classroom. "What was Derek's deal?"

"No clue." Sadie thought about the wound. It did seem bigger at first. A lot bigger. But she must have been mistaken. *Or maybe...*

"Promise me, whenever you decide to turn Derek into a toad, you'll invite me over to watch." Nessa laughed.

Sadie pushed on the door to the girl's bathroom. "You'll be the first call I make." She stepped up to the sink and stared at her hands as the water flowed over them. She scrubbed them with soap and checked them from every angle. Her hands were the same as they had always been.

"Yoo-hoo," Nessa said. "Earth to Sadie."

"Oh sorry." Sadie turned off the water. "Did I miss something?"

"I said if you could have any magical power or whatever, what would it be?" Nessa pulled the door open.

Sadie followed her out. "I have no idea."

"Because I would choose the power to make any food appear whenever I wanted it," Nessa said. "Like in sci-fi movies. They say what they want and some machine thingy gives it to them. Except I don't want to bother with a machine."

"That's a good one." Sadie wished she could change the subject.

"Or invisibility," Nessa said. "But I don't get how you can run around everywhere without clothes on and not freeze. I would totally freeze."

"Do you have something to read?" Sadie asked.

"What?"

"While we're in the library for the rest of the period." Sadie turned the corner.

"Yeah, as long as it doesn't have to be my Biology book."

"I think you're good," Sadie said.

Nessa smiled. "Sweet."

✳ ✳ ✳

After school, Sadie headed to her Tae Kwon Do class, glad to not miss a second week in a row. When class was finished, she gathered her things and hurried to Mrs. Fallon's house. She wanted to talk to Mamo about what happened with Derek.

"Mamo." Sadie called as she entered the front door.

"In the kitchen."

Sadie dropped her bag at the foot of the stairs and continued down the hall. "I need to talk to you about—"

Merinda and Conner sat at the kitchen table. Mamo stirred something on the stove.

"What is it?" Mamo asked.

"Uh, it can wait." She held up her hand. "Hi."

Merinda waved back.

Conner stood and moved toward Sadie. "Hello, my dear." He gave Sadie a hug.

"Oh." Sadie adjusted herself and hugged back. "Hi."

"How was school today?" Conner returned to his seat.

"Uh, fine." She looked at Mamo.

"They're joining us for dinner," Mamo said. "Might as well make the best of it while they're in town. And you can get to know them a little better since they are family."

Sadie tucked her hair behind her ears. "Okay...but I don't want to talk about any of the stuff. Not Yowies or Callings or anything."

"Fair enough," Conner said.

Sadie raised an eyebrow. "Okay. Good." She crossed the room and kissed Mamo on the cheek. Red sauce simmered in the pot.

"So I shouldn't ask you if you left any fur patches around school from all your shedding?" Mamo smirked.

"That's not funny," Sadie said.

"It's a little bit funny." Mamo covered the sauce with a lid.

"Oh my gosh, seriously." Sadie got a glass out of the cupboard. "Wait—is that why so much of my hair comes out in my hairbrush? Because of Yowie shedding?"

Conner and Mamo chuckled. "No, sweetie," Mamo said. "That's normal human shedding. I was just teasing you."

Sadie relaxed. "Oh. Okay. But maybe we save the teasing for another time." *Or never.*

"Too soon," Mamo said. "Got it. Are you hungry?"

"Very," Sadie said. "Is that your yummy spaghetti sauce?"

"It is indeed. Would you please set the table?" Mamo handed placemats to Sadie.

"Sure. Where is everyone else?" She put the placemats on the table.

Conner straightened the mat in front of him. "Your young man, Brandon, got a surprise visit from his parents and they took him out to dinner."

"He's not my—" Sadie lifted plates out of the cupboard and set them next to the stove. "Anyway, that's nice."

Mamo removed a foil package of garlic bread from the oven. "They seem like lovely people."

"And interesting," Merinda said.

"Wow, so everyone met them." Sadie filled glasses with water.

"You just missed them," Conner said. "They left not a minute before you walked in the door."

Brandon probably didn't want them to meet me anyway.

There was a scratch at the back door. Sadie moved to open it but Mamo stopped her.

"The dogs are in the backyard for the time being. Merinda feels a bit...uncomfortable." Mamo fixed her gaze on Merinda.

"That's not fair," Sadie said. "This is their home."

"Oh, you know, she's right." Merinda stood. "Maybe I should go."

Mamo motioned her back into her chair. "No need to go, but I agree with Sadie as well—this is their home. I'd like to let the dogs in."

Merinda bit her bottom lip.

"Don't worry. I have chew bones for each of them, so they'll be plenty interested in something besides you."

Sadie opened the door and Mamo handed each dog a bone. She turned back to Sadie. "Kyle is at a friend's house. As usual."

"So, it's just us." Sadie wished she could eat dinner in her room.

"Not your first choice of dining companions, I'm sure," Conner said. "But I myself am delighted to be here spending time with you, especially now that all the secrets are out."

"Me too," Merinda said.

"As am I," Mamo said. "I've missed being connected to our extended family." Mamo washed her hands and dished up spaghetti.

Sadie carried over plates and a fresh salad from the counter. Dinner passed with small talk about the weather, gardening, and how long they'd had the beehives. Conner mentioned he and Willy kept bees as kids. He still lived in the same house where they grew up but didn't keep bees anymore.

"Why not?" Sadie asked.

"In high school, I decided I was too busy for it, and I never went back to the bees after that," Conner said. "But seeing your hives has inspired me. Perhaps I'll pick up the hobby once again."

"I saw your yearbook photo," Sadie said. "At least I think it's you."

"If it's a picture of a handsome and strapping lad, then it is most definitely me." He grinned and slurped spaghetti.

"I'll bring the pictures down after dinner," Sadie said. "What about you, Merinda? Where do you live?"

"Not far from Conner." She bit into a piece of bread. "Have you decided?"

Sadie stopped spinning noodles onto her fork. "Huh?"

"Merinda." Mamo pursed her lips.

"What? I know we weren't supposed to talk about Yowie," Merinda said. "But I didn't know I couldn't ask Sadie personal stuff."

"If the personal stuff is about being Yowie, then of course you're not to ask about it." Mamo looked at Sadie. "I'm sorry. Let's change the subject. I have pie for dessert so I hope everyone is saving room."

"No, it's fine." Sadie turned to Merinda. "I'm not choosing Yowie. I'm not accepting the Calling. And I'm not going to change my mind."

"Seriously?" Merinda's brows cinched together. "That seems so stupid."

"Merinda..." Conner shook his head.

"What?" Merinda put her napkin on the table. "She's got the chance to help hundreds in our Clan, and she's going to say no? Like she's turning down a prom dress she doesn't like or something?"

"It's not that simple, and you know it," Mamo said.

"Seems pretty simple to me," Merinda said. "Help your family or don't help your family."

Sadie's chest ached. "But I—"

"No, I get it." Merinda stood. "You're more important than any of us. Your needs come first. And if the princess doesn't want to help, the princess doesn't have to help." She moved toward the hall. "I gotta go." Her steps stomped away and the front door slammed.

Sadie slowly swirled her fork through sauce pooled on her plate.

"Oh, uh...well, given the situation, it seems I'd better get going too," Conner said. "I'll try to talk to Merinda. Thank you for the invitation to dinner, Willy. I'll see myself out." He kissed Mamo on the cheek and left.

Tears blurred Sadie's vision. She shoved herself away from the table and hurried out of the kitchen.

"Sadie." Mamo scooted her chair back. "Hold on."

Sadie stopped at the foot of the stairs.

"Come talk to me." Mamo directed her toward the living room. "Please?"

"She's right. I'm horrible. I haven't thought about the rest of the family for more than two seconds."

"You're not horrible," Mamo said. "Come and sit."

Sadie staggered into the living room and fell onto the couch. Mamo snuggled in and put her arm around Sadie, pulling her close.

"What am I supposed to do?" Sadie asked.

"You do exactly what you want to do," Mamo said. "Whatever is in your heart. And what anyone else thinks about your decision, well, let them think it. It's none of their business anyway."

"But it is their business if I can help them and I don't do it." Sadie sniffed. "And I let members of our family die."

"Now you listen to me." Mamo tightened her arm around Sadie's shoulders. "Even if you choose Yowie and accept the Calling, your powers have to develop and that takes time. The Clan would still have to deal with that, and they'd have to deal with it on their own. You can't help them before then."

"Okay..." Sadie used the cuff of her sleeve to wipe her eyes.

"And another thing—you're certainly not letting anyone die. Bad people are doing bad things and that's no fault of yours."

Sadie nodded. "But I'm still horrible. I mean, the idea of changing into something so scary, and so ugly, and being so different from everyone else I know. What if I change and I get stuck that way? And I have to live in the woods forever? And I scare everyone and people shoot at me and chase me and I can't ever come home again?"

She hiccupped.

"And I never go to college, or travel, or get married or anything? Look at Brandon. He knows I'm a freak and he hasn't spoken two words to me since he found out."

"Aw, sweetie." Mamo squeezed Sadie again. "I think you're overreacting maybe a little bit. And I doubt Brandon's actions are a reflection on how he feels about you. I think we have to give him more credit than that." She smiled. "And I do take a little bit of offense at being described as scary and ugly."

Sadie turned her face to Mamo's. "Oh, I didn't mean it like that. I—"

"You're overwhelmed. I get it. This is all too much for someone your age, no matter how brilliant and tough you are."

"I'm so not brilliant and especially not tough. This has been the worst couple of weeks ever," Sadie said. "I can't even go to school without the smallest thing putting me into a tizzy about stuff."

"Like what?" Mamo asked.

Sadie relayed the story about Derek in Biology. "I know he was just being his usual jerk self, but it bugged me when he acted like I'd done something to him."

Mamo was silent.

"Oh no, what is it?" Sadie asked.

"Did he say anything about how the wound felt? Anything like that?"

"Yes." Clamminess climbed into Sadie's cheeks. "He said it felt weird."

"When you were pressing on the wound?"

"Yeah."

Mamo smiled. "Your healing power is coming in. And early."

"How?" Sadie pushed herself to standing. "How can that happen when I haven't done anything?"

"You don't have to do anything. Power manifests on its own schedule."

"Shouldn't I be able to decide these things?" She grasped the hawk's eye pendant. "And shouldn't this be stopping it or something?"

"It can only balance the transition, smooth it out."

"But I don't want it. Any of it." Sadie slumped into a recliner. "I wish I didn't even know about it."

"I'm sorry, sweetie—"

"Please, make it stop. Do some magic Yowie thing and make it all stop."

Mamo stroked Sadie's hair. "There's nothing to be done. You choose Yowie and the Calling, or you don't. And whatever powers you receive in the meantime become part of you. And they are gifts, Sadie. Maybe you'll never need the ability to change someone's memories, but the power to heal is one you will treasure."

"Nothing feels like a treasure at the moment." Sadie leaned back and stared at the ceiling. "I want to make it official. Right now." She shifted her attention to Mamo. "I don't want to be a Yowie."

"Okay."

"So what words do I have to say?" Sadie asked. "Tell me."

"We'll need Conner here."

"Call him. Make him come back."

"And we'll need Lena's help, so we have to wait for her to get back from London," Mamo said. "She'll be home tomorrow."

Sadie huffed. "I thought you agreed with me but now it feels like you're trying to make me wait even longer."

"Sweetie, I'm on your side, no matter what choice you make."

"Made," Sadie said. "I made it already. Past tense." She regretted her tone. She did sound like a spoiled princess. Sadie paused. "I'm sorry."

"It's okay," Mamo said. "You're going through a lot."

"But still...I'm sorry."

"You're forgiven," Mamo said. "Can you manage to hold on a little longer? Until we get what we need in place?"

"Yeah, of course," Sadie said. "As long as everything's okay and nothing's going to explode or anything."

Mamo chuckled. "Explosions are definitely not a power of any Yowie in history, so I think we're safe there."

"That's good. And tell me about this healing power," Sadie said. "Could I have used it to fix you when you were so sick?"

Mamo nodded. "Yes, if it had been fully manifested. Once that happens you'll be able to give Haru a run for his money."

Sadie thought about the healing Haru had performed to help her and Jason, Finn, and Jason's uncle Alexander. Haru had been there when they needed him, and he helped them save the Rampart.

"That would be kinda cool." Sadie failed at forcing back a small smile.

"There's my girl, finding the positive." Mamo hugged her.

"And wait." Sadie stepped back. "Is your healing power the reason I never got chicken pox or strep throat or any of those things kids get?"

"Oh, you got them," Mamo said. "I just nipped them in the bud."

"Huh. I just thought I was super healthy."

"You are, with a little assistance when needed." Mamo patted Sadie's arm. "How about we do something fun, like watch a movie?

And since we were talking about explosions I suggest a good action flick."

"That sounds great." Sadie settled onto the couch next to Mamo and they curled up under a shared blanket. Mamo clicked on the television and scrolled through the movie selection. They picked one of their favorites, and soon the scene opened with green symbols flowing down a black screen as a lead character spoke on a telephone in the background.

Sadie tried to watch the movie but her mind wandered. It wasn't only a matter of choosing Yowie and the Calling or not. She still had to hide. Mamo said the Calling would cloak her, so agreeing to accept it meant she could stay in Salton with her friends. If she didn't choose Yowie and the Calling, she and Mamo had to leave and Sadie would never see her friends again.

Sadie pretended to watch the movie for Mamo's sake as she considered her options. She and Jason hadn't been friends that long, and he wasn't even reading her messages much less responding to them, so maybe he wasn't as good of a friend as Sadie thought.

Brandon made it clear he wasn't interested in being friends with Sadie since he found out about the Yowie.

And she'd been friends with Nessa for a long time, but it would be easier if Sadie didn't have to keep so many secrets from her.

Thinking through it again reaffirmed her choice. Decline being Yowie and refuse the Calling, move somewhere with Mamo, and start a new, normal life.

THIRTEEN
Bounty

The next morning Sadie didn't brush her hair, she didn't get dressed, she didn't get ready for school. She went downstairs.

Mamo sat at the kitchen table drinking her coffee and reading the newspaper. She looked up as Sadie entered. "Is it pajama day at school?"

"I'm not going to school." Sadie took a mug out of the cupboard and poured herself a cup of coffee.

Mamo removed her reading glasses. "What are you doing?"

Sadie carried the mug over to the table and sat. "I'm having coffee with my grandmother." She sipped the drink and suppressed a grimace.

"Since when do you drink coffee?" Mamo closed the newspaper.

"I'm making some big decisions," Sadie said. "I should also be doing more grown-up things." She choked down another swallow.

"Drinking coffee and not going to school—those are your grown-up things?"

"You drink coffee, and you don't go to school," Sadie said.

Mamo put on her glasses and returned to reading the paper. "Great."

"Great?" Sadie asked.

"Sure. I can use help paying the bills, which is a grown-up thing to do, so you'll have to get a job," Mamo said. "Though since you don't have a high school diploma, the job will be something like working as a maid where you get to clean other people's toilets."

Sadie grimaced again, but not because of the coffee. "I can babysit."

"Good point." Mamo pushed her glasses up. "You can do babysitting in the evenings, and clean houses during the day."

"Fine." Sadie took another drink of coffee but spit it back in the cup. "Seriously, why do you drink this stuff?"

Mamo peered into Sadie's eyes. "What's really going on?"

Sadie pushed the cup away. "I just want to be done with all of this, and I want to move, and I want to start over. And be different, but in a good way."

"You are Sadie Callahan." Mamo took Sadie's hands in hers. "And whether we move, or you drink coffee, or you become a maid or an astronaut, you'll always be Sadie Callahan."

"But once we're somewhere else, my decision not to be Yowie will be done, and no one will know about it even being a thing, and I won't have to think about Yowies anymore." She pressed into Mamo's fingers.

"I see..." Mamo stood and refilled her mug.

"Well, right?" Sadie asked. "Because I'm ready. I want to do this and stop thinking about everything." She swept her arm in an arch.

"And everyone?"

"No," Sadie said. "I'll think about you, you'll think about me. We can go back to how things were before."

"But before, I had secrets." Mamo took her seat. "From you."

Sadie shrugged. "And now you don't. So we're good."

"And you're ready to give up everything," Mamo said. "You'll go to a new school, make new friends, live in a new town. No more Nessa or Jason or Brandon."

"Yes," Sadie said. "When can we do the official no-Yowie thing? Today?"

"Conner is gathering some things, and Lena won't be home until later." She sipped her coffee. "She'll need a bit of time to recover from jet lag, so we can't do anything until tomorrow at the earliest."

Sadie's shoulders dropped.

Mamo fixed her eyes on Sadie. "And you're going to school today."

"What? No." Sadie sat up. "There's no reason since we're leaving anyway."

"This isn't open for discussion." Mamo flipped the paper over to the back page. "I suggest you hustle upstairs and get ready. I won't tolerate you being late."

Sadie *tsked*.

"And no attitude, please," Mamo said without looking away from the paper. "I'm still the grown-up, and you're still not."

Sadie surrendered and went to her room.

✳ ✳ ✳

School felt fake. Sadie went through the motions and took notes in class, ate lunch with Nessa in the cafeteria, and said hi to people she knew. But she did it for Mamo, not for herself. Sadie wanted to break the ties, move on, and stop pretending like she belonged at Salton High School.

After school, Brandon came out of Mrs. Fallon's house as Sadie was about to enter.

"Oh, hi." Brandon held the door.

"Yeah, hi." Sadie kept walking into the house. "Thanks." Shay and Finn trotted up and greeted Sadie.

"Uh, wait a sec." Brandon followed her in.

Sadie stopped in the foyer and turned toward him.

"So, there's been a lot of stuff going on..." He looked at his shoes.

"Yeah, I'm kinda in that loop." Sadie shifted her bag's shoulder strap.

Brandon focused on Sadie's face. "No, I mean, we were going to maybe do something this weekend."

"We were?" Sadie asked. "I don't remember." Her voice was cold, but her belly fluttered.

"Yeah, I thought so. But with all of your stuff, and my—"

"Don't worry about it," Sadie said. "I get it."

"Get what?"

"After hearing everything about me, I wouldn't want to hang out with me either." Sadie moved toward the stairs.

"What? No," Brandon said. "That's not what I meant."

"It's not a big deal," Sadie said.

"Yeah, it is." He shoved his hands in his pockets. "I wanted to tell you—"

"Right, I guess it is a big deal," Sadie said. "I mean the fact that I'm actually some hairy, ugly, creature-thing. Of course, that's a big deal. But you don't have to explain." She started up the stairs.

"Can you wait one second?" Brandon walked to the foot of the staircase.

Sadie didn't stop, and Shay sped past her. "I have tons of homework." She turned the corner, ducked into her room, and shut the door.

Sadie fell onto her bed and Shay jumped up next to her. Sadie's heart pounded.

I don't need Brandon to flat out tell me how weird he thinks I am. I already got that message, thank you.

Sadie stayed in her room and surfed the internet. She read celebrity gossip sites and watched videos with rescued puppies, and kittens, and ponies. She reviewed rescue sites and hoped she could talk Mamo into adopting a dog after they moved. She bookmarked a couple of dog postings who looked like they could be related to Shay. Sadie reached for Shay snoozing next to her and dug her fingers into her scruff. Shay would stay in Salton. She was another friend Sadie would lose.

Voices mumbled through the door. Sadie walked over and listened. Across the hall, Mamo was talking to Mrs. Fallon in her room, their voices low. Sadie cracked her door.

"They took him," Mrs. Fallon said. "I tried to talk them out of it."

"Is it only temporary?" Mamo asked. "They can't truly believe this is the best thing for him."

"She seemed intent on making it permanent." A drawer slid open. "Joseph wasn't as convinced." The drawer thumped shut.

Who is Joseph?

"And neither was Brandon," Mrs. Fallon said. "I think he agreed because he didn't want to disappoint his mother."

Brandon's gone? Sadie's heart sank. *Is that what he was trying to tell me?*

"That's ridiculous," Mamo said. "They have no business taking Brandon on a trip like that."

"She's worried about how much time they might have left to be together as a family," Mrs. Fallon said.

"Then cancel the damn trip and stay home." Mamo's voice pitched louder.

Mrs. Fallon's voice was barely above a whisper. "You know they can't do that."

Steps moved closer to Mrs. Fallon's doorway. Sadie scrambled to her desk. Shay jumped up and wagged her tail at Sadie's sudden movement.

She signaled Shay to lie down and the pup plopped to her belly. Sadie slipped into her chair and woke the screen on her computer, pretending to pay attention to the display. A light knock sounded from her door.

"Come in," Sadie said.

Mamo entered. Shay stood and wriggled. "How was school?" Mamo asked. "Is the cafeteria serving coffee with lunch these days?"

"Very funny." Sadie turned in her chair. "School was fine."

"Glad to hear it." Mamo scratched Shay under the chin.

"I still think it's a waste of time," Sadie said.

"And I don't. So we agree to disagree, and you keep going to school."

"Until we leave," Sadie said. "Did I hear Mrs. Fallon? Is she back already?"

"She is, and she's exhausted," Mamo said. "She needs to get some rest before we ask her for help."

"But if people or Yowie or whatever are looking for us, we need to move things along." Sadie grabbed a hair tie and pulled her hair into a ponytail. "And everyone is safer once we're gone, right?"

Mamo ignored Sadie's comment. "Speaking of gone, did you get a chance to say goodbye to Brandon?"

"Uh, no," Sadie said. "He left?"

"Yes, his parents picked him up a little while ago. They're taking him on a world tour."

"That sounds like kind of a long trip."

"They said they'd be traveling for at least a year." Mamo picked a piece of lint off her pants. "Should be a great experience for all of them. Once in a lifetime."

"Right...totally." *That's not what you said to Mrs. Fallon.*

"And that makes it all the easier for us," Mamo said. "One less person we have to miss saying goodbye to when we leave."

"Yeah," Sadie said, though somehow it didn't feel easier. "It's not like we even knew him that well anyway."

"Hmm. I suppose you're right." Mamo moved toward the door. "I told Lena I'd handle dinner tonight, and I need to pick up a few things from the grocery store. Want to come?"

"I have homework," Sadie said.

"Very responsible for a girl who thinks school is a waste of time." Mamo smiled. "I'll see you later."

Sadie returned to her laptop, but she didn't really look at it. Why didn't Brandon tell her he was leaving? Then again, why would he?

A pit hardened in her stomach.

Ping. A message arrived on Sadie's computer. She clicked the box.

The message was from Merinda: "Hey—I'd like to apologize."

Sadie frowned and didn't respond.

Another message arrived: "I was really dumb last night, and I want to tell you I'm sorry. Plus, there's something else I want to talk to you about."

She ignored Merinda's note and opened her Algebra book but couldn't think about numbers.

Her computer pinged again. "It's about Willy, about her health. They don't want me to tell you, but I think you should know."

Sadie snatched up her phone and typed: "What is it?" She could not let Mamo get sick again.

Merinda's next message arrived: "Better to talk in person about this stuff."

Sadie's thumbs flew across the phone: "Then come over."

"Willy might see me and stop me from telling you. And the dogs scare me."

"Ugh, I seriously think Merinda is the most annoying person I've ever met," Sadie said to herself. She didn't want to meet Merinda and risk another lecture, or who knew what else, but Sadie had to know about Mamo. She ran her hand down Shay's side.

Shay's tail thumped on the bedspread.

Sadie typed back: "Okay. Where?"

"How about Hartson park? But no dogs, please."

Hartson was Salton's largest park. One section was groomed, with grass, a playground, and a public pool. If you kept walking, the park morphed into natural terrain that flowed into the cottonwood forests with wild scrub oak and chokecherry bushes along a creek. The bike paths in town led to the park and trails through the woods. There would be a lot of people around so Merinda couldn't get too crazy.

Sadie replied: "I'll meet you at the swing set in twenty minutes."

"See you there."

Sadie threw her laptop into her bag, thinking she might sit at the park for a while after meeting with Merinda.

Shay jumped off the bed and followed Sadie downstairs. At the front door, Sadie told her to sit. Shay touched her butt to the floor and popped back to standing.

"No, Shay. Sit." Sadie pointed at the floor.

Shay hurried past Sadie and scratched on the front door.

"You can't come with me," Sadie said. "Back up."

She moved a few steps away but stayed close. Sadie asked Shay to sit again, but the dog wouldn't budge. She stared at the door.

"Okay, forget it." Sadie opened the door and Shay tried to rush out. Sadie blocked with her leg and wedged herself through, leaving Shay inside.

Shay whined and scratched on the door.

"I'm sorry, girl," Sadie said. "I'll take you for a walk later." Sadie headed down the porch steps. Shay scratched harder. Barking sounded from the house until Sadie was too far to hear Shay anymore.

✳ ✳ ✳

Merinda was swinging when Sadie arrived at the park. Several kids played nearby, and two wore Halloween costumes even though the holiday was more than a couple weeks away.

Children swinging on either side of Merinda tried to match Merinda's speed and height, and others waiting for their turn screamed for Merinda to go higher and higher. When Merinda saw Sadie, she leaped from the moving swing and the kids cheered.

Merinda hurried over. "Thank you for coming."

Sadie nodded toward the swing set. "Nice landing."

"Oh, thanks," Merinda said. "The swings were always my favorite. Still are, I guess."

"Yeah, swings are great." Sadie held up her hands. "So, I'm here. Tell me about Mamo."

"Right." Merinda gestured toward the path. "Should we walk?"

"Fine." Sadie followed Merinda's lead.

"I don't know how much Willy and Conner told you about me," Merinda said.

Sadie shifted her bag from one shoulder to the other. "Just that you lived with them for a while."

"A long while, really," Merinda said. "My parents were kinda messed up."

"Sorry." Sadie tried not to care about Merinda's story. She had her own problems to deal with, and she really wanted Merinda to get to the point.

"It's okay. Or it will be," Merinda said.

It will be? Does she still live with her parents?

Merinda rubbed her fingertips together. "My parents drank. A lot. They'd get so drunk they'd forget to feed me. That's why I couldn't live with them."

"Oh, uh..."

"And then after six years of living with Willy and Conner, my dad died. I guess that scared the crap out of my mom," Merinda said. "So she got herself cleaned up, and I moved back in with her when I was thirteen."

"That's good she got better," Sadie said. The scent of upturned soil from a nearby flowerbed wafted around them.

"It didn't last long," Merinda said. "She can't hold a job. She can't do anything but drink and pop her happy pills, as she calls them. I take care of her. I take care of us both."

Sadie wasn't sure what to say. "That's gotta be really hard."

"It is. But that's my life." Merinda stopped walking. Her gaze shifted to the empty pool, closed for the season. "I'm tired of it being so hard."

"I don't blame you." Sadie didn't feel right cutting Merinda off and asking again about Mamo.

"I'm trying to change things." She turned back to Sadie. "And Conner's helping me. He always helps me."

They started walking again.

"That's nice of him." Sadie was surprised by a moment of affection she felt for Conner.

"He's a nice person." Merinda stepped off the sidewalk onto a trail leading into the natural part of the park. "You're famous, you know."

"Huh?" Sadie thought she misunderstood.

"You're famous. Because of the Calling," Merinda said. "The Calling has been searching for you for a long time. But everyone thought you must be dead."

"Right," Sadie said. "Well, not dead. And the Calling can go find someone else and make them famous. But what did you want to tell me about Mamo?"

"I don't think the Calling works that way." Merinda kept her eyes on the path ahead. "I think you have to be really dead for the Calling to stop, like, calling for you."

Unease inched into Sadie's spine. "We should go back and sit on a bench. I don't want to get too far from home since they're expecting me back soon."

"I like it out here," Merinda said. "The breeze through the cottonwoods keeps me calm."

Calm is good.

They continued walking. Sadie slipped her cell phone out of her bag and into her hand.

"All that stuff they told you about Garrison Devine, and that he wants to eliminate you? That's true," Merinda said.

"Okay..." Sadie unlocked her phone.

"And what they said about him not knowing where you are yet, that's true, too." Merinda turned to Sadie. "Only Conner and I know you're here."

"So, Mamo and I are safe in Salton."

"For sure," Merinda said. "I'm not going to tell them where you are. Neither will Conner."

"Thanks," Sadie said. "I should be getting back. If you'll just tell me what you know about Mamo."

"I haven't apologized yet," Merinda said, continuing her walk down the trail.

Sadie stopped. "Then do. I need to go."

"Just a little farther." Merinda pointed to a group of boulders ahead. "I love sitting on those rocks."

The boulders weren't that much further. "Okay, but that's as far as I go." Sadie fell back into step with Merinda.

A moment later, they were at the boulders. Sadie tucked her phone in her pocket and climbed onto the sun-warmed rocks. The creek babbled behind them.

"This is the best place," Merinda said. "I feel like everything is okay when I'm sitting up here."

Sadie inhaled the fragrance of leaves and sunshine. "I see why you like it. It's a good spot."

"Yeah," Merinda said. "And it's a good place for me to take care of things. You know, apologize. I really wanted you to accept the Calling."

"I just can't—"

"No, I get it." Merinda scooted further up the boulder she was on. "Conner explained it to me. It's your decision. I'm sorry I got so upset with you."

"Oh, well, thanks," Sadie said.

"It just would have been better for me if you'd said yes." Merinda stared at the tops of nearby cottonwood trees.

"If I could just hand off the Calling or whatever, I would do it. I'd give you the powers, too. I don't want them."

"That wouldn't work for me," Merinda said.

"I thought you said—"

"I don't want the powers. I don't want to deal with all that shit." Merinda leaned into the rock behind her.

Sadie's muscles tightened. "Okay." She moved to climb down to the ground, "I need to go. So tell me what you wanted to tell me, and then I can get home."

"Yeah, well, I don't really know anything about Willy," Merinda said. "I know something about you."

"I seriously can't believe I fell for this," Sadie pinched the bridge of her nose.

"There's a bounty on your head," Merinda said.

Sadie looked at her. "Excuse me?"

"You're worth a lot of money." Merinda kept her eyes to the sky. "More if you had accepted the Calling and started receiving all of your powers."

"What are you talking about?"

"There's one fee if you're delivered before you accept the Calling," Merinda said, "and even more if you're delivered after you've accepted the Calling."

Sadie gripped the phone in her pocket. "Why would that matter?"

Merinda sat up. "Because the leader can siphon off your powers for himself. He just has to get to you during that in-between time, after you've accepted the Calling but before your powers are fully formed."

Sadie eased down the rock. "I'm not accepting the Calling."

"Right. So I won't get paid as much," Merinda said. "And that sucks."

Sadie dropped to the ground. "You told him where I am?" Her breath quickened.

"No." Merinda stood and stared down at Sadie. "Better if I deliver you myself. And I don't want Conner to get hurt. He's still a

Callahan, and the leader might take a face-to-face opportunity to eliminate him." She stretched her arms overhead. "Conner's always been good to me. So I'm going to take you to Garrison, and I'll give Conner his share of the bounty later."

His share? Conner is helping her?

Sadie scanned the area wondering if others were hiding.

"There's no one here but me and you," Merinda said. "And I'm not taking it easy on you this time." She bounded off the boulder and landed in front of Sadie. She grabbed Sadie's arm.

Sadie twisted out of the hold and kicked Merinda in the gut.

Merinda skittered backward and steadied herself with one arm against the rock. She screeched and rushed Sadie.

Sadie side-kicked, but Merinda was ready. She dodged and thrust her forearm up from under Sadie's kicking leg. Sadie tumbled to the ground. Merinda kicked Sadie's ribs.

Air gushed out. Sadie forced herself into a roll and scrambled to her feet, wheezing. She blocked Merinda's punch, left and right, but Merinda connected with a knee to Sadie's belly. She crashed to the ground.

"Had enough, little girl?" Merinda crossed her arms.

Sadie pushed herself up to her haunches. "Not yet."

Merinda ran toward Sadie.

Sadie tucked under Merinda's torso and propelled herself up, launching Merinda over her back and onto the ground. Sadie spun, ran forward, and stomped Merinda's leg. The bone crunched. Merinda screamed.

Sadie stopped. "Now I've had enough." She breathed hard.

"This isn't over," Merinda seethed.

"Looks like it's over to me. You can't even walk. I'm calling Mamo and she can deal with you." Sadie pulled her phone out of her pocket. The glass was cracked. "Great." Sadie tapped Mamo's number. The phone still worked.

Merinda grunted as she pulled herself across the dirt away from Sadie.

"You think you're going to crawl away now? You're just making it harder to get you out of here," Sadie said.

The call connected to Mamo.

"Hey, we need a ride," Sadie said. "Merinda attacked me and I kinda broke her leg."

"What? Are you okay?" Mamo asked.

"You did break my leg, you bitch!" Merinda wailed.

"Yeah, but she's kinda mad at me," Sadie said into the phone, still trying to get enough air into her lungs.

Mamo asked where they were and said she was on her way.

Sadie slipped her phone in her pocket and turned her attention to Merinda.

She wasn't moaning anymore. She sat motionless with her eyes shut.

"Hey, Merinda? Are you awake?" *Oh god, did I kill her?* Sadie took a step toward her.

Merinda's body shimmered and she pulled her arms close.

"Oh no," Sadie said. "No, you don't." She rushed over and grabbed at Merinda's ankle. Black feathers fluttered through her fingers. "No way. You are not getting away that easy."

The starling hopped across the ground, away from Sadie, flapping its wings against the dirt.

Sadie chased and snatched at Merinda but she slipped from Sadie's grasp. A second later Merinda was airborne. Sadie jumped and snagged a wingtip, but Merinda switched direction and angled away, freeing her wing from Sadie's hold. She soared into the air and disappeared into the trees.

"Crap." Sadie stomped her foot. Pain shot up her leg and she doubled over.

Double crap. She took a few deep breaths until the pain eased. She stood tall, picked up her bag, and made her way down the trail.

Mamo met her partway. She put her arm around Sadie and took some of her weight.

"Ah, careful." Sadie winced and shifted Mamo's hand down to her hip. "Super sore on that side."

"Sorry." Mamo adjusted. "Where's Merinda?"

"She turned into a bird and went bye-bye," Sadie said. "I tried to grab her."

"I'm surprised she had the energy. You're sure you broke her leg?" Mamo asked.

"Definitely. It wasn't pretty."

"We'll find her. And when I get my hands on that twit, well, that's another thing that's not going to be pretty."

"She said there's a bounty on my head."

"What?" Mamo's grip contracted on Sadie's arm.

"She wants to turn me in and collect the money." Sadie stopped and faced Mamo. "And she said she's splitting the fee with Conner."

Mamo's teeth clenched and her face darkened.

"Over my dead body."

FOURTEEN

Planning

Mamo and Sadie walked in the front door. Shay ran over and pressed her head into Sadie's thigh. The pup licked and licked and licked Sadie's hand.

"I know, I'm sorry," Sadie said. "That's the last time I don't listen to you. I should have let you go with me."

Shay sat and wagged her tail, then ran up the stairs.

As Mamo helped Sadie to her room, they passed Mrs. Fallon's empty bedroom.

"I'm surprised she's not resting," Sadie said.

"She had an unexpected errand," Mamo said. "And we've changed our dinner plans. Chinese takeout instead of me cooking. A few too many things going on so we decided easier was better."

"Sounds good to me." Sadie sat on the edge of her bed and examined her hands. They trembled. "The damage isn't as bad as I expected."

Mamo took Sadie's hands and stilled them inside her own. "There shouldn't be any damage. This shouldn't have happened." She brushed hair away from Sadie's eyes. "I'm surprised you went to meet her in the first place."

"She said she had something to tell me about you."

Mamo raised one eyebrow.

"I know, it was stupid," Sadie said. "It's just when she said she knew something about your health, I got worried." Her lip quivered.

"Aw, sweetie," Mamo said. "I promise, no more secrets between us, okay? One for two and two for one."

"Right. Yeah." Sadie swallowed. "I'll be okay. I'm just a little overwhelmed or something." She drew in a breath.

Mamo rubbed her back. "How is your leg?"

"It really hurts," Sadie said. "And she kicked me in the ribs, but they don't hurt any worse than when I've been injured in Tae Kwon Do matches."

"Try putting a little weight on your leg."

Sadie stood. Shay leaned into her, bracing against her weight. Sadie eased onto her leg. Nothing happened.

"Huh."

"Huh good, or huh bad?" Mamo asked.

Sadie put more weight on the injured leg. "I think huh good." She shifted all her weight over. She hopped. She wiggled her leg and hopped on it again. "I guess I was wrong."

Mamo pressed her arms into Sadie's torso. Sadie tensed for shooting pain, but none came. Mamo released her.

"But she kicked me. Hard."

"Remember that treasure we were talking about?"

Sadie thought for a moment. "The healing thing? That's what this is?"

"Sure seems like it to me," Mamo said.

Sadie's eyes widened. She jumped around her room like she was playing a screwy game of hopscotch. She slapped her arms into her sides. She looked again at her hands where she expected to find scrapes but saw only small red marks. "No way."

"Yes way," Mamo said. "And I'm happy to see it. Since my abilities are so depleted, I was afraid you were going to have to heal the old fashioned way. I was ready to tuck you into bed for a few days."

"Oh my gosh. Tae Kwon Do is going to be that much better from now on." Sadie grinned. "Am I going to be, like, unbreakable or something?"

"Well, that would be something," Mamo said. "But you'll still be very breakable. And there are limits to how much you can heal. Like you can't heal from dead. At least not yourself."

"Wait, are you saying I can heal other people, dead people?"

Mamo shook her head. "No, sweetie, I was just being a smart-aleck." She patted Sadie's arm. "Raising the dead isn't part of our gift."

Sadie shrugged. "Right. I figured. Like we need zombies running around."

"Exactly," Mamo said. "Let's keep this a zombie-free zone. Unless we can send them after Merinda. Then I fully support raising a zombie army."

Sadie sucked in a breath. "What are we going to do about her? Do we need to hide? Do we need to leave right now?"

Mamo frowned. "We don't need to worry about her just yet. With the kind of injury you gave her, and her shifting to bird form on top of it—I can't imagine she has the energy to return to human form. No Yowie would. She's holed up somewhere trying to recover. It will take at least a couple of days for her to shift back. She can't do anything until then."

"What about Conner?"

"I'll handle him."

Sadie folded her arms. "But you're barely back to being you, you've been so sick. And he's healthy."

"Big sisters are always tougher than little brothers," Mamo said.

"But how? If he's, you know, taller and stuff?"

"I've got this, sweetie. Don't worry." Mamo touched Sadie's arm. "I'm going to find out what he's up to without him even knowing I'm asking."

"Okay..."

"Willene?" Mrs. Fallon called from downstairs. "We're back. And we have dinner."

"We'll be right down, Lena." Mamo turned back to Sadie. "Get cleaned up. I think Lena may have a surprise for us."

"It's not Conner, is it?" Sadie asked.

Mamo chuckled. "Definitely a better dinner guest than Conner." She kissed Sadie's forehead. "I'll see you in a few minutes."

Sadie pulled a stray twig out of her hair, brushed out bits of leaves, and took a quick shower. She dressed in her comfiest lounge pants and a giant sweatshirt. She went downstairs to the kitchen.

Brandon was sitting at the kitchen table.

"Oh." Sadie stopped in the doorway. "Hi." She hid her happiness at seeing Brandon again and forced an attitude of indifference. "I thought you left."

"Change of plans," Brandon said. "I'm back."

"Okay." Sadie walked to the counter and spoke to Mrs. Fallon. "Can I help?"

Mrs. Fallon glanced at Mamo then back to Sadie. "How about you get out plates and utensils? We'll need serving spoons for each of the dishes."

"Sure." Sadie didn't look at Brandon. She hoped no one could see her heart thumping in her chest. The beats felt like they could throw her off balance. She opened the cupboard door.

"Uh, Mrs. Fallon? Could I borrow Sadie for a minute?" Brandon asked.

Sadie spun toward him. "Borrow me? Like I'm a cell phone or something?"

"I didn't mean it like that," Brandon said. "I just want to talk to you."

"Go ahead and talk," Sadie said. "It's a free country." She clanked a stack of serving spoons onto the counter.

"In the other room, if that's okay," Brandon said.

Sadie bit the inside of her bottom lip.

Mamo moved close and whispered in her ear. "Give him a chance."

"Fine." Sadie walked out of the kitchen and Brandon followed. She plopped into the recliner in the living room. "So talk."

He sat on the couch across from her. "A lot's been going on—"

"Didn't we do this part already?" She pulled her legs underneath her.

"No, because—"

"I get it," Sadie said. "I'm a freak and you don't want to be around me, and you left without saying goodbye. And now you're back for some reason, but you want to make sure I don't bug you."

"What? No," Brandon said.

"You don't have to worry," Sadie said. "I'm not going to be here that much longer."

"What are you talking about?"

"We're outta here. As soon as we do the no-Yowie thing, Mamo and I are gone." Sadie pulled a blanket from the back of the chair over her lap.

Brandon's jaw dropped. "You're seriously leaving?"

Crap. I wasn't supposed to tell. "You can't say anything."

He leaned into the couch. "Who would I tell? My parents? They don't even like me."

Sadie pulled her hair forward and held it for a second. "What?"

"My parents." Brandon rubbed his hands down his face. "Sometimes they're the best parents in the world, and sometimes they're the worst. And right now things are pretty bad."

"I...uh...I thought they were taking you on a trip around the world." Sadie tucked herself deeper under the blanket.

"It wasn't going to be a very fun trip." Brandon stared at the ceiling. "They just felt guilty about leaving me behind. Again."

"I thought you liked all their stories and adventures," Sadie said.

He looked at her. "The stories are great. But I'd much rather hear about them afterward. Besides, they go off to their digs or whatever and leave me in the hotel for days at a time. And when we're together, they fight constantly. It sucks."

"They just leave you? Alone?" Sadie asked.

"Yeah," Brandon said. "When this big project came up, where they're going to be gone for at least a year, I convinced them to let me stay with Jason through at least the rest of the school year. But I guess they got all stressed that Jason isn't here and that I'm staying with Mrs. Fallon instead."

"So their surprise visit was to come and get you."

"Yep. I begged them to let me stay," Brandon said. "Mrs. Fallon told them it was fine with her, but they didn't buy it."

"But you're back now."

"They had one of their classic arguments in the car on the way to the airport, and I lost it," Brandon said. "I told them they sucked as parents and I didn't want to go with them, and if they really cared about how I felt they'd let me stay here."

"They let you come back?" Sadie asked. "Just like that?"

"Not exactly." Brandon ran his hands through his hair. "There was a lot more fighting, and a long conversation with Mrs. Fallon, and then they left me at a diner. That's where Mrs. Fallon picked me up." He held his face in his hands. "I suck."

Sadie paused. "I don't think you suck." Guilt slithered through her about jumping to conclusions about Brandon.

He turned to Sadie. "I pissed off my parents and basically told them I hate them, and you think I hate you, so I pretty much suck."

"I—"

"And jeez, the whole reason I wanted to talk to you right now is to tell you I'm sorry," Brandon said. "I didn't plan to dump my whole stupid story on you."

"It's okay," Sadie said. "I'm glad you told me about your parents. But what are you sorry about? Your parents aren't your fault."

"No, but I got so caught up in stressing over them I haven't been a very good friend." Brandon held out his hands. "And you think I think you're a freak, and I so don't think that."

"Oh, I...you don't?" Sadie felt too warm and pushed the blanket off her lap.

Brandon scooted down the couch, closer to the reclining chair where Sadie sat. "Not even a little. I think you're great. I thought you sounded great before I met you, just from the things Jason told me. Then I met you and you're even more great than I thought."

"I am? I mean, but the Yowie..."

"I don't care about the Yowie," Brandon said. "You choose it, you don't choose it. You should do whatever you want. I just like hanging out with you."

"Oh, well, I—" Sadie's mind spun.

"Like hanging out with me too? I hope?" Brandon asked.

"Yeah." Sadie smiled. "Yeah, I do."

Brandon returned the smile. "So we're good?"

"We're good."

Brandon stood. "Back to the kitchen for dinner?"

"Yep."

He reached for Sadie's hand and pulled her out of the chair. "Let's get in there before Kyle gets home and eats everything."

"I know, right? For as much as he eats, he should be huge," Sadie said.

They walked into the kitchen and Mrs. Fallon hurried over. She grabbed Sadie's shoulders. "Willene told me what happened. Let me look at you." She scrutinized Sadie's face and examined her scalp and her arms. She poked Sadie's ribs.

Sadie giggled. "Stop. That tickles." She batted at Mrs. Fallon's hands.

Mrs. Fallon addressed Mamo. "She's completely healed. For real?"

"I don't think a lot of people giggle when they're in pain," Mamo said.

"Wait, what did I miss?" Brandon asked.

Sadie told the story about Merinda's attack and the subsequent healing.

"Holy crap, that is cool," Brandon said. "The healing part I mean. And you kicking ass as usual."

"Not all the ass, though," Sadie said. "I got a bit of my own ass kicked, which I didn't like at all."

"Okay, enough with the A-S-S word please," Mrs. Fallon said. "Everyone sit."

"Oh, c'mon, Lena," Mamo said. "If one kicks ass, one should be able to say they kicked ass."

Mrs. Fallon threw her hands in the air. "Okay, fine. You make a fair point." She set the containers of Chinese food on the table. "But maybe we can talk about something else. Or better yet, everyone dish up what food they want. Kyle is going to be here any minute, and there's no stopping the human food vacuum."

A few minutes later Kyle walked in and everyone chuckled.

"What did I miss?" Kyle asked.

"Nothing and everything," Mrs. Fallon said. "Sit down and have some dinner."

They brought Kyle up to speed while he ate. After dinner, Mamo said she was going to talk to Conner.

"I'm coming with you," Sadie said.

Mamo stood. "I think this is a better conversation to be had sibling to sibling." She carried her plate to the sink. "I need to find out what he knows, and he's more likely to talk one-on-one."

"But what if he tries something? Tries to hurt you?" Sadie stacked plates in front of Kyle.

Kyle raised his hands. "Hey, what's the deal?"

Sadie faced him. "Your turn to do the dishes." She turned back to Mamo. "I should come with you."

"You should get ready for bed," Mamo said. "You've had a long enough day as it is. And Conner isn't going to hurt me. There's nothing gained in that. I'll figure out what's going on, and I'll see how the plans are coming along for your ceremony to decline Yowie and the Calling."

"You're sure?" Sadie asked.

"Very." Mamo stopped at the hall closet and got her jacket. "I'll see you in the morning."

"Okay." Sadie walked her to the front door and watched her drive away.

Brandon stepped out of the kitchen. "Do you want to watch a movie or something?"

"Normally I would say yes, but I am done." Sadie yawned. "I'm going to go up and crash early."

"I don't blame you," Brandon said. "Maybe tomorrow. It would be cool if we got to watch at least one movie together before you, ya know...before things change around here."

"Uh, yeah. Totally." Sadie forced a half-smile. She was going to miss Brandon. "I'll see you tomorrow." Sadie went upstairs with Shay close behind.

※ ※ ※

There was a knock on Sadie's door. She forced open an eye and checked the time. It was five a.m. She let her eye shut and ignored the sound.

The door opened. "Sweetie? You awake?" Mamo whispered.

"No." Sadie pulled the covers over her head.

Shay stood and made three circles on the bed, then lay back down, tucking herself tight into Sadie's belly.

"I'm coming in," Mamo said. "But I won't turn the light on yet."

"I thought it was important to be well rested before school." Sadie's words were muffled by blankets.

"It is. But you got to bed early last night," Mamo said. "I want to talk to you before everyone else is up and about."

Sadie shoved the blankets off her head. "What." Her hair crackled with static.

Mamo sat on the edge of the bed and brushed Sadie's hair out of her eyes. "I talked to Conner. He had no idea what Merinda had planned."

Sadie blinked hard trying to get her sleepy eyes to stay open. "Are you sure?"

"I'm positive. And he came up with an idea to help us catch Merinda before she does anything else."

Sadie pushed herself higher in the bed. "What is it?"

"It's going to take some assistance from you," Mamo said.

"Okay."

"And patience."

Sadie sighed. "What kind of patience?"

"We need to draw Merinda out and get her to come to us. We want to use you as bait, in a sense," Mamo said. "Kind of like secret spy, undercover stuff."

"I'm not undercover if I'm bait," Sadie said.

"No, but there will be secret stuff going on. Conner's going to tell her you're accepting the Calling."

"But I'm not."

"That's the secret part," Mamo said. "If she thinks you're going to accept the Calling, we're betting she'll make another attempt at capturing you, but not until after the ceremony. She'll wait for the bigger payoff."

Sadie rubbed her eyes. "I don't want to go through with that ceremony." A twinge in Sadie's gut made her think twice. She rejected the thought.

"We won't have a real ceremony," Mamo said. "She just has to think we had one, and then we'll be ready for her when she shows herself."

"Okay, so where does patience come into this?"

"We can't do anything until Merinda recovers enough from her fight with you to be able to shift," Mamo said. "She has to be in human form since she can't very well carry you off as a starling."

The corner of Sadie's mouth ticked up. "I wouldn't be surprised if she tried."

"Sadly, neither would I." Mamo reached over and rubbed Shay's belly. "But Merinda knows she doesn't have any strength right now, starling or otherwise. She'll wait."

"So we wait."

"Yes, until the weekend," Mamo said. "Can you manage that?"

"I guess."

"I have another favor to ask."

Sadie raised an eyebrow.

"I'd like us to stay here. Safety in numbers, as they say."

Sadie pushed to sitting. "I thought we weren't in any danger?"

"We're not, yet," Mamo said. "I'm confident about that. I'm just thinking proactively rather than reactively. And being proactive means staying together."

A pang of disappointment at not going home weighed on Sadie. But at least she could spend more time with Brandon. "Okay."

"That's my girl." Mamo rubbed Sadie's cheek. "Now get up and get ready for school."

"What? I still have to go to school?"

Mamo stood. "Well not yet. You do have lots of time before school starts."

"But why do I have to go at all?" Sadie asked.

"We had this conversation yesterday," Mamo said. "Why would anything be different today?"

"Because I got my ass kicked? Because I agreed to be bait?" Sadie faked a pout.

"I believe you were more kicker than kickee," Mamo said. "And that tells me that acting as bait is a walk in the park for you—pun intended."

"Very funny."

"And going through your normal routine better sells our story to Merinda," Mamo said.

"Whatever." But Sadie knew Mamo was right.

"I'm making blueberry waffles," Mamo said.

"I think I'm feeling more motivated." Sadie asked Shay to scoot over, then pushed off the covers and swung her legs to the floor. "I'll be down in a bit."

Sadie got ready for school. The scent of vanilla and warm blueberries made her mouth water and she increased her pace. When she walked into the kitchen, Brandon was already there.

"Good morning," Sadie said.

Brandon's mouth was full. He hummed hello and waved.

Mamo handed Sadie a plate.

She took it and sat next to Brandon. "Why do you get up so early when you don't have to?" Sadie asked. "You can do your schoolwork whenever."

"First of all, hello, your grandmother's blueberry waffles." Brandon pointed to his plate. "And second, I got used to getting up early when I traveled with my parents. Now it's automatic. I like getting my stuff done early anyway. Then I can do whatever I want the rest of the day."

"I think I would relearn how to sleep in," Sadie said.

"You could try, but I doubt your dear old granny would put up with that for too long." Mamo smirked.

"Who are you calling old?" Sadie smiled and took a bite of waffle.

"You are indeed the best granddaughter in the world," Mamo said. "I'll keep you in my will."

✳ ✳ ✳

After breakfast, Sadie headed to school. Even though Mamo assured her she was safe, and that Merinda was incapacitated, Sadie stayed on alert. She paid attention to cars that drove by, checked to see if there was anyone on the sidewalk she didn't recognize. She even watched birds that fluttered from one tree to another. But she didn't see any starlings. Everything seemed fine.

Normal.

Sadie surprised Nessa at her locker and gave her a hug.

"There's my girl," Nessa said. "You were cranky pants yesterday."

"Yeah, sorry," Sadie said. "But today Mamo made blueberry waffles and all is right with the world."

Nessa's face fell. "I missed blueberry waffles? I want to marry your grandmother's blueberry waffles."

"I thought you wanted to marry Kyle."

Nessa thought for a moment as she closed her locker. "Nope. Blueberry waffles is definitely the leading candidate right now. Or is it *are* the leading candidate right now? But it can't be *are*, can it? Because that would give me multiple husbands and no way do I want to deal with that."

"Even if they're all blueberry waffles?" Sadie asked.

"That's a good point." Nessa linked her arm in Sadie's. "I am now pro-polygamy."

They passed Derek in the hallway. "I know what you are, witch." He veered toward Sadie.

She ignored him and kept moving.

"I think you need to consider a different spell for him," Nessa said. "Toad is too nice. Cockroach, maybe?"

"I like it," Sadie said. "I'll consult my spell book when I get home." Sadie wondered if her healing power could fix Derek's bad attitude.

Sadie dropped Nessa at first period and continued to her classes. She stayed on the lookout for anything unusual, at least more unusual than Derek. After school, Sadie walked home alone. She thought about how much she would miss Nessa.

But she still believed she was making the right decision. Sadie just wanted to be normal. She just wanted to be with Mamo. And saying no to all the stress that came with accepting the Calling was the only way to make that work.

Sadie entered the house and Shay came running. She rubbed her head on Sadie's legs, her butt wiggling.

"Hello, sweet girl." Sadie hunched and rubbed Shay's cheeks.

Finn walked up and snorted onto Sadie's neck. Shay ran to grab a toy.

"No offense, but *eau de Finnea* is not my first choice of perfume." Sadie smiled and scratched Finn's chest. Sadie's bag slid down her arm onto the floor.

"Let me grab that." Brandon lifted Sadie's bag.

"Thanks." Sadie stood. "I have to get in my after school snuggles."

"Lucky dogs." He hung the bag on the banister.

Heat flushed into Sadie's face. "Uh, how was your day?"

"Good. But I have some bad news."

Sadie's hand flew to her mouth. "What is it? Is Mamo okay?" She checked the living room and started up the stairs.

Brandon followed her. "Hold up—I'm sorry. It's not that kind of bad news."

Sadie turned toward him. "What do you mean?"

"Your grandmother and Mrs. Fallon aren't here. They're with Conner," Brandon said. "The bad news is that we have a babysitter tonight."

"What? I haven't had a babysitter since I was nine," Sadie said.

"You and me both," Brandon said. "But tonight we get Kyle."

"Are you sure it's not the other way around and we're supposed to babysit him?" Sadie asked.

"He seems pretty sure about it." Brandon gestured toward the kitchen.

Sadie headed into the kitchen and found Kyle with cereal boxes lined up on the counter. She stopped. "Uh...Kyle?"

He turned. "Oh good, you're home. I'm in charge." He picked up a piece of paper and read it. "Do your homework. Make your own dinner. Get to bed at a decent hour." He swept his arm past the boxes. "And I made the dinner part easy so you don't even have to open the cupboard."

"Seriously, dude?" Brandon pointed at the boxes. "That's dinner?"

"Yeah." Kyle grabbed one of the boxes. "It says it's enriched with vitamins and minerals. It's good for you."

"Okay..." Brandon leaned against the doorjamb.

Kyle thudded the box back on the counter. "Do what you want, it doesn't matter to me."

"Wow," Sadie said. "You're totally like a professional babysitter. Do you have any games to play with us?"

"Alright, whatever," Kyle said. "They didn't really leave me in charge."

"I'm shocked." Sadie crossed her arms.

"I just wanted to help," Kyle said. "Everyone else is helping with stuff. Grandma Lena is helping you and Mrs. C and Brandon. And Mrs. C is helping Grandma Lena and Brandon." Kyle pointed at Sadie. "And you're helping catch bad guys. Even the dogs are helping. And I'm just here."

"You're hardly ever here," Brandon said.

Kyle huffed. "Okay, but I'm here right now."

"And what bad guys?" Sadie asked.

"Your fake cousin, or whatever Merinda is," Kyle said.

"She's not really related to us. She was Mamo's and Conner's foster-sister. And I didn't stop her," Sadie said.

"But you will." Kyle sat on the counter.

"Dude, no one's stopping you from helping with anything," Brandon said.

"What can I do?"

"Just hang out." Brandon turned up his hands. "Be ready. There's no set plan or anything."

"That's it?" Kyle jumped off the counter. "Just hang out?"

"Yeah. That's all I'm doing," Brandon said.

"But you don't have to," Sadie said to Kyle. "I don't want you to feel like you have to be here all the time or anything." She tucked her hair behind her ear. "Still, it's super nice to know that you want to help if you can."

"I really do," Kyle said. "Whatever you need."

This was a side of him Sadie hadn't seen before. "Thanks, Kyle."

"You have my number, right?"

Sadie nodded. Mamo had made sure everyone exchanged numbers a few days ago.

"So, you need anything, you call me," Kyle said. "Okay?"

"Of course, yeah." Sadie didn't understand where this behavior was coming from.

"It probably won't happen," Brandon said. "I'll be here for her."

Sadie raised her brows and turned to Brandon.

"But if she does need something, she can call me," Kyle said. "That's all I'm saying."

"Yeah, I know," Brandon said. "But I've got this."

Sadie held up her hands. "Okay, hold on. We've all got this. We're all helping. Right?" She looked at Brandon.

"Right," he said.

"And Kyle? Right?" Sadie asked.

"Yeah, right."

"Okay. Now I'm going to do homework," Sadie said. "I'll see you both later, maybe over a bowl of delicious and fortified cereal."

✳ ✳ ✳

Sadie's homework didn't take long. She asked Shay if she wanted to go for a walk.

Shay sprang to standing and chased her tail. She raced out of Sadie's room. Less than a minute later she was back upstairs, panting through the harness in her mouth.

"So that's a yes?" Sadie asked.

Shay dropped the harness and sat, wagging her tail.

Sadie fastened the harness onto Shay and followed the dog downstairs to get her leash. Sadie thought she'd invite Brandon to go with her, but he wasn't on the main floor, and he must not have heard her when she called down the stairs to the basement. Sadie shrugged it off.

"Just us girls, Shay." She clipped on Shay's leash and they headed out the door.

Except for the occasional distraction like a sassy squirrel, Shay did well walking on leash. She'd come a long way in the few months since Jason got her as a puppy and started training her to help him with cryptids. Sadie wondered how much of her training Shay would still remember by the time Jason and his uncle got back from London. They'd already been gone more than two weeks. Sadie reminded herself to ask Mrs. Fallon about her trip the next time she saw her.

Sadie and Shay walked through the park, past the swings where she'd met Merinda. Sadie stayed alert, but she felt safe with Shay close. They stopped at the dog park, where Shay wrestled and chased and rolled in the dirt. She leaped into the doggie pool then climbed out and shook, spraying water on everyone around her.

Apparently, eau de dog is my signature fragrance today. Sadie laughed to herself and wiped drops of water off her neck. She tried to ignore the twinge in her heart at the thought of leaving Shay behind. Even though Shay wasn't her dog, Sadie loved being with her.

Sadie and Shay took the path home that skirted the edge of the park between the groomed and wilderness areas. They stopped at a bench in the sunshine to give Shay time to dry before they got back to the house. Shay stretched her back legs, then her front, and lay down. Sadie scratched Shay's chest and relaxed for what felt like the first time in days. She closed her eyes and let the sun warm her face.

A few minutes later, Shay vaulted to standing, startling Sadie. Shay's eyes were locked on a cottonwood grove in the distance. A low rumble rolled through her chest.

"What is it, Shay?" Sadie stared where Shay watched but didn't see anything unusual. She scanned the treetops for birds. The bare branches were empty.

Shay took two measured steps forward without breaking her gaze. Her hackles rose.

Sadie stayed close and kept her line of sight in the same direction as Shay's. A second later, something brown moved and stopped. Sadie's muscles tensed. Shay's growl grew deeper. The brown form moved again, pushing through the bushes and grasses that grew in the grove.

"Is that the bear?" Sadie glanced around to see if anyone was nearby. She wanted to get someone else's opinion about what they were seeing.

She and Shay were alone. Sadie refocused on the animal still moving slowly from right to left. "Maybe it's a lost dog or something." *It has to be a dog. Or a bear. It can't be anything else.*

The animal stopped and turned in a jerk, looking toward Sadie and Shay.

Shay yanked Sadie forward and barked loud and fast. She leaned into her harness, her paws digging into the ground.

Sadie held Shay's leash with both hands and dug in her heels. Shay lurched and gained distance.

"Shay, stop. Stop!" Sadie leaned backward.

Shay pulled harder toward the animal. The handle of the leash cut into Sadie's fingers. She moved to adjust it and the leash slipped from her grasp.

Shay bolted.

"Stop! Shay!" Sadie took off after her. Dog or bear, she didn't want Shay to get to the animal. She didn't want Shay to get hurt.

Shay moved through the grasses like a cheetah closing the gap. Sadie couldn't keep up.

"Shay!"

The animal turned away and ran, Shay close behind. A second later it rose onto two legs. It sprinted and increased speed until it outpaced Shay. And disappeared. For a few more seconds Shay barked at the empty space the animal left behind.

Sadie stopped and squatted, resting as her body recovered. Her hair stuck to her sweaty neck. Shay trotted up and sat, her tail wagging through the leaves and dirt.

"That...wasn't..." Sadie took a deep breath. "A bear." She shuddered.

Shay licked Sadie's face. Sadie stood and picked up Shay's leash dirty from being dragged.

Was that Conner? Or Mamo? Are they messing with me?

Sadie viewed the cottonwoods for another moment, then she and Shay hurried home.

FIFTEEN

Leaving

S adie unclipped Shay's leash, and she made a beeline for a bowl of water in the kitchen.

Brandon walked into the foyer carrying a bowl of cereal. Milk dripped off the spoon he held above the bowl. "You look...uh...did you go for a run?"

"Not on purpose." Sadie sat on the stairs. "Shay got away from me, and I chased after her."

"Squirrel?" Brandon stuffed a spoonful of cereal in his mouth. Milk dribbled down his chin and he wiped it with his sleeve.

"This wasn't a squirrel." Sadie told Brandon what happened. "I need to ask Mamo about it."

"You're sure about what you saw?" Brandon asked. "I mean, no offense, but we all have Yowie on the brain. Maybe your mind was playing tricks on you."

"I thought about that," Sadie said. "But there's no way. It was brown, furry, and it ran on two legs. What else does that?"

"Maybe gorillas escaped from the circus and are living in the woods?" Brandon took another bite of cereal.

"Yes. The circus," Sadie said. "Always losing their gorillas and leaving them behind to fend for themselves." She stood. "I guess it's good that there are still some ideas that sound crazy to me."

Brandon chewed and signaled a thumbs up.

Sadie started up the stairs. "I'm going to see if I can get hold of Mamo."

✳ ✳ ✳

Mamo and Mrs. Fallon were home less than twenty minutes after Sadie called. Conner was with them. Everyone gathered in the living room. Even Kyle joined them without being asked.

"Maybe I underestimated Merinda's abilities," Mamo said. "Could she be able to shift already?"

"I don't see how," Conner said. "That would be tough for either of us to do, and she's not a direct relative. Her powers aren't at the same level."

"So I didn't see one of you guys out there?" Sadie snuggled closer to Mamo.

"No," Mamo said.

"I can vouch for them," Mrs. Fallon said. "All Yowie were present and accounted for."

"So it had to be her, didn't it?" Brandon asked. "Or is Salton known for Yowie sightings? Or Bigfoot sightings since we're not in Australia."

Mamo nodded. "Right. Years ago an old rancher swore he saw Bigfoot out on his property, just outside Salton. But like today, we were all present and accounted for," Mamo said. "And there haven't been any sightings since then so I'm guessing the rancher was just looking to tell a good story."

Mamo addressed Conner. "Brandon makes a good point." She raised her hand. "Sadie had to have seen Merinda in Yowie form."

"I don't know..." Conner leaned back in the recliner.

"Have you sensed anyone else?" Mamo asked?

"Sensed?" Sadie asked.

"We usually know when other Yowie are near," Conner said. "Unless, of course, you're off your game for some reason, like Willy when she was ill. Merinda and I arrived in town without an inkling of alarm."

"That's old news, Conner." Mamo flitted her hand. "Stay on topic, please."

"Fine," Conner said. "To answer your question, no, I haven't sensed anyone else. The Yowie energy around us is the same as when we arrived."

"So somehow Merinda shifted into her Yowie form after her injury," Mamo said. "And she's hiding in the woods."

"I guess so." Conner leaned forward. "But I can't explain how she did it."

"How do we get her?" Kyle asked. "Shay can track her, and I can rig a net or something. They have those big nets in movies you know, where someone steps on the trigger or whatever it is, and the net scoops them up? That would work."

Mrs. Fallon walked over to Kyle and pressed her hand on his forehead.

"What? Is something wrong with me?" Kyle pressed his hands into his face.

"That's what I'm trying to find out," Mrs. Fallon said. "For a second you sounded like you wanted to help."

Kyle stepped away from Mrs. Fallon's hand. "I do want to help."

"Just when I thought we had enough strange things going on," Mrs. Fallon said. "Kyle is growing up."

"C'mon, Grams." Kyle puffed his chest.

Mrs. Fallon put her arm around him. "This is a good thing, and I appreciate your idea. But let's put it on the back burner and see if we can come up with something less...swashbuckley."

"Yeah, okay." Kyle sat on an armrest of the couch.

"I don't think there's anything else to be done for now," Mamo said. "We stick with the original plan and wait for Merinda to return to human form. Conner will keep trying to reach her, and he'll tell her Sadie's chosen Yowie and the Calling. Then we move ahead with the fake ceremony and catch Merinda when she makes her move."

"If she makes her move," Sadie said.

"As much as I've tried to help her over the years," Conner said, "she continues to make poor choices. I'm sad to say I believe this will be another one."

Sadie grasped the hawk's eye pendant around her neck. "Then we wait."

"And we all go through our normal routines." Mamo patted Sadie's knee. "School included."

"I got it, I got it," Sadie said.

Mrs. Fallon yawned. "My goodness. The jet lag is finally catching up to me."

"Yeah, how was your trip?" Sadie asked. "Did you see Jason? And Uncle Alexander?"

"I did see them but didn't talk to Jason for more than a few minutes," Mrs. Fallon's forehead creased. "Alexander isn't doing too well, I'm afraid. But the League assures me he's on the mend. Jason is keeping busy with his dad and Della."

"Oh, are they sightseeing or something?" Sadie didn't understand why Jason was too busy to reply to her texts.

"I wish they were, but the League has them involved in some projects, and Della is still receiving treatment," Mrs. Fallon said. "They tell me it's important she continue her treatment a little longer to ensure she doesn't backslide after she comes home."

"Yeah, makes sense." Sadie picked at a cuticle.

"And Jason still doesn't have proper phone service, so he hasn't received messages from us," Mrs. Fallon said. "I don't understand why the League can't handle that for him. They're so good at dealing with difficult projects, yet the simple ones seem to get lost in the shuffle. But I'm not letting that one go anytime soon."

Sadie felt lighter. Jason wasn't totally ignoring her after all.

"Go get some rest, Lena." Mamo eyed a bowl on the coffee table with dried bits of brown flakes. "Looks like Conner and I are going to join the kids in a hearty bowl of cereal."

"Or I can make us some tasty grilled cheese sandwiches," Conner said.

Sadie and Brandon voted for grilled cheese.

Kyle raised his hand. "Me too."

"The kitchen is yours," Mrs. Fallon said. "I'll see you in the morning."

✳ ✳ ✳

The next two days passed without anything strange happening. Sadie went to school, she laughed with Nessa, and she managed to avoid Derek and his comments about her being a witch.

In the evenings, everyone ate dinner together and closed out the night with a movie. Sadie sat on the couch with Shay on one side and Brandon on the other. On the second night, Brandon's knee touched Sadie's. She didn't move away.

Saturday morning arrived along with a call from Conner. Mamo gathered everyone in the kitchen and said Conner had heard from Merinda. He told her he didn't believe she had attacked Sadie, and he gave Merinda the false information about Sadie accepting the Calling. Conner invited Merinda to join them for the ceremony later that day, but Merinda declined. She said she hoped the ceremony would go well, and that she'd talk to him afterward.

"So that's it," Mamo said. "Mission Merinda is a go."

"Mission Merinda?" Sadie's brows raised.

"Well we can't call it plan-to-catch-Merinda-and-stop-her-from-spilling-the-beans, can we?" Mamo asked.

"That is a mouthful," Brandon said.

"Exactly," Mamo said. "Brandon understands the art of words."

"I don't know about that," Brandon said. "But okay."

"Wait—what do we do with Merinda if we catch her?" Sadie asked.

"*When* we catch her." Kyle poured himself a glass of orange juice. Mamo gave Kyle a double-take. Mrs. Fallon chuckled.

"What?" Kyle asked. "That's what they say in movies. You know, to be all positive."

"Right you are, Kyle," Mamo said. "*When* we catch her, we'll wipe her memory."

"Oh," Sadie said. "I guess I didn't think about that."

Brandon put two slices of bread in the toaster. "What if she shifts into a bird?"

"We have a net and a cage ready," Mrs. Fallon said. "Plus, Finn's trained for these things. She won't let Merinda get away, and Shay will get to see how it's done. A little real-world experience."

"You've thought of everything, huh?" Sadie dug her spoon into a cup of yogurt.

"I hope so," Mamo said. "Oh, and Sadie, once we take care of Merinda, we can move home. So pack up your things, okay? We can finally get out of everyone's way."

Sadie forced a smile. "Yeah. Great."

"You don't have to go, Willene." Mrs. Fallon crossed her arms. "In fact, I think you should stay."

"You've been too good to us already and it's best for us to move on," Mamo said.

"Can we talk about it?" Mrs. Fallon asked. "I don't want you to feel like you have to rush off."

"My mind is made up," Mamo said.

"Is Sadie's mind made up?" Mrs. Fallon turned to Sadie. "Are you ready to leave?"

Sadie knew Mrs. Fallon was talking about more than Mamo and Sadie moving back to their house. She glanced at everyone in the room. "Uh, whatever Mamo says is fine with me. It's good." Sadie's chest winched tighter and tighter like she'd never be able to inhale again. "I gotta…" She pushed away from the table and rushed to her room. She sank onto the floor at the foot of her bed.

Mamo entered, closing the door behind her. "Are you all right?" She sat on the floor next to Sadie.

"Can we please stay in Salton?" Sadie shoved down a lump in her throat. "Please?"

"Only if you accept the Calling so you'll be cloaked." Mamo pulled Sadie close.

"Maybe I should do that," Sadie said. "And I'll just never change into a Yowie—I don't have to, right?"

"You'll have to do it at least once, but—"

"Okay, so I'll do it once, and then switch back and be me. And I'll be cloaked and safe and we can stay here," Sadie said. "No one will find us."

"The cloak only works until your powers are developed," Mamo said. "Then you accept the Calling and assume your role as leader."

"Which means what, exactly? I mean, besides dealing with the whole Garrison Devine thing. What does a normal leader have to do?"

"Listen to the members of the Clan, consider laws and regulations and how they benefit membership, represent the Clan as a liaison to the League of Governors, work with a team of advisors and—"

"And try to make things better," Sadie said. "Good. For everyone."

"Yes," Mamo said. "But that's not the situation we're in. If you accept the Calling it would be one battle after another. Garrison will send mercenaries after you, after all of us."

"But he's older than you, right? A lot older. Maybe he'll…maybe he won't be around that much longer. He could be gone—he could die—before the cloak wears off."

"I wish that were likely but Yowie are long-lived," Mamo said. "Barring an unforeseen development he has many decades of life left."

"Then after I get all of my powers, maybe I could beat him, them, whoever, and make the whole thing stop. You said I'd be strong."

"I don't want you in that kind of danger. And more often than not, you'd have to be in Yowie form to fight. If you got injured, like Merinda, you could get stuck."

"Merinda didn't get stuck."

"Her injuries were nothing compared to the kind of battle we'd be fighting," Mamo said.

"But everyone here, I don't want to leave them. I don't—" Sadie pressed her lips together. "I'll miss them," she whispered.

Mamo hugged her. "I know, sweetie, I know. I feel the same way. We care about them." Mamo released Sadie and looked into her eyes. "Which is another reason we have to leave. You'll be safer, and they'll be safer, too. If we're not here they can't get hurt."

If something happened to Mrs. Fallon or Brandon or the dogs, any of them, because of her, Sadie would never forgive herself. "Okay," she said, her voice froggy. She cleared it. "Okay, you're right. We have to go."

Mamo hugged Sadie again. "That's my girl, always thinking about others. I promise you, you're making the right decision."

Sadie sat back. "Yeah, I know."

"As soon as we catch Merinda and wipe her memory, I'll walk you through the process to decline the Calling," Mamo said.

"Why can't we just do that now?"

"Because a communication would be sent to all Yowie about your decision, including Merinda. She'd know Conner lied."

"But does that matter if we leave?" Sadie asked.

"We can't risk her reporting Conner to Garrison," Mamo said.

"Right." Sadie sniffed. "Have I mentioned how much I don't like Merinda? Because I really, really don't like Merinda."

"Welcome to the club." Mamo reached for a package of tissues sitting on Sadie's desk. "She and I never got along very well. And she never learns from her mistakes." She offered a tissue to Sadie. "Then again, Conner always bails her out rather than letting her fail, so how can she learn?"

"Maybe she's not smart enough to learn," Sadie said.

"Everyone is smart enough to learn," Mamo said. "But some choose not to because it's easier than going through the hard stuff." Sadie leaned into Mamo.

Mamo stroked Sadie's hair. "Feeling better?"

Sadie nodded. "When are we leaving?"

"The sooner we go, the easier it will be," Mamo said. "I think we should head out tonight after everyone goes to bed."

"Okay," Sadie said. "I'll make sure I have everything packed."

Conner joined them for an early dinner. Mrs. Fallon served baked fish, salad, and steamed broccoli with melted cheddar. Sadie picked at her food.

"Not hungry?" Mrs. Fallon asked.

"Not really," Sadie said.

"Well that's a relief," Mrs. Fallon said. "I thought maybe you didn't like my cooking." She winked at Sadie.

"Oh no, I love your cooking." Sadie took a bite of fish and set down her fork. "I guess I'm just nervous about tonight."

"I'll eat it." Kyle reached across the table for Sadie's plate.

"There's plenty more." Mrs. Fallon batted the back of Kyle's hand. "Let her be."

"No, it's okay." Sadie handed her plate to Kyle. "I can't eat it."

"And this way it doesn't go to waste," Kyle said. "Win-win." He jabbed a chunk of broccoli with his fork and shoved it in his mouth.

"No food ever goes to waste with you around," Mrs. Fallon said.

Kyle grinned and jammed in another bite of food.

"We have time before the ceremony starts." Mamo eyed Kyle. "You could actually chew the food before you swallow it."

224

"Ah mm ewing it." Dark green mush showed through Kyle's lips.

"Dude," Brandon said, "you are totally gross."

Kyle swallowed. "What?"

Sadie stood. "Is there something I can do to get things ready?"

"I brought a box of candles up from the basement," Mrs. Fallon said. "Set them up in the living room, would you? But don't light them yet."

"And shut the blinds," Mamo added. "We want Merinda to be able to see the mood of what's going on, but not the actual goings on."

"Okay." Sadie went into the living room and distributed the candles. She put most of them on furniture near the walls, and a few small ones on the coffee table. She inspected the room, wondering if the candles were in the right places until she remembered they weren't doing a real ceremony anyway.

Brandon walked in. "Nervous, huh?"

"Yeah." Sadie plopped onto the couch. "I'll be glad when this is over."

"And then what?"

"And then Merinda doesn't bug us anymore," Sadie said.

"And then you're leaving." Brandon sat across from her.

Sadie sat on her hands. "You didn't say anything?"

"No, but I think Kyle's the only one that doesn't know," Brandon said. "And maybe Conner. Mrs. Fallon definitely knows."

"Yeah."

"When?"

Sadie shrugged. She couldn't bear to tell Brandon they were leaving tonight. She didn't want to think about it, much less talk about it.

Brandon stood. "I wish you weren't going." He headed downstairs to his room in the basement.

Sadie held her face in her hands. Her gut twisted. Leaving Salton would be the hardest thing she'd ever done.

Mamo entered and Mrs. Fallon followed.

"All right, chop chop." Mamo clapped her hands twice. "Thirty minutes to show time. What else do we need to do? Do we have the bird cage?"

Mrs. Fallon gestured to a corner. "Right there. With the net."

"Good," Mamo said. "Where are the dogs? Finn? Shay?"

Finn and Shay hurried in from the kitchen and sat next to Sadie.

"Excellent," Mamo said. "Conner, anything new from Merinda since you spoke to her this morning?"

"Nothing," Conner said. "As far as I know, she's resting in her hotel room."

Kyle hurried up from the basement. "I have my baseball bat." He held it high.

"That won't be necessary," Conner said. "Merinda won't have much strength to fight, and certainly not against this many of us."

"What if she goes all Yowie on our asses?" Kyle swung the bat.

Conner stepped backward. "Again, not likely to have the strength."

"Put that in the corner with the net," Mrs. Fallon said.

"Sure thing." Kyle crossed the room and set down the bat. "I'm sitting on this side of the room so I can get to it fast."

"Only if there is an emergency," Mrs. Fallon said. "And there won't be an emergency."

"Okay, but if there is, I'm ready," Kyle said.

Mamo lit the candles. "We'll get started in a few minutes."

"Get started how?" Sadie asked. "We're not really doing anything."

"We thought it would be fun to share some Yowie stories," Mamo said. "Conner found some of the best stories about fake sightings. Seemed appropriate since we're having a fake ceremony."

"Did someone say Bigfoot hunters?" Brandon came up from the basement. "I'm in." He sat next to Sadie and smiled.

"Bigfoot, Yowie, Sasquatch—we have a balanced selection of fascinating stories to tell," Conner said. "Or should I say tale? Get it? T-A-L-E?" He chuckled.

Everyone else groaned.

"I hope the stories you picked are better than that joke," Mamo said.

Conner put on his reading glasses and began reading the account of a Bigfoot hunt by three men in Washington State. They told of giant footprints they found in the snow outside their cabin, and how the prints came up to the window as if the beast had spied on them while they slept. They followed the steps away from the cabin until the trail disappeared, as if the creature had evaporated into thin air. And they described moaning and howling at night that they'd never heard before. Then one night, there was a scratching sound on the cabin window.

Finn's head perked and she looked toward the kitchen.

"It's just a story, Finn," Sadie whispered and stroked Finn's head.

Conner continued reading.

Shay raised her head and growled.

Goosebumps crawled over Sadie's skin.

Finn, still zeroed in on the kitchen, bumped her muzzle on Shay's. Shay silenced.

Sadie checked the time. The fake ceremony was supposed to last an hour and it had only been ten minutes. Was Merinda here already?

Finn stood, her gaze still fixed. Shay followed.

Conner kept reading but his eyes flashed at Mamo. She nodded.

Sadie's heart pounded.

Merinda limped in from the kitchen. "You really should keep your doors locked." She wore black leggings with a tear across one thigh. She had on her black boots, a black jacket, and long red sweater. In her right hand, she carried a silver blade.

"You decided to join us after all," Conner said. "I'm glad to—"

Merinda swung the blade stopping it shy of Conner's throat. "I thought you liked me."

"I do," Conner said. "Of course I do." He moved to push the blade away.

Merinda pressed it into his skin. "Don't."

Conner held his hands up.

"I'm not stupid," Merinda said.

"Of course you're not," Conner said. "No one here thinks that."

"She does." Merinda pointed at Mamo with her free hand.

Mamo pressed her mouth tight.

"That's not true, not true," Conner said. "Tell her, Willy."

Merinda rolled her eyes. "Shut up, Conner. I was in your room the whole time. I heard everything."

"What?" Conner's mouth dropped open. "How did you—"

"I couldn't very well get into my own hotel room after her highness over there busted my leg and made me shift to starling." Merinda sneered at Sadie. "So I followed you into yours. Thanks for noticing by the way."

"You could have signaled me," Conner said. "I would have helped you."

"Yeah, well, I passed out in the closet," Merinda said. "Next thing I know, I wake up and hear you plotting against me."

Mamo stood. "It was hardly a plot." She brushed the front of her pants. "We just wanted to lure you out so we could talk to you. And here you are." Mamo held her arms wide. "Now let's stop this nonsense and have a chat."

Merinda reached into her jacket and pulled out a second knife, this one longer than the first. "Sit down."

Mamo sat.

Kyle leaned and reached behind him.

"And stop right there, jock boy. What's your name again?" Merinda asked.

"Kyle."

"Yeah. Jock boy," Merinda said. "You touch that bat, I cut his throat."

Kyle looked from Merinda to Conner. "Okay. You're in charge." He shifted forward.

"That's right," Merinda said. "I'm in charge. That's finally sinking in with you people." She addressed Mamo. "Did you hear that, Willy? I'm in charge."

"Merinda..." Mamo reached one hand toward her.

"Say it, Willy," Merinda said. "I want to make sure you understand."

"Fine." Mamo dropped her hand. "You're in charge. What is it you want?"

"I want you to sit quietly, and speak only when you're spoken to, for one." She swept the knife through the air. "And two, I want to take a little trip with darling Sadie."

"That's not going to happen," Mamo said.

"No, she's wrong." Sadie's hands trembled. "That can happen. That can totally happen."

Brandon turned toward her. "Sadie, no."

Mamo stood again. "You will not touch her."

"I don't want anyone to get hurt." Sadie's voice pitched up. "I'll go with you."

"You won't." Mamo's voice boomed.

"Shut up!" Merinda yelled.

Conner cried out and everyone stopped.

Sadie gasped.

A trickle of blood ran down Conner's throat.

Merinda sighed. "Now see what you made me do?"

Conner's bottom lip quivered. "It's okay. I'm okay. It's not...it's not deep." Blood seeped into the collar of his white shirt.

Mamo's hands covered her mouth and she stared at Conner.

"What's this? The great and powerful Willy is scared?" Merinda smiled. "I think now's about the time you would tell me these things are not toys." She tapped the flat side of the blade on Conner's neck

229

to emphasize each word. "But oh yeah, I'm in charge, not you. Back in your seat."

Mamo sat and placed her hands in her lap.

"And you, Mrs. Fallon. You sit next to her." Merinda directed Mrs. Fallon across the room. "Good. Now I can see everyone's face. Except for dear Conner's here." She tapped his neck again. "But I bet I know what he's thinking." She took a deep breath. "So here's what we're going to do. Willy's going to do the mumbo jumbo stuff needed for Sadie to accept the Calling. I'll supervise to make sure you don't miss any steps."

"But she doesn't want to accept the Calling," Brandon said.

"Shut. Up." Merinda pushed the blade harder into Conner's neck. Brandon's jaw clenched.

"As I was saying, we're going to do the fancy little ceremony so the princess gets all her magical powers. Then you're all going to take a nice nap, and Sadie and I are going on a road trip." Merinda hopped on her good leg. "Ooh, maybe we can totally sing along to the best music, and eat the best snacks, and totally be best friends." She snickered while her eyes glared.

"Fine," Sadie said. "Whatever you want."

"Got that right," Merinda said. "So what's first, Willy."

"I need some things from the hutch near the kitchen."

"Go ahead. But I'm watching you, and the handle of this blade on Conner's neck is feeling slippery." Merinda ran her tongue along her teeth.

Mamo stood and walked to the hutch.

Merinda's attention stayed locked on her.

Mrs. Fallon snapped her fingers.

Finn leaped from behind the couch and clamped her jaws on Merinda's arm, throwing her to the ground and forcing her to drop one blade.

Conner scrambled clear.

Merinda swung her other arm and stabbed Finn in the side. She yelped and let go, falling sideways. Merinda pulled herself up.

"No!" Sadie rushed to Finn and put pressure on the wound. Blood gushed. Brandon dropped to his knees next to them. Sadie searched for Shay but didn't see her.

Metal clanged from behind and Sadie turned. Mamo swung her own weapon at Merinda, a blade of gold.

Sadie put Brandon's hands on Finn's wound. She grabbed the blade Merinda had dropped, the one with Conner's blood on it, and ran to Mamo's side.

"Sadie, get back." Mamo pushed Sadie behind her.

"I can help. I can stop her."

"Says you." Merinda held onto a chair, balancing against her injured leg, and thrust her blade at Mamo.

Mamo skittered backward.

Sadie rushed forward and blocked Merinda's swing. She countered. She pushed Merinda back.

Merinda grimaced as her weight shifted onto her bad leg. She raised her blade over her head and screamed.

Sadie prepared to block the blow but Mamo shoved Sadie aside and blocked it herself. "Help Conner and Finn." The weapons banged together again. "Get everyone out of here."

"But I can—"

"Do it." Mamo blocked another swing and skittered back. She charged and swung at Merinda.

Merinda blocked.

Sadie started back to Finn and Conner when a guttural moan sounded behind her. She spun on her heel.

Mamo held her belly, her eyes wide. She dropped to one knee.

Kyle dashed for the bat and spun toward Merinda. Mrs. Fallon snatched up Mamo's dropped blade and charged.

Merinda scurried out.

Sadie ran to Mamo and grabbed her before she fell. "No, no, no. Mamo, no." She eased Mamo down. She pressed her hands on the wound. "You can heal." Blood gushed. "Make it stop. Make it stop." Sadie willed her healing powers.

Mamo gripped Sadie's arm. "Be safe. You be safe."

"You have to stay with me." Sadie pushed harder but the blood didn't slow. "You have to take care of me."

"You're strong," Mamo said, her voice whispery. "Stronger than I thought. I love you."

Mamo's eyes closed. Her arm dropped.

"It's not working. Call 9-1-1." Sadie yelled to Conner over her shoulder. "You have to do something. Make her heal."

He hurried over. "I don't have that power."

"She does. Make it work." Sadie patted Mamo's face. "Wake up."

"She can't," Conner said. "She's drained."

"But she can't die!" Sadie kept one hand on the wound and clutched Mamo's hand with the other. "Wake up, wake up."

"There's maybe one thing..." Conner said.

"What. Tell me."

"Accept the Calling," Conner said. "The healing power you have right now isn't enough. The Calling will initiate an immediate boost to your powers, though it's uncertain which ones, or if it will be enough."

"But the ceremony, we don't have time." Sadie tightened her grip Mamo's hand.

"There's no ceremony. Just words."

"But—"

He shook his head. "You need only speak the words."

"Fine." Sadie panted, trying to get enough air. "Give me the words. Give me the words!"

"Repeat after me," Conner said.

Sadie nodded fast.

"Through Water, Fire, and Air, Sun, Moon, and Earth."

Sadie said the words.

"I accept the Calling to serve with Honor, protect with Power, and bring forward Light and Love."

Sadie finished the sentence. "Okay, what's next."

"That's it," Conner said.

"But I don't—"

Light shot into Sadie. Her breath stopped. Her back arched. She heard someone yelling her name. And as fast as the light came, it doused. Sadie's eyes adjusted and she focused on Mamo.

Blood pooled around her. "Okay, c'mon, Mamo. C'mon." Sadie pressed her hands into the wound. "Please..." She glanced at Conner. "What do I do? Am I doing it wrong?"

He shook his head, barely moving it.

Sadie shook Mamo's shoulders and yelled her name. She shook again. "Wake up. Wake up!"

Mamo didn't move. The color of her skin faded.

"No..."

Mrs. Fallon hunched next to Sadie and touched Mamo's cheek. "She's gone, Sadie."

Sadie didn't take her eyes away from Mamo's face. "She can't be. She can't leave me." Sadie threw herself over Mamo's chest and sobbed. "She can't. She promised." Sadie sat up and pulled Mamo's shoulders toward her. Mamo's head lolled. Sadie hugged Mamo's neck. "Please, please come back. I did the Calling, I can fix you. You can't die." She bawled into Mamo's body. "Don't leave me alone."

Mrs. Fallon placed her hands on Sadie's shoulders and gently lifted her up, away from Mamo. She pulled Sadie into a hug. "You're not alone." Mrs. Fallon stroked Sadie's hair. "I promise you you're not alone."

SIXTEEN

Yowie

Sadie's skull pounded. She didn't want to leave Mamo's side. Air hiccupped into Sadie, forcing oxygen in between sobs. Noise and chaos tornadoed around her.

Mrs. Fallon spoke but Sadie couldn't hear over the whooshing that filled her head. Mrs. Fallon put her arm around Sadie's waist and pulled her up, and away, directing her into the kitchen.

Cold water ran over Sadie's hands. Mrs. Fallon adjusted the knobs and the water warmed. She rubbed soap onto Sadie's skin. Bloody streams, mixed with tears, flowed down the drain. Mrs. Fallon rinsed off the soap and dried Sadie's hands. Someone put a blanket around her shoulders.

Sadie couldn't stop crying.

Mrs. Fallon led her to a seat at the table. She rubbed Sadie's arms and spoke but Sadie didn't understand. Mrs. Fallon wadded tissues and wiped Sadie's tears. She stuffed more tissues in Sadie's hand.

Blurry figures darted back and forth.

Nothing made sense.

Mrs. Fallon tucked Sadie's hair behind her ears. She offered Sadie a drink but Sadie couldn't answer. She didn't know the answer.

Mrs. Fallon led Sadie outside. She opened the car door. Sadie sat. Mrs. Fallon fastened Sadie's seat belt. Blue and red lights flashed from somewhere nearby.

Sometime later, she wasn't sure how long, Sadie was home, in her room, her real room, at the house she shared with Mamo.

Mamo...

Mrs. Fallon held a mug to Sadie's lips and she drank.

✳ ✳ ✳

Morning light woke Sadie. Her eyelids felt thick as she blinked against the brightness.

Thumping sounded on the bed behind her and Sadie rolled over. Shay belly-crawled close and licked Sadie's face. She settled her head on Sadie's chest and blew air through her jowls. Relief flowed through Sadie. Shay was safe.

Nausea filled Sadie's belly knowing Mamo was not.

Mrs. Fallon peered through the doorway. "You're awake."

Sadie nodded.

Mrs. Fallon came in and sat on the edge of the bed. "I'm not sure what to say. I know it's not a good morning, and I know you feel horrible. So do I." She brushed away hair that lay across Sadie's cheek.

"You can say it was all a nightmare, that it didn't really happen." Sadie's voice cracked.

"I wish I could," Mrs. Fallon said. "I would give anything to be able to say that to you right now."

Sadie's eyes filled with tears. "How is Finn?"

"She's going to be sore for a few days, but she'll be okay." A hint of a smile formed on Mrs. Fallon's face. "Your healing power saved her. You saved her."

Sadie shifted and pushed herself to sitting. "But Mamo...I failed and she's..." Tears rolled down Sadie's cheeks.

Shay repositioned her head and whimpered. Sadie draped her arm over Shay's back.

"You can't blame yourself for what happened," Mrs. Fallon said.

"You mean what didn't happen. Mamo didn't get better. She—"

Sadie's vocal chords locked. She wiped her tears and squared her shoulders. "She died."

"Yes," Mrs. Fallon said. "Because of Merinda, not you."

She bit her lip and released it. "And now we just...what?"

"We'll figure that out," Mrs. Fallon said. "But you're cloaked, so you're safe here."

Sadie checked her hand for signs of being Yowie. "Even from Merinda?"

"The police are looking for her."

"But even if she doesn't come after me, even if the police catch her, can't she just call someone else and tell them where I am?" Sadie asked.

Mrs. Fallon shook her head. "The cloaking prevents that. She can tell anyone she wants but the message is immediately wiped from records and memories."

"Except her own."

"While she's here, yes," Mrs. Fallon said.

"You mean, if she leaves Salton, she forgets about me and Salton?"

"She won't forget about you," Mrs. Fallon said. "But she won't know you're in Salton for at least as long as the cloaking lasts."

Shay lifted a front leg and touched Sadie's arm. Sadie suppressed a sob and rubbed the top of Shay's head. "How is everyone else?"

"They're okay," Mrs. Fallon said. "Conner is at my house with Kyle and Brandon. They're taking care of things over there."

Taking care of things. Sadie pictured the blood and damage. And Mamo lying on the floor.

She wrestled down another cry. She had to be strong. She had to be prepared.

"We'll stay here for now." Mrs. Fallon ran her hand down Shay's back. "The boys and Finn will stay here too until things get settled."

Settled? Nothing would ever be settled again.

It was so unfair—she'd accepted the Calling. It was supposed to make things better. It was supposed to help Mamo. But it didn't help and Sadie was alone.

So stupid.

Mrs. Fallon squeezed Sadie's hand. "Do you feel like eating something?"

"No."

"Would you try to eat something?"

Sadie shrugged.

"I'm going to make some eggs. And Shay needs her breakfast."

Shay's ears perked.

"I hope to see you downstairs in a little bit, okay?" Mrs. Fallon stood and called Shay.

Shay nuzzled Sadie's neck.

"It's okay," Sadie said. "I'll be right here." *For now.*

Shay jumped off the bed and followed Mrs. Fallon out of the room.

Sadie listened as their steps moved away and down the stairs. She rolled face down onto her pillow and cried.

✵ ✵ ✵

Sadness engulfed Sadie and pushed her to head downstairs. She needed to do something else to help ease the misery swirling inside her. Maybe food or people or a changed environment would break the cycle, if only for a moment.

Mrs. Fallon sat at the kitchen table with her phone. Next to her was the empty chair where Mamo used to sit.

Sadie's heart wrenched. Her hands trembled.

Mrs. Fallon plunked down her phone and sprang up. She hurried to Sadie and put her arm around Sadie's shoulders. "I'm glad you came down. Can I make you some eggs?" Steam rose from a mug of coffee.

"I guess so." Sadie sat in her spot at the table. She averted her gaze from Mamo's chair, and watched Mrs. Fallon open Mamo's fridge, use Mamo's pans, take out Mamo's utensils. Sadie had seen Mrs. Fallon cook in Mamo's kitchen before, but this time it was different. Sadie wanted to tell Mrs. Fallon to stop, to leave Mamo's things exactly where they were. She clenched her teeth and stayed silent.

"Conner and the boys took Finn to the vet this morning after they checked out of the hotel," Mrs. Fallon said. "He'll bring everyone over here after they're done."

"I thought you said she was okay."

"She is. It was just a precaution." Mrs. Fallon dropped butter into a hot skillet. "He's bringing the dogs' stuff as well." She cracked an egg. It sizzled in the pan.

"What about Mamo?" Sadie opened her shoulders, refusing to let her chest knot tight.

Mrs. Fallon stopped and looked at Sadie. "What do you mean?"

"Where is she?" Sadie asked. "What do we do with her?"

Mrs. Fallon paused. She cracked another egg. "She left directions, her wishes, in case anything ever happened to her." She put a lid on the pan. "She asked to be cremated."

"And then what? We put her on a shelf?" Sadie focused her energy on locking down a scream that threatened escape.

"We'll do something lovely for her," Mrs. Fallon said. "She left a few ideas about where she'd like to have her ashes scattered."

"She likes the garden." Sadie's hand went to the hawk's eye pendant. "And the bees."

"Yes, she mentioned both of those places." Mrs. Fallon dished the eggs onto a plate. She added fresh fruit and a cup of yogurt.

"She never told me her wishes," Sadie said.

Mrs. Fallon set the plate in front of Sadie and sat next to her. "Grown-ups don't like to talk about their passing with kids. It can be scary." She rubbed Sadie's back.

Sadie understood the scary part. She'd never been as afraid in her life as she was right now. She poked an egg yolk and watched the yellow flow over the white.

"But you don't need to worry," Mrs. Fallon said. "Willene spelled out everything she wanted, and I'll make sure it's all taken care of for her, and for you."

Sadie nodded once. "Why do we have eggs?"

"Do you want something else to eat?"

"No. I just don't know why there's food here," Sadie said. "No one lives here. There shouldn't be any food here." Her nostrils flared. "This is Mamo's house, and we moved out, and no one lives here anymore." She dropped her fork.

Mrs. Fallon grabbed Sadie's hand. "This is your home, Sadie."

She pulled her hand away. "It's not. It's Mamo's. And she's dead. She didn't buy groceries. She's dead." Her bottom lip quivered.

"I asked Conner to bring a few things over this morning," Mrs. Fallon said, her voice calm.

"But we shouldn't be here without Mamo."

"This is your home, Sadie," Mrs. Fallon said again. "Even without Willene, this is still your home. But if you don't want to be here, we can stay somewhere else."

"I think that would be good," Sadie said. This wasn't home without Mamo. Sadie didn't have a home.

"Okay." Mrs. Fallon touched Sadie's hand. "Can we talk about where we'll go later? After everyone gets here?"

"Yeah. Fine." She picked up her spoon and scooped yogurt then dumped it back in the cup.

"Why don't you try to eat something? I think it will help you feel a little bit better," Mrs. Fallon said. "I'll talk to Conner and let him know what we're thinking, okay?"

Sadie agreed to eat, but she didn't want to feel better. She didn't deserve to feel better.

She'd let Mamo die.

✳ ✳ ✳

Sadie sat on the back porch with Shay until everyone arrived a couple hours later. She and Shay met them in the foyer.

Finn entered first, her gait slow and limping. She'd been shaved around her wound, and black stitches crisscrossed her pink skin. She wagged her tail at Sadie.

Sadie hunched down and hugged her. "I'm so sorry you got hurt." Sadie wiped away a rogue tear and blinked back others.

Brandon patted Finn's butt. "She's a tough girl. The vet was impressed with how well she was doing, considering how deep the wound was." He scratched her behind the ears. "I think we both know why."

Sadie stood and shrugged. "Like you said, she's a tough girl."

"And she has some tough, and special, friends," Brandon said.

Sadie glanced at him but didn't acknowledge his words.

"The vet tried to put the cone of shame on her, but she refused," Kyle said, a cautious smile on his face. "No way Finn was wearing that thing."

"Cone of shame?" Sadie asked.

"You know, the plastic thing that goes around a dog's head to keep them from licking their stitches," Kyle said. "The vet gave one to us in case Finn bugs her wound, but I don't think she will. She's pretty cool about stuff."

Shay approached Finn. She moved slowly, sniffing Finn's backside, then her ears and mouth, and making her way to Finn's fresh-shaved skin. Shay's nose traveled from the first stitch to the last, then back. She stopped sniffing and licked Finn's cheek.

"Where was Shay last night?" Sadie asked Mrs. Fallon.

"It was too much for her," Mrs. Fallon said. "She's not ready with her training. Once I saw Merinda with a weapon, I sent Shay to the basement."

"How did I miss that?" Sadie asked herself more than anyone else.

"There was a lot going on," Brandon said. "I'm so sorry about your grandmother." He stepped forward and gave Sadie a hug.

"Yeah, that totally sucks." Kyle half-hugged Sadie with two pats on her back. "And sorry."

Conner came in the front door and dropped two dog beds on the floor. His eyes were puffy and red. He turned to Sadie. "My dear girl." He opened his arms wide.

Sadie walked over and threw her arms around his belly. Her tears gushed.

Conner hugged her tight. "This is a terrible day, my dear. A terrible day."

Sadie nodded against his shirt, then let go. "I'm glad you're here."

"Oh my dear, I wouldn't be anywhere else right now." He addressed Brandon and Kyle. "We have a few more things in the car if you boys wouldn't mind giving me a hand?"

Sadie watched them carry in suitcases and a bag of dog food. *What are they doing?* She didn't understand why they unloaded the car if they were going to leave and stay somewhere else.

Conner handed a box to Mrs. Fallon and she carried it into the kitchen. Kyle set two suitcases near the foot of the stairs.

The doorbell rang and Mrs. Fallon answered it. The next door neighbors came in and handed off a casserole. They told everyone how sorry they were, and offered any help that might be needed. Sadie took a seat in the living room. A few minutes later, more neighbors arrived and repeated the routine. Then it happened again, and again a little while later, and one more time after that. Sadie felt like she was on display.

Conner's phone rang several times. Sadie heard him talk about cremation and preparation and scheduling services. He suggested flowers. He suggested music. He asked Mrs. Fallon's opinion. He told Sadie what they'd decided and said he believed Mamo would love it.

How could he know? Before a couple of weeks ago, Conner hadn't seen Mamo in fourteen years.

And how could Mamo love anything? Mamo was dead.

Nessa texted twice and left a voicemail message. Sadie didn't respond.

Why is everyone okay with moving on like it's any other day?

Mrs. Fallon suggested Sadie go upstairs and lie down, but Sadie declined. She didn't want to lie down. But she didn't want to be here either.

Mrs. Fallon assigned Brandon and Kyle different tasks around the house from dusting to vacuuming to wiping down counters. It was another warm October day so she opened windows to air things out. And in the middle of the afternoon, Mrs. Fallon heated a casserole left by one of the neighbors.

"I'm sorry I didn't get out some of this food earlier," Mrs. Fallon said. "The day got away from me."

Sadie felt like the day had slogged by, and it wasn't even two-thirty.

"There's a lot to be done," Conner said. "And no good way to do any of it other than to just keep at it."

"Where are we going from here?" Sadie asked.

"Well, we have to get through this week and the services on Friday," Conner said. "Then we can regroup."

"No, I mean where are we going to stay? I don't want to stay here," Sadie said.

Conner's brows raised and he looked at Mrs. Fallon.

"I apologize, Sadie," Mrs. Fallon said. "I haven't had a chance to talk to Conner yet."

"Can we go back to your house?" Sadie asked, then realized she hadn't been thinking.

"It will be a few days before it's ready," Mrs. Fallon said.

"Yeah, there was blood, like, everywhere." Kyle waved both

hands in the air. "I have no clue how that cleaning company is going to deal with it."

Mrs. Fallon directed a firm stare at Kyle's face.

Kyle's mouth dropped open. "Uh...sorry. I didn't mean—"

"So, we'll go to a hotel." Sadie crossed her arms. "But we're not staying in Mamo's house."

Conner patted Sadie's shoulder. "But this is your home. Willy would want you to be in your home."

Sadie shrugged out from under his touch. "How do you know? It's not like you've been around."

"Perhaps not, but I still know my sister," Conner said. "And she'd be happy to know you were living here."

"With who?" Sadie asked. "With you? Is that part of the deal? You get the house but you have to let me live here too?" She backed away from the group.

Conner held up a hand. "Sadie, I'm not here for—"

"Why are you here?" Sadie's voice pitched higher. "Everything was good before you showed up. You brought Merinda here, and you pressured me when Mamo didn't want you to, and you made me accept the Calling, and it didn't even help. And now I'm a Yowie and Mamo is dead." Sadie sucked air deep into her lungs. "Mamo is dead and it's your fault." She pointed at Conner.

Sadie grabbed her hoodie. "I wish you had been the one that died."

She rushed out of the house, slamming the door behind her.

Sadie shoved her hands in her pockets and pulled up her hood. She headed for the cove.

She crawled through the gap between thick branches and flung herself onto the ground. Bushes entwined above her, forming a natural dome with a bed of downed leaves. She took out her phone and texted Jason: "How do you just not respond to me? What kind of friend are you?" She didn't wait to see if the message was delivered or read. She knew he'd ignore it.

Sadie pushed the phone back in her pocket and covered her eyes with her arms. She wished for a power to bring Mamo back. She called from her mind to some Yowie force, to the Sovereignty, to anyone who would hear her and grant her this one wish. Bring Mamo back. Sadie promised to do whatever the Yowie, or the Sovereignty, or whoever wanted, to be the best Yowie, to live in Yowie form her whole life if that's what it took. Just bring Mamo back.

A breeze blew through, shuddering the dry leaves that clung to their branches.

Sadie smacked both hands into the ground. "Like I have any idea what I'm doing. I accepted this stupid Calling and I have no idea how it works. Mamo promised she'd teach me. She promised." Sadie smacked the ground again and threatened the tears that were building, forcing them to retreat.

She thought about what she'd said to Conner and dropped her face into her hands.

I'm a horrible person.

Conner had brought Merinda to town, but it was Sadie's fault that Mamo was dead. Sadie could have saved her. She could have fought Merinda. And Sadie was one hundred percent sure she would have saved Mamo. Even if Sadie lost to Merinda, at least it would be Sadie waiting to be cremated instead of Mamo.

Why didn't I listen to myself? Why did I let Mamo fight?

Sadie dug her fingers into her scalp. "I am so stupid."

She wasn't going to let that happen again. She was on her own now, and she'd listen to herself and take care of herself. That's all that mattered.

Sadie's phone buzzed. She had text messages from Brandon, Mrs. Fallon, and Nessa. She opened Nessa's: "Where are you? I'm at your house."

Sadie closed the message. She scanned the texts she'd sent to Jason. They were still unread. Even without phone service, he should have emailed her or something by now.

He's just one more person I can't count on.

She checked Brandon's note: "Can I meet you somewhere?"

What was the point in that? He wouldn't always be here for her. She didn't write back to him.

Mrs. Fallon sent a note asking if Sadie was okay. But she had her own family to deal with. Sadie wasn't going to bother Mrs. Fallon with her problems anymore.

Sadie would get through this on her own. Alone.

An empty pit grew in Sadie's stomach. As the sun set, she crawled out of the cove and headed back to her house.

Sadie walked in and found Mrs. Fallon sitting in the living room with Shay. Shay greeted Sadie as if she hadn't seen her for days. Finn slept on a dog bed near the fireplace.

"Oh, thank goodness." Mrs. Fallon stood and embraced Sadie. "I'm so glad you're home safe."

"I'm cloaked, remember?" Sadie hung her hoodie on the banister.

"I wasn't worried about that. Can we talk for a minute?" Mrs. Fallon gestured for Sadie to sit.

Sadie shrugged and took a seat.

"I am sorry about today," Mrs. Fallon said. "I thought you would like to be home right now, and I thought it would be good to be surrounded by people who love you. But I was wrong."

Sadie didn't say anything.

"I still believe being here, in your home, would be better for you right now than being in a hotel room," Mrs. Fallon said. "And I'd like to stay here with you." She motioned toward Finn. "Plus, this is a better place for Finn to heal, and we can both help take care of her."

Sadie's heart twinged thinking about Finn's injury.

"But I asked Conner and the boys to stay at a hotel, so it's just us. You, me, and the dogs," Mrs. Fallon said. "I hope that's okay. But if it's not, we can go to the hotel, too."

Sadie looked around the room at everything familiar, everything Mamo. She watched Finn sleeping, her feet twitching like she dreamed about chasing squirrels. Or probably cryptids. Sadie turned back to Mrs. Fallon. "Okay. We can stay. For Finn."

Mrs. Fallon exhaled. "Thank you. You're doing a nice thing for her."

Sadie stood. "I'm going to bed."

"You don't want something to eat first?"

"I'm tired," Sadie said.

✳ ✳ ✳

Sadie stayed in her room for the next few days. She started each morning and ended each day by examining her body in the mirror. She searched for new hairs, changes in her skin, differences in her eyes and mouth. She checked for long toenails, or odd fingernails, or teeth that looked more like fangs. If she started turning into a Yowie, she wanted to be prepared. She wanted time to hide before anyone saw her. And she was determined to try and figure it out alone.

She was excused from school due to Mamo's death, and Sadie refused to see anyone but Mrs. Fallon. And then it was only for meals if Sadie bothered to eat. She even stopped taking Shay for walks. Sadie asked a few times about Merinda but no one had seen her.

Mrs. Fallon suggested Sadie spend time with Conner to learn about the Calling and the Callahan family but Sadie declined. She couldn't bear to see him, and she was certain he wanted nothing to do with her after she said she'd wished him dead. Sadie stayed in her room, researched Yowie on her own, and ignored unfinished homework. There wasn't any point in doing it since wherever she ended up, it wouldn't be in Salton.

The day of Mamo's memorial service arrived. Sadie put on a sleeveless black dress with black leggings. She crossed the hall to Mamo's room and went into her closet. Mamo's smell enveloped her. Sadie inhaled and hugged a stack of sweaters sitting on the shelf.

Her heart hurt but Sadie refused to cry. She'd had enough crying. She wanted to be strong.

She turned to Mamo's lightweight sweaters. Sadie flipped through the hangers, searching until she found the one she was looking for. It was a white cardigan with splashes of abstract black and yellow meant to resemble honeybees. Mamo loved it and said it was as much a piece of artwork as it was clothing. It was one of Sadie's favorites, too.

She slipped it on over her dress and buttoned it halfway. Her silver charm bracelet tinkled as it fell through the sleeve. Sadie shifted the hawk's eye pendant from inside the dress to outside. It hung in a V against the black background and sparkled. Sadie sat on the end of Mamo's bed and took a deep breath, then another. She closed her eyes and pictured Mamo's face smiling back at her.

A few minutes later, a car picked up Sadie and Mrs. Fallon. They drove in silence to the church. Conner met them at the door and Sadie barely glanced at him. He escorted them to seats in the front of the church where Kyle and Brandon already sat. Sadie scooted into the pew next to Brandon. Mrs. Fallon sat on her right and Conner on the end.

"Hi," Brandon whispered to Sadie.

She nodded.

"Your grandmother was really loved," he said. "I think the whole town is here."

Sadie hadn't noticed the crowd when they walked in. She scanned the space around her and returned her attention to the front. "Yeah, everyone loved her." She swallowed hard.

"I'm really sorry," Brandon said.

Sadie nodded again and shifted her gaze to her lap.

The pastor stepped up to the podium. He said something about love and kindness and goodness of spirit. He said Mamo embodied all of these qualities. He talked about her contributions, he talked about her love of nature, and he asked God to help her family find peace.

Sadie wondered if she could ask God for that, too.

Conner stood and walked to the front. He told stories about growing up with Mamo, and how she often took the big sister thing a little too far, telling him what to do, making him do her chores. The congregation chuckled. He relayed the story about her sneaking off to Woodstock and returning with a peace symbol tattoo on her thigh. It wasn't until their mother got flustered and threatened boarding school that Mamo admitted the mark was ballpoint pen ink. Sadie smiled.

"She brought something else home from Woodstock, something even worse than the tattoo, or so our parents thought at the time," Conner said. "A boyfriend." Another chuckle came from the congregation. "But my parents grew to love him, as did I. He was wonderful to my sister, and they got married and started a family. They raised a fine son, and he, in turn, found a wonderful woman, and the two of them gave us the greatest of gifts, my Great-Niece, Sadie Callahan." He looked at Sadie with tears in his eyes.

Sadie's eyes flooded.

"Willy loved you with all of her very being," Conner said. "And she was so proud of you. You were her light, her happy star, the goodness she saw in every day." His smile quivered. "She described you as joy personified, and there was nothing she wouldn't have done—" His voice caught and he cleared his throat. "There's nothing she wouldn't have done for you. Your smile made her smile. Your happiness brought her happiness. And even though she's not physically with us any more, I guarantee she's sitting right beside you, holding you up. One of the best guardian angels in Heaven watches over you, my dear girl. Love surrounds you from Heaven and earth." Conner gave a slight nod and stepped away from the podium.

Sadie wiped at tears on her cheeks and her eyelashes. Mrs. Fallon handed her a tissue. Brandon took her hand in his. Sadie squeezed it.

After the service, Conner and Mrs. Fallon hosted a reception at Mamo's and Sadie's house. People from Salton flowed in and out, offering condolences and hugs, sharing memories of Mamo, and assuring the family they were there to help, though how Sadie had no idea. Brandon stayed close to Sadie throughout the day but didn't push. Kyle offered to bring Sadie food. And Shay shadowed Finn who was near fully recovered.

As the crowd dwindled, Sadie slipped away to her room. She needed some time alone. But she wanted to be outside in nature, something both she and Mamo loved. Their garden was too crowded with visitors, so Sadie changed her clothes, opened her window, and climbed onto the trellis on the side of the house. It had been years since she'd done this, and then she'd been caught by Mamo as soon as she made it to the ground. She hoped the trellis would still hold her weight.

Sadie weaved her fingers into the vines and pushed with her toes to find footing. She eased her way down. A crosspiece cracked but held. Sadie climbed further. About three feet above ground she jumped.

So far, so good.

Sadie scrambled across the side of the yard and ducked behind the neighbor's bushes. She knew they wouldn't see her because they were at her house. She hurried through their yard, over their back fence, and down the alley toward the path.

A few minutes later, Sadie found herself in the cottonwood forest, moving farther and farther away from town. The fragrance of fall filled her head and leaves crunched under her feet. She stopped on a sunny rock near the creek. She slipped off her shoes and socks and dunked her feet in the water.

Icy cold shot into her. Sadie pressed her lips tight. She kept her feet submerged. Seconds passed and the temperature adjusted, morphing from freezing to refreshing.

Sadie leaned back and closed her eyes. Her lids weighed heavy as if they had small anchors attached. The gurgles of the creek soothed her. She tried not to fall asleep but lost the battle.

✳ ✳ ✳

Shay ran toward Sadie. She grew bigger as she approached, then raced past and shrank as she moved away. Sadie called her name but Shay didn't respond. She kept running. Sadie called again and Shay finally stopped but she didn't come to Sadie. She didn't turn toward Sadie. She faced away and barked over and over and over. Sadie took a step forward and fell into a hole.

Her body jerked.

"Wha—" Sadie braced her hands on the rock and realized she'd been dreaming. Tension eased out and she sat up. Her feet, now dry, were covered with bits of leaves and grass.

She checked the time on her phone. She'd been gone for more than two hours. "At least I was smart enough not to freeze my feet off." She had four messages asking when she'd be home, two from Conner and two from Mrs. Fallon.

Sadie didn't respond to the messages. She'd go back soon enough and no one needed to worry about her. She could take care of herself. But she was glad the messages were only questions about timing, and not about how she was doing.

Sadie was tired of people asking her how she was doing.

A dog barked in the distance.

"Shay?" Sadie held her hand up to block the low sun. She searched the area around her.

Another bark. Sadie adjusted her line of sight. A white form held its ground, its tail up. Sadie yelled Shay's name but she didn't respond.

She leaned back and closed her eyes.

Shay barked again, louder and faster. Sadie ignored her. Shay kept barking.

"Shay, go home," Sadie yelled, not moving from the rock, not opening her eyes. She was done with Shay. Sadie needed to move on and Shay needed to take care of herself. Besides, she was Jason's dog.

Shay barked more, now with deeper tones, more urgency.

Sadie huffed. "Jeez, what is her problem?" She tried to ignore Shay but couldn't. She brushed off her feet and put on her socks and shoes. She walked toward Shay and called her name again, firmly this time. Shay stayed in place and kept barking.

A low, brown form near Shay moved from side to side. Sadie froze. Shay growled.

Sadie ran, crashing past branches and leaping rocks. "Shay!"

Shay stopped barking but didn't turn. She stayed fixated on the brown form. Sadie was close enough now to see it was a Yowie, and it was only about thirty feet away from Shay.

Merinda.

Sadie stopped at Shay's side. "Okay, it's okay." Sadie breathed hard. "C'mon, Shay." Sadie pushed her hand against Shay's chest but she didn't budge. "Let's go home. I'll get you a treat. Do you want a treat?" Shay's focus stayed locked. Sadie'd never known Shay to choose something else over a treat.

Merinda, still low to the ground, took a step forward.

Sadie rose up and pointed. "Don't you even try it, Merinda. Or I'll make it so you never shift again. Do you understand me?" Sadie's heart raced. Would Tae Kwon Do work on a Yowie?

Merinda rose on two legs. Even at that distance, Sadie could see how Merinda towered over her. She had to be at least seven feet tall.

Sadie's instincts said run. But no way would she leave Shay.

"Fine, Merinda." Sadie flung her arms up and stepped in front of Shay. Shay adjusted her position to again be at Sadie's side. "You want to fight? Fine. You think I'm scared of you?" She flicked her wrist. "Well, you look pretty damn-scary-ugly, so yeah. But I'm not backing down. I'm not letting you hurt anyone else I care about."

Merinda's head tilted to the side. She seemed to be looking at Sadie's bracelet.

"What? You like shiny things?" Sadie wiggled her arm. "You think you're going to take this too? Give it a try. I promise I won't make it easy."

Merinda took another step forward.

Sadie sprang into her fighting stance.

Merinda looked at Sadie and sniffed the air.

What is she doing?

Sadie searched for rocks or a branch. She mapped out two positions where she could pick up rocks small enough to throw, but large enough to still do damage. She saw nothing that would work as a club.

Merinda took one more step.

Sadie braced herself. Adrenaline zipped through her.

Merinda sniffed again, stared, then turned and lumbered away, deeper into the cottonwoods.

Sadie dropped her fists to her side. Shay sat.

"What just happened?"

Shay wagged her tail.

Sadie hunched and examined Shay for wounds. "Are you okay?"

Shay licked Sadie's face.

"You ready to go?"

Shay stood and headed toward home.

Sadie followed but kept checking over her shoulder for any big, brown beasts.

She saw nothing.

SEVENTEEN
Home

Adrenaline drained from Sadie's system as she headed home. Shay scampered ahead but periodically stopped and waited for Sadie to catch up. Once she did, Shay again hurried ahead.

Sadie smiled at Shay's antics and realized the dog made her smile every day, even on the saddest ones. Even when Sadie pushed her away and locked her out of her room, Shay would do something goofy to get Sadie's attention.

Sadie stopped walking. Her heart hurt like it was tucking in on itself.

She couldn't lose Shay.

Sadie dropped to the ground, her legs folded beneath her. Her mind spun.

What Conner said during Mamo's service...he didn't hate Sadie. Why didn't he hate her? She'd said horrible things to him. And Mrs. Fallon had done so much to help her, before and after Mamo's loss. Even Kyle wanted to help. And Nessa.

And Brandon.

Shay galloped up and skidded to a stop, kicking dirt onto Sadie's pants. She grabbed Shay's head and kissed her between the eyes. "I love you, you know."

Shay snorted and wriggled her body. She bounced in place until Sadie stood.

She had to figure out a way to stay in Salton. Even after everything, she did care about Conner, and he seemed to care about her. Maybe he'd stay in Salton? Mamo would want them to stay close.

Sadie picked up her pace and followed Shay toward home.

A new text arrived as Sadie walked in the front door of her home. It was from Mrs. Fallon: "Fallon house is done. Helping Conner and boys move stuff. Drop off Shay and come over."

Sadie's brows scrunched. Sadie hadn't taken Shay with her, she just happened to find her. And why did Mrs. Fallon call it "Fallon house?"

Sadie chalked up the weirdness to grown-ups and text messaging. She replied: "Ok. Be there in a bit."

Finn sauntered up and greeted Sadie and Shay. Sadie sat on the floor, rubbed Finn's belly, and examined her stitches. She was nearly healed. Sadie lightly touched the pink, puckered skin. Heat radiated from her fingertips and she yanked her hand back.

She turned her hand over and checked her own skin. Nothing different, nothing glowing, nothing red from heat. She studied her other hand. Same as it ever was.

Sadie eased her hand back over Finn's wound. Her palm warmed. She placed a fingertip on a stitch. Heat intensified. Sadie ran her finger down Finn's puckered skin.

The stitches dissolved.

The skin smoothed.

Sadie's jaw dropped.

All that remained was a light pink line surrounded by stubbly fur. Sadie repeated the process using her whole palm. Finn's fur filled in like it had never been shaved away.

Sadie covered her mouth with her hands then dropped them. She eyed them again but they were just hands. Her hands. With a special gift inside.

A small smile came to Sadie's face when she remembered Mamo's words: The power to heal is one you will treasure.

Finn jumped up and licked Sadie's face. Finn chased Shay and tackled her in the foyer. Shay play-bit Finn's ankles and wriggled from under her then ran upstairs, Finn close behind. They both bolted back down and zoomed into the kitchen. Sadie heard them slurping up water.

She walked into the kitchen and opened the door for the dogs. Bags of trash from the reception sat on the patio, the only sign there had been so many people in the house earlier. She went upstairs and showered, still feeling sticky after everything that happened with Shay and Merinda. Sadie dried off and got dressed, put her wet hair into a ponytail, and went downstairs. She brought the dogs inside, giving each a treat and a snuggle. Sadie shut the back door and headed for Mrs. Fallon's house.

A police car was sitting in the driveway when Sadie arrived. She hurried up the front walk.

Mrs. Fallon sat in the living room with two police officers. One of them stood.

"Is everything okay?" Sadie asked. She stood on the edge of the living room, near the stairs. She didn't see or hear anyone else.

"Uh, these...officers believe they know where Merinda is." Mrs. Fallon's voice was void of warmth.

"Oh." Sadie turned to the officer who was standing. The back of his shirt was untucked. "Great. Did you arrest her?"

He tilted his head. "Not yet. You're Sadie?"

Sadie glanced from the policeman to Mrs. Fallon and back. "Yeah...do you know where she is?"

"We sure do," the policeman said. "This is going to be a very good day."

"Yeah, after you catch her." Sadie looked at Mrs. Fallon again.

Mrs. Fallon raised her brows.

A quiver rolled through Sadie's gut.

The standing policeman smiled and put his hand on his chest. "I'm Samuel. And my partner there is Hank."

Hank stood. He was a few inches shorter than Samuel and his uniform hung on him like it was a couple sizes too big.

"I can't tell you how great it is for us to be in the same room with you," Samuel said.

Sadie stepped back. "Well, that's nice. But where is everybody? In the kitchen maybe?" She gestured toward the kitchen with one hand and grabbed the phone in her pocket with the other.

"Oh, I almost forgot your cell phone," Samuel said. "You can give that to Hank."

Hank held his hand out.

Sadie didn't move.

The corner of Samuel's mouth ticked up. "Now, Sadie, don't make a thing out of this. We have weapons and you don't. But we don't want anyone to get hurt, so just hand over the phone."

"Why are you doing this?" Sadie flicked her eyes from Samuel to Mrs. Fallon and back. She put her phone in Hank's hand. "Policemen are supposed to help people."

"I can't disagree with you there," Samuel said. "But there are bad policemen."

Hank chuckled. "But we're not bad policemen because we're not policemen."

"Right you are, Hank my man," Samuel said. "So we cannot be blamed for tarnishing the fine reputation of local law enforcement. We just borrowed these uniforms."

"It took a little persuading," Hank said.

"Yes it did, yes it did." Samuel narrowed his eyes at Sadie. "We are very talented at persuading people."

Sadie's heart beat in her belly. "What do you want?" She moved toward Mrs. Fallon but Samuel stopped her and told her to stay where she was.

"It's safer for everyone if you stay right there where we can see you," Samuel said. "We don't need any surprise memory wipes, or whatever other trick you may have up your sleeve."

Sadie wished she was still making people fall asleep. But that didn't happen anymore, and she never knew how she made it happen in the first place. Sadie wasn't sure how memory wipes worked, but she thought she had to touch someone to do it.

The back door slammed. "How long do we have to wait for that twerp?" Merinda entered from the kitchen, fully human, and stopped when she saw Sadie. She clapped her hands. "I spoke too soon. Our payday has arrived."

"You're looking better since the last time I saw you," Sadie said.

"I might have had a few hairs out of place after Willy attacked me, but no worries," Merinda said. "I'm feeling good. Strong." She sneered. "Lovely service, by the way."

"You were there?" Sadie hated the idea that Merinda had seen any part of Mamo's memorial service.

"Let's just say I was like a little birdie on the wall. I couldn't resist offering my good riddances." She walked over and sat next to Mrs. Fallon. "I see you met my new friends." She flicked her hand at Samuel and Hank.

"I thought you were loopy when you told us Sadie Callahan was here," Samuel said. "But she's the real deal and I'm seeing dollar signs." His lip curled.

"You can't believe how hard it was for me to recruit some help," Merinda said to Sadie. "That stupid cloaking stopped every message I sent. Except the last one." She leaned back. "I offered these two something else, something only I could give them. Something that had nothing to do with you, princess. And given the sorts of boys they are, they took me up on the offer. It wasn't until they arrived in Salton that I was able to offer them a share of the bounty on you instead. Lucky for me, they accepted the trade. And bonus— they brought me a few little pills that helped me get my strength back. No wonder my mama likes these things so much."

Sadie's skin crawled. "So now what?"

"You get to go for a long ride in a police car," Samuel said. "And if you're a good girl, we'll even turn on the siren for you."

Mrs. Fallon stood. "She's not going anywhere with you."

Merinda yanked on the back of Mrs. Fallon's shirt. "Sit down."

Mrs. Fallon spun and slapped Merinda hard. "You should be ashamed of yourself after everything Willy and Conner did for you."

Merinda sprang up and jutted her chin. "Did for me? Willy pushed me around and never said I was good enough. It was always 'try harder try harder try harder.'" She poked Mrs. Fallon in the chest. "Maybe she should have tried harder to be nice to me."

"You're wrong," Mrs. Fallon said, her voice stern. "You should have listened. You should have tried harder. Willene believed you could be better."

"I'm better than Willy ever was." Merinda's voice screeched.

"Seriously? You're a murderer." Sadie squared her shoulders. "And you'll pay for everything you've done."

Merinda back-handed Mrs. Fallon, shoving her down onto the couch. "Not today, princess. Today is all about you."

Sadie clenched and unclenched her hands. "Are you okay, Mrs. Fallon?"

She nodded.

"This is a lot of fun, ain't it, Hank?" Samuel elbowed his partner. "We may just get ourselves a full-on catfight."

"I'd pay to see that," Hank said.

"That's just it," Samuel said. "We'll get the show, plus the reward

when we collect our bounty. Basically, we're getting paid to play."
He crossed his arms and grinned.

Sadie forced her expression to appear neutral. "Where is everybody else?"

"What do you mean?" Merinda smacked her lips.

"Did you do something to them?" Sadie's muscles twitched.

"Not yet," Merinda said. "But we can change that if you don't do what you're told."

"You've got me, Merinda." Sadie pointed at Samuel and Hank. "You've got two guys with guns, plus your Yowie-ass self. What can I do against that?"

Merinda scrunched her brows. "You're not going to fight?"

"Fight with what? My invisible, bullet-deflecting shield?" What Sadie wouldn't give for an invisible bullet-deflecting shield right now.

"Well, that's no fun." Merinda stomped her foot. "I wanted to threaten to hurt your friends and make you all upset before we left."

"Just..." Sadie pressed her hands together. "Where are they, Merinda?"

Merinda tipped her head at Hank. He took out his gun and went out the back door. A minute later, in came Kyle, Brandon, and Conner, all with their hands duct taped together. Conner had a piece of duct tape over his mouth. All three had tears in their shirts and spots of blood soaked through. Hank lined them up against the wall behind Mrs. Fallon and opposite Sadie.

Sadie rushed forward.

Samuel aimed his weapon. "Nope."

Sadie stopped.

Samuel directed her back to her spot by the stairs.

"What did you do to them?" Sadie glared.

"They wrapped us in razor wire so we couldn't move," Brandon said.

Sadie cringed. She needed to get the crazy people away from the people she cared about.

"And Conner would not stop blabbing at me," Merinda said. "Even after I tightened the wire."

Conner had more blood on him than the others. He was pale and seemed to be shaking.

"Okay, Merinda," Sadie said. "I'll go with you now."

Brandon stepped forward. "No, Sadie."

Hank clocked Brandon in the head with his gun. Brandon staggered.

"Stop, stop." Sadie held up her hands. "I said I'd go. Don't hurt them anymore."

"Sadie..." Mrs. Fallon's eyes watered.

"I'm going." Sadie heard a noise behind her in the basement. "It's better for everyone this way."

Mrs. Fallon mouthed, "No."

Sadie looked at Mrs. Fallon and Brandon and tried to reassure them. She was at a loss.

"Fine, let's go then." Merinda stood. "I am looking forward to getting paid."

Sadie turned toward the front door. Samuel and Hank came behind her with their guns pointed at her back.

A louder noise came from the basement and Sadie stepped to the side.

Shay rocketed from the landing and clamped her jaws onto Samuel's arm. He wailed and fell, dropping the weapon. A second later his body shimmered. Shay sank her teeth into his neck. The shimmer faded and Samuel's eyes rolled up.

Brandon jumped onto Hank, throwing his bound arms around Hank's neck. He leaned back, choking off Hank's air. Hank fired his gun past Brandon's head into the wall behind him. Sadie kicked Hank's knee, then his thigh. He dropped to the floor unconscious.

Mrs. Fallon ran to help Conner who'd fallen to the ground.

A gunshot fired.

"Enough!"

Everyone froze. Merinda held Samuel's gun in the air. "I hate that dog." She aimed the weapon at Shay.

"No!" Sadie launched herself at Merinda but Finn was faster. She leaped onto Merinda from behind, knocking her forward. The gun fired, a glass vase shattered, and Merinda dropped the weapon. She scrambled away and shimmered. But she didn't switch to starling.

Merinda shifted to Yowie.

Finn clamped onto Merinda.

Merinda flicked her arm, throwing Finn off her and into the back of the couch. Finn lay stunned. Merinda moved toward her.

Sadie rushed over and blocked Merinda's path. "You will not hurt anyone else."

Merinda swung.

Sadie ducked. "Everyone get out of here." Adrenaline spiked through her. Sadie felt hot.

Merinda swung again and Sadie blocked with her right arm. Merinda's eyes widened. Sadie punched Merinda in the gut and doubled her over. Sadie hit her with an upper cut then front kicked her in the chest. Merinda crashed into the wall and slid down.

Merinda shimmered and shifted to starling. Shay snatched Merinda out of the air, clamped her jaws, and shook her head until the bird's neck snapped. Shay spit Merinda onto the floor.

Sadie stared at the bird to be certain it didn't move. She scanned the room to make sure everyone was safe. All eyes were fixed on her.

"What?"

Kyle looked at the ceiling. "Nice...uh...punches." He sat with Brandon on an unconscious Hank, his taped hands pressing down.

Mrs. Fallon hurried over and threw a blanket around Sadie.

"It's okay, I'm not cold." Sadie looked down. She was naked. "Oh my gosh." She snugged the blanket tight around her. "What happened? Did Merinda do something to me?"

Mrs. Fallon pressed her lips together. "Not Merinda, Sadie. That was all you."

Kyle snickered.

Mrs. Fallon gave him a look that said, "grounded forever unless you stop."

The grin dropped from Kyle's face.

Sadie noticed torn clothes on the floor. She scurried into the kitchen away from everyone.

Mrs. Fallon and the dogs followed. Mrs. Fallon removed a pair of scissors from a drawer. "I'm going to cut them loose. I'll be right back." She returned a minute later and handed Sadie sweats and a sweatshirt. "I borrowed these from Brandon." She held up the blanket and Sadie dressed behind it.

"What happened?" Sadie sat on the floor with the dogs.

Mrs. Fallon pulled up a chair near them. "You shifted."

"I couldn't have. I didn't notice anything." Sadie examined her hands.

"But you did," Mrs. Fallon said. "Full Yowie. Gave Merinda quite a shock."

Sadie remembered the heat, remembered the look in Merinda's eye. "That's why I...she wasn't taller than me."

Mrs. Fallon stroked Finn's head. "I think you had at least a foot on her."

"And my clothes..." Sadie covered her mouth with her hands.

"A little bit of a size difference," Mrs. Fallon said. "One of the many reasons Yowie choose to live their lives in one particular form, usually human. Saves on the clothing bill." She smiled.

"Everyone saw me naked," Sadie said. "I can never leave this kitchen again. I can't ever face any of them again for the rest my life."

Mrs. Fallon stroked the back of Sadie's head. "It was one moment, and as embarrassed as you feel right now, this too shall pass. I promise." She stood and got two glasses out of the cupboard. "Besides, being the granddaughter of a woman who met her husband at Woodstock, I think you'd be pretty comfortable running around in your birthday suit." She filled the glasses with water and handed one to Sadie.

"Comfortable in my own house, when I know who is around, sure," Sadie said. "But not in front of...them." She swept her arm in the direction of the living room.

"I know it's hard, but try to let it go," Mrs. Fallon said. "I'll talk to Kyle about being respectful, but I don't think you need to worry about Brandon. And Conner knows how Yowie shifting works—he won't give it a second thought. Just remember the good you did, that we all did. Merinda can't bother us anymore, and Hank's memory will be wiped. You're safe. We're all safe."

Sadie ran her hands down the backs of both dogs.

"Okay?" Mrs. Fallon asked.

Sadie paused. "Was it horrible? Was I...was I horrible? A monster?" She kept her eyes on the dogs.

"Not hardly," Mrs. Fallon said. "I think you were rather spectacular."

"You have to say that."

"Hmm," Mrs. Fallon said. "I believe I've acquired enough wisdom and self-confidence that I don't have to say anything I don't want to say." She touched Sadie's chin and turned her head to see her face. "I'm sticking with spectacular."

"Spectacularly ugly," Sadie said. "I'm surprised the dogs didn't take off running."

"Let's think about this for a minute." Mrs. Fallon held out her index finger. "One, the dogs didn't run when they saw you as Yowie, and they're trained to defend against bad cryptids."

"Yeah…"

"And two, you used your ability to defeat bad people, which is a very not-ugly thing to do," Mrs. Fallon said.

"Yeah, but—"

"And three—how did you feel when you were Yowie?"

"What do you mean?" Sadie asked.

"Did you feel uncomfortable? Smelly? Ugly?"

"I didn't feel anything different," Sadie said. "I didn't even know I'd changed. I felt like myself."

"Because you were yourself," Mrs. Fallon said. "You are Sadie Callahan, period. Yes, you have the ability to present yourself in two different forms, and maybe someday you'll have even more forms to choose from. But you're always Sadie Callahan."

"I guess."

"Well, I know," Mrs. Fallon said. "Your Yowie form is merely another shell you can choose to wear. And you wear it well."

Sadie let out a small laugh. "Like a fur coat."

"An animal-friendly fur coat." Mrs. Fallon winked. "And a powerful one at that, seeing as how you saved the day."

"I am glad about that part for sure," Sadie said. "Mamo always said to look for the bright side in every challenge."

"She was a smart woman," Mrs. Fallon said. "That philosophy has served us both well over the years." She petted Finn's head. "Speaking of bright sides, I noticed Finn's stitches were gone."

Sadie held up her hands and waggled them. "My gift."

"Ah. One of many you'll have, I suspect," Mrs. Fallon said. "Spend a few minutes working on them now, would you?" She gestured toward Shay and Finn. "And after we're done with the sheriff, and if you can bear to look at Conner and the boys," Mrs. Fallon smirked, "you can heal their punctures and other wounds."

"What about you?" Sadie asked, holding her warm hands over the dogs. "Are you okay?"

"Wrenched wrist, a few bruises," Mrs. Fallon said. "Add me to your queue, but let's take care of them first. Kyle doesn't do well with pain."

Sadie smiled. "Will do."

"Now I've got a dead bird to dispose of before the police arrive," Mrs. Fallon said.

"And we'll let the police believe Merinda is on the run again?" Sadie asked.

Mrs. Fallon nodded. "It's easier than trying to explain a dead starling in the house."

For a moment Sadie thought that might be the easiest part to explain, but changed her mind. "I guess it would be weird to talk about the attack and then have to make up something about a bird suddenly flying in from nowhere."

"Exactly," Mrs. Fallon said.

✳ ✳ ✳

The police arrived and blue and red lights flashed outside of Mrs. Fallon's house for the second time in a week. After Sheriff Gunderson's team got everyone's statement, he told them they were free to go and asked that they stay somewhere else for a few days while the police conducted their investigation.

They all went to Sadie's house and discovered the back door open. It answered the question about how the dogs got from here to Mrs. Fallon's house—at least one of them knew how to use the lever door handle. From there they easily entered Mrs. Fallon's house through the downstairs dog door.

Everyone soon went to bed but Sadie couldn't sleep. She tiptoed down to the kitchen to make a cup of tea and found Mrs. Fallon sitting at the table nursing one of her own.

"You gave up counting sheep?" Mrs. Fallon said.

Sadie took a mug from the cupboard and filled it with hot water from the teakettle Mrs. Fallon already had on the stove. "I've never understood why that's supposed to work. I think too much about the sheep. Are they black or white or both? Why are they jumping the fence? Is it some kind of game or are they going somewhere? Or running from something?"

"I can see why that doesn't work for you," Mrs. Fallon said, chuckling. "You have an analytical mind."

"Well, whatever it is, tonight my mind will not stop thinking." Sadie opened a drawer and got out a bag of orange-ginger tea, one of Mamo's favorites.

"I'm guessing Willene's on your mind?" Mrs. Fallon asked.

Sadie sat and set the mug of steaming tea on the table. "I feel like losing Mamo is going to hurt forever."

Mrs. Fallon put her hand on Sadie's. "I know the feeling."

"And then there's the other stuff too," Sadie said. "Like why didn't Mamo or Conner fight as Yowie, and how do I figure out this Yowie stuff and the Calling and what all that really means, and what's the next Calling thing that's going to happen, and where I'm going to live, and all without Mamo." She shoved down tears.

"I can help you," Mrs. Fallon said, "but first, what do you mean where you're going to live? Didn't Willene ever talk to you?"

"Talk to me about what?"

Mrs. Fallon looked up and shook her fist. "Willene Callahan, if you can hear me up there, know that I'm very cross with you right now." She turned her face to Sadie's and held both of Sadie's hands in hers. She took a deep breath. "Do you remember me saying Willene had taken care of things in case something happened to her? That she'd left instructions?"

"Yeah, that she wanted to be cremated and stuff," Sadie said.

"Yes, but that's not all," Mrs. Fallon said. "When you told me she hadn't talked to you about things, I assumed it was only the funeral arrangements. I didn't realize she'd told you nothing."

"Nothing about what?"

"Sadie, Willene and I made arrangements for me to be your legal guardian in the case of her death. The paperwork is all in order, everything is set." Mrs. Fallon squeezed Sadie's hands. "So if it's okay with you, I'd love to have you officially be part of our crazy family."

Sadie felt like she was floating. "Seriously?"

"Yes. Seriously," Mrs. Fallon said.

Sadie sprang from her chair and threw her arms around Mrs. Fallon's neck. "Thank you."

Mrs. Fallon hugged back. "So, that's a yes?"

Sadie returned to her chair. "Yes, yes. Triple yes. Yes, infinity." Her heart pounded.

Mrs. Fallon smiled. "That makes me very happy." She rubbed Sadie's arm. "And you poor thing, I'm sorry I didn't make things clear earlier. I was insensitive."

"It's okay," Sadie said. You didn't know. I'm just so happy right now. And relieved. And still really sad but also happy. Is that even possible?"

"Emotions are a tricky business," Mrs. Fallon said.

"Okay, well, at least in this moment, I feel a lot of happy, Mrs. Fallon."

"And I'm very glad about that, but let's get a couple of things straight right off the bat." Mrs. Fallon leaned back in her chair. Her expression became serious.

Sadie's hands felt shaky.

"First, no more calling me Mrs. Fallon," she said. "It's way too formal. Please call me Lena." Her smile returned.

Tension slipped out of Sadie's shoulders. "I can do that."

"And second, and you don't have to decide now, but you own this house, and I think it would be nice for you to stay here and be close to your happy memories of Willene," Lena said. "You'd still have the garden, and the beehives, and everything you shared here with her. There's nothing tying me to my house, and I'd love to move in here with you. But if you think that would make you uncomfortable—"

"No, I like it," Sadie said. "I would love that."

"You're sure?"

"Definitely," Sadie said.

"Then it's settled," Lena said. "I'll make the arrangements. And if for some reason you change your mind, you let me know."

Sadie agreed, but she knew she wouldn't change her mind.

"As for your other questions," Lena said, "Conner will teach you about the Calling. You're not alone in that."

"Okay." Sadie was a little worried about Conner after everything that happened. "But is he all right? I mean, I don't want to make him more stressed."

"You are never a stress to any of us," Lena said. "Don't give that another thought. Conner will be right by your side."

"But he's worn down, and he didn't shift to Yowie," Sadie said. "He and Mamo both could have fought as Yowie and then she might..."

A sad smile formed on Lena's face. "Shape-shifting is like a muscle—if you don't use it, the muscle weakens and shifting becomes more of a challenge. Willene and Conner lived their lives as human and their ability was compromised." She brushed aside a piece of hair. "Though I think Conner tried. I'm guessing that's why Merinda wrapped them in the razor wire, to prevent him from changing."

Anger rushed into Sadie as she thought about what Merinda had done, what she had taken from Sadie. She wasn't sorry Merinda was dead.

Lena touched Sadie's hand. "Are you okay?"

Sadie looked at Lena, thankful that she wasn't alone. "Yeah. Well, no. But I think I will be." Sadie hugged Lena tight.

EIGHTEEN
Reunion

Sadie slept late the next morning. As she woke, she rolled over and soon smelled eggs, bacon, and pancakes. Her stomach growled.

Shay pushed open Sadie's door and jumped on the bed. She rolled onto her back for a belly rub.

"How do you know I'm awake every single time?" Sadie rubbed Shay's pink skin. "Are you spying on me?"

Shay's tongue lolled out the side of her mouth and she wiggled side to side. Sadie gave her one more good scratch on the chest.

"Alright, time to get up."

Shay went back downstairs and Sadie got dressed. She headed to the kitchen but stopped at the bottom of the stairs. Butterflies flit through her belly. Brandon and Kyle were both in the kitchen. Sadie had barely talked to either of them after she'd lost her clothes. After they saw her naked. She avoided looking at them any more than she had to when she healed their wounds. But now she'd have to spend time with them.

Comments from Mamo played in Sadie's head: It's just a body. Everyone has one. We're too uptight. Skin is skin. Who really cares?

I really care.

But Sadie couldn't avoid Brandon and Kyle forever. She couldn't even avoid them through breakfast.

She held up her head and walked into the kitchen. "Good morning." Sadie picked up a plate.

"Good morning," Brandon said.

"Hey." Kyle waved his fork.

"The pancakes smell good," Sadie said. "And the bacon. And everything." She stabbed two pancakes and put them on her plate.

"Yeah," Brandon said. "And they are good. Right, Kyle?"

"Right," Kyle said. "Good pancakes. And bacon." He crunched into a piece.

"So, I slept well," Sadie said. "Did you guys sleep well?" She dished scrambled eggs into a bowl. She didn't like them to touch the syrup.

"I slept great," Brandon said. "How about you, Kyle?"

"Okay, this is dumb," Kyle said.

Sadie set down the syrup. "You didn't sleep well?"

"C'mon, you know what I mean," Kyle said.

Sadie felt her face flush.

Brandon punched Kyle's arm. "Dude, leave it alone."

"And then what? We act all weird around each other forever?" Kyle asked. "Dad says you should confront your fears. Just say out loud what you think is too scary to say out loud, and then it's not scary anymore."

Sadie shut her eyes and wished she could disappear.

"Not this time," Brandon said.

"Totally disagree," Kyle said. "So I'm doing it. We saw Sadie naked."

Sadie dropped her face into her hands.

Brandon punched Kyle's arm again. "You're embarrassing her."

"How can I be embarrassing her?" Kyle asked. "She was there. She knows what happened."

"But she probably doesn't want to think about it," Brandon said.

"Okay, but when you really *do* think about it, it's not a big deal," Kyle said. "I mean, sure, it was surprising, but she'd just saved our asses, so I think that is the bigger deal."

Sadie lowered her hands.

"No way was it the kind of moment where you're like, oh look, there's a naked person." Kyle took another bite of bacon. "It was more like hey-thanks-naked-person-for-saving-my-ass."

Brandon canted his head from side to side. "That's true." He swallowed a bite of pancake. "And if the Incredible Hulk can do it, why can't Sadie?"

Sadie carried her plate over and eased into a chair. "Doesn't the Incredible Hulk at least get to keep his pants on? How does he do that?"

Brandon and Kyle smiled at her and she laughed. "I can't believe I'm going to say this out loud, but Kyle is right. Talking about it does make it way less scary."

"Hah," Kyle said. "Chalk one up to good parenting from dear old Dad. I knew it would work since that's how I got over my fear of people finding out I was afraid of kittens." He took a drink of orange juice.

Brandon's eyebrows raised. "Kittens?"

Kyle held up his hands. "What? I was, like, four years old. I got over it." He picked up his fork and pointed it at Sadie. "But you're right about the Hulk and his pants. That's weird."

✳ ✳ ✳

The next day, everyone helped move more of Lena's things to Sadie's house. During a break, Conner asked to speak to Sadie on the patio.

She sat next to him on the outdoor sofa. "Are you feeling okay?"

"I'll be honest, I miss my sister," Conner said. "I barely got her back before I lost her again."

Sadie's lip quivered. "Yeah, I get that. But I'm glad you're here, and I'm sorry about everything I said before—"

He placed his hand on Sadie's. "Don't think about that for another second. Emotions were running high, for all of us. Still are for that matter."

"But still—"

"Not another second," Conner said. "We're family. And family loves, and supports, and forgives. And I hope you can forgive me."

"For what?" Sadie asked.

"For not being able to do more to save Willy." Conner swallowed hard. "And for pushing too hard about the Calling. I never intended to make it a burden for you, but I fear I did."

Sadie shrugged. "Everything felt like a burden. Moving, or hiding, or accepting the Calling...it was all going to be hard, no matter what I chose."

"Regardless, I hope you'll give me another chance," Conner said.

"I don't know what you mean."

He tipped his head to the side. "My dear, you truly are a treasure to me, not because of the Calling, and not because we lost Willy, but because you're my great-niece. I've long wanted to be part of your life." He sighed. "When your parents announced they were expecting a little girl, well, there was no greater celebration in our family, that is until the day you were born."

"Oh, I didn't realize..." Sadie glanced at the wrinkles on the back of his hand. "I didn't know you knew them that well."

"I loved them like they were my own kids. We were still

reeling from the loss of your parents when you and Willy disappeared," Conner said. "I understood why she did it, but it hurt. I immediately started looking for you both and I didn't stop. I just wish I'd found you earlier, before the Calling, before this whole mess." He rubbed the top of his forehead. "Maybe things would be different."

"Mamo would say that it's where we are that matters, not what might have been." A twinge needled Sadie's heart.

Conner pulled his hands down his face. "I've put you through so much. I'm so sorry about that."

"It's not your fault. And I'm not mad, not anymore," Sadie said. "I do have a lot to figure out. Maybe you can show me some things or give me some pointers before you go. Or if there are books I should read or stuff on the internet, I can read that. And maybe we can talk on the phone sometimes?"

"I hope I can do more than that," Conner said. "If you'll let me."

"What do you mean?"

"I'd like to stay in Salton and give us a chance to get to know each other better," Conner said. "And I'll be able to help you with the Calling, and your powers, and whatever else you need."

A small smile crept onto Sadie's face. "For real?"

"Yes," Conner said. "For real. Lena's already offered her former home to me, but I told her I wanted to talk to you first and get your okay."

"It's totally okay," Sadie said. "But you could move in here with us."

"I would like that," Conner said. "But for now I think it's best to let you ladies adjust to your new family unit while we all figure out how we best work together. Besides, I can be something of a slob, and no one needs that kind of roommate thrust upon them." He smirked.

Sadie stood and threw her arms around his neck. "Thank you."

"Ah, my dear, no need to thank me." He hugged her back. "I'm doing this for purely selfish reasons. I get to spend time with you and make a few new friends in the process." He squeezed Sadie tight.

✳ ✳ ✳

The next few days were spent packing up Mamo's clothes and donating them to charity, a request she'd made in her will. Sadie kept a few items of clothing, like the sweater she'd worn to Mamo's service. At Lena's suggestion, Sadie also kept all of Mamo's jewelry. Sadie could decide over time what pieces she wanted to keep, and what she might want to give away.

Sadie spent time reconnecting with Nessa, and enjoying time with Brandon. The more she and Brandon talked, the more Sadie realized how much they had in common. Feelings of sadness and happiness continued to mix and wave through her.

The next day, Lena got an urgent call and had to head to London. She brought everyone together in the living room. "Things have gone a bit sideways and I need to go. Now."

"Is everyone okay?" Sadie asked. "Is Jason okay?"

Lena took a deep breath. "Not right now, no. But I think we can change that. I'm determined to bring them home." She turned to Conner. "You can stay here with the kids?"

"Of course."

"Thank you," Lena said. "I'll update you all as soon as I know anything, but if everything goes according to plan, we'll have them home soon."

Sadie's mouth parched. "But what if...what if you don't come back?" She didn't know if she could deal with losing Lena when she was just barely able to get through a whole day without crying about Mamo.

Lena placed her hands on Sadie's shoulders. "First off, I'm not tackling this alone. I have help waiting for me in London. And we have a plan." She stayed focused on Sadie's face. "But even if something happens and I don't come back, believe me when I say you are one of the strongest people I know. You can get through anything, and you won't do it alone. Don't forget you also have Conner, and Kyle, and Brandon."

Sadie nodded.

"And Yowie-you," Lena said.

Sadie smiled.

Lena hugged her. "Don't worry." She released her hold. "I'm determined not to let this family get smaller."

Later that day, Sadie sent another text to Jason: "Your grandmother says you're in trouble. Sorry about earlier messages. Hope you're okay."

She tapped send.

※ ※ ※

Lena was gone for a couple of days, then texted Sadie and told her they were on their way back to the United States.

Jason was finally coming home.

Sadie texted back: "Great news."

Lena thought it would be easiest for everyone to meet at her old house and asked Sadie to arrange it.

The car pulled up in front of Lena's house around seven-thirty p.m. Lena walked in first, followed by Jason. Lena hugged Sadie. Shay tackled Jason in the foyer.

Jason dropped to his knees and pushed the top of his head into her scruff. She wriggled and swerved to lick Jason's cheeks and eyelids and neck.

"I have missed you so much, Shay." Jason scratched her ears and her back. Shay mouthed Jason's wrist and fell onto the floor for a belly rub. "Good girl. It's so good to see you, you have no idea."

"I don't need a belly rub, but I'd love a hug," Sadie said.

Jason jumped up and hugged her. "Are you okay? Grandma Lena said things have been tough. I'm sorry I didn't get your texts."

"That's okay," Sadie said. "But I'm really glad you're back. For a while, I thought you'd bailed on me and decided to live in London forever."

"No way," Jason said. "I'd much rather hang out here."

Sadie recalled Jason's past assessment of Salton. "Wait—are you saying boring old Salton is better than London?"

"Believe it or not, there is nowhere I would rather be than right here in Salton. You won't believe half the stuff I have to tell you about what happened over there," Jason said. "But first, how are you? What's been going on?"

"She didn't tell you?" Sadie asked.

"No. Grandma Lena thought it would be better if I talked to you myself."

"Okay. In a little bit," Sadie said. "You should say hi to everyone first." She gestured to Brandon.

"Bro, so good to see you." Brandon gripped Jason's hand and half-hugged him with a pat on the back. "Things got rough in London, huh?"

"You could say that," Jason said. "Lots to tell. But sorry I wasn't around when you got here. Are you staying for a while?"

"A couple more months at least," Brandon said. "Parents are on a long assignment."

"Cool. We can totally catch up."

Finn pushed her head into the back of Jason's leg.

He turned toward her. "Good girl, Finn." Jason scratched Finn's chest and she kicked a back leg indicating he had a good spot. "Did you take care of Shay while I was gone? Teach her a few new tricks?"

"She did a very good job with Shay," Lena said. "She probably has a few surprises for you."

"I can't wait." Jason looked at Sadie. "Mrs. C go to bed early or something? Don't tell me—she has some crack-of-dawn beehive thing to do tomorrow, right?" Jason chuckled.

Before Sadie could answer, the front door opened to everyone else who'd arrived from London. There were greetings and hugs and plans made to get everyone together the next day for dinner and long conversations. But now it was time to get some rest.

Jason stepped forward. "But I wanted to talk to Sadie—"

"No, it's okay," Sadie said. "You guys are all exhausted, and one more day isn't going to hurt anything. We can talk tomorrow."

"Are you sure?" Jason asked.

"Yep, absolutely." She nodded.

"Okay. I'll come by your house," Jason said.

Sadie glanced at Lena then back to Jason. "I'll come to your house instead, okay? You'll probably still be tired, adjusting to the time change and everything. Text me when you're up, and I'll swing by."

"Yeah...okay," Jason said.

Brandon took Sadie's hand in his and squeezed.

Everyone said their goodbyes.

Sadie dropped and scratched Shay's ears and kissed the top of her head. She whispered in her ear. "Between you and me, I think you're going to give Finn a run for her money."

Shay wagged her tail and licked Sadie's cheek.

✸ ✸ ✸

Lena held the door for Sadie as she walked into the house that was now their home. She hugged Lena and told her she was happy Lena was back from London, safe and sound. With exhaustion setting in, Sadie said goodnight and went up to her room.

Sadie gazed at the picture of her and Mamo at the fair. For a moment it triggered a pain in Sadie's chest like it had every day since Mamo had died, but the pain faded.

Sadie thought about her new family, one that she loved, and it was also a family Mamo wanted her to have. But somehow the family didn't seem that new. It was more like they'd always been there, but Sadie simply hadn't noticed. And with Jason home, the family was restored. Sadie felt more of the happiness than the sadness that lived inside her.

She climbed into bed. It felt cold without Shay curled into her. Sadie fingered the hawk's eye pendant around her neck and pulled the covers closer. Tomorrow she'd talk to Lena about adopting a dog. And Sadie would get Finn's and Shay's approval, too.

The scent of roses and vanilla wafted through the room. Sadie reached down and pulled a throw over her, one that used to sit on the foot of Mamo's bed, and now sat on hers.

Sadie was home.

***

Sadie woke in the middle of the night. Her left hand hurt and tingled.

Crap. I must have slept on it wrong.

She moved her arm from under the covers and shook it. Prickles shot through her.

Ow, ow, ow. She waved her arm harder. A few seconds later, the stinging eased.

Sadie relaxed and closed her eyes until her bladder decided it was time for a trip to the bathroom.

She whipped off the covers and stepped out of bed. Cool air sent shivers across her skin. Sadie pulled her arms in close and headed down the hall. The bathroom doorway glowed with the night light inside.

Sadie shut the door and kept the regular light switch off. She flushed the toilet and moved to the sink to wash. Sleep goop messed with her eyes in the low light—she could only focus on one of her hands under the water. She scrunched her eyes trying to clear the gunk, but still her eyes didn't clear. She dried her hands and rubbed her eyes, but her vision didn't balance.

Jeez, annoying.

Sadie grabbed a tissue but it made no difference. She finally turned on the light so she could better see to wipe her eyes.

She gasped.

She grabbed her left arm.

She gripped her left hand.

Her arm and hand were there, and it wasn't her vision that was the problem.

Sadie's left arm was invisible.

THE END

PREVIEW:
THE LEAGUE OF GOVERNORS

ONE

Trouble

Jason's first few weeks back at school were weird. Carrying the secret of his mom's death and how she'd tried to destroy every person at his school, actually every human on earth, made him feel like he wore a neon sign flashing: "I'M HIDING SOMETHING." Questions from friends like, "What are you doing this weekend?" made him anxious, and interest in how his burned hands were healing made him cautious. Did people know more than they were letting on? Did they know he was now a Rampart Guard and could shoot electric bolts out of his hands? Were they testing him with questions? In time Jason settled into the fact that he, Sadie—his best friend at Salton High School, and his brother, Kyle, were the only people at school who knew anything about the Rampart and Jason's role in saving it.

And Jason was good at keeping secrets.

Jason met Sadie at their lockers. "From Mamo." She handed him an apple from her grandmother's garden.

"All this healthy stuff is going to kill me." Jason grinned, took a bite. "Tell her thanks, as usual."

"I will. And she'll be glad to hear you are actually eating what she sends." Sadie snapped her locker shut.

"Hey, if it's good, as in tastes good, I'll eat it."

Sadie and Jason headed to the lunchroom where Jason tossed the apple core in a trash bin near the door. They grabbed seats and Sadie unpacked her lunch. Jason pulled a protein bar out of his bag and peeled back the wrapper.

"Seriously, that's all you're eating?" Sadie asked.

"I had an apple."

Sadie rolled her eyes. She looked across the room. "Ugh. Here comes Derek Goodman."

Jason looked over his shoulder. His lip curled.

Derek sneered. "What are you looking at?" He and two of his friends stopped behind Jason.

"I was trying to figure out what smelled so bad," Jason said.

Derek sniffed the space above Jason's head. "It's you, the slimeball that beats up his own weakling brother."

Jason bolted out of his seat and stood inches away from Derek. "Take that back."

"Or what?"

Jason pressed his fists into his thighs. His chin jutted. "Take—That—Back."

"Not—Gonna—Happen. For all we know, you've done something to your sister, too. I heard she hasn't been in school for like a month."

Sparks zapped inside Jason's hands. He battled the urge to singe Derek Goodman. And to slug him hard in the gut.

"Jason?" Sadie's voice was half-anxious, half-warning.

Jason shook his head. "You're not worth it."

"No? How about now?" Derek shoved Jason into the table.

Jason sprang into a fighting stance. Sadie rushed to his side of the table.

"What's going on here?" Coach Martel grabbed Derek's shoulder from behind. "You. To the principal's office."

Derek moved toward the exit. Coach turned to Jason. "Are you all right?"

"Yeah. Fine." Jason straightened and relaxed. His hands cooled.

"Okay. Good man." Coach patted Jason on the back. "Don't forget basketball tryouts are in a couple of weeks."

"Thanks, Coach." Jason wouldn't be trying out for the basketball team. He wanted to stay focused on his training for the Guards.

Coach Martel nodded. "Now, if you'll excuse me, I have a problem to escort to the principal's office. Again." The last word he said under his breath.

Lunch period was almost over and most of Jason's classmates left for their next period. His adrenaline eased and he gathered up what remained of his lunch.

"Della's still having a hard time?" Sadie asked.

Jason wadded his trash and hooped it into the nearby bin. "Yeah. She's awake half the night, she starts crying at the weirdest times. She was playing fetch with Shay yesterday and lost it when Shay wouldn't drop the ball for her."

"Is there anything I can do?" The bell rang and Sadie picked up her lunch bag.

Jason looked at his hands. The skin on his palms was shiny and tight, newly healed from being burned when he'd tried to save his mom. "Nah. Dad's trying to figure it out. Thanks, though." He turned toward his next class. "See you later."

"Yeah, see ya," Sadie said.

✳ ✳ ✳

After school, Jason and Shay headed to Uncle Alexander's. Jason opened the front door. Shay rushed in and tackled Finn. They rolled and lunged and growled like they wanted each other's blood.

Jason checked their body language. This was all fun and games. Reading the dogs' signals was one of Jason's early lessons as a Rampart Guard, along with how to consistently summon the right amount of power for whatever repair the Rampart needed. Too much energy directed at a small problem meant a small problem became a big one. And a big problem meant severe damage to a segment of the Rampart, and risk to humans from the energy of cryptids living among them. Nothing like that had happened for more than two hundred years, and Jason wasn't about to be the Guard that ruined that record and helped the rest of the world discover that the cryptids they'd thought were myths, like Loch Ness, the Dover Demon, and Skyfish, were real and living among them.

Shay and Finn continued their wrestling match with a slam into the leather couch.

"Hey, Uncle A." Jason collapsed on the couch.

Uncle Alexander poked his head out of the kitchen. His brown hair looked windblown. Jason figured he'd been riding his scooter.

"Did you study the League's guidelines and laws?" Uncle Alexander asked.

"Yep. Until I fell asleep. Which took about five minutes."

"I know it's not the most riveting read but you have to learn it. It's important to understand how the League oversees the relationship between cryptid and human populations worldwide."

Jason tipped his head back and closed his eyes. "I promise I'll get to it. Maybe this weekend."

"What about Morse code?"

"I almost have the full alphabet down, but I still think it's a waste of time. We have messaging apps, you know. And phones. And paper and pencil," Jason said.

"Your protest has been noted. Keep studying the code."

Jason huffed. "Fine. And maybe next you can teach me smoke signals."

Uncle Alexander tapped Jason with a water bottle. "No smoke signals. But definitely the Rampart distress signals."

He sat up. "Those are much more interesting. I'm now on the lookout for sun dogs, moon dogs, rings around the sun, changes in electromagnetic field noise, extra-bright double rainbows, and a few more things I can't remember. And Sadie's going to keep an eye on the internet for any hey-look-here's-a-picture-of-me-with-Bigfoot or whatever postings."

"Good. I'll quiz you while you work the bag. Let's head down to the gym." Uncle Alexander clasped Jason's arm and pulled him to his feet.

"I'm on board with the training, but I still don't get why so much of it is self-defense when we can shoot electric bolts out of our hands," Jason said.

"As I said when we first started training, it's part of the code of the Rampart Guards. No using powers against those who are without powers."

"Right, but if they attack you first—"

"No using powers against those who are without powers." Uncle Alexander rubbed his temple.

"You okay, Uncle A?"

"Yes, just remnants of a headache from earlier today."

Thanks to dear old Mom. Jason wondered if Uncle Alexander would ever be one hundred percent healthy after being poisoned by her for so long.

Gotta work harder. Gotta be ready.

In the gym, Jason kicked and punched, defended and attacked, and practiced methods to escape choke holds and bindings. During breaks, he rehearsed Shay's basic commands and started her on cryptid scent identification. Finn assisted when Shay was stumped.

When he and Shay got home that evening, like every evening after training, they headed to the kitchen. Kyle sat at the table doing homework. Shay bee-lined to her water bowl, slurped up a sloppy drink, and caved onto her kitchen bed—one of several dog beds placed around the house.

"Must be nice." Jason plunked a pile of books onto the table. "No homework for you." He bent down and rubbed Shay's cheek.

"Seriously nice," Kyle said. He stretched his arms overhead.

Dad walked in. "I'm glad you're both here. We need to talk."

"What's up?" Kyle asked.

"Della . . . the League of Governors. They're worried."

"What do they have to do with anything?" Jason took leftover chicken out of the refrigerator.

"Because of the Guards. Because of the remaining power she still has," Dad said.

"Okay." Jason bit into a chicken breast, not bothering with a plate.

"I'm taking her to them."

"What? Why?" Kyle asked.

"They may be able to help."

Jason shifted his weight and swallowed. "I don't get it. Why them?"

"She needs to talk to someone but she can't meet with a regular therapist. Since the League is fully aware of cryptids and the Rampart, Della will be able to speak freely about what she's been through. Plus...the League is worried she might be going down a path like your mother's."

Jason straightened. "Della is not crazy."

Dad shook his head. "No, I know. But she needs help dealing with everything she witnessed, what your mom did."

Dad always referred to her as "your mom" now, never by her name, Adrienne.

"You two and Shay will stay with Uncle Alexander, okay?"

"C'mon, Dad. I can watch Jason," Kyle said.

Jason huffed. "Hey. I don't need watching. You do."

"Whatever, dude. I'm practically sixteen—"

"Enough." Dad used the voice you didn't question. "You both need watching and you're both going to Alexander's."

"Yeah, fine." Kyle shut his notebook. "When are you leaving?"

"Tonight. Three-hour drive to the airport then we catch the red-eye. GQ is picking us up at Heathrow."

Dad's uneasiness quashed the amusement Jason usually found when he heard Grandad Quentin's nickname. "Wow. Okay. I'll get my things together." Jason snagged an apple and scooped his books off the table. He headed toward the hall.

"Me too." Kyle followed.

Shay led them upstairs and leaped onto Jason's bed. Jason tossed shirts and pants and underwear into a duffle bag. He packed his bathroom stuff. At the last minute, he remembered socks. He yanked open the drawer and scooped a few pairs into the bag.

He noticed a balled T-shirt stuffed in the corner. "I forgot all about this." Jason pulled it out and a broken chess piece—a rook—and an old metal coin fell to the floor.

Jason set the coin on his dresser and examined the two parts of the rook. It was from the antique chess set his dad gave him for his fourteenth birthday. The piece broke when he'd handled it, and he'd found the metal coin inside. Not wanting his dad to know he'd damaged the set, he'd tucked them all in his drawer, out of sight.

Jason examined the two pieces and slid the notch into its matching slot. The pieces locked like they'd never been apart.

What the . . . why didn't that work before?

He twisted the rook, trying to remove the base again. He pressed on the bottom, he pressed on the top, but the pieces held fast.

Weird. Jason returned the rook to the chessboard and glanced at the coin with the letters L-E-X embossed on the surface. He slipped the coin in his pocket.

"Ready, Jason?" Dad called from downstairs.

"Yeah. Coming." Jason grabbed his bag. "Let's go, Shay."

Shay jumped off the bed and trotted downstairs. Della, Dad, and Kyle waited in the hallway with their suitcases. Della's eyes were puffy.

"Lucky you, Dell, going to London." Jason dragged his duffle behind him as they headed to the garage.

Della sort of smiled. "Yeah. I guess."

"Well, I'm jealous. You get to have fun, and I get to go to school."

Della nodded. Jason wondered if she was about to start crying again. He wanted to say something to make her feel better, but everything seemed to make her feel worse.

Dad loaded the bags into the van. They arrived at Uncle Alexander's a few minutes later. He and Finn greeted them in the driveway.

Dad got out and helped unload the bags. "Thanks, Alexander. I appreciate this."

"Not a problem. It gives us more time to train." Uncle Alexander winked at Jason.

"I can help toughen him up." Kyle smirked and punched Jason in the arm.

"So not funny." Jason faked a punch at Kyle's chin.

"Boys, please behave yourselves and don't torture your uncle. I'll call you as soon as we arrive." Dad hugged Kyle and Jason then stroked Shay's chest and gave Finn a quick scratch behind her ears.

An October wind whisked into Jason's shirt and goosebumped his skin. "Okay. Have a safe trip." He reached into the passenger window and mussed Della's hair. "Talk to you soon, Dell. Have fun."

She batted at his arm. "Not the hair again. Now it's going to be all staticky." She raised the window.

Dad backed out of the driveway. Jason, Kyle and Uncle Alexander waved them away.

Jason shoved his cold hands in his pants pockets. *Crap. I meant to ask him about the coin.*

The next day, Jason woke early and ran with Shay, a ritual he practiced as part of his personal regimen. When he got back to Uncle Alexander's house, he texted Sadie to let her know he couldn't walk to school with her since Uncle Alexander's house was off the route they usually took: "See you at school. Staying at Uncle A's. Dad and Della headed to London."

Jason wolfed down a protein bar and chugged water, then jumped into the shower.

Later in the day after completing his afternoon training, he and Kyle sat down to dinner with Uncle Alexander.

"Have you heard from your dad?" Uncle Alexander passed a bowl of roasted veggies to Jason.

"No. I thought maybe he'd called you or Kyle."

"Nada on my phone," Kyle said.

"I haven't heard from him either. He probably got sidetracked with something. The League has a way of doing that." Uncle Alexander held up a serving plate. "Salmon?"

"Yeah. Thanks." Jason's mouth watered at the scent of the maple glaze. He dug into the meal and tried to ignore the weird jitters in his stomach.

"Do you want more? How about some bread?" Uncle Alexander picked up a loaf of garlic bread wrapped in foil.

Jason waved. "Nah, I'm good."

"Jason, you're in training and doing even more than I've asked. You need to increase your calories, get more nutrition." Uncle Alexander took a piece of bread for himself. "I'm concerned about your weight. And your energy levels."

"I'm fine. I'm strong." Jason admired the veins on his forearm.

"Looking strong and being strong isn't the same thing. Plus, if you don't keep your energy levels up, your health could be compromised. Please eat something more."

Kyle dropped his fork. "And besides, don't you want guns like these?" He flexed both of his arms.

"Only if I'm entering a scrawniest arms contest." Jason smirked.

"I'll show you scrawny. Later. When you're busy trying to walk your skinny ass down the hall or something." Kyle picked up his fork and took another bite of salmon.

Jason rolled his eyes, but he'd be on alert the rest of the evening. "Seriously, Uncle A. I'm fine. I feel good. Eating plenty, I promise." He took a drink of water.

Uncle Alexander sighed.

Jason changed the subject. "Hey. Did you ever find out anything about the guy Mom kept talking about when she was trying to destroy the Rampart? Sewell Kendrick?"

Uncle Alexander shook his head. "There is a Sewell Kendrick in the system, but records show he passed away some years ago." He stabbed lettuce and tomato with his fork. "I suspect the Sewell Kendrick your mother mentioned was fabricated, a way for her to do the things she was doing without taking full responsibility. Perhaps she read about the real Sewell Kendrick in some League documents and took a liking to the name."

"So as far as we're concerned, she made him up," Kyle said.

"I think so." Uncle Alexander ate the bite of salad. "And the numbers of disruptions in the Rampart have dropped significantly, back to normal levels. That's another indication Adrienne was the driving force behind the attempted destruction."

Jason picked out the green beans and pushed them around on his plate. "Well, great. She was the big bad all along." He shoved back from the table and took his plate to the sink, rinsed it and put it in the dishwasher. He rubbed the new skin on his palms. "I guess we can stop worrying about it and all go back to normal."

✳ ✳ ✳

The rest of the evening passed without a call.

Jason dialed Dad's cell. It went straight to voice mail. "Hey, just checking in. Hope the flight went well. Give me a call . . . whenever. Love you guys." Jason pressed "end call" and crawled into bed. Shay curled up close.

"They must have gotten busy with something, huh girl." Jason stroked Shay's fur from nose to forehead. "He'll call tomorrow. Right?"

Shay wagged her tail.

"Good girl." He switched off the light.

✳ ✳ ✳

Heat broiled Jason awake in the middle of the night. He kicked off the covers. His T-shirt clung to him, sweaty and soaked. Shay panted hard.

Intense light nearby caught the corner of Jason's eye.

Fire?

He grabbed Shay's collar and scrambled away.

He turned back. Shielding his eyes, he saw the source of the heat, the light. But it wasn't fire. At least not yet.

It was the coin.

The coin with L-E-X embossed on its surface, sitting on the nightstand next to Jason's bed.

It glowed bright red.

Read more of THE LEAGUE OF GOVERNORS,
available at your favorite bookstore.

ACKNOWLEDGEMENTS

So many people go into the creation of a novel, and I treasure every one of them. Each person mentioned here contributed and influenced this story in the best possible way.

Thank you, Jeffery Deaver, for your encouragement after reading a sampling of my work, and for validation when I shared my idea for two book twos—two completely different stories, one for Jason and one for Sadie, which occur on the same timeline. And thank you for the idea to have same scenes in the beginning and ending of both books from the respective characters' points of view. The conversation with you solidified my conviction to try something different, and I'm delighted with the results.

Thank you to these talented artists, experts, masters of their craft, who provided their respective services:

Lisa Miller: I've said it once and I'll say it again and again, her class, Story Structure Safari, is unequalled.

Steven Novak: The brilliant, and patient, designer of the cover, including the transformation of the Lex coin from an image in my head to one for all to see.

Steve Parolini: Who knew so many words could be cut to make a story stronger? This guy. The NovelDoctor is more like an elite novel surgeon.

Susie Brooks: Not only a smart and sassy copy editor but a dear friend as well.

Dale Pease: Talented interior designer who also has a gift of patience.

Brian Callanan: The man's got skills and brings the books to life with his audio narration.

Thank you Pikes Peak Writers—yours was the first writing conference I ever attended and I was overwhelmed and mesmerized. And thank you Rocky Mountain Fiction Writers for giving me the opportunity to give back.

Thank you to my Racca's critique group of Kim Byrne, Judy Logan, and Terri Spesock, who provide me with thoughtful and enlightening feedback even when I bombard them with pages. And thank you Racca's for the continued welcome at your restaurant, for a menu of deliciousness, and for sharing Marilyn with us. She's not only the best waitress but also a friend.

Thank you to my Tattered Cover critique group of Mark Lehnertz, Sue Duff, Chad Mathine, Bob Biniek, Matthew Woolums, and Todd Leatherman who are always supportive, helpful, and available when I need them. Can't ask for more than that.

Thank you to many more people who continue to support me from near and far. Please know how much I love and appreciate you. A few I must mention here are:

Kelly Hindley who is a beta reader, supporter, and has been a friend forever.

Dianna Cannon who wows me with her support, her feedback, and is the third member of the friends forever triumverate.

Meghan Mortimer who never ceases to believe in me.

Katie Terrien who proved to be a skilled beta reader, and is clearly the best mother-in-law in the world.

Corinne O'Flynn who listens when I'm frustrated and cheers as hard as I do when success comes.

Kevin Terrien who enthusiastically tells everyone about his wife's (that's me) books.

Maggie who warms my feet under my desk.

Shea who makes me laugh every single day.

Boon whose history as a misunderstood pit bull mix (he's a lover no matter what) inspired me to make both Finn and Shay pit bull mix dogs.

A special shout out to two readers I met after writing THE RAMPART GUARDS—Yusuf and Maryam. It's been fun staying connected on Goodreads. Keep me posted on the Bigfoot hunting!

Most of all, thank you to all the readers out there, not only of this book but all books. Authors write books because we love the stories, but there's nothing like learning that others enjoy the stories, too. If you love a book, any book, I encourage you to write a review on your preferred bookselling site or sites and help that story be found by more readers. Plus, you'll delight your favorite authors, too.

All the best to everyone, and may you always be surrounded by golden Skyfish.

ABOUT THE AUTHOR

Wendy Terrien received her first library card at age two and a few years later started writing her own stories. Her debut novel, *The Rampart Guards* (February 2016), earned a Kirkus starred review and was named to Kirkus Reviews' Best Books of 2016. The novel is a Foreword INDIES Book of the Year Award Finalist, a Next Generation Indies Award Finalist, and is the first in her intriguing urban fantasy series.

In addition to her novels, Wendy published a short story, "The Fate Stone," in the award-winning *Tick Tock: Seven Tales of Time* (March 2016), and "Light" in *Off Beat: Nine Spins on Song* (April 2017), both from Wicked Ink Books.

Wendy graduated from the University of Utah (go Utes!) and moved to Colorado where she completed her MBA at the University of Denver. She focused her marketing expertise on the financial and technology industries until a career coach stepped in and reminded Wendy of her passion for writing. Wendy began attending writers' conferences, workshops, and retreats, and she hasn't stopped yet.

She regularly participates in two critique groups and is the Secretary of Rocky Mountain Fiction Writers, and a member of Pikes Peak Writers. In 2014, Wendy was a finalist in the San Francisco Writer's Contest.

Wendy lives in the Denver area with her husband, Kevin, and their three dogs: Maggie, Shea, and Boon. All three of her dogs are rescues, and Wendy is passionate about promoting shelter adoptions. If you're in Colorado, you may even be able to spot her by her "Adopt a Shelter Pet" license plates.

Learn more about Wendy by visiting her website: wendyterrien.com

More Wendy on the web:
Facebook: facebook.com/wendyterrien
Twitter: @wbterrien
Instagram: instagram.com/wendyterrien
BookBub: https://www.bookbub.com/authors/wendy-terrien